story to read on 9-16-2019

Stop on   9 - 17-2019

Marrying
CHRISTOPHER

Marrying CHRISTOPHER

MICHELE
PAIGE
HOLMES

Mirror Press

Interior Design by Rachael Anderson
Edited by Angela Eschler, Michele Preisendorf, Cassidy Wadsworth, and Jennie Stevens
Cover design by Rachael Anderson

Cover Photo Credit: Lee Avison/Trigger Image
Cover Photo Copyright: Lee Avison
Ocean Background Photo: Shutterstock.com #113710504

Published by Mirror Press, LLC
ISBN-10: 1941145434
ISBN-13: 978-1-941145-43-2

To LuAnn—
Whose patient corrections
and sometimes brutally honest words
taught me so much about writing.
I will always hear your voice in my head
and be thankful of it.

CHAPTER

Yorkshire, England, July 1828

Christopher Thatcher leaned casually against the mantel in Mr. Samuel Preston's drawing room. A smile played upon his lips as he studied the room's other occupants—his two sisters, Grace and Helen, and their husbands—and thought of another night, not long ago, when he had stood in this same spot and contrived a plan to unite his sisters with the men they loved, Lord Nicholas Sutherland and Mr. Samuel Preston.

Nicholas's transformation over the past months had been nothing short of miraculous, but then Grace had always been a worker of miracles, raising her younger siblings alone as she had. That she had brought the tall, handsome, dark-souled earl to his knees had not surprised Christopher, and he felt inordinately pleased to be witness to not only Grace's happiness but to Nicholas's release from the grief that had too long consumed him.

Samuel, on the other hand, had a more gentle nature and was the perfect match for Helen. Samuel had coaxed her from years of shyness and timidity, and she had truly blossomed these past months so that her personality shone as much as her outward beauty.

Brilliant work, Christopher silently congratulated himself. In spite of a few glitches along the way, all had turned out to be the happiest of endings for his sisters—almost. There was one more item to be resolved before he felt he could go about his life and no longer worry about their welfare. *Sir Edmund Crayton.*

The pirate had to be dealt with. Since Grace's and Helen's recent weddings, they had all been somewhat on edge, aware as they were of the vile transaction that had taken place between Crayton and their late father. Though the £3500 Crayton had paid—Christopher still shuddered at the many depravities their father's gambling debts had brought into their lives—for the "right" to Helen had been returned to the scoundrel, neither she nor Grace would be completely safe until he was permanently *relocated*. So long as Crayton remained in England, Christopher felt that his protection must remain also—a situation that he felt had become almost unendurable.

It was not his sisters he wished to escape. He loved them dearly and felt it was his sacred duty to protect them from Crayton, just as Grace had protected him as a child. But his sisters had husbands now, and despite the fact that he had lost much of his sense of purpose when they'd gained safety and love, Christopher still could not pursue a new purpose— or sense of self—until the threat was vanquished entirely. And yet, he was impatient to leave England.

In spite of my sisters' husbands' generosity. The two had gone so far as to even offer him a fair piece of property, a parcel of each of their own adjoining estates. His sisters had been most disappointed when he did not accept the offer. He wanted property, yes. But he wanted to earn it on his own, not have it handed to him. He wanted to make something of himself, to be free to pursue whatever he may, to make his own name and fortune. America had freed herself from England, and he intended to do the same.

But first . . .

Christopher caught Lord Nicholas Sutherland's eye and gave him an almost imperceptible nod. It was time to present their plan. Christopher had chosen to share his idea with Nicholas first, as, of his two brothers-in-law, Nicholas was the one more likely to take risks and action.

"I have the weekly report on Crayton," Nicholas said when there was an appropriate break in the conversation.

Helen tensed at once, and Samuel, ever attentive, took her hand in his.

"Crayton's activities this week have not taken him from London. He had several meetings—a few with his own solicitors, one with a ship's captain, and two with . . . ladies of ill repute."

Samuel shot a look of disapproval at Nicholas. "You needn't share *all* the details. Telling us that he was not in Yorkshire is sufficient."

Nicholas ignored him. "Crayton also attended the theatre this week."

Helen gave a resigned sigh. "It is almost as if he knows we are tracking him and shows himself at the theatre just to mock me. I fear we shall never be able to go again."

"You won't," Christopher said. "Unless something is done—something more *permanent*."

"What have you got up your sleeve this time?" Samuel asked, his eyes narrowing as he studied Christopher.

"You act as if my past schemes have come to no good," Christopher said, feigning offense. "And yet, look at you— sitting there with my lovely sister fawning all over you."

"I am not—" Helen straightened quickly, blushing as she extracted her arm from beneath Samuel's.

"What did you have in mind, Christopher?" Grace asked, likely more to draw attention away from Helen than from anything else. Her instinct to protect her younger sister still ran strong.

"Nicholas will tell us." Christopher left his place before the fire and drew up a chair closer to the four of them. Glancing over his shoulder, he checked to make sure the drawing room doors were still closed and no servants had entered. He did not want the conversation to leave their circle.

Nicholas cleared his throat once, then began in a strong, assertive tone. "Christopher has proposed that we trap Crayton at his own game."

"You would like us to purchase him and plan for his abuse just as he did for Helen?" Grace teased.

"This is no trivial matter," Nicholas gently reminded her. "At the very least, your sister remains in danger. And I do not doubt Crayton would take any opportunity to snatch you as well."

"Not to mention the bounty price still on Christopher's head," Helen said quietly.

"Yes." Nicholas nodded. "You'll recall that, in addition to debauchery, Crayton has also, for some time now, been quite adept at using his fleet to overrun merchant ships. These he boards and takes control of, slitting the officers' throats and taking the rest of the crew captive, to be pressed into service for the Royal Navy."

"The cargo he keeps as his own," Samuel said. "At a great financial loss to those it belonged to." He spoke from experience, Christopher knew.

"I have a friend," Nicholas said. "Captain Merlow has his own fleet and a vested interest in the East India Company. And—as he both owes me a favor and is only too eager to remove Crayton's threat from the seas—he is willing to assist us." Nicholas paused, his gaze traveling around to each of them, as if to judge how they were receiving the plan thus far.

"Continue," Samuel said.

Christopher took over. "On Monday next, Crayton will be delivered of the news that the second Saturday in August Captain Merlow will be crossing through French waters with a rather *valuable* cargo." Nicholas and Samuel exchanged a knowing look.

"Opium," Samuel guessed, his expression grim. "Crayton's taste for it was mentioned in the solicitor's report."

"I thought the opium trade went south," Grace said, "to China. Grandfather called it the Crown's futile attempt to keep English silver at home."

"It is futile because there are plenty of Englishmen—Crayton included—who are addicted to it as well," Samuel said.

"And while much of the opium does travel from India to China, a fair amount makes its way to European ports and here as well," Nicholas said. "Though Captain Merlow isn't actually going to be in possession of the opium when he meets Crayton. He'll leave port with it, and Crayton will no doubt have a man in place to verify that. But once at sea, Captain Merlow will be transferring the opium to another vessel that *is* headed south. During this exchange, his ship will take on arms and additional men, employing twice the usual protection for a ship that size."

"That's a rather large expense to incur on the off-chance Crayton will bite." Samuel leaned back against the sofa as if he'd just dismissed the validity of their plan.

"Oh, he'll bite, all right," Nicholas said assuredly. "Aside from wanting some for himself, Crayton knows how and where to sell the opium, so it's as good or better than a shipment of gold. And switching the cargo in exchange for men and weapons isn't costing Merlow a penny."

Grace turned to Nicholas abruptly. "How much?" she demanded. "How much has this cost *you*?"

"Very little when I consider your safety." He trailed his

fingers down the side of her face. "No amount would be too much to keep you safe."

Grace took his hand, her gaze softening, and held it to her lips as they looked at one another.

"Well, then." Christopher cleared his throat uncomfortably. *Such ardor from two of the most sensible and levelheaded people I know. May I never fall victim to such wiles.* "In summary, Crayton will attempt to meet up with the shipment of opium, Merlow and his crew will detain him, and then Crayton will be on his way to the Continent, where he shall be pressed into service for La Royale."

"You intend to send him to *France*?" Helen said.

Grace clapped her hands. "How perfectly delightful."

"Pressing him into service for England would not gain us much," Nicholas said. "He has too many important 'friends,' despite his thievery on our own waters. It would only be a matter of time before he was released—and more dangerous than ever."

"But in the French navy, Crayton would be the lowest of the low," Christopher explained. "He has pirated in their waters, too, and many a Frenchman has been his victim."

"You don't think they'll kill him, do you?" Helen asked, sounding rather alarmed.

"If we're lucky," Nicholas said, earning frowns from both women.

"It's doubtful they will harm him too much," Christopher said, though he silently agreed with Nicholas's assessment. "Crayton will be worth more alive, strong and able as he is."

"There is the risk of ransom," Samuel said. "If the French learn who he is, might they not write to the king and request payment for Crayton's release? After all, he was knighted for his *service* to the crown."

"I have thought of that already." Christopher felt inordinately pleased that their dialogue was going so well. *This just may work.* "More than a dozen years have passed since he was knighted, and during that time he has somewhat fallen out of favor with those who brought him to power. In addition, he has incurred the wrath of many others. While you have all been off enjoying your wedding trips, I have been busy traveling to London and beyond, speaking to seamen and captains, listening carefully in taverns, and discovering just how many enemies Crayton truly has."

"And risking your own foolish neck," Samuel muttered.

"Better mine than yours." Christopher grinned. "I daresay Helen favors you more."

Helen sat on the edge of her seat, a distressed look upon her face, evident by the wrinkling of her pert nose. "I should be distraught if anything were to happen to either of you—to anyone in this room."

"No harm is going to befall any of us," Nicholas said. "Christopher has planned this most thoroughly."

"Indeed, I have," Christopher said. "Happily, the number of Crayton's enemies likely equals or exceeds that of his obligated allies. Even the crown itself has tired of him in recent years. His talents are not valued as much now as they once were. We are at peace with both France and America; the continual need for men to be pressed into service has greatly diminished."

"Pirating among his own has become a nuisance rather than a benefit. If he is removed, no one will mourn his absence," Nicholas concluded.

"You have been busy," Grace said, eyeing Christopher suspiciously.

He shrugged. "I may have learned a few tricks from solicitors, given all the time I spent in court awaiting news of our inheritance."

"Not to mention what you learned while skulking about in pubs all the years you had to chase your father down." Samuel had unfastened the top button of his waistcoat and was beginning to roll up his shirtsleeves, a sure indication that he was ready to go to work.

"There was that too," Christopher admitted with a half grin. "Well?" he asked. "Are we all in agreement?"

"What is there to agree to?" Samuel asked, his voice wary. "It sounds very much as if the cogs are already in motion."

"They can yet be halted," Christopher said. "We must all be in agreement before we proceed. Because if any part of the plan goes wrong, if just one person involved sways loyalty, we could all be in great danger."

For the first time since the discussion had begun, Nicholas exhibited signs of discomfort, tugging on his cravat and avoiding eye contact with anyone, especially Samuel.

"Those you've hired know the origins of this plot?" Samuel asked. "They know we are behind it?"

Christopher shook his head. "I have been careful to avoid any use of your name or Nicholas's. But a few know who *I* am. And that puts us all in danger."

"We are all already in danger and have been for some months," Helen said. "I, for one, would like to be able to roam about the garden with Beth as we used to."

Christopher knew she dearly missed these excursions with Samuel's four-year-old daughter—just one of the many reasons they had to proceed.

"The constant need for a guard at the gate, these weekly reports—" Helen waved her hand toward Nicholas. "They are wearying. I think Christopher is right to do this. We must act instead of waiting and watching for Crayton to."

"Well said." Christopher sent her an approving smile. A year ago Helen would never have been so bold. "All in favor?"

Grace spoke first. "I agree with Helen."

"And it is a foolish man who disagrees with his wife," Nicholas said, sharing a rather sultry look—one Christopher wished he had not seen—with Grace.

"Let us proceed," Samuel said, "and pray all goes as you have outlined."

"But if it does not . . ." Grace glanced at each of them as the long-assumed burden of worry and responsibility flashed in the depths of her eyes. As eldest, she had spent her life looking out for her younger siblings.

"Then you shall all have to join me on my journey to America." Christopher reached into his pocket and retrieved the ticket he had purchased just two days earlier, deciding that now was as good a time as any to share news of his imminent departure. "I intend to leave as soon as this business with Crayton is completed. The ship I am traveling on leaves from Liverpool the fourth of September, and I have it from the captain himself that there are still plenty of cabins available."

CHAPTER 2

Christopher laid his fork across his plate and set his serviette upon the breakfast table as four pairs of eyes followed his every move. The dining room had never been so silent, and he wished little Beth had been allowed to join them this morning. She certainly would not have been as solemn as the others in the room.

"I thank you for breakfast, Samuel—and for your hospitality these many months." Christopher cleared his throat, uncomfortably aware of the constriction building within. "It is time. I should go." The servant hovering behind him pulled his chair back, and he stood.

"You should *not* go." Helen's voice elevated to an unnatural pitch, and a quick glance her direction confirmed that the tears, which had been threatening all morning, had at last spilled over and were now streaming from her eyes. Grace reached over and took her hand.

"We must allow your brother to direct his own life," Samuel said firmly but not unkindly. He put his arm around Helen, supporting her as she rose from her chair. "You will always be welcome here, Christopher. Our home is yours."

"I know. And I thank you." For a fraction of a second, Christopher wished he could avail his brothers-in-law of their generosity. Parting with Grace and Helen was not going to be easy for him either. But the pull he felt to America's shores grew stronger daily and could not be ignored.

He turned, quickly exiting the dining room and entering the foyer as a great hiccupping sob reached his ears.

Grace. Oh no. He'd expected tears from Helen, but he'd hoped Grace would maintain control of her emotions this morning. The chorus of sobs following behind him indicated his hopes were in vain. Christopher crossed the foyer and stepped outside into the crisp morning air before stopping, hoping the coolness might do them all a bit of good and somehow soothe the bitterness of his departure.

He waited on the top step, then turned and shook hands with Nicholas, then Samuel, as they arrived. Grace and Helen stood beside them, hugging each other and crying.

"I cannot thank either of you enough," Christopher said to his brothers-in-law, his throat swelling once more as he fought the tide of his own emotions. "I could not have chosen better men for my sisters."

"I thought you did choose us," Samuel drawled with a half smile.

Christopher clasped his arm. "Too right. So I did." He grinned and sent Samuel a silent thanks for his attempt at lightheartedness.

"Take care," Nicholas said. "And be sure to write often, or Grace shall insist upon being shipped off after you to monitor your welfare."

"Oh no," Christopher said with mock seriousness. "She is your responsibility now. Do not dare let her anywhere near a dock or a ship."

"I do not intend to." Nicholas nodded once more, then stepped backward, retreating over the threshold and into the foyer, along with Samuel, so that Christopher might say his farewells to Grace and Helen in private.

He wasn't certain whether or not he felt grateful for this courtesy. His sisters would need their husbands to comfort them, and he needed to keep his own emotions in check—a feat made more difficult without the worry of acting a ninny in front of the other men.

"You *had* best write often and tell us of your adventures." Grace clasped his right hand tightly in her own as Helen claimed his left.

Christopher glanced over his shoulder at Harrison, their driver, who stood beside the Sutherland landau. Harrison merely shrugged, as if to say, *Good luck getting them to let you go now.*

Instead of fighting his sisters' grasps, Christopher stepped nearer so that the three stood closely. "It is you who must take care, Grace. And you must be sure to write as soon as you are safely delivered of your child."

Her eyes widened. "How did you know? We have not spoken of it in front of you. I did not wish to worry you or cause you to delay your trip."

At her words, Christopher knew his sisters would let him go, but he also knew they believed his journey was merely a lark, a young man's adventure, from which he would soon return. They could not have been more wrong. He intended to settle in America and make a life for himself there.

"It was impossible *not* to notice your condition," Christopher said, earning a scowl from Grace as she glanced down and pressed a hand to her still-flat stomach.

"You don't *appear* different," he clarified. "But for the past month Nicholas has been treating you like a fragile china doll. He does not even allow you to walk up the stairs by yourself. What else was I to think?"

"I see." Grace pursed her lips, but Christopher knew she was pleased with his assessment of her husband's attentiveness.

"And you, Helen—" Christopher turned his gaze upon

his younger sister, who thankfully had stopped her sniffling during his exchange with Grace. "I hope you feel better soon. I've not any experience with women who are increasing, but Samuel tells me the illness usually passes after a month or two."

Helen and Grace gasped at the same time.

"When were you going to tell me?" Grace demanded.

"I only just realized myself this week." Helen's eyes narrowed at Christopher. "Samuel told you?"

Christopher chuckled. "Do not scold him for confirming what I had already guessed. The sounds from your chamber each morning and your lack of appetite at breakfast made your condition rather obvious."

"Oh, dear." Helen blushed prettily as her hand flew to her cheek. Christopher squeezed her other hand gently.

"You will need to take extra care of your husband during this time as well."

"I know." A fresh set of tears escaped Helen's eyes. "He is so frightened of losing me."

As well he should be. Christopher attempted to push aside the fear he felt for each of his sisters. When he'd realized Grace was expecting, he had considered delaying his departure until she was safely delivered and he had met his niece or nephew. But the weather would be poor that time of year, and he would likely have had to wait a few months more. *And it would only be harder to leave.* His sisters had their lives, and it was time to go in search of his.

"And how do you feel about a child of your own?" Christopher asked Helen gently, hoping to coax her from her sorrow.

"Beth is like my own," she said. "But, oh, I am ever so happy." She smiled through her tears. "A child, Christopher—I shall soon have a child!"

He laughed. "Well, let us hope that's what it is." At this Helen released him, wrenching her hand from his in mock anger, then flung herself into his arms and sobbed upon his shoulder. Grace followed suit, and the lapels of Christopher's coat were soon wet with their tears.

Just as he began to feel desperate, Nicholas and Samuel reappeared in the doorway. They came up behind their wives and gently pulled them away, Samuel turning Helen into his embrace, and Nicholas kissing Grace's forehead, then wrapping his arm about her.

"Go," Nicholas said, waving Christopher toward the carriage, "while you still can. I'm not certain how long we shall be able to hold them off."

This elicited a teary laugh from Grace, and with a last, fond gaze at his sisters, Christopher turned away and hurried into the carriage.

"Wait! You cannot leave without a bit of sustenance for your journey." Their longtime servant, Miranda, ran down the front steps carrying a large basket in her hands. She handed it to Harrison, who, Christopher noticed, took entirely longer than necessary in removing his hand from Miranda's as he relieved her of the basket. He passed it into the carriage, and Christopher made an exaggerated show of hefting it to the seat.

"What have you got in there—rocks?"

"No—not that you don't deserve them, leaving your sisters as you are." Miranda placed her hands at her hips and bestowed her sternest look upon him, causing Christopher to smile. He leaned forward out of the carriage and placed a quick kiss on her cheek. "I will miss you as well, Miranda. You had best take good care of her, Harrison."

"I intend to," he said, sending a coy look in Miranda's direction.

Harrison closed the carriage door, and a moment later they were off. Christopher turned his face to the window and waved, watching as long as he could, until the carriage turned from the drive onto the road and his family disappeared from sight.

Whatever am I doing? How can I possibly leave them?

Alone with his thoughts, the severity of his decision crashed down upon him, its weight suffocating. *When—if ever—shall I see Grace and Helen again?* Yet, still, he felt he must go. England did not hold his future.

America—independent, as he longed to be—did.

CHAPTER  3

Manchester, England, September 3, 1828

"*M*iss Abbott! Miss Abbott, wait!"

The door had only just closed when the summons pulled Marsali from the longed-for solitude within the coach. *What now?* She leaned her head back against the seat, partly from exasperation, partly from exhaustion. Her aunt and uncle had scarcely given her time to pack yesterday—not that she had much *to* pack—and had awoken her well before dawn so she might complete the morning work before she left.

"Miss Abbott!"

Marsali drew the curtain back from the window and peered out to see one of her aunt's maids waving an envelope as she ran toward the coach.

The steps had not yet been put up; neither had the coachman ascended his perch, and to Marsali's dismay, he opened the door, allowing the servant girl to enter the carriage. This she did, thrusting the letter at Marsali.

"Post just came, and this for you. From *America*."

"Thank you." Marsali accepted the letter warily, worried that it was some trick of her aunt's to detain her further. But a quick look at the postmarks confirmed the letter was indeed from America and had been sent some three months earlier. "From my sister." Marsali smiled. "She promised to write and tell me what I must expect upon my arrival."

"Might you want to open it now—just in case it's something else. Bad news, perhaps?" the maid suggested.

Marsali's eyes narrowed, and though she very much wanted to open the envelope, she made a show of tucking it into her reticule instead. "What it says is of no consequence. Even if ill has befallen my sister"—her stomach clenched at the possibility—"I should assume my journey anyway. There is nothing here in England for me. You may tell my aunt I said that." She sat up tall in her seat.

The maid bobbed her head obediently, but not before Marsali glimpsed the empathy in her eyes.

Likely she wishes she was leaving too. Save for a paltry wage, the servants were treated no better than she, the niece thrust upon her aunt and uncle four years earlier. Well, they'd made good use of her, hadn't they?

"Good luck to you, then, miss." The maid backed out of the coach.

The door closed once more, and Marsali willed the driver to hurry aboard and be off before her aunt could think of anything else to delay her. She glanced at a corner of the envelope peeking out from her reticule. *Post just arrived— doubtful.* It was far more likely that her aunt had already had the letter in her possession for weeks—if not longer. *Little wonder she did not open it herself,* Marsali thought, half suspecting that her aunt actually had opened the letter and read its contents before resealing it. Once more, a feeling of unease stirred within her. *What if it really is bad news?*

It took a great deal of effort to dismiss the thought and to leave the letter untouched. It was likely just some ploy of her aunt's, hoping that no news, or bad news, from Charlotte might dissuade Marsali from following through with her plans.

No chance of that. The vehicle lurched forward suddenly, throwing Marsali's head against the seat. She did not push aside the curtain to see if anyone stood at a window watching her leave. She did not wish for one last glimpse of the street or house. She was leaving Manchester and all of England behind forever. And she couldn't have been happier.

Closing her eyes and doing her best to dismiss any worry over her sister, she promised herself that she *would* wait until she was aboard the ship and they were underway before she opened her letter. For now the wheels rolling along the cobbled streets and the swaying carriage soothed her. *I am on my way. With each passing minute, Charlotte is closer.*

Near the noon hour, the coach stopped at an inn near Warrington. Three other passengers had joined them along the way, and Marsali waited until each had departed the carriage before she stood and shuffled stiffly toward the door. Squinting against the sun, she accepted the coachman's outstretched hand and stepped outside into the midday brightness. The difference in the air hit her at once, and she inhaled deeply, smelling the moist, salty air of the ocean. They weren't that far now. A few more hours and she would be aboard the ship.

A smile curved her lips as she followed the others toward the Elm Tree Inn, an ivy-covered building that boasted two large windows up front. She had slept much of the morning away but now felt rejuvenated and looked enthusiastically forward to new experiences and a life free— for a few weeks, at least—from the burden of constant labor.

Just outside the inn door Marsali paused, wondering if there would be anything on the menu she might purchase with the little money she had left. Deciding she might at least be able to afford a cup of tea, she tentatively entered the pub, allowing one of the gentlemen who had shared her coach to hold the door for her. A woman traveling alone could not be too cautious and had reason to be wary. Her aunt and uncle might have easily offered her the use of their coach and servants to accompany her, but then, that would have been a kindness—a word unknown in their vocabulary or lifestyle.

Inside, the light shone nearly as brightly as it had outside, streaming as it was through the two southern-facing windows. Seating herself near one of these, at a tiny table with only one chair, Marsali felt a little more of the tension leave her.

I am away from them. I am this much closer to America—and Charlotte. To a new home.

Christopher emerged from the hackney, paid the driver, then waited as his trunk was unloaded from the back. After two consecutive days of traveling, it felt good to be standing on solid ground, though that feeling wasn't to last long. But acquiring sea legs had to be easier than sitting cramped inside a coach for hours on end.

He took in the scene about him at the Liverpool docks, lively with midmorning activity, men loading and unloading cargo, ships leaving anchor, and a friendly bustle of commerce all about. The brick buildings lining the waterfront advertised all manner of merchant ships and services, from coopers to sailmakers. Men—many of them with the hardened look of sailors—loitered about, likely looking for work. Christopher eagerly scanned the names on the weathered shop signs, hoping to see one proclaiming "Thomas and Gower, Steamship Service," but there was no such sign.

Not yet, anyway. But in years to come—maybe even next year—there will be. He was excited at the prospect of steam travel and especially being able to make the trans-Atlantic journey in nearly half the time it took the standard sailing vessels.

A long line of people snaked along the boardwalk and

up the gangway of the large sailing ship to his left. Babes in arms cried, and tiny children clung to their parents' legs or peered warily from between them. A group of young boys skipped about in some sort of game. The older youth and gentlemen near his own age wore expressions of cautious optimism, while the older adults stood tiredly, many looking defeated already.

And their journey has yet to begin. From their thick accents, Christopher guessed they were Irish. From their poorly patched and threadbare clothing to the baskets and bundles in which they had secured their meager belongings, he guessed them to be even poorer than he.

And all heading to America as I am. She does not care that we arrive without wealth. Though he *was* to be fortunate in his travel, crossing the Atlantic under considerably better conditions than most. Christopher's gaze slid to the smaller, yet good-sized vessel docked beside the immense sailing ship and felt an almost palpable excitement. History was about to be made. *And I am to be a part of it.*

The coachman and driver had succeeded in retrieving his luggage. "You sailing on that newfangled ship?" Both men looked toward the vessel attached to the nearest gangplank.

"I am," Christopher said, proud rather than concerned, as the men seemed to be.

"I hear they're calling her a steam *coffin*," one remarked.

"Steam and the speed that comes with it do not necessarily equate with death," Christopher said, though he knew much of the public held that view. It was the reason he'd been able to purchase such an affordable passage on the *Amanda May*, one of the first steamships set to cross the Atlantic and in record-breaking time.

"For your sake, I hope you are right," the coachman said, his voice so full of doomsday that Christopher had to work to hold in a laugh. The coachman and the driver hefted the trunk between them and, still looking wary, followed

Christopher along the dock and to the gangway. For a half second he wondered if they were going to deposit his trunk there and leave him to find someone else to help with it. But after a few surreptitious glances at the ropes securing the *Amanda May*, they started up the ramp and boarded the ship.

For all the activity bustling on the docks below, the ship's deck appeared deserted. Christopher nodded to a spot out of the way, and the coachmen put his trunk down and were off, hastily retreating the way they'd come.

Christopher held back the urge to chuckle as they practically ran down to the dock. He didn't see why the addition of a *paddlewheel*, steam engine, and smokestack to a sailing ship should cause such a stir. But Captain Gower had done just that with his "newfangled" invention. Christopher could only feel thankful for that and for the advertisement he'd happened upon when he'd been in London last spring.

"Our first passenger." Christopher turned as Gower himself strode across the deck. Christopher had met him once before, nearly two months ago, when he'd come to the public viewing of the *Amanda May*. Grey peppered the hair at the captain's temples, and his skin had the weathered look of a sailor, but his round face appeared jovial, the corners of his eyes crinkling as he smiled.

"Welcome." Captain Gower stuck out his hand, and Christopher took it, pleased to feel that the captain's grasp was strong and solid.

"Christopher Thatcher, sir," he said. "Eager to be off."

"Not a fugitive, are you?" the captain asked in a tone that didn't reveal whether or not he was in jest.

"No. But I had to fight my way from my sisters' grasps, and I'm feeling somewhat relieved to have that behind me." A fleeting discomfort pulsed through Christopher's chest as he recalled their tearful farewell. He'd known Helen to cry a lot, but he couldn't recall Grace having ever shed so many tears. He tried to take comfort in knowing that he'd left both of his sisters in more-than-capable hands.

And with Crayton shipped off to France now . . . There was no longer anything holding him back from his dreams. *From here on out, I make my own way. I am bound by no one and nothing. The choices I make will be my own, not anything I am compelled to.*

"Well then, welcome aboard," the captain said once more. "Marc, our cabin boy, will help you stow your trunk." As if on cue, a lad of about fourteen appeared on deck, just behind the captain.

"Take any cabin you'd like on the port side—take all of them, if you want," Captain Gower said, grunting. "You're the only male passenger we've got this voyage. Cowards, these Englishmen are. I've no doubt I'll fill her full on the return trip from America. Little wonder she won her independence fighting against a bunch of pasty Englishmen." He shook his head. "Three women will be joining us, and we've got a fine crew, but you'll have plenty of time to yourself for the next four weeks." Pivoting sharply, he strode away in the direction he'd come, as if he'd had all of the talking that he could stomach.

Christopher called a thank-you anyway and reached down to lift one end of his trunk. The cabin boy, Marc, already held the other, and together they lifted it easily, Marc's end rising so quickly that his face registered surprise at the trunk's light weight.

"I don't have much with me," Christopher said by way of explanation. "Probably less than most who travel across the Atlantic."

"Less than them women coming aboard," the lad said, staring past Christopher.

Turning so he could walk sideways, Christopher caught sight of the procession coming up the gangway. Two men appeared at the top of the ramp, then four, then six, then eight. Each pair carried a large trunk between them, and piled on top of these trunks was an assorted array of parcels—paper-covered packages wrapped with string, fancy carpetbags, and hatboxes.

The last pair of men, struggling with their load, stepped aboard the ship as two ridiculously feathered hats appeared behind them, bobbing up the ramp above their owners. Christopher turned away before the faces beneath the hats came into view. He hurried his step. The last thing he wanted right now was to be around women—especially any as frivolous as it appeared these two must be.

He loved his sisters fiercely and had done his best by them, but now—at last—it was *his* time. Time to pursue the life he'd dreamed of for as long as he could remember. And he refused to do any little thing that might risk complicating it. Women, in his opinion, tended to complicate a man's life. Some day far into the future—after he owned his own land and established a successful farm, when he'd built a fine house and had a solid bank account, then he might be interested in a complication of the female sort. But that time was years away. Today he was gloriously single and free from all worries over any female.

And I intend to enjoy it. He might only be twenty-one, but he'd not had the youth others were afforded. He'd been shouldering responsibility since he was old enough to wander away from home and find his way back again—practically his whole life.

Marc paused as they came to a door. Holding his side of the trunk with only one hand, he reached his other toward the knob. "Which cabin would you like?" he asked as he pulled the door open and started inside. Christopher followed, careful to duck beneath the low doorway as they stepped down into a long saloon lined with a good two dozen doors on each side and tables and benches running down the entire length of the middle.

"Which cabin is farthest from the women's quarters?" Christopher asked.

"Over there." The boy inclined his head toward the end of the row on the opposite side. "It's the one closest to the captain as well."

"Perfect," Christopher said. "I'll take it."

CHAPTER 4

*T*he coach rolled to a stop, jarring Marsali from a troubling dream in which she was back at her aunt and uncle's house. The carriage rocked as the driver hopped down, and Marsali winced as her head—tender already from hours of knocking against the side—hit the carriage wall again. Thoroughly awake now and grimacing, she pulled the curtain back, eager for her first sight of the wharf.

But instead of a bay full of ships at anchor, her eyes met a dirty and rather deserted street corner. *Lime Street and Pembroke.* She did not recognize either name and supposed the coach must be stopping to take on another passenger. The two gentlemen and the lady who had been her traveling companions for much of the journey had disembarked at the last stop, somewhere in the heart of Liverpool. She had guessed that her own stop at the docks would not be long after.

The carriage door swung open, and the coachman poked his head in. "Last stop. All out."

"You must be mistaken," Marsali said. "I am the only one left, and this is not my destination."

"Docks'r over there." The coachman pointed through the carriage to the window on the other side.

"Oh. Of course." Marsali hurriedly climbed down, embarrassed at not having thought to look out the other window. Somehow she had expected the scene to be different—louder and busier, full of people all as excited as she was, eager to be leaving behind this forsaken island.

"That'll be another shilling for your trunk," the coachman said, his hand held out.

"But I paid you already—when we left this morning." What kind of fool did he take her for? She'd been sleepy today, not forgetful.

"Right. You paid me at the first. An' you pay me at the end—unless you don't want your trunk, that is."

Marsali clutched her reticule tightly to her and frowned, furious with both herself—for not knowing whether or not she was being cheated—and with the unfeeling coachman, who had done nothing that she could see to earn that extra shilling.

"In your advertisement, it stated clearly that the price for transport from Manchester to Liverpool was exactly six shillings."

He nodded. "And so it has been."

"But you charged me an extra shilling this morning to load and transport my trunk. And the driver charged me another as well." *For who knows what.* Without a driver there would have been no transport of any kind. It seemed rather logical that his fee, at least, should have been included in the original cost. "Then I was assessed a third shilling for the change of horses at noon."

"Yep." The coachman nodded again, exaggerating his movements as if she were daft and was having difficulty understanding. "A shilling at the start, and a shilling now, for me to take your trunk down and restore it to you."

"That isn't fair," Marsali said. "Such a fee was not advertised. You ought to have been more clear up front."

He shrugged. "I guess we'll just be keepin' your trunk, then." He tipped his cap at her, then turned to close the carriage door.

"Wait!" Marsali held her hand out. "I'll pay it—or what I can, anyway." She loosened the strings of her reticule and reached inside, reasoning that she *had* to have her trunk. It wasn't as if she could sail across the Atlantic or arrive in America with no underclothes or without so much as a sleeping gown or shawl.

"I haven't a shilling. Only a sixpence." She held her hand out, the coin on her palm.

The coachman snatched it up. "At'll do. Right, then. Let's get your trunk." He walked around to the back of the carriage, and Marsali followed. The driver was already waiting there to help, and Marsali worried that he, too, would assess some last-minute fee—in which case she would have to give him one of her belongings as payment. And threadbare as most of her garments were, it was doubtful he would accept such.

Yet I am here. What can he do? Eager for her first sight of the ship she was to sail on, Marsali walked past the men around to the other side of the carriage. But there was no water in sight. She turned a hurried circle. No water anywhere.

"Wait. There's been some mistake." She whirled around to stop the coachman from untying her trunk before it was too late. "This is not my stop. My ship departs from the Waterloo dock, and I don't see any docks *anywhere*."

"I know." Something about the coachman's nonchalant manner alarmed her.

"Then why have you not taken me there?" she demanded, turning quickly searching for the driver, who had disappeared again. "It is what I paid for."

He shook his head. "No. You paid for transport to

Liverpool. If you want to go to the docks, it'll be an additional shilling."

"I haven't an additional shilling," Marsali said, her panic escalating. "I've just given you the last of my coin—for the *arduous* task of removing my trunk."

"Guess you'll have to walk, then," the coachman said, ignoring both her sarcasm and her plight. Her trunk was untied and fell to the ground with a none-too-gentle thud. Whistling, the coachman flipped her sixpence casually into the air once, then dropped it into his pocket, where it jingled merrily against the other coins resting there.

"It is quite a racket you have going," Marsali huffed in a last, desperate attempt to wrangle his conscience—supposing he had one. "To strand a lady as you are—"

"It's not my custom to strand *ladies*." His face twisted in a sneer as his gaze roved over Marsali as if she was the vilest creature. "But a woman like you is a different matter. Your uncle said to leave you where you belong. And so I have. Be glad you've a bit of daylight left. Maybe you've still a chance of making that sea voyage—as some pirate's chattel, if you're lucky." His harsh laughter echoed down the street.

Marsali reeled backward as if struck. His stinging words sank deep, revealing her true vulnerability just when she'd believed she was at last beyond her aunt and uncle's reach.

Will I ever be beyond it? Will I ever be free?

The coachman stepped up on the side of the coach, gave a shout, and it rolled away. She sat woefully on her trunk as the carriage and the last of her money disappeared. Quickly she scanned the buildings and signs hanging over them. Madame Kelner's Girls for Hire, Palace of Pleasure, The Starlight—Showgirls and Spirits. She felt suddenly ill. *Your uncle said to leave you where you belong.* It wasn't here, just as it had not been in his arms or in his bed, though he'd tried on more than one occasion to persuade her to that end.

Her head jerked to the other side of the street as she fought panic. Surely there had to be other sorts of establishments here. The Lion Tavern—Women and Ale, Moll's Club for Men, Archer and Sons' Wine and Spirits.

No. Marsali wanted to squeeze her eyes shut against the obvious, but fear kept them wide open, darting to and fro. Dusk settled quickly over the lonely street. Several buildings down, a lone female figure emerged and came to stand beneath a lamppost, leaning against it in such a way, and facing the street, so as to be easily noticed by any passersby.

Worry over reaching the ship suddenly paled in comparison to the more immediate problem of getting off this street. Before long it would be full dark.

And I will be here alone—or worse.

CHAPTER 5

The medical inspector dabbed his napkin to the corner of his mouth. "A fine meal, Captain. If your cook is able to provide such tasty fare throughout the voyage, I daresay your ship will find success based on the merits of its cuisine alone."

"Mr. Tenney is an excellent cook," Captain Gower agreed. "And we are well supplied with a pen for chickens and a stall for a milk cow to sustain us with fresh eggs and cream throughout the journey. We've barrels of salted meat and sacks of grain—even nuts and dried fruits. The shorter length of travel makes all of that much easier to provide and store." He eyed his pocket watch for the seventh time in the last hour; Christopher had been counting.

It had seemed a long hour to him as well. They had all dined together—Captain Gower, the medical inspector, Lady Cosgrove and her daughter, and himself. Only Miss Abbott, the one passenger yet to board, had been absent. Lady Cosgrove had excused herself shortly after the main course, citing a headache as her excuse for retiring early and requiring her daughter to come along to assist her.

The meal had become a bit more pleasant after that. At least the captain and inspector were able to carry on a proper conversation now that the chatty Miss Cosgrove had left.

"Blasted woman is going to delay us," the captain muttered beneath his breath, but not so quietly that both Christopher and the medical inspector failed to hear it. The latter's eyes went to a clock on the wall behind the captain.

"Surely you don't mean to wait for Miss Abbott," the inspector said, placing his napkin on the table as if making ready to leave.

"I may not have a choice *but* to wait for her." More than a hint of irritation tinged the captain's voice.

"Why?" the inspector asked. "It's not as if one *less* person on this ship is going to make any difference, though she does account for a quarter of your passengers." He chuckled at his own joke.

Captain Gower attempted a smile, though Christopher caught a glimpse of a desperate sort of bitterness beneath.

"The girl is indentured to Mr. Thomas," the captain explained. At the inspector's blank look, he clarified. "Mr. Thomas is the wealthy Virginian who financed over 80 percent of the *Amanda May*. It would seem that the least I can do—seeing how I have failed at attracting passengers— would be to deliver his servant."

"Ah." The inspector nodded. "So Miss Abbott is not just *any* passenger."

"Not at all," Captain Gower said. "She is to serve as a lady's maid for Thomas's daughter. Her current maid's term of indenture has recently ended, and he was unable to secure a proper replacement. He seems to feel that a young woman from England is the best choice."

"Does that not strike you as odd, Captain?" Christopher asked. "I should think America would have plenty of young women, both those born there as well as a great many immigrants recently arrived, who would be pleased to have such a position." He thought of the Irish ship docked beside them. "Why should a man have to advertise and send away, as it were, for a maid?"

"I do not pretend to know." Captain Gower tugged at his cravat as his mouth turned down, exhibiting mild discomfort and causing Christopher to suspect that he was not being entirely truthful.

"I cannot imagine what might have happened to delay her," the captain said, glancing at his watch yet again.

"Most unfortunate," the inspector said, pushing back his chair and rising.

An abrupt, forced smile appeared on the captain's face. "Let us at least enjoy ourselves while we wait, gentlemen." His gaze moved from the inspector to Christopher, a silent plea in it.

"I've a fine bottle of port waiting to be opened in celebration of our departure, and I am most eager to show off some of my latest acquisitions."

"Well, now . . ." The inspector brought a hand to his chin as he considered.

Christopher felt somewhat surprised at being included in the invitation, but then he *was* the only male passenger, so it wasn't as if the captain had many choices if he wished for more company to keep the inspector lingering.

"Fine port, you say? It would be a shame to pass that up." The inspector patted his rotund belly affectionately, as if promising it yet another treat.

When he has already eaten a double portion of everything. Good that he won't be joining us on this voyage, or the rest of us might go without.

Christopher stood and followed the two men into the captain's quarters, two generous-sized rooms, the first of which featured a wide, cushioned seat with a large, paned window behind it. Ornate wood trim framed both the window and the seat and matched the gleam of the polished floors and beams overhead. But the main features of the room were the large tables on the opposite side. These were built in an octagonal shape to fit the space and held an enticing array of objects—none of which Christopher could identify.

"I collect inventions," Captain Gower said, striding over to the tables, his chest puffed out as if they were his greatest pride and joy. "A few are my own; several belonged to others who never realized their potential; and one I will be showing to American investors for a friend of mine—Joseph Niépce. Perhaps you have heard of him?"

Both Christopher and the inspector shook their heads.

"He has invented a heliograph," the captain said, as if they ought to know what such a thing was. He moved to the second table and pointed out the box sitting at the end.

The inspector came closer and bent over, examining it. Christopher lingered behind, interested as well but not wanting to interrupt the inspector's distraction. He had the idea that this was exactly what the captain had intended, bringing them in here to stall for time until Miss Abbott arrived.

If he was unable to detain the medical inspector, if the inspector left without clearing all of the listed passengers, their departure would be delayed—something Christopher wanted as little as the captain. He would do all he could to assist Captain Gower in assuring they sailed tomorrow.

Captain Gower left the inspector to his examination of the objects on the tables and went to a cabinet near the window. He removed three glasses and set them on the sideboard below. From a wine rack built into the sideboard, he withdrew a somewhat dusty bottle.

Christopher watched as the captain removed the cork, sniffed it appreciatively, and with a nearly concealed sigh, began to pour out.

"I say, Gower. You must be the vainest captain I've met," the inspector said. "With your ship that can move without sails and a special stand of mirrors with which to preen." He moved closer, attempting to peer into one himself.

"Ah, but they are not for preening." The captain crossed the room and handed a glass of port to the inspector.

"What are they for, then? And what is that box supposed to do?"

"The heliograph was Joseph's first attempt at making a picture. The mirrors are used to reflect the light of the sun in order to capture the image."

The inspector's look turned skeptical. "Since when can a mirror paint?"

"I did not say a portrait, but a picture—an image." Captain Gower set his drink aside, then carefully picked up two parchments from behind the invention. "A sun drawing, if you will." He held the parchment out, and Christopher came closer for a better look.

The first was a landscape, or a likeness of one, but nothing like Christopher had ever seen. The second was a grainy image of a man with a horse.

"This one was made with Joseph's camera obscura, another invention he is still working on," Captain Gower said.

"I've seen much better paintings," the inspector said, and the captain exchanged a look with Christopher as if to suggest that men in the inspector's line of business obviously had no imagination.

"A camera obscura produces a likeness," Captain Gower attempted to explain once more. He held up the landscape. "Joseph took this one out the window of his house, but a sun drawing can be made of anything. One could just as easily capture you as you are right now, standing there."

Drinking some of my best port, Christopher imagined the captain thinking as he watched the man's eyes narrow at the rate the inspector was downing his drink.

"Most intriguing." The inspector's glass was nearly empty. "Any future in it?"

"Mr. Niépce seems to think so." Captain Gower returned the images to the table. "Joseph and I first became friends several years ago, when he and his brother invented the Pyréolophore. It was a mechanism, a machine, if you will, for powering boats upriver. He and I, we think alike." Captain Gower tapped a finger against the side of his head. "There are better ways to do things, faster ways to get places. We've just got to find them."

"And this Niépce, have his boats found success?" the inspector asked.

The captain's face fell. "No." He waved his hand dismissively. "Joseph and Claude did not give the Pyréolophore the time and attention it needed. Their patent has run out, and now Joseph believes this creating of pictures is the future." The captain chuckled. "Though, in truth, I cannot see how making an image of a person is more important than the speed with which that person can cross the Atlantic, but we shall see. I am to deliver Joseph's invention to some American investors in an attempt to procure financing to continue his project."

The mention of American investors brought to mind their current problem—Mr. Thomas's missing servant—and Christopher felt relieved when the captain offered to refill the inspector's glass. If Miss Abbott failed to arrive before the inspector left, and if the captain truly intended to wait for her, who knew when they would be able to start their journey to America.

But the inspector had taken up a second drink and appeared completely untroubled by the inconvenience of having to linger while waiting for the last passenger to arrive.

Christopher stood behind the two men, only half listening as the captain eagerly expounded on the merits and possibilities of each of the inventions he'd collected. Usually Christopher would have found this sort of thing most interesting, but his thoughts kept returning to the missing passenger and the possibility that something had gone wrong or would go wrong to delay them. If, for some reason, the *Amanda May* did not sail, if he had to return to Yorkshire and begin again to arrange for another passage, he was not at all certain he would be able to part from his sisters a second time.

Leaving them once had felt like tearing a piece of his heart out. He rubbed a hand absently against his chest, as if that might erase the ache—and the loss and the guilt—he felt. It was necessary, he knew, if he was to have this opportunity to start over, to have a fresh slate and a better life.

To make the name Thatcher into something noble and good.

But knowing a thing must be done and doing it were proving to be two entirely different things. He needed to get on with the rest of it now. The hard part had been leaving; he was eager for what came next. He'd been imagining America's shores for so long now, imagining working the land with his hands, earning his own, fair wage, and saving and purchasing his own property. But none of that could begin until he reached America. And it appeared the captain would not begin their journey until Miss Abbott arrived.

The inspector also appeared to be reminded of her absence, and the late hour as well. He set his empty glass on the table. "I'd best be off now."

"But if Miss Abbott arrives—"

"I've got a ship full of Irishmen to examine tomorrow morning," the inspector said. "I'll check in with you briefly just before. With any luck, you can still make your departure time—with Mr. Thomas's servant aboard."

"Thank you," Captain Gower said, the sincerity of his gratitude evident in his voice. Christopher supposed this was a generous offer on the inspector's part.

"Good eve to you, then." The inspector tipped the hat he had just placed upon his head.

"Good evening," Christopher said and followed the captain and the inspector out of the captain's quarters. Captain Gower saw the inspector safely off of the ship while Christopher waited on deck, all the while busily scanning the wharf for any sign of the missing woman.

Marsali sat on the edge of her trunk and waited nervously inside the foyer of Madame Kelner's Girls for Hire, both the closest establishment to where the coach had dropped her off and the one with the possibly least-offensive name. Under normal circumstances, or on a different street, "for hire" might mean any number of things. The red-velvet wallpaper, dim chandeliers, and heavy scent of perfume told her that it did not mean any of those other things here, but still, Marsali reasoned, this had to be better than stepping inside the Palace of Pleasure, farther down the street.

"This way, and bring your trunk." The young woman who'd first answered when Marsali had rung the doorbell a few minutes earlier had returned. She inclined her head toward a side door off the foyer and walked toward it, clearly expecting Marsali to follow. This she did, dragging her trunk behind her with the same terrible scraping noise it had made as she'd lugged it across the street.

The woman opened the door, and Marsali moved awkwardly past her into a cozy sitting room. Decorated in subtle tones of green, the room was considerably less offensive to the eye than the foyer had been, and Marsali left her trunk just inside the room in favor of sitting in one of the chairs before the empty fireplace. She sank into its softness and felt herself relax just slightly. Holding her hands out before her, she realized they were both freezing and shaking, and she wondered that she'd not noticed before now just how cold she'd become.

From fear. The temperature itself was warm enough this time of year. Whatever the cause, she felt grateful for this temporary shelter. Behind her the door clicked shut, and Marsali removed her gloves and stretched her fingers.

"Used to hard work, are you?"

Marsali started at the voice above her. A woman considerably older than herself and considerably more beautiful stood behind Marsali. She came around in front of her, a purple satin gown swishing about her ankles. A matching necklace lay at the base of her throat, pointing down to the V of her dress, a far more daring décolleté than any Marsali had ever seen. Feeling most uncomfortable, she forced her eyes to the woman's face and noted the careful application of rouge and powders, which Marsali suspected were intended to conceal the woman's actual age. White-blonde curls were piled high atop her head, with a few kept down on either side of her face. She reached out, taking one of Marsali's hands in her own and examining it.

"These hands will need some healing. It will be a while before I could use you. Gentlemen pay for soft hands—not rough."

"Oh no." Marsali extracted her hand from the stranger's as she shook her head vigorously. "You misunderstand. I haven't come looking for . . . work. It's only that I'm in a bit of trouble."

The woman arched an eyebrow. "With child?" She leaned forward and took Marsali's chin, turning it, so her profile was presented. "What a pity. You would be popular. Though the other girls wouldn't like it." She let go abruptly and sat back in her chair, her gaze drifting to Marsali's waistline. "How far gone are you? It's possible it could still be taken care of. Though that would mean even longer before you could work."

"I am *not* with child," Marsali said. "And I do not wish—"

"Well, I've no need for any more maids right now, especially not one as pretty as you. It would only cause problems." The woman stood, indicating their conversation was over.

Marsali resisted the urge to rub both her hand and chin where the woman had touched her. Instead she stood as well. "I am not here applying for a position as a maid—or anything else," she quickly added when the hopeful, speculative expression reappeared on the woman's face. "My coach mistakenly dropped me off outside your . . . establishment, and I am in need of transport to the Waterloo dock. I have passage on a ship that is to leave tomorrow morning." She held her breath, waiting to see if the woman might offer any help.

"What do you expect me to do about it?" she asked haughtily, her eyes still appraising Marsali in a way that made her most uncomfortable.

"I thought, perhaps, I might offer you something in my trunk in exchange for a coach to take me."

"Have you anything of value?" The woman seemed possibly interested again.

Marsali's mind reviewed the contents of her trunk—scant compared to those she'd arrived at her aunt's with four years earlier. And scant compared to the opulence—however distasteful—she'd glimpsed upon entering Madame Kelner's establishment. She wondered suddenly if Madame Kelner herself was standing before her.

"Well?" the woman asked, impatience in her tone.

"I do not have much," Marsali admitted. "But the trunk itself, perhaps? In exchange for an old carpetbag or even a sackcloth in which I might carry my things."

The woman shook her head. "What need would I have for a trunk, and an old one at that? No one around here is going anywhere. I am afraid I cannot help you. Now, if you would be so kind as to remove yourself from my premises. Customers will be arriving soon, and you wouldn't want any of them becoming confused about you, would you?" She smiled in a knowing sort of way, and Marsali had the uncomfortable feeling that the woman had guessed every thought and revulsion she'd felt since first walking through the door.

Still, inside Madame Kelner's had to be better than out alone on that street. Two more women had taken up their posts before she had made her way inside. She did not want to be out among them and the men who would soon be arriving to peruse the offerings. "Please," Marsali begged. "I have nowhere to go."

"I am not running a charity."

So she is Madame Kelner.

"The girls around here work for their keep. *You* could work for yours as well." Madame Kelner stepped closer, her eyes boring into Marsali's. "I could fetch a high price for you—even if it was just for one night. I would even see to it you had a proper gentleman."

"No." Marsali shook her head and backed away.

"Then get out." Madame Kelner's hand shot forward, narrowly missing Marsali's face. "See that you are gone immediately, lest I receive an offer for you too good to pass up." Madame Kelner swept past her in a swirl of satin. "Kimberly will show you out."

She exited the room, and the young woman who had shown Marsali in returned.

"This way," she said quietly and bent to pick up one side of the trunk. "We've a back entrance. It will be a little better than going straight out to the street right now."

Marsali nodded, swallowing back the tears she felt threatening. Lifting the other end of her trunk, she followed the girl out of the room, through the foyer, and past the long staircase leading to the upper floor. They entered another door and crossed through a kitchen. Marsali's stomach growled with hunger as they passed by an oven and the scent of baking bread overtook the other, less pleasant aromas of the building. They left the kitchen and came to a narrow hall with several doors leading off it.

"Wait here," Kimberly said, lowering her end of the trunk. She turned away, hurrying down the hall and disappearing through one of the doors. Marsali sat on the trunk and tried to think what she must do next. She had no idea whatsoever which direction the wharf lay, and even if she did, it wasn't as if she could pull her trunk along with her.

Kimberly reappeared in the hall, something folded over her arms. She came closer, holding the offering out to Marsali.

"I overheard your conversation with Madame, and I thought you might be able to use this." She shook open the bundle, and Marsali saw that it was a large cloth sack, the kind flour was sometimes delivered in.

"Thank you," she said, only slightly relieved. She still had no idea how she was going to reach the docks. "And I shall give you my trunk in return for coach fare?"

Kimberly shook her head. "I haven't any money. I'm sorry. I still owe Madame for . . ." Her voice trailed off, and Marsali was left to surmise what might have incurred the debt.

"But I can tell you how to get to the docks," Kimberly said. "And you can carry your belongings—some of them, at least—in this. It will be easier than your trunk."

"Thank you." It wasn't much, but it was a better option than any she could think of, and Marsali felt a rush of gratitude for the young woman, likely risking more trouble with Madame by helping as she was.

She fished the key out of her reticule and unlocked the trunk. Kimberly held the sack open while Marsali made instant decisions about which items she must take and which she could live without. Her hairbrush, yes; woolen petticoat, no. Hopefully her employer would provide her with another when winter came. Two of the three dresses she owned, beyond the one she wore, yes. Her least favorite, no. Nightgown and cap, yes. Underclothes, yes. Books, no. Sewing kit, no. She held back tears and suppressed a sigh. She pulled her cloak and a heavy woolen shawl from the trunk and set them aside, knowing neither would fit in the nearly full sack. No doubt it would have held more had she had the time to fold and arrange things properly, but she'd shoved each item in as quickly as her shaking fingers would allow.

The last item in her trunk was a bundle of mostly faded hair ribbons, one of the last gifts from her father. Marsali placed these in the flour sack, and Kimberly helped her tie the string tightly around the top.

"Hold this," Kimberly instructed, handing her the sack. She snatched the shawl from the edge of the trunk where Marsali had placed it and hurriedly tied two large knots at the back. Then she draped the shawl over Marsali's shoulders and tied it securely in front. When this was accomplished, she layered the cloak over the shawl, pulled the hood up over Marsali's head, and tied it as well.

"Walk hunched over, with your head down, and it will appear as though you've a hump on your back," Kimberly said. "Shuffle your feet, keep your face covered as much as possible, and it's likely the only people who will take notice of you will be the lads who loiter by the wharf—and they'll only taunt you about being old and decrepit or throw a rock or two."

"Will this really work?" Marsali asked as she clutched the sack to her and pulled the cloak tight around it.

"Aye. I've done it myself a time or two. It's important you keep your head down and walk just so." She took a few shuffling steps down the hall and back again. "See how it gives the appearance of the old and infirm?"

Marsali nodded, though she wasn't certain her performance would be as good. *It had best be. My very life may depend upon it.*

"You must make sure to keep your head down. And if someone approaches you, don't look up, but start coughing and gagging. Spit on the street if you must—anything so it appears you're very ill. Go now." Kimberly turned Marsali toward the back of the hall and pushed her along toward a door at the end.

"But I don't know how to get to the docks," Marsali said, her panic returning at the thought of being thrust into the alleyway alone.

"I'll draw it out for you." Kimberly stepped in front of her, opened the door, and went outside. She searched around a moment and found a broken bottle, then picked up a jagged piece of it, bent to the dirt, and began drawing.

"We're here." She marked the spot with an *X*. "You're going to walk to the end of the passageway, then turn left. You'll be on Lime Street again. Stay on Lime until you get to Hanover. Go right on Hanover, and stay on it a good long time until you reach the docks. I'm not sure which direction your ship will be, but you can walk up and down until you find it."

"How long do you think it will take me?" Marsali asked, loath to leave this small security yet anxious to be gone as well.

Kimberly shrugged. "An hour or two, I'd think. Longer, perhaps, if your ship is at one of the far docks."

"Thank you," Marsali said, looking into the girl's eyes. "May God bless you for helping me."

Kimberly shook her head. "That's kind of you, miss, but it ain't likely to happen. One good deed against my many sins is not likely to balance out. But I thank you just the same. Be gone now." She waved her hands, as if shooing away a pigeon or a stray cat. Her heart aching, Marsali turned away. *Why does life have to be so unfair? So difficult for so many?* Were circumstances different, she felt the girl might have been a friend.

Had Papa still been alive. And had Kimberly had a

father to see after her as well. *We might have taken tea together in the afternoons and gone on carriage rides around the park.*

Leaning purposely forward, Marsali shuffled down the alleyway. *But those things are not to be. Not for me. Not for the women on this street. Who has time for tea or going to the park when simply surviving requires so much?*

CHAPTER 6

*C*hristopher sat on a crate alongside the rail, where he could easily see the comings and goings on the dock below. In the hours since the medical inspector had left, the wharf had grown quieter and the street darker as the business of the day had been completed, excepting the boardwalk taverns, from which an occasional burst of raucous laughter came whenever a door opened.

"Rethinking your decision?" Captain Gower hung a lantern on a nearby post and came to join him.

"Not at all," Christopher said, though his thoughts had been turning to home—or his sisters' homes, at least. He had no qualms about traveling to America aboard a steamship, and neither did he regret his decision to leave England. He only wished there might have been a way to bring Grace and Helen. He missed them, their companionship, their evenings full of talk and laughter. "I was simply enjoying the solitude you promised," Christopher said. "I admit to being unaccustomed to such. It may take some getting used to."

"That it does," the captain agreed. "When I am long from the sea, I find myself yearning for it, for quiet hours at the ship's wheel with nothing to disturb me except the cry of a gull or the fin of a dolphin skimming through the waves. But then, when I'm out on the ocean, when all is calm and quiet, I cannot help but think of home, of my wife and wee'uns and how desperate I feel to return to them. It seems a man—at least one destined to sail—cannot ever feel entirely satisfied."

"I suppose it is good, then, that I am not destined to be a sailor," Christopher said, half jesting, though the captain's words had struck a chord of discomfort. He wanted to believe he could be entirely happy in America. But was that possible having left his sisters behind as he had? He'd not been happy in England, so this was the better choice—was it not? He frowned, weary of thinking on it and wishing the ship had sailed already.

Captain Gower chuckled. "You may not be a sailor, but I reckon you know just what I mean."

"It would seem that I do," Christopher admitted. "But I have placed my hope in America—that her freedoms and opportunities will be my happiness and a better life than I could ever live here."

"She is the reason we stand on this ship," Gower said. "If I cannot get any Englishmen to sail on her, it's certain I'd not have convinced any to finance her."

"What will your American investors think if we do not sail as planned tomorrow?" Christopher asked.

"We'll make up that day or die attempting to," Gower promised, and Christopher felt the first inkling of uncertainty in his gut. *Speed does not necessarily equate with death*, he'd told the coachmen just this morning. But might it, if the captain grew careless?

"Miss Abbott may yet arrive," the captain said, lighting a pipe he had pulled from his pocket but sounding less hopeful than he had earlier.

Christopher followed his gaze, scanning up and down the boardwalk, and saw that a lone figure—cloaked and with hood drawn around the face—*was* approaching, walking slowly past the Irish ship next to theirs. With the captain, he watched as the individual moved laboriously along the wharf, not stopping at the larger vessel but glancing up at the *Amanda May* and continuing toward them. It was apparent now that the individual was a female—a rather small one, and possibly deformed. She was hunched over and shuffling along as if with great difficulty.

"How old *is* this Miss Abbott?" Christopher asked.

"Young enough to serve at least four years after this voyage," Captain Gower said. "Or at least that is what Mr. Thomas was led to believe through their correspondence."

The woman paused at the gangway, said something to the guards stationed below, then started up the ramp.

"A new passenger, perhaps?" Christopher suggested.

"Let us hope so," the captain said, taking up the lantern once more and heading toward the gangway. "For as much as I want Miss Abbott to arrive, I should like her to look a bit more *alive* when she does."

Christopher followed the captain to midship, then hung back so as not to interfere with the interrogation soon to take place. The woman was taking an extraordinarily long time to ascend the ramp, and Christopher wondered if they ought to offer assistance. But at last her head appeared, hidden in the folds of a winter cloak, her face down, as if keeping her balance required that she watch her every step.

She stood on the deck a moment, then dropped the bundle she'd been carrying—a sack of flour, it seemed. Captain Gower extinguished the pipe he'd lit just moments before, then stepped forward, lantern held up in one hand, his other on the pistol at his waist.

"State your name and your reason for boarding my ship."

The woman straightened, raised her hands, and pushed back the hood of her cloak, revealing a startlingly young and beautiful face.

Christopher held back a surprised gasp but was unable to suppress a smile.

"Marsali Abbott, sir. A Mr. Joshua Thomas arranged for my passage."

A passage that has just become far more interesting.

"He arranged for more than that," the captain said. "Are you not contracted to be a lady's maid to his daughter for a period of four years?"

"I am." Miss Abbott stood a little taller yet.

"Mr. Thomas is my colleague, and I would hate to think that he is being cheated," the captain said. "In addition to having a difficulty with reporting on time, it appears you may have infirmities which prevent you from fulfilling your duties."

"I have *no* infirmities, sir."

"Yes, well, it is a pity the medical inspector left hours ago and is not here to refute your claim. He is set to return tomorrow morning—at the cost of one of my finest bottles of port, mind you—but I am of a mind not to bother having him back when it is clear you cannot even walk properly."

"I have been walking for over two hours," Miss Abbott said. "On brick and cobblestone roads in worn slippers not meant to traverse great distances. I assure you, under normal circumstances my feet and legs move quite well. As for the other—infirmity—you speak of." She untied the strings of her cloak, removed it, and set it on top of the bundle she'd dropped earlier. She turned away from the captain, revealing a knotted shawl bunched at the base of her neck.

"My journey here was somewhat perilous; this disguise allowed me to make it safely. It seems no one wants to bother with an old, deformed woman." She turned to face him once more.

Christopher smiled to himself and wished he might applaud Miss Abbott's ruse. It reminded him very much of something Grace might have done in days not long ago, when her situation was perilous as well.

Miss Abbott's must be very grave indeed, he thought, noting the sack that lay at her feet. He'd brought little with him, but his possessions seemed extravagant compared to what little Miss Abbott owned.

And what will she think—how will she feel—when she meets our other passengers, Lady Cosgrove and her daughter? Christopher had had the misfortune of meeting them earlier, and his first impression was that both the lady and her daughter were as ridiculous as the number of trunks and parcels they'd brought with them on this voyage.

"I see." The captain cleared his throat uncomfortably. "I may have judged your condition wrong, but that does not excuse your tardiness."

"It is not my habit to be late," Miss Abbott said. "The coach refused to take me the entire way, and I was forced to walk from . . . the center of town."

Christopher caught the slight hesitation in her voice and guessed the captain had as well. *What is it she is not telling us?* he wondered, then mentally scolded himself for his curiosity. The last thing he wanted was to be interested in this woman's affairs—no matter that it appeared she'd had a difficult time of it.

She is not Grace or Helen, he reminded himself. *And therefore not my responsibility.* He took a step backward, intending to retreat before either party could take notice of his presence. He had a book waiting for him in his cabin—on loan from Captain Gower, who had invited his guests to make use of his shipboard library, small though it was. *An evening reading is just the thing to distract me from thoughts of home.*

"Please, Captain Gower, sir. I am fairly exhausted and would be ever so grateful if you would show me to my lodgings. I believe with a bit of bread and a good night's rest I'll be better able to answer your questions and pass the medical inspection." Miss Abbott bent to pick up her cloak and sack.

"Meals are served promptly on this ship; supper is always at seven o'clock. As you have missed it this evening, you will have to wait until breakfast tomorrow—at eight o'clock sharp—for something to eat." Captain Gower's tone brooked no arguing and was more stern than Christopher thought necessary.

"Very well," Miss Abbott said, sounding weary.

Christopher glanced at her and felt a swell of pity and wanted to protest on her behalf. He knew what it was to go hungry—had felt that gnawing, stabbing pain in his gut, had frequently known the dizzying weakness caused by hunger quite often during the first fourteen years of his life. He recognized the pained look in Miss Abbott's eyes and guessed—by her thin frame—that she was no stranger to hunger herself.

"Might you show me to my quarters, then?" she asked the captain. "Unless I have missed the appointed hour for retiring for the night and must wait until the morrow for that as well?"

Weary, but not done for. Christopher turned away, hiding his smile.

"This way," Captain Gower said gruffly.

Hurrying ahead, Christopher reached the door to the saloon first. He pulled it open and stepped aside, allowing first Miss Abbott and then the captain to enter.

"Miss Abbott, this is Mr. Thatcher, another of our passengers this voyage." The captain's introduction was stiff, as if he hadn't really wanted to make it. "Mr. Thatcher, Miss Abbott."

"Welcome aboard," Christopher said, feeling grateful for more than the renewed possibility of tomorrow's departure.

"Mr. Thatcher is as glad as I am that you have arrived at last," Captain Gower said, addressing Miss Abbott. "He is most eager to be away from England and would not have been pleased if we had been detained longer."

"Then Mr. Thatcher and I have something in common," Miss Abbott said. "I have been counting down the days until I never have to see England again." She dipped into a graceful curtsey, even cumbered as she was by the large sack. "Mr. Thatcher."

"Your cabin is this way," the captain said. "I've put you close to mine so as to see you come to no harm. Mr. Thomas and his daughter are most eager for you to arrive safely and have given me that charge."

Miss Abbott made no comment to this but followed the captain down the women's side of the saloon, while Christopher walked down the other side, toward his own cabin, also near the captain's quarters on the other side.

So much for not being near any women, he thought when Miss Abbott was shown to the room directly across from his, though he found this did not bother him nearly as much as he'd thought it would—or as much as it would have if Lady Cosgrove or her daughter were situated so closely to him.

"Good night, Captain, Mr. Thatcher." Miss Abbott went inside her cabin and closed the door behind her.

"Not sure she's what Thomas is expecting," Captain Gower muttered and headed for his own quarters at the end of the long room.

"Good night, sir," Christopher said, then stepped inside his room and closed his door as well. He hesitated but a moment, then retrieved the bundle on the top of his trunk. Miranda had sent him with enough food to last a week, and though it wasn't as fresh as it had been three days ago, the crusty bread and cheese would be better than nothing. Quietly, Christopher stepped outside his cabin, leaving his door ajar so as to make as little noise as possible.

Instead of walking down the aisle to the end of the tables and the narrow passage in front of the captain's quarters to the other side, Christopher climbed on top of and over the benches and table in front of him, stepping quietly onto the floor in front of Miss Abbott's cabin.

He raised his hand, intending to knock softly, when he heard weeping from the other side of the door. He tensed, then withdrew his hand and stood there, undecided.

What am I doing? Had he not—just this morning— made a vow to enjoy his freedom from responsibility for any female? To enjoy worrying about no one but himself? To keep his life completely uncomplicated? And yet here he was, about to do something that would likely displease Captain Gower. *Something that at least borders upon meddling in his affairs—and Miss Abbott's.*

She was not his responsibility. Christopher knew this, and it alarmed him that here he was, acting as if she were anyway. Her hunger and hardships and anything else having to do with her were not his concern.

So why am I here? Why could he not turn around and go back to his cabin and pretend he had not noticed the hunger and the sadness in her eyes, pretend that he did not hear her heart-wrenching weeping this very moment?

Because I cannot—not when I am able to do something to assist her. To ignore Miss Abbott's distress would have meant disappointing Grace. And she had raised him better than that—as had his grandfather, having finished what his sisters had so well begun during the six years they had lived with him.

The true mark of a gentleman, Christopher, lies in how he treats others—both his peers and those who have less than he. Titles and fortune have nothing to do with it. How a man regards those less fortunate than he is determines who and what he really is.

Christopher raised his hand once more, knocking as quietly as possible on Miss Abbott's door.

The weeping on the other side ceased at once, followed by a series of hiccupping breaths.

The cabin walls are rather thin. I'll do well to remember that.

"Who is it?" Miss Abbott's teary voice asked.

"Mr. Thatcher," Christopher whispered. "I've some food for you. I'll leave it outside your door." He set the bundle down and returned the way he'd come, sliding over the table and benches quickly and entering his own door just as he heard Miss Abbott's open.

She glanced down at the parcel at her feet, then stooped to pick it up. Christopher started to push his door closed.

"Thank you." She sounded bewildered, as if no one had ever before done her a kindness.

"You're welcome." Christopher opened his door a hair more and met her gaze across the width of the saloon. "No one deserves to go hungry." He smiled encouragingly. "I hope the food does you good."

Miss Abbott clutched the bundle to her and nodded, then retreated into her cabin once again. Christopher closed his own door as well, then walked across to the bed and collapsed on it, hands clasped behind his head and a smile on his face.

No doubt about it. His heart felt lighter than it had since leaving Yorkshire. *Since leaving Grace and Helen.* Miss Abbott was not his sister, and it certainly wouldn't do to become too close to her or too involved in her problems, but perhaps he could do her a bit of good—show her a bit of kindness—during their journey.

There would be no harm in it, he reasoned, as she already had a post to go to—an arrangement of indenture for the next four years. But for the next few weeks, he might try being her friend and lightening her burdens—whatever they were—inasmuch as he could while they sailed together. If doing so assisted her, he would be glad of it.

He felt glad of it already, and a bit foolish as well, to realize he'd not separated himself from the responsibility for his sisters quite as much as he'd believed he had. *Apparently watching out for females in distress agrees with me after all.* Grace and Helen would have laughed to hear him admit that. But, then, he supposed, they had both probably realized it already.

CHAPTER 7

With reluctance Marsali placed Charlotte's still-unread letter on the table beside her bed, then left the security of her cabin and stepped out into the connecting hall. It seemed an unusual arrangement, with nothing separating the women's quarters from the men's excepting the long row of rectangular tables running down the middle of the room. Perhaps, as with the modern steam engine employed on this ship, this arrangement of closely clustered cabins was also in vogue. If nothing else, she knew it had to be better than the other option—traveling below deck in steerage, as her sister had four years earlier. The difficult voyage had nearly killed Charlotte—one of the reasons she'd been so reluctant to have Marsali make the same journey.

But I am making it now. And in none too shabby conditions. Her cabin, while tiny, was private—the first room she'd enjoyed all to herself since a child. The bed was comfortable, and the washbasin and stand appeared new. Had she still been in possession of her trunk, it would have fit nicely along the wall. And the louvered, circular window at the rear of the cabin let in sufficient light that she might sew or read—had she any books, or anything with which to sew.

Holding back a sigh, Marsali tried not to think of her trunk and belongings left behind yesterday. She was aboard the *Amanda May*, they would shortly be traveling toward America, and that was all that mattered. In a few short hours the ship would be underway, and she would be reading Charlotte's letter and learning all about America and Virginia, where her sister lived.

The common room was empty, and Marsali worried she'd missed breakfast. But it couldn't possibly be eight o'clock yet. She'd watched the sky turn from dark to pink through her window this morning. *I am early. That is all,* she told herself, then walked the length of the room and stepped outside into the morning sunshine.

The air felt warm and muggy already, and she guessed it would be another hot day. *And I shall not have to spend any of it hidden beneath my winter cloak.* Marsali shuddered, yesterday afternoon's frightening situation still all too close.

She pulled the door closed behind her and set out to explore the ship. The majestic smokestack was almost directly to her right, and this she stared up at, impressed already by its height and girth. She would have liked to see the pipe installed and imagined that it must have been quite the feat to set it in place.

A short distance past the smokestack was the wheelhouse. It was this feature that had helped her locate the ship last night, as none of the other vessels at dock had any such contraption. Moving to the rail, Marsali leaned over the side, studying the immense wheel and trying to comprehend what it would take to set such enormous paddles churning. She'd no doubt that once they were, the ship would move in record time. Rather than feeling frightened by this, she found the sight and possibilities exhilarating.

"You're up early."

Marsali looked over her shoulder and found Captain Gower standing behind her. She turned to face him, her back against the rail.

"I am *always* up early. I do not believe I could sleep late if I tried."

"That is well, as you'll not have much opportunity for that beyond this voyage."

Marsali forced a smile, though she did not appreciate the reminder of the period of servitude that awaited her. She hoped Captain Gower would not treat her differently than the other passengers, that he would not continuously refer to her indenture, but it seemed that perhaps he would.

No matter, she told herself. *I will simply have to earn his good graces.*

"Your ship is splendid," she said sincerely.

"I rather think so." Captain Gower smiled, and it changed his face completely, giving Marsali hope that there was a fair man within.

"Mr. Thatcher has asked for a tour of her once we are underway. You may join us in that if you like."

"Yes, please." Marsali's hopes soared. Perhaps the captain *would* treat her as the other passengers. *And I should like to see Mr. Thatcher again.* The thought caused a queer little flutter inside, as had his unexpected kindness the previous night.

"Breakfast will be served shortly, and you can meet the other passengers. Perhaps you and the young Miss Cosgrove will get on well. She looks to be about your age."

Marsali's smile broadened. This was more than she had hoped for. To make a friend on this voyage would be lovely—to have idle hours in which she might enjoy visiting with another female. *To sit at tea and live as I once did—even if only for a few weeks.* "I should like that very much."

"Then let us go in." The captain held his arm out to her, and Marsali hesitated but a second before she placed her hand upon it. *How long has it been since a gentleman offered me his arm?* She had not expected such a courtesy from the captain, of all people, but she took it as a good sign—that perhaps he regretted being so gruff with her the evening before.

They returned to the common room and found that the table closest to the captain's quarters had been set with linens, plates, and silverware. The captain seated himself at a lone chair at the head of the table, and Marsali slid onto the bench to his right, uncertain of where she should sit. It seemed odd that just this one table had been set when there were so many cabins. *Where is everyone else to eat?*

Mr. Thatcher's door opened, and he stepped out into the hall. "Good morning, Captain, Miss Abbott." He nodded to each, then joined them at the table, sitting directly across from her.

She had not realized or noticed last night how tall he was or how broad his shoulders were. He wore the clothing of a gentleman, but his stature somehow bespoke a man used to physical labor. Neither had she noticed the deep blue of his eyes—eyes that held a hint of good-natured mischief as they met hers briefly, giving Marsali the impression that he knew she'd been appraising him.

"Good morning, Mr. Thatcher," she murmured, keeping her gaze downcast and noticing that his hands did not have the finely aristocratic look her uncle's and his associates' did. In spite of herself and her inherent wariness of men, she felt intrigued by Mr. Thatcher. At the least, she wanted to thank him again for his kindness but sensed she should not say anything in front of the captain. After all, it had been he who had scolded her as if she was a child and then sent her to bed hungry.

The doors closest on either side of the captain's quarters swung open, and two ship's boys entered, each bearing a large tray laden with various bowls and platters. The smaller of the two boys struggled under the weight of his tray but managed to set it safely on the table.

The captain pulled a pocket watch out of his vest. "Eight o'clock sharp. Good work, lads. You may tell Mr. Tenney I said so as well."

"Yessir," they said in unison and left the same way they had come.

Punctuality, Marsali realized, *is of great importance to the captain. No wonder I incurred his wrath last night.* She would make certain not to do so again.

The captain removed the lid from a platter and began dishing eggs onto his plate. Marsali's stomach grumbled with hunger, and she glanced away, taking her time with unfolding her serviette so as not to appear too eager. She doubted she could expect a hearty breakfast like this every day throughout the voyage, but this morning, at least, it appeared they were to eat very well.

So long since I have done that either. The captain finished with the platter of eggs and passed it to her.

"I've already explained to the other passengers that we're not as fancy as some are used to here. The men I've hired to crew this ship have better things to do than stand here and pull out chairs and pour drinks. And I don't see the need for washing more dishes than necessary. One plate, one fork, one knife, one cup per meal. Keep it simple, I say. And we're all able-bodied and can fend for ourselves, aye?"

"Of course," Marsali said, feeling only gratitude that *she* was not expected to serve. But she wondered about the other passengers, as it was obvious the majority had yet to take their meal. *Who will serve them, and where will they eat?*

At the far end of the room, the second to last door on Marsali's side banged open. A woman emerged, her petticoats making their entrance before she herself did. Trying not to stare, Marsali watched from the corner of her eye as the frilly, canary-yellow dress and the woman in it made their way toward the table.

"Ah," Captain Gower said. "Miss Cosgrove has decided to join us. Her mother informed me yesterday that an eight a.m. breakfast time was unacceptably early, but perhaps at least half of their party has changed her mind."

Marsali followed the young woman's progress toward them, noting that her excessively full skirts barely fit between the benches and the wall. Marsali could see what it was that had likely changed Miss Cosgrove's mind about breakfasting at eight. Her eyes at once sought out Mr. Thatcher and were now riveted upon him. Somehow, Marsali doubted he had shown Miss Cosgrove the same kindness he'd shown her in offering food, but he must have done something—aside from being dashingly handsome—to attract her keen interest.

This disappointed Marsali, though she couldn't exactly say why or even feel justified in her disappointment. She was also discouraged to realize this was the young lady Captain Gower had suggested she might be friends with. Already Marsali could see that prospect was doubtful.

The way Miss Cosgrove's hips swayed as she walked begged to be noticed—as if her bright dress was impossible to ignore. And she wore nearly as much powder on her face as some of the women Marsali had seen on Lime Street yesterday. Her hair was perfectly coiffed, her nails groomed, and an almost overbearing scent of lilacs announced her arrival, lest her other tactics failed.

Captain Gower rose from his chair and went to greet her. "Good morning, Miss Cosgrove." He bent over her hand, kissing it briefly. "May I present Miss Abbott, who joined us late last evening. Miss Abbott, this is Lady Cosgrove's daughter, the lovely Miss Lydia Cosgrove, whom I was telling you about."

"Hello." Marsali smiled, then rose from her chair in unison with Mr. Thatcher. She braced herself for rejection as she turned to Miss Cosgrove. *It is apparent I am only a servant.* But for these few weeks at least, she longed to be treated as equal with her fellow passengers. She'd been beneath everyone and everything—including her aunt's dogs—the past four years, and she was dearly tired of it.

To Marsali's surprise, Miss Cosgrove returned her smile, and it appeared genuine. "Oh, I am ever so glad you've come. What a dreary voyage this would have been with only Mama for company." She clasped Marsali's hands in hers and squeezed them. "I hope we shall become the dearest of friends." She released Marsali and, with a flounce of skirts, seated herself on the bench.

Somewhat dumbfounded at such a hearty, enthusiastic greeting, Marsali followed suit.

"There," Captain Gower said as he returned to his seat. "Just as I said. You'll be good for each other."

Marsali was not at all certain about that, but she could not deny that it felt pleasant to not have been instantly looked down upon. None of the ladies who visited at her aunt's house had ever said they were glad to make her acquaintance, and certainly none would have reached out in a gesture of affection as Miss Cosgrove just had. *And surely she had to have noticed my simple, far-less-expensive and less-fashionable dress.*

Yet she does not seem to be judging me for it. Nonplussed by such unusual behavior from a woman of an obviously higher social class, Marsali began passing the platters of food her way.

"I slept ever so well, Captain," Miss Cosgrove said. "I know we're not at sea yet, but I felt the water rocking me all the same. It was so *very* peaceful and soothing. I just love it. I believe I shall love every moment of this voyage. What time shall we be off today? Might I stand beside you at the wheel, Captain, as you direct us out of port? Shall we require a tug to tow us out, or will we steam out on our own accord? Do you think many will come to watch us depart? If so, I think I should like to be at the rail waving a handkerchief at them all. Oh, aren't we all so fortunate to be here?" She glanced around the table at each of them in turn.

Her smile was infectious, and Marsali's initial—*and unjustified and unfair*, her conscience scolded—assessment of Miss Cosgrove changed. "We *are* fortunate," she agreed, feeling suddenly light and happy. England was all but behind her, and a great adventure lay ahead. Being a lady's maid could not possibly be half as difficult as serving in her aunt and uncle's home had been. And Miss Cosgrove, with a personality as bright as her frilly morning gown, promised to be great entertainment during the voyage.

"Would that more people had your optimistic outlook," Captain Gower said, raising his glass to Miss Cosgrove. "Would that they do in the near future, or I shall very shortly cease being the captain of anything larger than a rowboat." He seemed in jest, yet Marsali detected an undertone of seriousness.

"Not everyone is as impressed by your ship?" she asked warily.

The captain set his cup on the table and faced her. "I had forgotten that you were unaware of our lack of passengers. I explained to the others as they boarded yesterday afternoon."

"You were not able to fill all of the cabins on this native voyage?" Marsali guessed, wondering if this might have contributed to his irritation at her tardiness.

Captain Gower scoffed. "We did not even come close. Those you see here—excepting Lady Cosgrove—are the sum total of our passengers. It is rather the opposite reaction I had hoped to receive, given the success of the American steamer, the *SS Savannah*, several years ago, though I gather she was not well received at first either. She made the voyage from shore to shore in thirty days, and it has baffled me since why no one else has rushed to follow suit. Why must we be at the mercy of the wind and weather when we might have a capable engine with which to propel ourselves? Why waste additional weeks when both cargo and passengers might make the journey more quickly? *Why*"—Captain Gower pounded his fist upon the table, causing the plates and silverware and glasses to jump—"are the English so blasted superstitious and afraid? So much so that I could not fill even a fourth of this ship's cabins?"

"You answered that yourself, Captain." Mr. Thatcher managed to respond before Miss Cosgrove, though her mouth hung open with whatever she had been about to say.

"We're a superstitious lot," Mr. Thatcher continued. "Your ship claims to travel faster than the weather—to no longer be at the wind's mercy, or Mother Nature's. I would venture to say that there are many who see that as challenging God Himself. And what is to stop Him from destroying a ship that claims to be able to outrun His forces?"

"I had not considered it in that light—or that great of detail," Captain Gower admitted. "But what is to be done to change public opinion? To change a people's perspective or belief?"

"Time?" Mr. Thatcher suggested. "That, and evidence of your ship's success. This *SS Savannah*—is she still running? I've not heard of her, but I should think that her continued success would only aid your cause."

Gower leaned back in his seat and shook his head. "She would not. The *Savannah* had her moment of glory in 1819. But her luck turned after that. She wasn't kept as a steamship, and she wrecked off of Long Island in the New York Harbor in 1821."

"Wrecked! Goodness. How positively dreadful." Somehow even Miss Cosgrove's clear dismay came off sounding somewhat upbeat.

Mr. Thatcher pursed his lips, and his gaze turned thoughtful. "Most unfortunate."

"Yes. Well, we will not have the same misfortune, even modestly begun as we are with but a few *fortunate*"—he paused to beam at Miss Cosgrove—"passengers."

Breakfast was finished and the dishes cleared away—by

someone other than her—before Marsali had the opportunity to catch Mr. Thatcher alone to thank him. Miss Cosgrove had monopolized both the conversation and Mr. Thatcher throughout the remainder of the meal, though in such a way that Marsali had a difficult time feeling bothered by her. Rather like a new, excitable puppy, Miss Cosgrove seemed to love everything and everyone. *That she only took my hands and did not lick me is perhaps a miracle,* Marsali reflected after having spent an hour in the young woman's presence. But such a genuine interest in everything and a love of life was something to be admired—if not envied. Marsali wondered if she had ever been that innocent or happy. She believed she must have been once, but so many years had passed since then that she could not recall.

She came to stand beside Mr. Thatcher at the rail in the spot Miss Cosgrove had only just vacated when her mother had summoned her.

"I wanted to properly thank you," she said, not meeting his gaze but staring out at the churning waters of the bay, where another ship was being towed out to sea. "I hadn't anything at all to eat yesterday, and—"

"*Nothing?*" Mr. Thatcher's gaze shifted from the water to her face, the concern evident in his deep blue eyes.

Unused to anyone caring at all about her or for her, Marsali felt a peculiar catch in her chest, the same she'd felt last night when she'd opened her door and found his offering at her feet and heard his kind words. "There wasn't time before my journey started, and I could not afford to purchase anything when the coach stopped at an inn for lunch."

"Then I am doubly glad to have shared my meager offering last night," he said. "I hope that is the last time you will go hungry. I know from experience, it is not pleasant."

"No," she agreed. "It is not." Curiosity prompted her to ask under what circumstances he had experienced the same, his fine suit and manners indicating that he came from a better station than she. "I hope a very long time has passed since you have suffered thus. It is difficult to believe that a man of your stature—status," she quickly amended, but not before she felt her face grow warm, "has ever gone hungry."

If Mr. Thatcher caught her blunder he was kind enough to pretend not to notice. "It has been many years, but hunger is not something one forgets. As to my social status . . ." He pulled at the lapel of his jacket. "My sisters gave me this suit as a farewell gift. They did not wish me to arrive in America looking quite the pauper I am."

The news that he was also poor further buoyed her spirits, though she felt badly for it. But the thought that she had met someone who might understand misfortune as she did was comforting. "Your sisters are talented seamstresses, and they must have saved long to purchase such fine cloth. It seems they care for you very much."

Her declaration coaxed a smile, albeit a somewhat wistful one. "I've no doubt they love me—my coat has barely dried from their outpouring of tears when I left them three days ago." Mr. Thatcher glanced toward his shoulder. "And they are both talented with a needle and thread, but this suit was purchased. My sisters are married, you see. To fine men who can provide well for them. Grace married an earl and lives on a grand estate. My younger sister, Helen, married his neighbor, Mr. Preston, who is in possession of great wealth and has a fine home of his own."

Mr. Thatcher's comments sounded anything but resentful, yet Marsali sensed sadness in his words. She wanted to ask him about this, if he was displeased with his sisters' choices in their husbands, but did not think it her place. Instead, she directed her attentions to the harbor once more, though still very much aware of his presence beside her. He politely turned his gaze outward as well.

So long have I been out of society that it is likely I have forgotten how to control my tongue. How am I to ever get used to polite conversation again? The topics covered among the servants downstairs at her aunt's home had been any and every, and conversations were often gossipy and crude—two traits she did not wish to carry with her into her new life.

Instead, she wished desperately to return to the manners and ways she'd possessed up until her fifteenth year, when life had taken a tragic turn. But already she could see that resuming the ways of a lady was not to be as simple as she had supposed. She hoped her new post would help with that, and watching the young lady she was to serve might be the way to relearn those manners and delicate behaviors she had lost.

She'd been grateful for the captain's mandate of simplicity at breakfast. It had brought a measure of relief, as she would not be required to remember who served what and from which side and with which utensil each course was eaten and when it was appropriate to begin eating.

Her aunt had never allowed her in the dining room— even to serve. That was too good a task for anyone as low as she; instead, Marsali had been assigned the daily emptying and scrubbing of the chamber pots, the clearing of the table scraps into the slop buckets, the cleaning of ashes from the fireplaces, and every other undesirable chore her aunt could heap upon her.

Marsali worried—and rightly so—that she might have trouble as a lady's maid. She wasn't at all aware of fashion, and she was only familiar with a few basic hairstyles—her own hair having been kept short the last few years—but she could sew. It was perhaps the thing that might save her. She would be able to care for a lady's clothing, to sew and mend anything. To alter or let out or even design a gown. It was the only way she'd managed to keep herself in clothes during her time at her aunt's house. And it was the skill that had allowed her to secretly put aside the ten shillings for the coach to take her to Liverpool.

"I'm afraid I am poor company," Mr. Thatcher said quite suddenly. Marsali turned to him, uncertain as to his meaning.

"Here I have told you of my family but asked nothing of yours. Are you the first in your family to make this voyage—the brave one to travel to America?"

"You are not poor company at all," Marsali said. "I was lost in thought, as I believe you were as well." She smiled at him, realizing how perfectly comfortable it had felt, standing at his side, neither of them speaking. Their silence had not been awkward but companionable. "And just because you fed me, do not feel obligated to entertain as well. I daresay Miss Cosgrove will take care of that for both of us—for the entire ship."

Mr. Thatcher laughed, easing her worry that she'd spoken rudely already.

"I did not mean to sound unkind," Marsali hurried to say. "Miss Cosgrove is lovely and vivacious."

He leaned closer. "And a person in her company can hardly get a word in edgewise. If one is to have a conversation on this ship, I fear it will have to be when she is busy attending to her mother. So you had best hurry and answer my question, or I shall be left curious in the event Miss Cosgrove returns. *Do* you leave family behind?"

"No one," Marsali said, letting out a happy breath. Her aunt and uncle didn't qualify. She held her arms open wide. "This ship is my passage to freedom."

"I thought . . . are you not making the voyage under indenture?" The concern in Mr. Thatcher's voice touched her.

As if I might have already forgotten I will owe four years for these four weeks of freedom. "I am," Marsali said. "My sister, Charlotte, arranged the indenture for me. She and her husband traveled to America four years ago. I have been waiting to join them ever since, and finally I am going. A Mr. Joshua Thomas has paid for my voyage, and in return I am to be his daughter's lady's maid for a period of four years."

"That seems a rather hefty price for one crossing."

Marsali shrugged. "It was the best Charlotte could find.

Oft it is five to seven years that are required. Do not feel pity for me," she said, noting Mr. Thatcher's solemn look. "I am quite happy with the arrangement. Being a lady's maid will be far better than serving at my aunt and uncle's home."

"Your own relatives treated you as a servant?" His brows drew together, and his lips turned down even more.

"*Servant* is perhaps a generosity when describing how they treated me, but let's not speak of that." She forced a smile. "It is behind me, and my sister will be waiting at the end of my journey. The plantation I am to serve at in Virginia is not so very far from her, and I have hope that we shall be able to visit fairly often. As Miss Cosgrove so perfectly expressed at breakfast, I *am* very fortunate."

"As am I," Mr. Thatcher agreed, and Marsali felt relief that the subject of her background was—hopefully—safely behind them.

"But you are leaving your sisters behind, not going to them," she said, feeling far more concern over his situation than her own. She finally dared ask what she'd wished to earlier, hoping that if he did not wish to speak of it he would simply tell her. "Were you displeased with their choices, with the men they married?"

"Heavens, no," Mr. Thatcher exclaimed. "I spent a great deal of the previous year working to see them wed to such fine men. It was a love match for both, and I couldn't be more pleased."

"Yet you are leaving them," Marsali said. "And feeling sad for it."

He turned back to the rail, leaning his elbows upon it, and glanced at her sideways. "You are too astute, I see. I shall have to be wary of you."

"I am sorry," Marsali rushed to apologize. "I did not mean to pry."

"And I did not mean to sound so harsh." He placed a hand over hers on the rail for a brief second, then pulled away. "No harm done," he assured her. "I have been rather surprised by my own melancholy. I have wanted to go to America for so many years now, have dreamed of it and planned for this day. But it seems I did not consider how difficult it would be to part with my family."

"Your parents remain in England as well?" Marsali asked, then bit her lip as she realized she'd pried yet again.

"My parents are both dead," Mr. Thatcher said. "My mother died when I was quite young—I do not remember her, truth be told. And my father died last year—at no loss to my sisters and myself. He was not a good man. It is perhaps because of him that I feel compelled to leave England. I want to begin anew in a place where *Thatcher* is not a name that precedes itself in a poor light."

"You have begun well, then," Marsali said, glancing at the hand he had touched. "For when I think of the name Thatcher, forevermore it will bring to mind a kind, generous man."

CHAPTER 8

After her pleasant visit with Mr. Thatcher, Marsali strolled about the deck, careful to stay out of the way of the men readying the ship to leave port. Captain Gower seemed to be everywhere, barking instructions about checking the mooring lines and the sails and asking repeatedly for a final measuring of coal. More than once Marsali heard a bit of murmuring from his men, wishing the captain would trust them to see to their tasks themselves.

But he cannot, Marsali surmised. This ship was his life, and its future and Captain Gower's largely depended upon the next twenty-five days.

Only twenty-five more days, and I shall see Charlotte. Marsali looked to the west, enjoying the cool breeze and once more anticipating the promises of her new life.

"Captain Gower, those clouds do not bode well."

Marsali glanced behind her toward the unfamiliar feminine voice and caught her first glimpse of the woman who had to be Lady Cosgrove. She stood beside Captain Gower near the wheel, one gloved hand extended, finger pointing toward the western horizon. Marsali followed her gaze and noticed the clouds for the first time. As it was not yet midday, they weren't blocking the sun, but their dark grey did appear rather ominous. The wind picked up, blowing wisps of hair about her face, and she realized the breeze *was* turning to something more serious.

"The wind may not be blowing favorably," Captain Gower said. "But for us that is of no consequence. We can make headway regardless of any ill wind or weather."

Lady Cosgrove's pout showed clearly that his words had not comforted her. She allowed her hand to drop, where it hung limp at her side. Marsali resumed walking and wandered toward the back of the ship, where additional coal—as ordered by the captain this morning—was being loaded.

A stout, well-dressed man strode up the gangplank, spied her, and promptly smiled. "Miss Abbott, I presume." He carried a black medical bag.

"Yes," she answered, at once wary.

"You had the captain quite worried last night. I daresay you're his most valuable passenger."

Marsali didn't see how that was possible, as she was his only nonpaying passenger. But she refrained from saying so. "And who might you be?"

"Medical inspector." He held up his bag. "Promised the captain I'd return today, and so I have. I imagine he was mighty glad to see you. He has to deliver you to a Mr. Thomas in America, I believe."

"Yes." Did everyone know of her situation? That this stranger knew of it bothered her. But Charlotte *had* mentioned a brief medical examination in one of her letters telling Marsali what to expect of the crossing. *I will answer his questions, and he will be on his way, and that will be that.*

"What do you wish to know?" Marsali held her chin high and looked at him unwaveringly. He was her last obstacle to leaving England. She thought herself very healthy, but if, for some reason, this inspector did not, he could force her to stay.

And what would I do then? It did not bear thinking of. Silently she prayed that he was honest and that her aunt and uncle hadn't somehow met and coerced him into doing their will, as they had the coachmen yesterday.

"Shall we go into the saloon?" he asked, then led the way. Marsali followed, her unease growing by the minute. According to Charlotte, this should be but a cursory examination, to ensure she hadn't the morbid sore throat or measles or lice. *Could not all of that have been determined outside?*

The inspector held the door open for her, and as she had the previous night with Captain Gower, she preceded him into the long room. She stopped at the first table, wanting to be near to the door and not anywhere near her cabin with this stranger.

The arrangement must have been satisfactory, for he set his bag on the table and got right to work. "Name, please."

"Marsali Elise Abbott," she said, thinking the question ridiculous when he'd already ascertained who she was.

He wrote her name on a form of some sort. "Country of birth."

"France."

The inspector's brows rose at this, but he recorded her answer on the paper.

"Are both parents living or—"

"Deceased." Saying that didn't hurt as much as it used to. Soon she would no longer be alone in the world.

So long as he lets me go, that is. He was looking at her suspiciously, as if having deceased parents made her somehow less than worthy of this journey.

"Are you in possession of all of your teeth?"

"Yes," Marsali said, insulted he would think otherwise. Must lack of money always be associated with lack of anything else, including caring for one's hygiene? She forced an overbright smile, showing off as many of her teeth as possible.

"Open your mouth," he said. She obeyed, and he pressed a small, flat stick of wood on her tongue to hold it down. "Mmm. Very good. No sign of infection."

Of course not. She'd been blessed with very little illness her whole life—a good thing, as her aunt and uncle quite certainly would not have paid to have a doctor care for her.

"I have always been very healthy," Marsali assured him.

"We'll see," he said, sounding as if he believed the opposite to be true. "Breathe in deeply, please."

She did, then held her breath and exhaled when he instructed her to. He listened intently, a frown upon his face the whole while.

What? she wanted to ask. *What is wrong?* Her heartbeat quickened, and she willed it not to, lest he think something amiss with her heart, too.

Please let me go. Please, she chanted silently in her head.

He examined her arms and hands. He snapped his fingers in the air near each of her ears, after which Marsali turned to him, not knowing whether to laugh or express irritation. *Perhaps one becomes a medical inspector when he does not do well enough in school to become a physician.*

He stepped close and peered into her eyes. "Can you read at all?"

This was too much, and his insult overtook her fear that he might make her stay. Marsali took a step back and looked directly at him. "I read. I write. I can figure sums in my head. I am fluent in three languages, enjoy reciting poetry, play the pianoforte reasonably well, and can sing better than most." Or she used to be able to sing. Until her aunt had forbid it. "Are those qualifications satisfactory enough to allow me to sail on this ship?"

"Perhaps," he said, annoyance in his tone. "Most fortunate for you that humility is not a requirement."

This infuriated her more, and she fumed inwardly.

She'd not been trying to boast but merely prove a point— that she oughtn't be treated any differently from the other passengers simply because she was traveling under indenture. *Wealth, or lack thereof, does not make a person good—or bad.*

"What other language do you speak, aside from English and French, I presume."

"Gaelic." Marsali loved her late grandmother's language almost as much as her native French.

"Hmph." The inspector snorted. "That is no longer a language."

"Simply because one may be ignorant of something doesn't mean that it does not exist."

This earned her another shrewd look. "Take your hair down."

"What—why?" Marsali demanded. This seemed an entirely inappropriate thing to ask. She might no longer be aware of each and every one of polite society's rules, but she knew enough to realize she was of an age when she ought to wear her hair up and that any man who asked her to take it down was not one she wanted to be near. She looked past him toward the door, trying to decide what she should do.

"I've got to check you for head lice," he said impatiently.

"I haven't any," Marsali said. As much as her aunt loathed her, she would have loathed having lice in her house even more, so Marsali had at least been afforded the privilege of bathing regularly.

The medical inspector folded his arms across his chest and gave her a hard look.

"Oh, very well," Marsali grumbled. At least no one else was in the common room to see. Her fingers searched for her hairpins and hurriedly removed them. She shook her hair free, then bent forward so he might better see her scalp.

He stepped closer and leaned in to examine her head for several long seconds; all the while Marsali fretted continuously and hardly dared to breathe. *What if I picked up something on Lime Street yesterday? What if the seat in the coach was infested? What if—*

"You may stand," he said after a minute. "Your hair is quite short for a woman. Are you certain you haven't had lice in the past, and your hair was chopped off to be rid of it?"

"I am *quite* certain," Marsali said. Her hair touched her shoulders now. If he thought that short, he would have been appalled to have seen it a year and a half ago, when her aunt had first taken her shears to Marsali's braids as she slept. After that, Marsali made sure to keep her door locked at night *and* to push a chair beneath the knob. The servant girls she shared a room with had not objected to this after they'd seen the way her aunt had butchered her once-beautiful hair.

"My aunt did not wish me to wear it long," she said, not intending to elaborate to this stranger, whom she soon hoped never to see again.

"Very well," the examiner said. "You are fit enough to sail on this ship, though it is apparent you've not been well nourished or trained to this point. You're too thin by half and do not have the disposition of a good servant. Let us hope your employer in America feeds you more and teaches you your place." He packed up his bag and left the room without another word.

When the door had closed behind him, Marsali sank onto the bench and leaned over the table, her face buried in her arms. Slowly her heartbeat returned to normal as the panic of the past several minutes ebbed away.

At the other end of the saloon someone cleared his throat. Marsali lifted her head and saw Mr. Thatcher emerging from his cabin. She sat up quickly and reached for her scattered hairpins.

He strode toward her, stopping on the other side of the table and seating himself across from her again.

"You must excuse me," Marsali said, doing her best to reform her bun without a brush or looking glass. "The medical inspector was here and—"

"I heard," Mr. Thatcher said. "I apologize. I did not mean to eavesdrop; I'd left my door open in the hope of gaining a bit of a breeze in my cabin. And once I heard the start of your conversation, it seemed best I listen to the remainder, lest the inspector act as rudely as his words. He seemed rather a bully. Are you quite all right?"

"Yes, thank you." She ought to have been bothered that Mr. Thatcher had overheard her conversation, but instead she felt oddly touched at his concern.

"It was most unfair of the inspector to ask you to take your hair down. He did not ask the same of me at all."

Marsali's head snapped up, and she caught the mischievous twinkle in Mr. Thatcher's eye and the twitch of his lips.

"Well, I hope he at least asked why you keep yours so short as well," she said, teasing him back. "After all, your hair does not even brush your collar."

"Entirely improper for a gentleman," Mr. Thatcher agreed with mock sincerity.

"For a woman, apparently, her hair must fall at least to her waist." Marsali placed the last pin and lowered her hands.

"The more I hear of your aunt, the more she sounds rather like an evil character from the stories my grandfather used to read. Are you familiar with *Grimm's Fairy Tales*?" Mr. Thatcher asked.

"No, but I do love to read." Marsali frowned. "I owned a few books but had to leave them behind yesterday, along with my trunk and the rest of my belongings. It was either that or risk missing this ship, which I could not do."

"Are they close by? Might there still be time to go and retrieve your things?" Mr. Thatcher leaned forward, hands braced on the edge of the table, as if he was ready to spring into action. *And to my rescue again.*

For a moment Marsali felt the hope in such an idea. Then she remembered where her trunk had been left and knew she could never risk returning there again. Nor would she want Mr. Thatcher to learn that she had been not only on Lime Street but inside one of the establishments there.

"I am afraid the trunk and my books are lost to me forever," Marsali said resignedly. Perhaps they would do Kimberly or one of the other girls at Madame Kelner's some good.

"In that case, you must borrow some of my books during our voyage," he offered. "And the captain has a small library we are to make use of as well."

"You are too kind, Mr. Thatcher." She met his gaze once more and felt comforted. "I imagine your sisters must miss you every bit as much as you miss them, if you were even half so good to them as you have already been to me."

"Grace and Helen and I are very close," he said. "We only had each other growing up, and so, of necessity, our bond became strong."

"How very fortunate you were to have each other," Marsali said. "I would have given much to have my sister with me these past four years."

"You shall have her soon." He rose from the table. "Wait here, and I shall fetch a book or two for you. What is it you like to read?"

"I am not particular," Marsali assured him. She hadn't had much time to read at all while at her aunt and uncle's. And though their library was vast, they had not allowed her to borrow any of the books in it. She'd risked it once and been caught, and the consequential beating had hurt enough that she never dared try it again.

"I've only a few volumes with me, but you're welcome to any of them. I'll be right back." He'd started toward his room when shouting from outside caught their attention. Captain Gower's voice—and another she did not recognize—carried through the door into the common room.

Fear seized Marsali. *What if the medical inspector lied? What if he has told the captain I am not fit to go?* Or worse, what if her aunt and uncle had somehow discovered which ship she was to sail on? It was entirely probable, as she had told both the driver and coachman which dock she was to be delivered to.

She stood quickly and went to the door. Mr. Thatcher had already retraced his steps and held it open for her. They ascended the stairs to the deck and found the captain engaged in a war of words with a stranger.

"I'm telling you that it does not matter whether or not you're able to leave of your own accord. As of this moment, all ships scheduled to depart this afternoon are required to stay in port. We'll not chance the storm taking any lives before you're out to sea. After that, it's your own neck you're risking. But here, we've the authority to say who stays and who goes and when you do it." The man stood with feet planted wide. One hand held his cap in place to keep it from blowing away in the strong wind.

"Port authority," Mr. Thatcher whispered, nodding to the badge on the front of the man's jacket.

Marsali brought a hand to her own head, feeling wisps of her hair escaping from her hastily repined bun. "We're being delayed, then?" *What now? What else?*

Captain Gower's lips pressed together, his face beet red, as if it was about to burst. Marsali was well acquainted with looks of rage and did not wish to be anywhere near. She took a step back, retreating into the saloon once more, but not before a quick glance at the sky confirmed that it had darkened and that the ominous clouds were closing in.

Mr. Thatcher followed her and closed the door behind them, pushing it hard to secure it against the wind. "May I suggest that a rainy, stormy day is one of the best kind for reading?"

"And staying in one's cabin is likely the best course when the captain's mood is foul," she added.

"That too," Mr. Thatcher agreed, a wry smile curving his lips. "Let's see about getting you a book."

CHAPTER 9

*T*he storm passed quickly, the thunderclaps and downpour lasting less than an hour, but Captain Gower's mood remained foul the remainder of the day and into evening, as Christopher suspected it would until they left port. Quite possibly the captain would remain upset until they'd made up the time they had already lost.

Twenty-five days. Could they really cross the Atlantic in such a short period of time? He hoped so and yearned— possibly almost as much as the captain—to find out and especially to see America's distant shore.

Along with the captain's mood, the storm had altered the air so that it was warm and muggy. In the narrow cabin it felt particularly stifling, and so Christopher left his room, intending to go up on deck, where the air might feel a bit cooler. Cautiously, he peered into the common room, wary lest the door on the opposite side at the far end might open as well. Miss Cosgrove had been his shadow much of the day, save for those times her ailing mother had summoned her, and warm though his cabin was, he felt he might prefer that over any more of Miss Cosgrove's chatter tonight.

In the space of less than twenty-four hours, he believed he had learned her entire life history and much of her ancestors' as well. Lady Cosgrove's second husband—not Miss Cosgrove's father—had died six months earlier, necessitating the removal of Lady and Miss Cosgrove from their luxurious town house in London. As their fortune had been tied to Lady Cosgrove's husband, they were forced to seek new means of support, and that had come in an offer of marriage—for *Miss* Cosgrove—from a Mr. William Vancer, a thirty-four-year-old American businessman and old family friend.

Christopher could not help but feel sorry for the man and hoped that either his business took him frequently from home or he was indeed a very good family friend and well aware that his soon-to-be bride could talk the hind leg off a donkey, as Miranda would have put it.

Chuckling to himself, Christopher recalled his dear servant's use of the phrase. *She'd been speaking of me.* At fourteen he'd been rather curious and quite a handful for his grandfather to take on. And, as Miranda had almost always been with at least one of his sisters during those first relief-filled years, free of their father for a time, she'd been with Christopher as well. *And let me know just how she felt about that duty.*

He frowned, suddenly worried that he had not changed all that much from that boisterous, unschooled boy. Perhaps Miss Abbott had thought him as annoying as he found Miss Cosgrove when earlier today he'd rambled on about his family while neglecting to ask anything about hers. He would have to do better when he saw her tomorrow—assuming Miss Cosgrove took a breath long enough for either of he or Miss Abbott to speak.

After a moment of waiting in the saloon with no one else having appeared, Christopher reached behind him and shut his door as quietly as possible. Instead of traveling to the far end of the long room to the entrance most often used, and the one nearest Lady and Miss Cosgrove's rooms, he opened the door to the right of the captain's quarters. This brought him through the galley, vacant now, save for the cook, dozing on a cot near the barrels of salted pork.

Christopher walked past the cook and opened another door, this one with steps leading to the upper deck near the bow of the ship.

With a quick glance at the wheel, he saw not the captain but one of his men positioned there, guarding it from any mischief, Christopher supposed. He could only feel glad to not have run into the captain. A glance behind him at the gangway showed crew members stationed at the top. Likely more were at the bottom as well, the captain wanting to take no chances on acquiring any last-minute stowaways.

Four other men sat by the mooring lines, one nodding to Christopher as he turned from them, intent on making his way to the other end of the ship. He found it preferable to look out at the water and imagine what was waiting beyond it than to look to shore and continually recall those he had left behind.

He was not the only one who'd had the idea of escaping either the heat or the past or both, as Miss Abbott already stood at the rail, close to one of the lanterns hanging overhead and at nearly the same spot where she'd joined him this morning. He felt pleasantly surprised to see her—rather the opposite of how he felt whenever Miss Cosgrove approached. For half a second he wondered if Miss Abbott had been waiting for him, then immediately chided himself for the thought.

She could not have known he would come up on deck, and even if she had, it wasn't as if she had sought out his company, other than once this morning, to thank him for his earlier kindness. She'd spent the afternoon in her cabin, seeming to prefer to be alone. But Christopher supposed it might be all right to ask her how she had enjoyed the book he'd lent her earlier.

He approached her from behind, then stopped suddenly as he noticed one of the crew sitting a short distance away, knife in hand, as he cleaned his fingernails and stared intently at Miss Abbott.

Feeling a lurch of alarm, Christopher resumed walking, lengthening his stride until he came up beside her. "Miss Abbott," he began.

"Good evening, Mr. Thatcher." She smiled, not seeming the least bothered by his intrusion.

"Pardon me," he continued. "But I do not believe it is safe for you to be out here alone like this at night."

"But I'm not alone." She smiled, then looked over her shoulder at the man Christopher had just spied watching her. He no longer sat a short distance away but had moved closer and was standing now, his eyes on Christopher.

"Mr. Murphy has had the misfortune to be assigned my chaperone by Captain Gower."

Murphy scowled as if recalling that particular conversation. "State your business with the lady, an' be off," he mumbled.

"No business," Christopher said. "I was just out to enjoy the cool air and thought to make sure she was safe."

"Would that I'd had the two of you to watch over me previously." Miss Abbott sighed, and her lips turned down. "But I do thank you for your concern, Mr. Thatcher." To Murphy she said, "I assure you he is perfectly harmless. Please allow him to stay so I might enjoy his company."

Murphy grunted his assent, then moved back into the shadows near an enormous coil of rope.

"Pleasant sort of fellow, isn't he?" Christopher remarked under his breath.

"I cannot blame him," Miss Abbott said. "Being saddled with the task of looking after me cannot have been in his job description."

Christopher chuckled. "I suppose not. Good of the captain to think of it, though."

"It is only because he is concerned that I arrive in good health for Mr. Thomas. I gather they are business colleagues of some sort."

"I believe so." The previous evening Christopher had tucked this piece of information away to be considered later. Perhaps if he made a good impression, the captain would put in a word for him with his associates in America. Christopher knew he would need to find employment within a week or two of arriving. He hadn't allowed either of his sisters or their husbands to give him any money for the voyage or for starting over on the new continent. Accepting the clothing Grace and Helen had presented him with had been difficult enough.

"Listen," Miss Abbott said as if he'd been speaking loudly instead of standing in silence beside her. "Do you hear that?"

"A violin, you mean?" Its strains seemed to be coming from the tall ship beside them, the one overloaded with Irish immigrants. It, too, had been detained today.

Miss Abbott turned toward the sound, her profile silhouetted in the moonlight. "It's pretty, isn't it?"

Much like you. The thought came unbidden, as it had the previous night when she'd first removed the cloak from her face. She had a delicate stature, aristocratic features in her high cheekbones and brows, and full lips. He found the combination of her fair skin and dark hair stunning and had not been surprised to learn that she was French.

But the last thing he wished or needed was to feel attracted to or interested in a woman—even one as sensible and pleasant as she.

After a few minutes, more instruments joined the first, and the tune turned from melancholy and soulful to a vibrant jig. The sounds of stomping feet soon accompanied this, along with joyful singing and the occasional shout.

Christopher almost imagined he could see the larger ship swaying with the rhythm of the dozens of stomping feet inside her.

"Are they—?"

"Dancing," he confirmed. "See the light coming from the windows below deck? That'll be where their quarters are—one big open area. No private cabins like we have, but plenty of room for dancing."

"My sister sailed on a packet like that. She said it was dreadful."

"It likely is a good deal of the time," Christopher said. "But for tonight, at least, all is merriment. They've left their homeland behind and are about to sail toward the hope of a better life."

"Ooh, listen. They've a piper, too." Miss Abbott's face lit as the sound of bagpipes carried over the water. Her toe began tapping in time with the fiddles.

"I don't see why they should be the only ones having a jolly good time of it tonight," Christopher said, having difficulty keeping his own feet still. He wasn't usually one for dancing, but this wasn't a crowded ballroom filled with a bunch of gossipy, giggling women.

"Would you care to dance, Miss Abbott?" He asked the question almost before he'd considered it fully.

"Here?" She glanced about, her eyes darting to and fro over the deck.

"Why not?" He shrugged. "We've got to have a bit of shipboard entertainment—aside from Miss Cosgrove, that is." Christopher looked over his shoulder. "I'm going to dance with the lady," he called to Murphy. "Join us if you care to."

Murphy grunted acknowledgment and continued cleaning his nails—toenails now—confirming his lack of interest.

Christopher bowed to Miss Abbott. "May I have this reel?"

"*Is* it a reel?" She angled her head, listening carefully.

"A reel, a jig, a step dance—a *waltz*. Does it matter?" Christopher said, finding the idea of dancing with her more appealing by the minute.

"Indeed it does." She laughed at his ignorance. "I should like to see you try waltzing to such a tune."

"We shall see who is laughing and who is fastest on their feet and still standing at the end of the night," he challenged, holding his hand out.

Miss Abbott took it at once as her eyes narrowed and her lips pressed together.

She is not one to deny a challenge, he remembered, recalling her earlier conversation with the medical inspector.

She gave a slight curtsey. His fingers curved over hers. He would never have been so bold back in Yorkshire or London. But England was behind them now, or nearly so— no matter that her shore was still but a stone's throw away. Aboard the ship for these few weeks, the rules were different. He knew it, and he sensed Miss Abbott did too.

"I haven't danced in years. I'm not sure I remember how." She cast her eyes down and suddenly tried to pull away. He wouldn't allow it.

"I've *avoided* dancing for years." Christopher grinned. "In England I employed every tactic to avoid the gentlemanly pursuits of balls and dancing. So this ought to be good." He captured her other hand so that they stood facing one another. "Ready?"

After a brief hesitation she nodded, and their eyes met as they listened for the right point to enter with the music.

"Now," Miss Abbott declared, and by some unspoken communication, they began skipping sideways down the deck, out of the swath of lantern light, then back again. On their second turn they traveled farther, passing Murphy, who looked at them as if they'd both gone mad.

As they reached the edge of the upper deck and paused to return the other direction, Christopher kicked up his heels in an attempted jig—and failed miserably, landing sideways on his ankle and nearly falling. Only Miss Abbott's firm grip kept him from making a complete fool of himself.

"We shall see who is still standing." She repeated his earlier words, then pulled one of her hands away to cover her mouth in an attempt to hide her laughter.

"I meant to do that," he said. "Trying to make you feel more confident." Christopher released her other hand and began clapping and high-stepping in a circle around her.

She held her skirts at the sides and began a jig of her own, pointing her toes in front of her as she skipped about.

"Not bad," he said. "Are you sure you're not Irish instead of French?"

She shook her head. "But I've Scottish blood, too," she boasted. "And my grandmother was a fine dancer."

"That explains it." Christopher looped his hand through the crook of her arm, and, facing each other, they began to circle about. Her smile was infectious, and he felt his own grin broaden.

Grace told me dancing was enjoyable, but I never believed her.

They passed beneath another lantern, and he saw that Miss Abbott's face was flushed. Her eyes were bright and merry, and when they locked on his for the merest of seconds, something in her look set his heart racing.

"Ooh, what are you doing? May I join you?" Miss Cosgrove's shrill, overexcited voice put an abrupt end to the moment and whatever it was he'd been feeling.

"How fun! Are they having a party on the other ship? I simply adore parties—and balls. And dancing. What a lovely idea. And in the moonlight too. I shall have to write to all of my friends and tell them I attended a midnight dance on deck only my second night aboard ship."

"It's not midnight," Christopher cut in before she could say more. She stood before them, hands clasped in front of her and still overdressed in the ridiculous ensemble she'd appeared in at dinner. How many cabins did she and her mother have, anyway? *Where do they store all those clothes?*

"Of course you may join us," Miss Abbott said, freeing her arm from his and stepping aside. "Mr. Thatcher is a most excellent dancer." She cast a sly look his direction, almost giving him the impression she knew of his discomfort.

"Oh, that is good to know," Miss Cosgrove gushed. "You can practice with me so I may be ready for the soirees I shall be attending once we reach New York. Mr. Vancer is to host a ball to welcome me. And Mother says his family always holds another at the year's end—a masquerade ball. Can you imagine?" She whirled about. "Everyone comes wearing a mask, so you cannot tell who anyone is. It sounds delightful."

Christopher thought it sounded like she ought to need a drink after such a long speech. He was beginning to feel he needed one just from listening to her.

"Go on and dance," Miss Abbott said. "The musicians are just starting another piece." She stepped backward, leaning against the rail, and Christopher could have sworn he saw a bit of mischief in her brown eyes.

Reluctantly he turned from her and faced Miss Cosgrove. "If the lady would care to."

She giggled—a most annoying sound. *Whereas Miss Abbott's laughter is . . . refreshing.*

Miss Cosgrove walked toward him, her hips swaying dramatically as they were wont to do whenever she moved. He wondered who had taught her such an outlandish swagger and how long it had taken her to master. He was quite certain he couldn't walk thusly, no matter how he practiced.

He held his hands out, intending to promenade about with her as he had Miss Abbott, but Miss Cosgrove moved too close for that and placed her hand at his shoulder.

Panic flared inside him as his nose wrinkled and his eyes began to water from the strong scent of her perfume.

"This is not a waltz. It's a reel." He most certainly did know the difference and was not about to pretend otherwise with Miss Cosgrove as his partner.

"I know that, silly." She swatted the air with her free hand, then placed it upon his other shoulder. "Hands upon shoulders thus, now we slide to the side."

Now we end this. "Mr. Murphy over there will have my head or report me to the captain if I dance so closely with you ladies." Christopher jerked his head toward Murphy and found the man had fallen asleep, his back propped against the rope.

"He won't care. He won't even notice." Miss Cosgrove giggled again.

"Might not your fiancé have something to say about us standing so close if he was about?" Christopher suggested.

Miss Cosgrove opened her mouth, presumably to argue, but was interrupted before she could say another word.

"Perhaps if I show you." Miss Abbott stepped forward.

Coming to my rescue?

Her smile seemed a bit smug as she linked her arm through his and steered him away from a crestfallen Miss Cosgrove.

"You owe me," he muttered when they'd begun to sashay down the deck.

"I?" She feigned a look of innocence. "What have I done but rescue you from an awkward situation?"

"Which you landed me in first." But he could not truly be angry with her, not when conversing with her and feeling the slightest touch of her arm against his set him to feeling so strangely pleasant.

"Please do try to be kind," Miss Abbott whispered. "She has had a difficult time of it and is attempting to make the best of her situation."

"Difficult?" Christopher asked, certain they could not be discussing the same woman. "Miss Cosgrove is to be married to one of the wealthiest men in New York."

"Who is quite a bit older than she is, and whom she does not know. Not to mention she's just left her home and her friends and everything familiar behind forever."

Miss Abbott's insight left him speechless. Where he'd seen only a spoiled, petulant young woman, Miss Abbott had seen suffering. As they made their way back toward Miss Cosgrove, the pout upon her face almost made him feel guilty. *Almost.*

Miss Abbott stepped aside once more, this time shrinking into the shadows, away from the lantern light. Christopher bowed to Miss Cosgrove. "Milady, shall we try once more? This Irish dancing 'tis a wee bit different, but nothin' the likes of which ye cannot handle." His false brogue elicited a smile, and she linked her arm through his as her knee raised in a hop.

They galloped about the deck, nearly kicking poor Murphy on one turnabout, until Miss Cosgrove's initial disappointment seemed to have fled.

"This is ever so enjoyable. I've never danced as the Irish before. Mama says they're a filthy people and she wouldn't ever sail on a boat they're on, but I feel their music is lovely. And their singing, too. I should like to have pipes at my wedding, I think. I wonder what Mr. Vancer would think of that. Maybe he could hire one of the men from that ship? Maybe I could ask him when we arrive—but no." Her pout returned. "We're going to get there *weeks* before that other ship does." She sighed heavily, then brightened at once. "But no matter. Surely there are droves of Irish folk in New York. See how many are on that ship alone. I'm sure I can find at least one to play his pipes for us."

"I am certain you can," Miss Abbott said, joining them again and rubbing her eyes tiredly. "But now we had best get to bed. We have worn poor Murphy out, and he's a long day ahead of him tomorrow."

"Yes," Miss Cosgrove agreed, turning away from Christopher as if he was not there at all. "And we mustn't be late for breakfast. Captain Gower is already cross about our delay."

Miss Abbott neither agreed with nor denied this statement but carefully steered Miss Cosgrove toward the common room. Christopher lagged behind, wanting to enjoy the cool breeze he'd come outside for in the first place.

When they'd gone several paces, Miss Abbott stopped, then turned back suddenly. "Just a moment. I forgot something." She ran back and knelt beside Mr. Murphy. "Thank you, sir. You may 'wake up' now. I'm taking Miss Cosgrove inside."

To Christopher's astonishment, one of Murphy's eyes cracked open, and half of his mouth curved upward. "Thank ye, miss. Couldn't take no more of that one tonight."

"I know," Miss Abbott whispered, then stood.

"How come you let him pretend to sleep, while I had to dance with her?" Christopher muttered under his breath as she passed.

Miss Abbott shrugged. "Because you're a gentleman—whether you like it or not."

CHAPTER 10

Surprisingly, Captain Gower's mood had improved by breakfast the next morning. Christopher had been awake when the Liverpool Port Authority had come aboard early and given the captain clearance to depart at ten o'clock. Only, the larger ship, the one docked beside theirs, was scheduled to be tugged out before the *Amanda May*.

"Doesn't matter," Captain Gower said confidently as he spooned oatmeal into his bowl. "The whole lot of ships here could leave before us and we'd overtake them within a few hours."

"Exactly how fast can your ship travel, Captain?" Miss Abbott asked.

"We've tested her at six knots per hour when the sea is calm. Of course, she'll be a bit slower with the wind against us and much faster with the wind in our favor."

"I should like her to go *very* fast," Miss Cosgrove said. "I do hope the elements will be with us on our journey."

"We shall need more than the elements on our side," Lady Cosgrove said sourly, sounding as much the opposite of her daughter as one could. Looking at her furrowed brow, pinched nose, and pursed lips was almost painful, and Christopher noted that her skin held a greenish tint this morning. She wasn't eating much either, aside from the small corner of toast she'd nibbled at.

"Sea legs—that's what you need," Captain Gower said. "Some of you will get them faster than others. We've buckets for those who feel they will be ill. I suggest all of you take one to your cabins today. Stay abed if you're not feeling well. A day or two out, and most will be right as rain."

Most was not likely to include Lady Cosgrove, Christopher guessed.

"Oh, I don't think I'll be needing to stay in my cabin," Miss Cosgrove said. "And a bucket won't be necess—"

"But it's good to have you all together at breakfast today," the captain said, effectively cutting off Miss Cosgrove before she could get going on another of her breathless monologues. "Lady Cosgrove and Miss Abbott, I do not believe you have been properly introduced to one another yet, so allow me. Lady Cornelia Cosgrove, this is Miss Marsali Abbott. Miss Abbott, Lady Cosgrove."

Miss Abbott turned to Lady Cosgrove with a warm smile. "It is a pleasure to meet you. I have enjoyed your daughter's company immensely already."

Christopher thought the word *immensely* might be overdoing it a bit. *If Miss Cosgrove merits such praise, how would Miss Abbott describe her interactions with me thus far?*

"Marsali . . . such an uncommon name. It wouldn't happen to be *Scottish*, would it?"

Christopher saw at once through Lady Cosgrove's seemingly innocuous question. It appeared that Miss Abbott—Marsali, a name as pretty as she was—did as well. Though he had known her less than two days, he recognized the fighting look that now flashed in her eyes. It was the same she'd given him last night when he'd challenged her to see who could dance the best. But this morning, behind her intense gaze, Christopher thought he glimpsed vulnerability as well.

"I am named after my grandmother, Marsali Mac-Donald, *of Scotland.*"

"Ah, I see." From Lady Cosgrove's tone Christopher saw that she did not care for this information. He wondered if her distaste for Scots was such that she would no longer allow her daughter to associate with Marsali on this voyage.

Perhaps I should claim to be from Scotland as well.

"And how is it you came to be in England?" Lady Cosgrove continued.

"My grandmother and her family left Scotland in 1745, after the failed attempt to restore the Stuarts and Bonnie Prince Charles to the throne. They fled to France, where my grandmother later married. My mother was born in France, as was I. But my father was English, and some years ago we moved to Manchester."

"And now you are traveling to America. It would seem that your family moves quite frequently. Looking for a place in which they fit in and are welcome?" Lady Cosgrove suggested as she looked down her nose at Miss Abbott.

Christopher set his glass down rather forcefully on the table and shot a look at the captain to see how he was taking to one passenger verbally abusing another. But Captain Gower seemed oblivious and was busily consulting his pocket watch and a chart he had laid out before him.

"Yes," Miss Abbott said. "You could say that we have been searching for our place. And England was most certainly not it. France was lovely. I should not have minded if we had continued on there. And I have always wanted to see my grandmother's homeland. Her stories and descript-tions of the Scottish highlands were enough that I think it must be the loveliest bit of ground on earth. But it is America that my sister calls home now, and so it shall be for me as well."

"Well said." Christopher raised his glass in a toast, catching Miss Abbott's eye across the table.

"Oh yes," Miss Cosgrove chimed in as she raised her glass as well. "I do so love to travel. We've been to ever so many places, and it's always a glorious time meeting new people and having new adventures. America promises to be the grandest of all. Where does your sister live, Miss Abbott? My Mr. Vancer lives in New York, in one of the largest mansions ever built there. He designed it himself, and it has twenty-seven bedchambers, which, I am told, is quite a large number for America. It also has a grand garden. But, of course, Mr. Vancer still travels to England and Europe every couple of years as well, so I shall be able to return to visit."

Christopher caught the tiniest bit of yearning in her last sentence and glanced at Miss Cosgrove sharply. Her smile was as bright as ever, but he saw through it to the sadness Miss Abbott had told him of the night before. *She was right.* He felt certain he would never have noticed Miss Cosgrove was anything but annoyingly cheerful had he not been told otherwise. For some reason this bothered him.

Here he'd been feeling so pleased with himself for noticing Miss Abbott's distress and coming to her rescue and befriending her, when the other young lady on board had been distraught as well. Considering that he had always prided himself on his ability to look out for, protect, and especially to be intuitive about anything to do with his sisters, his lack of intuitiveness in this situation seemed almost shameful.

But neither Miss Abbott nor Miss Cosgrove are my concern, he justified. *It is time I stopped behaving as if they were. This is my time, my freedom, and I have earned it. I have no place being concerned about their affairs.* Christopher pushed back his chair and stood. "If you'll excuse me, ladies, Captain." He had a book with him already and tucked it beneath his arm. "I believe I shall take advantage of being out of doors before we leave port—in case I am predisposed to being ill, as the captain has warned. Good day." He turned toward the door.

"What a splendid idea, Mr. Thatcher. May I join you?" Miss Cosgrove practically jumped out of her chair. "What is it you are reading? Perchance, might it be poetry? I *adore* poetry."

Perchance might a man have five minutes peace on this voyage? Christopher gritted his teeth and forced a smile. He looked back toward Miss Cosgrove and happened to catch Miss Abbott struggling to hold back a grin—or outright laughter?—as she pretended great interest in her bowl of porridge.

"Of course you may join me," Christopher said in his most pleasant voice. "And shall we invite Miss Abbott as well?"

At this her head snapped up, and she exchanged a look with him.

Do not think to foist her off on me all day, he sent her way.

I wasn't!

Maybe not, but you were certainly enjoying my discomfort.

Guilty. Miss Abbott glanced away.

Christopher's look turned smug. "Shall we, ladies?" He took a step toward the door. Miss Cosgrove was already prancing down the aisle, and he heard the reluctant scrape of Miss Abbott's chair as she stood to join them.

They are not my responsibility, he repeated to himself. *But if I must endure the company of one throughout this voyage, I should at least be allowed the companionship of the other as well.*

CHAPTER 11

"Fire her up, Mr. Jones!" Captain Gower called from the top of the stairs leading below deck. An answering bellow carried up to him, and Marsali watched as he left the stairwell, crossed the deck, and proudly assumed his place at the wheel.

Mr. Thatcher and Miss Cosgrove both stood at the stern, the latter busy waving two handkerchiefs at once and calling farewell to the crowd assembled below. Marsali preferred standing at the side of the boat, close to where the gangway had been. Holding the rail, she leaned over, eager to see the first churning of the wheel.

A trickle of steam had been spouting steadily from the smokestack for some time, but all of a sudden this turned to puffy white clouds, growing larger by the minute. People standing on the dock pointed and exclaimed, causing Miss Cosgrove to become even more animated, her handkerchiefs flapping and snapping in Mr. Thatcher's face. Marsali smiled to herself, all the while feeling guilty for having abandoned him to such a fate. But she'd spent over an hour walking the deck with them this morning and felt she had earned a moment alone.

Shouts came from below, and Marsali peered over the rail in time to see the first movement of the wheel. This coincided with the first movement of the ship as she turned away from the docks. Most in the crowd cheered, though she noted more than a few somber faces.

And not because they are sad to see us go. There were those, the captain had explained earlier, who wished the *Amanda May* ill, for if she succeeded, she stood to challenge—even pose a threat to—the other shipping lines.

"The steam engine is going to change the world," Captain Gower had predicted. At this moment, Marsali couldn't help but think he was right.

Fascinated, she watched as the wheel gained momentum. Quickly the distance between shore and ship increased. Steam puffed from the tall stack, and the wheel churned through the water at a steady pace as the *Amanda May* moved away from the harbor and out to sea.

First Officer Luke stood beside Captain Gower at the wheel and the helmsman on the other side. Marsali guessed that Captain Gower wanted his moment of glory as they left port—and likely another when they arrived in New York—but that much of the work of steering the ship would be left to his officers in between. She'd been introduced to these men and others shortly before departure and had quickly discovered that Mr. Luke was one to avoid. He could easily match Miss Cosgrove for dialogue, but his was even more self-centered. Listening to him—as Marsali had been trapped into for a good ten minutes earlier—one would think Mr. Luke was the captain and had built the entire ship himself, with his bare hands. She hoped his duties would keep him very busy throughout their voyage.

Captain Gower, on the other hand, continued to impress her. When all had been assembled on deck he offered a prayer for their safe journey.

Marsali would not have guessed him to be particularly religious, but when he had petitioned the Lord not only for their safety but for the safety of the families they left behind, she had seen him in a different light. The *Amanda May*, Mr. Thatcher had explained, was named after the captain's wife, and she and their two children would be anxiously awaiting his return. Marsali wondered if the captain's obsession with speed had anything to do with a desire to see his family more frequently.

I shall have a family to see soon as well. Charlotte was a mother now, to a little boy who had just turned one. Marsali had liked Charlotte's husband, Matthew, when she'd known him in Manchester, and the thought of sitting at a table with the three of them—with *family*—filled her with yearning that felt almost like a physical ache.

Holding to the rail, she carefully made her way to the bow, having no desire for any further look at England and her past, though she could not deny the air of excitement on board and on the docks behind them. She felt glad for this, for the captain especially. His ship may have met with superstition, but those watching her leave port of her own accord, without any tug or wind to aid her, had to be impressed.

Marsali stood at the bow a few minutes more, looking back toward the wheel a time or two and enjoying the breeze on her face. What a wondrous thing it was to have time in which to simply stand and do nothing but appreciate the blue of the sky and the ocean, the feeling of being alive. She hadn't seen much of the outdoors the past few years—there hadn't been time for anything but work—and she found that her senses craved it. The cry of a gull, the spray of the water, and the salty scent of the ocean all filled her with joy. It felt as if her life had finally begun—just now, at this very moment.

I am coming, Charlotte. As much pleasure as she took in standing on deck and feeling the wind in her face, Marsali felt even more enthusiasm for the letter now tucked inside her pocket. She'd put it there this morning, anxious to read it at last, as soon as they were underway.

She left the bow and walked to midship, where she settled on a crate in the shade beneath the main sail. Eagerly, she withdrew the precious paper, careful to hold it tightly. She didn't want to chance having the wind catch the letter and blow it away, but neither did she wish to return to the stuffiness of her cabin when the day was so fine. The breeze here beneath the sail was not too strong and felt refreshing. Wisps of hair that had previously blown about now fell softly on either side of her face. Marsali took one of these and twirled it around her finger a moment—an old childhood habit—before summoning the courage to open the letter.

The last one I shall have from Charlotte before I see her again.

"Miss Abbott, would you care to join us as we bid farewell to England? She'll not be in our sights much longer."

Marsali looked up from the envelope she'd been about to open and found Mr. Thatcher standing above her, eyes screwed tightly in a rather desperate look—one that begged for assistance. Miss Cosgrove hovered just behind him, but her eyes were puffy and her cheeks red and splotchy, as if she had been crying.

"No, thank you," Marsali said as kindly as she could. She'd indulged them after breakfast, when really all she had wanted to do was go to her room and continue reading the marvelous book he'd lent her. But her conscience had not allowed her to abandon Mr. Thatcher to a morning alone with Miss Cosgrove. Though Marsali found her quite amusing, as well as a great insight to the intricacies of society, she could also appreciate that Miss Cosgrove's non-stop chatter could grow wearisome, especially for a man. And now it appeared that her chatter had been replaced by tears. Marsali very much doubted that Mr. Thatcher had particularly enjoyed those either.

Notwithstanding he has a fine shoulder to cry upon. Her gaze flickered over him briefly, looking as handsome in his frock coat today as he had yesterday when describing to her his discomfort as he took leave of his sisters. *And as fine as he looked last night when we danced.*

What a pleasant diversion that had been. Though there had been that moment when he'd faced her, when their eyes had met and their fun had seemed to turn to something more—something that both frightened and excited her. Marsali supposed she was a coward for not lingering in the moment and exploring it more closely, but Miss Cosgrove's timely arrival had seemed the perfect excuse to end whatever it was that had passed between herself and Mr. Thatcher.

I am not free to be interested in any man. Charlotte had been eighteen when she'd met Matthew, fallen in love with him, and married. *But I do not have that luxury. I am not allowed feelings of my own yet, other than the feelings of responsibility to those to whom I am committed.*

"I am truly sorry to decline your invitation," she said to both Mr. Thatcher and Miss Cosgrove, as they were clearly both waiting for an explanation. His face registered disappointment, though he attempted to hide it. And Miss Cosgrove let out a dejected sigh. Marsali picked up the envelope in her lap. "It is just that I've been waiting until we were at sea to read this." She could not bear to think of waiting even a half hour longer. The letter had been on her mind almost constantly since her aunt's maid handed it to her two days earlier. A dozen times she had picked it up and been on the verge of opening it, only to tell herself that she should wait. But with their ship underway and England's shores at last safely behind them, there was no longer a reason to delay reading it.

"Oooh." Miss Cosgrove's eyes widened with delight, and she rose up on her tiptoes, leaning closer for a better look. "Who is it from? Have you left a beau behind, or is there one awaiting you in America?"

"It is a letter from my sister," Marsali explained. "She promised to write and tell me what I must expect upon my arrival in New York and on my journey to Virginia."

"Oh, do tell us what she says, please." Miss Cosgrove left Mr. Thatcher's side and with a flounce of skirts—pink today—seated herself on the crate beside Marsali.

"Perhaps Miss Abbott would like to read her letter in private," Mr. Thatcher suggested.

Marsali sent him a look of gratitude. "That would be—"

"But I haven't ever had a letter from America," Miss Cosgrove said. "Mr. Vancer only ever wrote to Mama, not to me. I should love to have a sister waiting for me, especially one who has lived in America for *four* years. She must know everything about it."

"Likely not," Marsali said. "Charlotte lives on a modest plantation in Virginia. And I fear—"

"Oh, you needn't worry I'll be bored." Miss Cosgrove leaned in close—so close her chin nearly rested on Marsali's shoulder.

"Very well." Marsali held back a sigh. "You may stay as well, Mr. Thatcher," she said as she caught him sneaking away.

They exchanged a look similar to that which they'd shared at breakfast, only this time it was Marsali who came away with the point. *As if we are playing a game of badminton and Miss Cosgrove is the shuttlecock.* The image brought a smile to Marsali's face as she remembered playing the game with Charlotte ages ago.

Charlotte. Without further hesitation, and heedless of her audience, Marsali tore into the envelope, breaking the seal and extracting the letter. With greater care, she unfolded the parchment. Her smile widened as she recognized her sister's fine script.

"What does it say?" Miss Cosgrove asked. "The sun is blinding, and I cannot see."

Marsali held the paper up at a better angle and began to read.

My Dearest Marsali,

It is with great urgency that I write to you and tell you that you must not make your journey as we had planned.

"Oh, dear!" Marsali reread the line again and wondered what trickery of her aunt's this was. Every one of Charlotte's previous letters had been counting down the years and then months and weeks until Marsali might join her. "She can't mean it," she said, glancing from Miss Cosgrove to Mr. Thatcher. "If Charlotte even wrote this at all. My aunt must have copied her handwriting."

I have learned that Mr. Joshua Thomas is not to be trusted. Friday last I discovered quite by accident that his daughter's previous lady's maid had passed away suddenly.

"How dreadful!" Miss Cosgrove exclaimed.

Turning her body away and bending her head low over the paper, Marsali continued to read silently.

As you might imagine, I found this news rather sorrowful, though not too distressing, as I had met her only once previous, when we were both waiting on ladies in attendance at the same ball.

I inquired of our visitor who shared this news, a Miss Pettigrew of Edgewood, what had befallen the maid and was told that she had developed a sudden pneumonia and died within a few days. I thought this rather odd, as pneumonia in the middle of summer here is quite rare, especially in an otherwise healthy young woman. But as we both know, unusual occurrences are often more common than one would believe.

Marsali knew Charlotte was referring to their mother's illness. Charlotte still believed their mother had simply fallen ill and died of consumption. Marsali had attempted to tell her the truth in a letter—that their mother had been poisoned—but Aunt Ada had intercepted it and thrown it into the fire. After that, Marsali had to carefully choose her words and write only vague hints of the situation at her aunt's house, or she would not be allowed to write to her sister at all.

Unusual occurrences often have more to them than one might believe, Marsali thought, her concern elevating as she returned to reading Charlotte's letter.

> *I would have thought no more of the incident, had Miss Pettigrew's maid not taken me aside later, as I was out taking in the wash.*
>
> *What she told me—whether truth or falsehood, though I have since had reason to believe her words to be true—has left me frightened for you, sister. The woman told me that Miss Thomas's previous two lady's maids have all perished shortly before their term of service was to end. Other servants working on the Thomas plantation have suffered similar fates, and some have simply disappeared.*
>
> *Following this report, Matthew and I undertook an investigation on our own, and what we discovered has been extremely disturbing. Mr. Thomas is not a good man. He is known for his cruelty to both slaves and servants alike. To the outside world he is a well-respected businessman, but those living under his hand tell quite a different tale.*
>
> *Marsali, you must not come to America. I fear you shall be in terrible danger—even more so than you are while still at Aunt Ada's mercy. Please stay in Manchester through the winter. You shall get through somehow. I know it. And Matthew and I will do our*

*best to save every penny we can to pay for your
passage ourselves.*

    *I am as sorrowful as you over this turn of events,
but I should rather be sad than frightened for your
life. Please remember I love you dearly.*

       Yours affectionately,

       Charlotte

Marsali's fingers went limp, and the letter slipped from them, falling to her lap. She squeezed her eyes closed, but the awful words still swam before them. Just as in Manchester, there was no escaping. And there was no doubt it was Charlotte who had written the letter. Had her aunt tampered with it, there would certainly have been no mention of her cruelty.

"What else did your sister say?" Miss Cosgrove peered over Marsali's shoulder, attempting to get a good look at the letter.

"Miss Abbott, are you quite all right?" Mr. Thatcher's voice pulled her back to the present, to the ship that was taking her toward even greater danger.

Marsali looked up through wet eyelashes and had the absurd thought that she must not cry in front of him. He had heard her doing so once already. And he had endured Miss Cosgrove's tears this morning.

"Charlotte says that I am not to come," Marsali said numbly.

"But you are already coming," Miss Cosgrove said.

"She thinks it dangerous," Marsali said.

"Oooh! I just knew it," Miss Cosgrove exclaimed. "It is as Mama said—we are journeying to the uncivilized world. Are the natives uprising again? What has happened there in Virginia where she lives? That's the wilderness, isn't it? It isn't like New York, which at least is somewhat close to becoming as refined and cultured as London."

"Miss Cosgrove, please," Mr. Thatcher said sharply. He

squatted in front of Marsali so that he was at eye level. "Are you all right? And your sister? No harm has befallen her?"

"No." Marsali shook her head and it cleared a bit. There was something to be grateful for—Charlotte was well. "My sister is quite all right. The ill has befallen my predecessor. Here. I do not care to read it again. And I see no harm in either of you knowing." She held the letter out to him, and after a second's hesitation he took it, then stood once more and began reading. Miss Cosgrove stood and joined him, nosing her way in to read over his arm.

Marsali folded her arms across her middle, hugging herself. The breeze that had felt good moments ago now seemed chilling. And the voyage she had so looked forward to had lost its appeal.

"But you can't turn back now," Miss Cosgrove exclaimed just a second after starting to read. This was followed by several gasps of varying severity. Mr. Thatcher finished the letter, lowered the paper, and looked at Marsali.

"What do you intend to do?" he asked.

"Nothing." She shrugged. "I haven't any choice but to go and to honor my indenture." It wasn't as if she could dive off the ship and swim back to England. *Not that I would go back.* Mr. Thatcher returned the letter, and she quickly refolded it, though the words seemed etched in her mind already.

Mr. Thomas is not to be trusted . . . He is known for his cruelty . . . maids have perished shortly before their term . . . Marsali clutched the tail end of the thought as if it was a life raft.

"Charlotte did not say that any of the maids had perished at the beginning or middle of their time of service. It was only when they were about to be released from their contract. Surely I will be safe for a good three years or more." She gave a half smile, trying to make light of the situation. Mr. Thatcher and Miss Cosgrove did not return her smile. Even the latter was astonishingly quiet.

Say something, Marsali begged silently. *Move me to distraction with your chatter.*

"You should not go," Mr. Thatcher said, his mouth drawn and his blue eyes looking as solemn as Marsali had ever seen them.

"I haven't any choice," Marsali said. "I've no other way to pay for my passage, and I shall owe Mr. Thomas for it upon my arrival."

"But your sister said he is a cruel man." Miss Cosgrove's eyes welled with tears, and her lip quivered as if frightened. Marsali wondered how much the display of emotion had to do with Miss Cosgrove's own worries—about the fiancé and the new life awaiting her in New York.

At least I am not betrothed *to Mr. Thomas.* Marsali suppressed a shudder and stood abruptly, taking one of Miss Cosgrove's hands in her own. "You must not worry for me. I shall be fine."

"But—"

"As for Mr. Thomas's supposed cruelty . . ." Marsali sighed, feeling rather more discouraged than fearful now. "It is not something I am unused to. Both my aunt and uncle loathed me. Having been subjected to their treatment the past four years, I am doubtful that Mr. Thomas shall be any worse."

Only please don't let him be as bad.

Mr. Thatcher had not said anything further during this exchange, but Marsali could see that he was troubled. His brows pinched together almost painfully, and his lips were turned down. Had she a penny to her name, she might have offered it for his thoughts.

"Come," Marsali said, linking her arm through Miss Cosgrove's. "Let us see if England is truly behind us now or if we can still make out her shore." She steered Miss Cosgrove toward the back of the ship. Mr. Thatcher lingered behind, and when Marsali glanced back at him, she saw that he had turned the other direction. Strangely, this relieved her. She did not want his pity, and she could not afford to get used to his assistance—as he had offered at her late arrival that first night.

I cannot depend upon anyone but myself. There is no one to rescue me. I am still alone in this world.

These circumstances were not anything different from those she had dealt with previously, but the thought of continuing on that way for another four years was disheartening. All of the enthusiasm she'd felt for this voyage, and her excitement for seeing America and even seeing Charlotte, had fled. Silently Marsali cursed the maid who had rushed to bring her that letter.

It would have been better had I not known. At least I could have enjoyed these few weeks. Now, instead of eagerly counting down the days until they arrived in New York, Marsali would be marking them off as the last days of her safety.

No matter, she told herself bravely as they reached the back of the ship. She released Miss Cosgrove's hand and clutched the rail as she looked out at England's rapidly receding shores.

"Aren't you afraid to work for Mr. Thomas?" Miss Cosgrove asked, her voice subdued in both volume and animation.

"Yes," Marsali answered honestly. "But many times in my life I have been afraid. And I have survived them all." *Some just barely.* She glanced at Miss Cosgrove and saw her lip quiver.

"And you are frightened as well?" Marsali asked. "About what awaits you in America?"

Miss Cosgrove nodded and sniffed loudly. She turned to Marsali, her eyes brimming with unshed tears. "Mr. Vancer is so much older. What if he doesn't care for me? What if he is cruel like your Mr. Thomas?"

"He is not *my* Mr. Thomas," Marsali said, then regretted it when Miss Cosgrove gave a hiccupping sob.

"I'm sorry," Marsali said, sliding her arm around Miss Cosgrove's shoulder in a gesture of comfort. "Mr. Vancer will not be cruel to you. And he does like you. He would not have offered for you otherwise."

"He doesn't *know* me," Miss Cosgrove said. "He hasn't seen me since I was twelve, and I don't remember much of that visit."

"But he must," Marsali said, praying she was right and was not about to make the situation worse. "You must have made a very good impression upon him, so that all these years later he has sent for you to come and be his bride."

"Oh, I do hope you are right." Miss Cosgrove managed a tiny smile along with the tears streaming down her face. Even with her cheeks red and her eyes puffy, she still managed to look very pretty. Marsali withdrew her arm from around Miss Cosgrove's shoulders and stepped back. She knew a moment of longing as she took in Miss Cosgrove's golden curls and the jeweled combs in her hair that matched her dress. Surely Mr. Vancer would be pleased with her appearance at least. She hoped very much that he would be pleased with the rest of his bride as well—that he would enjoy her vivaciousness and appreciate her enthusiasm for most everything.

And if he does not . . . It troubled Marsali to think of a subdued Miss Cosgrove, of the light and happiness within her put out.

"Your mother will be with you as well," Marsali said, searching for something she might say which was true. "She would not let you marry someone who would be unkind to you."

Miss Cosgrove rolled her eyes. "I think that Mama might let me marry a *rock* if it had enough money." She giggled.

Marsali laughed with her and felt better for having offered comfort. "Such an unfair lot we women have," she said as much to herself as to Miss Cosgrove. "It seems we must either marry—and often not for love or because we wish to—or we must spend our lives serving others and subject to their treatment."

"I think you are certainly the one with the more difficult time of it," Miss Cosgrove said in a rare display of altruistic thinking. "I wish you could come with me and be *my* lady's maid. I would treat you kindly, and we would be the dearest of friends—sharing my sweets, staying up late at night talking together, gossiping about the ladies I'd met at the ball or the gentlemen who had come to call on us."

"It sounds lovely," Marsali said, indulging in the fantasy even further, where she was not the maid but a resident of such a household and of equal status. "But no doubt your Mr. Vancer has a houseful of servants already, with one picked out especially for you."

"And she is probably old and stuffy." Miss Cosgrove wrinkled her pert nose and stuck out her tongue.

Marsali laughed. "Oh, Miss Cosgrove, you are a dear. You have cheered me considerably, and I thank you for it."

"Lydia," Miss Cosgrove said. She reached out, turning Marsali to her and placing her hands upon her shoulders. "We are friends now—in sorrow and fear as well as happiness—so you must call me by my Christian name."

"Lydia is a lovely name," Marsali said, thinking how well it fit her. "You may call me Marsali."

"Marsali the brave!" Lydia quipped. "Facing her fears with far more courage than I. Though I don't know how you shall."

"Do not worry for me," Marsali said once more. "I have been on my own for a long time. I can care for myself." *And I will.*

She'd had to in the past. And she would have to again. At least this time she would be on the same continent as her sister.

CHAPTER 12

"She's the most modern ship in more ways than one." Captain Gower stood just outside the door to the saloon, ready to lead those passengers who were interested on the promised tour of the *Amanda May*. Christopher had been pleasantly surprised to discover that Miss Abbott was one of those passengers, whereas it appeared that Lady Cosgrove and her daughter were not.

"I am certain Lydia—Miss Cosgrove—wanted to join us," Miss Abbott said as they moved toward the stairs that would lead them below the ship's main deck.

"I believe her mother was not feeling well and required Miss Cosgrove's assistance this afternoon," Captain Gower said, much to Christopher's relief. What a contrast the two young women were, he thought as he walked alongside Miss Abbott, who showed no sign of tears, no sign at all that anything was amiss or might be troubling her, in spite of the distressing news she'd received yesterday. Had that same letter been delivered to Miss Cosgrove, no doubt she would have been given to a fit of hysterics on the spot.

Miss Abbott, on the other hand, had seemed to recover from her shock quite rapidly. She'd declared herself ready to face whatever hardships lay ahead and did not seem wont to wallow in either self-pity or worry. *She is much like Grace,* Christopher thought with a smile and a swell of admiration for his new acquaintance.

He allowed Miss Abbott to go before him on the stairs and noticed the frayed hem of her gown as she held it up and began her descent.

Do I admire her because she, too, has known a difficult life? And am I so critical of Miss Cosgrove because hers has been one of privilege? Christopher did not wish to think himself so judgmental, yet examining his readily formed opinions about each lady, it appeared he was.

Something I'd best watch myself with in America. His grandfather would have said harboring prejudice against the fortunate was no different than believing the worst of those without means.

It was not your father's lack of money that made me dislike him, Grandfather had once confided in Christopher. *It was his lack of ambition.*

Help me not to lack either ambition or compassion, Christopher silently prayed. *And let me find a way to assist Miss Abbott once she is in America.*

Captain Gower paused at the base of the stairs and took up a lantern to guide their way here, below deck, where the light was dim. "The deck, planking, and keelsons are of hard pine, but the *Amanda May's* frame is made of seasoned white oak. And her hull is diagonally braced with iron. She's not only fast, but strong." He held the lantern low, over the polished floor, and Christopher whistled appreciatively.

The wood was beautiful, as yet largely unmarred, and the boards fit together perfectly, the only imperfections being that of the pattern of the grain.

"Not an inexpensive ship, is she?" Christopher said.

"On the contrary, no expense was spared." Captain

Gower's voice held more than a touch of pride. "You'll not find a better-made ship sailing the Atlantic. All the keelsons and waterways are scarfed and keyed. She's got thirty-two beams under the lower deck and thirty-four under the main." He held the lantern aloft, illuminating one of these as they moved down the corridor. "Her bulwarks are built solid, like those of a warship."

"This is most impressive, Captain," Miss Abbott said. "I have nothing to compare your ship to, never having sailed before, but I must say I feel extremely safe aboard her."

"That you are," Captain Gower said, while Christopher wondered at her choice of words—if she was thinking of the coming dangers on land more than she let on.

They ducked as they entered another part of the hold, and Captain Gower pointed out an impressive five-thousand-gallon water tank. Christopher wondered if he'd had it completely filled, considering their shortage of passengers, but he thought it better not to ask.

"And here we come to the heart of the ship." Captain Gower stepped aside and indicated that they should go before him. Miss Abbott stepped up over the entrance to the engine room, her face alight with curiosity as she looked about, taking in all the apparatus. Christopher had been most interested in seeing this room but now felt his eyes sliding repeatedly to Miss Abbott, as he found himself enjoying her reactions nearly as much as what was being shown them.

"Through here you'll see the stokehold and beyond that the boilers." Captain Gower had followed them into the engine room and pointed to another door at its side. "Every man has an assigned job. Some fire, and others trim, and each knows exactly what is needed and when."

Christopher leaned through the doorway, peering into the hot room and the as-yet fresh faces of those within. He very much doubted they'd appear the same after spending four weeks at their tasks. Through yet another doorway beyond, he glimpsed the mounds of coal and did not envy the men their labor of retrieving it and constantly feeding the fire.

"Mr. Jones is in charge down here. I believe you've met." Captain Gower nodded to the taller, redheaded man. "He'll be joining us for dinner every few days and making certain the other men have their turns up top as well. We're not in such a hurry that we'll lose men to poor working conditions. As well as the best ship, I intend to have the best crew, and that requires they be treated better than the competition."

Christopher listened as Mr. Jones described the basic principles of a steam engine and explained each of the dials and meters on the panels before them.

It *was* fascinating, this glimpse of the future, and once more Christopher felt excited to be a very small part of it. The world was on the brink of change. He'd felt it in London and guessed that America would be much the same in that regard. And while he might not be an inventor himself, he was reinventing himself and his family name. The idea of starting from scratch, with no prejudices against him and nothing between himself and his dreams but hard work, was exhilarating.

Beyond the endless horizon outside were endless possibilities. He could be and do anything he wanted, with nothing to hold him back.

Yet his dreams were so different than his grandfather's had been—he'd no desire for a title or any sort of recognition. Neither did he wish for wealth or a mansion like Mr. Vancer's. *Twenty-seven bedrooms. Ridiculous.* He did not want a house full of servants. Just a house—one he built himself, preferably. And land, lots of land, where he could grow the things his family needed.

My someday family. His gaze strayed to Miss Abbott once more. Someday, sometime far off from now, he supposed he would find a woman he could admire, one who cared for him as well. And then he would marry and start a family.

When I'm thirty ought to be about right. Eight and a half years seemed time enough for him to establish himself and enjoy life a bit.

And what will Miss Abbott be doing during those years? It was exactly the sort of thought he did not wish to have— and couldn't seem to help but having.

What will *she do when faced with Mr. Thomas's cruelty?* Though Christopher tried not to, he could not seem to keep himself from thinking of his sisters and making comparisons between them and Miss Abbott.

If I had not arrived to stop Crayton when he found Helen at home alone . . . If I'd not intercepted Lidgate when he tried to follow Grace the night she fled his house . . . If I hadn't been at the theatre with Helen when Crayton approached her . . . Any of those situations—and many others—could have ended horribly for his sisters. All those years of accompanying Grace to deliver and pick up the laundry she took in had been particularly difficult—especially as she had grown older and more beautiful and he had not yet been old enough or big enough to properly defend her. More than a time or two he'd hobbled home, his nose bleeding and his gut aching from the blows he'd taken to ensure Grace wasn't harmed.

He hadn't been completely jesting when, at his sisters' weddings, he'd told them he was ready to be through watching over them.

Nor, apparently, had he been wrong when he'd suspected his life would become dreadfully boring without that responsibility.

And what is wrong with boring? he asked himself. *Why can I not be content to carry on without worrying over someone—some female? Miss Abbott?*

He could not be content because his conscience would not allow it. *Miss Abbott does not have a brother to look out for her. And now that I know of her plight, I cannot ignore it or pretend that she—and her difficulties—do not exist.*

"It would seem much to endure, working down here." Miss Abbott fanned her hand in front of her face.

Not as much as four years of servitude to a man known for cruelty.

"That's why the men working below have shorter shifts," Mr. Jones explained. "Four hours on and eight off."

"And what of your shifts?" she asked. "Are you allowed the same?"

He gave her a half smile. "Not quite. I've got to oversee it all, and I worry when I'm not down here. Wouldn't want an accident to happen. Don't want to disappoint the cap'n, and we need to keep everyone safe."

"That's very noble of you." She returned his smile, and Mr. Jones's grin engulfed his face as a blush stole across it to match his hair color.

Christopher couldn't entirely fault the man. Being the recipient of Miss Abbott's smile had threatened his own resolve a time or two already.

They left the engine room and returned to the deck, where Captain Gower continued to point out the finer features of his ship. "The masts hoist the auxiliary sails. Her riggings are fashioned of the best Russian hemp."

"It must be a spectacular view from the top." Christopher eyed the rigging, imagining how grand it would be to climb and wondering if the captain might allow him to.

"It's not a task for the faint of heart," Captain Gower said, a knowing look in his eye, as if he realized the direction of Christopher's thoughts. "Even in calm waters, the ship sways. The effect only multiplies when you're up so high. Many a seasoned sailor has lost his life falling."

"How dreadful," Miss Abbott said. "But I must also agree with Mr. Thatcher. How splendid it must be to look out over the ocean from such a vantage point."

"*Nevertheless*," Captain Gower said. "We shall all have to enjoy the view from the deck."

Christopher exchanged a disappointed look with Miss Abbott.

Too bad.

Women are never allowed to do anything, he imagined her saying.

"A single suit of sails requires over twelve thousand yards of canvas," Captain Gower continued, steering the conversation away from the temptation of the rigging.

"Have you any idea how many *gowns* might be fashioned from twelve thousand yards of fabric?" Miss Cosgrove's high-pitched voice and sudden arrival put an abrupt end to Christopher's musings and the pleasant time he'd been having with only the captain and Miss Abbott for company.

Have you any idea the amount of time it would take to launder all those gowns? His thoughts returned to his sisters and the meager upbringing they'd had, scraping together an existence by doing the laundry for ladies of means in the years before their grandfather had discovered them. He fought a scowl as he turned to greet Miss Cosgrove, strutting, as it were, around the sail, an air of appraisal about her.

She spoke of dresses, whereas Miss Abbott spoke of climbing riggings. Was it any wonder that he favored one lady's company above the other?

"How is your mother?" Miss Abbott asked, linking her arm through Miss Cosgrove's as if they were the closest of chums.

At least it stopped her from parading about with that painful swagger. Christopher wondered if that hadn't been Miss Abbott's intent all along.

"Mother is quite unwell," Miss Cosgrove said. A second later her face brightened. "But she is sleeping now, so I am free to join you. What have you seen without me?"

"Captain Gower has constructed a most marvelous

ship," Miss Abbott said, earning a nod of approval from the captain. "He has spared no expense for our safety. Indeed, this is the most well-built vessel to be found upon the Atlantic, is that not right, Captain?"

"Indeed it is." He pulled out his pipe and began filling it. "But you've seen about all that will interest you ladies. Pumps, windlasses, and winches all look about the same, but rest assured ours are the most modern to be found."

Christopher thought the captain's abrupt end to the tour a bit surprising, and by the curious look upon Miss Abbott's face, he gathered she did as well. Miss Cosgrove seemed oblivious, still chattering away at Miss Abbott, the captain—anyone who would listen.

"I wonder how many yards of fabric would be found at Almack's if all of the ladies' gowns there were tallied together. Of course, none would be so rough and coarse as this canvas. You'd find only the best fabrics, like silk."

"Captain Gower," Miss Abbott quickly cut in. "Do you ever envision a time when a ship might be propelled only by steam and without any sails at all?"

"Possibly," Captain Gower said, his tone skeptical. "But sails do more than provide auxiliary propulsion. In rough seas they'll help keep an even keel, ensuring that the wheel remains in the water and we travel a straight line." He doffed his hat. "If you'll excuse me now. Miss Abbott, Miss Cosgrove." He turned toward Christopher. "Mr. Thatcher. It has been a pleasure introducing you properly to the *Amanda May*, but I must be back to running her now."

"Thank you for showing us," Christopher said. "It was most impressive and interesting."

"Good day, Captain. And thank you for your time," Miss Abbott said. Captain Gower replaced his hat and left them.

"Oh, but I just got here." Miss Cosgrove's lip jutted out in an exaggerated pout.

Christopher caught Miss Abbott's eye and shrugged,

then bowed as he took his own departure. She shook her head as if letting him know she was disappointed at his sudden departure as well.

She obviously suspected that he, like Captain Gower perhaps, was not anxious for Miss Cosgrove's company. Christopher had agreed to be kind to her, but that did not signify spending a great deal of time with her each day. And just now he wished for time alone in which to consider the direction of his thoughts.

The tour had been inspiring, and he felt goaded to action.

If men are able to propel a ship across the ocean using a steam engine and paddlewheel, if twelve thousand yards of fabric can be fashioned into a sail, if an oak tree can be cured, then stripped and planked and those planks made to curve in the shape of a hull . . . If such marvels were to be had on a single ship, then surely he was clever enough to come up with a solution to a problem as well.

It was neither his problem nor his affair, but Christopher had about given up that argument with himself as a lost cause. He felt compelled to find a solution, compelled to assist one very intriguing young lady with a certain matter regarding her safekeeping in the near future.

He was not at all sure how he would accomplish such a thing, only that it must be done. There had to be a way, and he was determined to find it.

In three-and-a-half weeks' time, when they all disembarked in New York, he intended to see to it that Miss Abbott would continue to be safe.

CHAPTER 13

Carrying a small lantern, Marsali left her cabin and crept stealthily down the length of the common room. For once she felt grateful for her old slippers, which, worn as they were, made not the barest sound on the wood floor. She did not wish to wake anyone, particularly Lydia, who would likely ruin Marsali's plans with her chatter. Most of the time she found Lydia's company pleasant enough, but tonight was different. It was what she had most looked forward to on this voyage, a quiet evening all to herself in which she might revisit the past and remember with fondness the happiness she had once known.

With care she opened the door and stepped out onto the deck, breathing in the cooler night air and lifting her head to the great display of stars spread magnificently across the black sky above. Tonight was the first night of the new moon, assuring that the sky was at the darkest it would be during their voyage and with the most stars visible. She felt most fortunate the sky was clear as well, with no clouds whatsoever.

With the chart she had borrowed from Captain Gower earlier that day tucked safely beneath her arm, Marsali climbed the steps to the front of the ship. As if he'd been expecting her, Mr. Murphy made his appearance, settling in for what appeared to be an evening of cleaning his teeth. The captain had likely advised him that she would be stargazing, and Marsali found she did not mind Mr. Murphy watching out for her—too much. She'd hoped that tonight he might be available to answer any questions she had, as it had been many years since she'd sat on a hillside in France and studied the stars with her father. But seeing the first bit of meat Murphy dislodged from his teeth changed her mind about moving any closer to him than necessary.

Sitting carefully a good distance away, she set the lantern down, tucked her skirt in around her, and unrolled the chart, spreading it out on the deck before her. It curled again at once, so she placed the lantern on one side of it to hold it down and tucked the opposite corner beneath her slipper until the parchment lay flat.

There they are. A shiver of excitement passed over her as she studied the patterns covering the page. Hercules and Pegasus, Orion and Cassiopeia. On Captain Gower's chart they were outlined the same as she remembered seeing them in the sky during her childhood. Her favorites were here, too, though brave Perseus and little Lyra would be harder to find in the sky. She would have to sit very still and concentrate to make them out as well.

With reverence her fingers traced the dotted shapes filling the parchment. She remembered the stories of each and could almost hear the rich timbre of her father's voice as he shared the tales with her. How magnificent they all were. How much she had loved sitting on the hillside behind their home, far into the night, as she and her father and Charlotte studied the stars.

She pictured them there—two little girls with a kindly, bearded man between them—and felt a lump rise in her throat. She wondered if her father was still able to see the night sky and enjoy it, or if heaven itself was among the stars. *Or even one of them?*

Pulling her eyes from the chart, Marsali tilted her head back and found the North Star, then the Plough quite easily. Pegasus was next, big fellow that he was.

"That is quite a different view than in London."

Marsali jumped and brought a hand to her pounding heart. "Mr. Thatcher. You startled me."

"My apologies." He inclined his head politely. "I did not mean to startle—or interrupt. Would you prefer that I leave you?"

"No," she said quickly. "Not at all. I—would like it very much if you would join me." She felt surprised to realize that she meant it. She'd wanted to be alone but somehow knew that Mr. Thatcher's presence would not take anything away from her night spent in memory. She patted the space beside her on the deck.

He hesitated. "Are you certain? I have the feeling I've just interrupted."

"You have." She grinned before he could look abashed. "I have been thinking of my father, remembering when he taught me about the stars and trying to recall his voice when he shared with me the stories behind the constellations." She patted the deck once more. "But I welcome your company. Dwelling overlong in the past does one no good."

"Well . . . since that is the circumstance—" Mr. Thatcher plopped down beside her—"I feel an obligation for keeping you from something that will do you no good."

"See. There you go, being a gentleman again," Marsali teased.

He scowled. "Never have I had such trouble avoiding gentlemanly behavior as since I've made your acquaintance, Miss Abbott. I must conclude that you are not at all a good influence upon me—though my sisters would likely claim the opposite."

Marsali laughed. "It is in your blood, as Lady Cosgrove would say, as she did at breakfast when she learned you are the grandson of a duke. I think you cannot escape that, no matter how much you may wish it."

"I have never wished to sever that tie, not in the manner you speak of, at least," Mr. Thatcher said politely. "I had no desire for the title, mind you, but the association with my grandfather is one I cherish. He was a fine man, a gentleman in the truest sense. It is the ties to my father and *his* name I wish to leave behind."

"You might have petitioned the courts to have your name changed," Marsali suggested. "It could have allowed you to stay in England with your sisters."

Mr. Thatcher appeared to consider this for a moment. "I think I should still have felt discontent. I cannot explain it exactly, but for many reasons, I felt compelled to make this journey, to see the new world and try my hand at a life there."

"You will do more than try your hand," Marsali predicted. "You will succeed at whatever it is you choose to do."

"Let us hope so," Mr. Thatcher said quietly, his eyes meeting hers with a look that felt oddly personal. "But here I have done what I told myself I must not when I approached you. I've interrupted your study of the stars. From this chart, I take it you are quite a serious student."

"Not really." She leaned forward, intending to roll up Captain Gower's map, when Mr. Thatcher's hand gently clasped her arm, stopping her.

"Don't put it away. Please go on with what you were doing. I promise to be quiet, but if I am disturbing you, you may send me away."

You are *disturbing me.* It felt as if a tiny, pleasant fire had started where his hand was touching her, much as she had felt that day he had placed his hand upon hers as they'd stood at the rail. The warmth spread quickly to her middle, a feeling of contentment mingling with something else—some emotion she was not familiar with. She glanced at Mr. Thatcher, and her heartbeat quickened inexplicably. As if he sensed the effect he was having, he withdrew his hand and leaned back casually, bracing himself on his arms.

Marsali looked down at the chart, trying to force her thoughts back to constellations while wondering what had just happened to make her react so.

I am not frightened of Mr. Thatcher, not in the least. She stole a second glance at him and found he had his face upturned as he studied the sky. *Good.* Perhaps he *hadn't* noticed how he'd flustered her.

Her fingers traced the chart once more before she raised her eyes to the sky, searching for Lyra. "The constellations are both easier and more difficult to find than I remember. My father was always the one to point them out, so I never had to do more than follow and search in the direction he pointed. Locating the shapes on my own isn't so simple."

"But the stars seem closer here, and brighter," Mr. Thatcher said.

"Yes." She nodded her agreement. "So even though I must find them on my own, once I make out their shapes, they seem clearer than I remember them being at home."

"There is nothing to block out their light here," Mr. Thatcher suggested.

"A unique experience we shall perhaps never have again," Marsali said. "On the Continent there were hills and village lights and trees and clouds to contend with. But our conditions tonight are as near to perfect as one might find. We should be able to locate most anything. Do you have a favorite constellation?"

He shrugged. "Not really. Or I've never thought about it, at least. I am guessing you do."

"Oh yes. I always found the stories of Perseus and Lyra most stirring, especially the way Father would tell them."

"Will you share them with me?" Mr. Thatcher asked.

"Surely you know them already," Marsali said. She couldn't imagine otherwise; neither could she imagine why he might wish to hear her renditions.

"I am not overly familiar with the stories." Mr. Thatcher crossed his legs and leaned forward, as a child anticipating a bedtime story might. "You must remember that I had no schooling or tutors until I was fourteen years of age. My sister taught me to read and write, but beyond that I had very little knowledge of the world—or skies above it. Grandfather did his best to remedy that, but I had much to learn and little time in which to do it, so some subjects—like astronomy— were neglected."

"I am sorry to hear that," Marsali said, feeling sad for him. "It must have been quite difficult not having a father who would teach such things to you." Her father had taken every opportunity to share the world with his girls. She and Charlotte had grown up knowing the names of the flowers and trees and the birds and insects that visited them. They had learned about the creatures inhabiting the sea as well as the stars residing in the sky. And every outing with Father had been simply delightful. The idea of learning about nature from a book or a tutor seemed nearly as terrible as not learning it at all.

"I did not know differently," Mr. Thatcher said. "It is you I feel sorry for—having lost your father, who cared for you deeply."

"I suppose we could both sit here and feel sorry for each other, or ourselves, but it does not do to dwell in the past," she reminded him.

"You seem to keep a rather tight rein on your thoughts," Mr. Thatcher observed. "You abstain from feeling overly melancholy regarding the past, and you refuse to worry over the future. I am left to assume that you are one who lives very much in the present, for the here and now."

"I think of the future as well," Marsali said. "But worrying about it will do me no good. For the duration of this voyage, I intend to enjoy every minute—every second—of freedom it affords me. It is a blessed thing to be able to use my time as I wish."

"Will you use it now to tell me the stories of Perseus and Lyra?" Mr. Thatcher asked.

"Of course." Marsali moved her foot from the chart and allowed it to roll back onto itself. "You have studied Greek mythology, I presume?"

"Somewhat," he said. "But I should like to hear *you* tell the stories—as your father told them. And in telling, perhaps it will assist you in remembering."

He was right, of course, as she had been right in believing that his company would not take anything away from her evening or memories. Rising up on her knees and tucking her skirts in around her once more, Marsali began. "It was Perseus who beheaded Medusa and then killed a sea monster to save the princess Andromeda."

"Medusa was the creature with a head of snakes?" Mr. Thatcher held up a hand and wiggled his fingers.

"It was actually her hair that was made up of snakes," Marsali said.

"Ugh." He pretended to shudder. "Can you imagine if each spoke as much as Miss Cosgrove does?"

"No. I cannot." Marsali pressed her lips together and attempted to appear stern. "That was most unkind, Mr. Thatcher. We must show compassion to our traveling companion, remember?"

"She is impossible to forget—or avoid," he said. "I timed her today. Miss Cosgrove spoke for six and a half minutes straight before taking a breath long enough for me to interrupt. And the worst of it is, I really have no idea what she spoke of during that entire time."

Marsali shook her head at him, indicating she thought him incorrigible. "You'll perhaps also recall that when a few drops of Medusa's blood fell into the sea, it mixed with the foam and became Pegasus, the flying horse. So you see, there is some good to be found in all of us if we but look for it."

"That seems to be a bit of a stretch in finding the moral to a story," Mr. Thatcher said good-naturedly.

Marsali ignored him. "Pegasus is easy to see, he's so large." She pointed to the sky, her finger tracing the lines that made up the great, winged horse.

"I see him," Mr. Thatcher said. "And which one is your Perseus?"

"Over there." She drew her finger along the outline of his body.

"Is he headless, then?" Mr. Thatcher said. "I do not recall that part of the story. I thought only Medusa lost her head."

Marsali rolled her eyes. "Have you no imagination? The stars only give a vague shape, or part of it. Your mind must supply the rest."

"Ah," he said and nodded as if a great mystery had just been revealed to him.

"Lyra, on the other hand," Marsali continued, "is quite small. But she has one of the brightest stars in the sky." Marsali stretched her hand once more, pointing to the tiny constellation above Hercules. "Lyra represents the harp that belonged to Orpheus. It was said that his music was sweeter than that of any mortal's. Even rivers changed course to be nearer his music."

"Interesting." Mr. Thatcher brought a hand to his chin as if deeply pondering a dilemma. "My tutor taught quite a different theory regarding the direction of rivers. Much more scientifically based, I must say."

"If you are going to mock me, I will not share any more of the story with you." Marsali folded her arms across her middle and turned away from him, pretending offense.

"I was only offering a second opinion, but I shall henceforth keep those to myself during the telling of these fascinating tales."

He spoke as if he expected her to share more than these

two, and an idea came to mind, that they might spend more evenings like this together, talking beneath a sky full of stars. The feeling that had begun with his touch swirled about inside her, a sort of warm anticipation. She hadn't had friends before this voyage. And inasmuch as she found Lydia amusing and felt grateful for her companionship, it was with Mr. Thatcher that she felt the greater connection. She enjoyed his teasing as much as his seriousness. Even just sitting beside him when they both were silent felt distinctly pleasant.

"Do go on," he said, sounding more repentant now that Marsali had gone a minute without speaking.

"No interruptions," she said sternly, looking back at him. "This is the tragic part of the story. You must listen well."

"You've my solemn promise. I am a great fan of tragedies."

Marsali bit her lip to keep from laughing at his pitiful expression. *It would be tragic*, she thought. *If I had not arranged passage on this ship and had not met him.* "Orpheus married Eurydice, but after their wedding, she was bitten by a snake and died."

"Was it one of the Medusa snakes—before Perseus took care of her?"

"No. And *no* interruptions," Marsali said. "This is the part of the story where you are supposed to feel terribly sad."

Mr. Thatcher turned his lips downward in a truly pitiful display.

"Orpheus loved Eurydice so much that he traveled to the underworld to beg for her return. Pluto's heart was softened by Orpheus's music, and he decided to allow Eurydice to leave. She was to follow Orpheus, who could not look back until both had left Hades and returned to the upper world."

"Oh, dear," Mr. Thatcher lamented. "I can well imagine

how impossible my brothers-in-law would find the task of not looking at their wives."

"Just before Eurydice reached the surface, Orpheus looked back at her, and she disappeared before his eyes. Orpheus wandered throughout Greece until he too was killed. After his death, Apollo placed his harp in the sky, and that is Lyra."

"To teach us . . . patience?" Mr. Thatcher guessed. "Or that beautiful music will not get you everything? Or . . ."

"I don't really know what the Greeks intended," Marsali admitted. "I just liked the story."

"What is there to like about it?" he asked. "And for the record, I've changed my mind. I am *not* a fan of tragedies." Mr. Thatcher's lips puckered as if he had just eaten something sour. "This is your favorite, you say."

"More for the harp than the story," Marsali explained. "Though now that I think of it, perhaps that is why I refuse to dwell on or in the past. Whenever my father told us that story, he always ended by saying that in life we must never look back, only forward. He said that whatever had happened in the past was of little consequence, but what happened today and then tomorrow was far more important."

"I believe that he and my grandfather would have regarded each other well," Mr. Thatcher said. "I should like to hear more of your father's tales—and wisdom."

"Another night, perhaps," Marsali said vaguely, though she had been hoping he would suggest that very thing. "It is late, and I believe Mr. Murphy has long since finished cleaning his teeth." She inclined her head toward Murphy, sprawled out on the deck, asleep, some distance away.

"He was awake when I arrived," Mr. Thatcher said. "I take it he really is sleeping this time, though. Which leads me to believe he has judged me and found that I am not such an unsavory character."

"That remains to be seen," Marsali said.

Mr. Thatcher rose from the deck and held his hand out to her. She took it and allowed him to pull her up. "*Tsk, tsk.* Behaving as a gentleman again. Well, I suppose that if Mr. Murphy has given his approval, then so must I."

"I am glad of it—even if it means I must use manners and act civilized when I am around you." Mr. Thatcher still held her hand, and they stood quite close, facing one another.

Marsali's heart had begun to race again. *It is this nearness to him.* She'd felt it the day she thanked him and he had first touched her, and again for a brief moment during their dancing. And then again tonight. *It is his closeness and his touch.* How peculiar it made her feel. *How good.* She was loath for him to let go, though she knew he must. "Good night, Mr. Thatcher."

"Good night, Miss Abbott. I bid you pleasant dreams." He released her hand, and his own fell away. Marsali resisted the urge to press hers to her cheek. But she took his wish to heart and guessed that tonight her dreams would be pleasant because they would be of him.

CHAPTER 14

"Marsali, wake up. *Please.*"

Marsali opened one eye to find her cabin dark save for a sliver of moonlight shining through her window.

"Marsali." The whispered plea came once more, urging her out of bed and to her door. She opened it to find Lydia standing in the common room, clad as Marsali was, in only her night shift.

"Mama is ever so ill. You must come." Lydia reached out and grasped Marsali's hand, pulling her from her room and out into the hall. Together they stumbled through the darkness to the other end of the saloon and Lydia's and Lady Cosgrove's connected rooms. Lydia opened the door, and Marsali stepped inside, her nose wrinkling at once as the stench of sickness overcame her.

"Has she a fever?" Marsali asked, covering her nose and steeling herself for what she knew would have to be done to care for Lady Cosgrove. *I spent four years cleaning chamber pots. I can clean up after Lady Cosgrove, too.*

"I don't know about a fever, but she's delirious. I'll light a candle." Lydia hurried across the room that was bathed in the striped moonlight coming through the slats of the louvered window. "Mama's been ill since the day we boarded. She doesn't do well on boats—it's the reason she chose the *Amanda May*. Fewer days at sea." Lydia succeeded in lighting the wick, and a small flame burst to life, illuminating the messy cabin, clothes strewn about the floor and bedsheets in disarray. "Mama can't even bear crossing the channel from the Continent without becoming ill. But today she took a turn for the worse, thrashing about in her bed and crying out. I've never seen her like this—Oh!" Lydia doubled over, clutching her stomach.

Marsali rushed to her side. "You're ill as well—how long?"

"Just this evening." Lydia continued to hold her stomach as Marsali helped her over to her adjoining cabin and into bed, all the while feeling guilty that she'd not checked on her when Lydia's absence had been more than obvious today. Instead, Marsali had spent much of the day alone, escaping into another of Mr. Thatcher's borrowed books. The stories promised a few hours of freedom from worry over her future. And that hadn't seemed so selfish or wrong—*until now*.

"I am sorry I did not come to see how you were getting on," Marsali said. Lydia had become a good friend during the first few days of their voyage, and Marsali knew she ought to have felt concern about her absence today.

"It's all right. I wouldn't have asked you to come now, except Mama is doing so poorly. I was caring for her well enough until this evening, when I started feeling a bit queasy."

"The sea was rougher today," Marsali concurred. Her own stomach had felt a bit unsettled at times.

"It was. So I drank that nasty tonic Mama bought from the peddler at the dock, and I've felt worse and worse."

"What tonic?" Marsali tucked the blanket over Lydia and brushed the hair back from her face. Her forehead felt clammy.

"It was supposed to keep us from becoming seasick." Lydia managed a wry smile, reassuring Marsali somewhat that she wasn't too ill—yet.

"Here is your bucket should you feel you're going to be ill." Marsali placed the pail next to the bed. "I'm going to check on your mother."

"Thank you." Lydia's eyes closed, and she moaned softly.

Marsali took up the candle and hurried through the connecting door. Lady Cosgrove lay upon her bed, unnaturally still and silent. Marsali stepped closer, her heart pounding.

Please don't let her be dead. Lydia wasn't strong enough for that. She needed her mother. *As did I.* Marsali held the candle up over Lady Cosgrove and gave a start as her face came into view. Her appearance was frightening—her skin appeared shriveled, her eye sockets collapsed, her complexion grey. She looked nothing like the woman Marsali had seen at breakfast four days ago.

"Lady Cosgrove?" Marsali summoned her courage and stepped closer to the bed, though what she really wished to do was flee. When Lady Cosgrove did not respond, Marsali bent closer and held a hand over the woman's mouth, letting out her own breath of relief when she felt Lady Cosgrove's weak one.

Not dead. Not yet. Nor will she be. Lady Cosgrove had not been ill until a few days ago when their voyage began, so she could not be *that* ill yet. Could she? Marsali set the candle on the washstand and rolled up the sleeves of her nightgown, prepared to go to work. Though two years had passed, her mother's illness and death were still fresh in her mind. *I'll not let Lydia suffer as I have.*

Marsali retrieved a cloth from the side of the basin and

dipped it into the tepid water. She held it over the bowl and wrung it out, nearly knocking over a before-unnoticed narrow, brown bottle at the back of the stand.

She picked it up and studied it, wishing it had a label. This might be the only medicine she had to work with. *But what is it?* Marsali put the washcloth down, then removed the stopper, leaned forward, and sniffed.

The faint smell of garlic wafted from the open bottle. Marsali jerked her head back, and the bottle slipped from her hand, shattering as it hit the wood floor. Shards of glass flew about the room, but Marsali paid them no notice.

Impossible. I only imagined . . .

Leaning over the bed, she pressed her hands into the mattress and her face close to Lady Cosgrove's. The garlic smell was stronger here, present with each shuddering breath she took.

No! Marsali tried to stand but nearly fell, bumping the table and causing the washbasin to tip precariously. Still holding the stopper in her other hand, she rushed from the room to Lydia's bedside.

"Is this the tonic you drank?" Marsali thrust the cork into Lydia's line of vision. "That bottle on your mother's washstand—did you drink from it?"

Lydia's head moved up and down against the pillow. "We were cheated. It doesn't work. Even when you take twice the dosage."

"*Twice?*" Marsali tried to keep the panic from her voice. "How much did you drink?"

Instead of answering, Lydia hung her head over the side of the bed and vomited.

"It hurts," she moaned. "So very badly." The blanket fell back as she drew her knees up to her chest. "Help me."

Marsali held Lydia's hair aside and tried not to panic.

It cannot have been for long. They were not ill just a few days ago. Lydia was not ill yesterday. Marsali stood abruptly, knowing she needed help. The captain had not mentioned a ship's doctor, but surely there had to be one. And surely he would know what to do to assist Lydia and her mother. "I'll return as quickly as I can. I'm going to get help."

Lydia leaned over the side of the bed, retching into the pail once more.

"That's good," Marsali told her. "Get it all out." *Every last drop.* Except she knew better. If what she suspected was right, assisting Lydia and her mother would not be so simple.

Loud pounding upon his door wrenched Christopher from a deep sleep. The room was dark, but he was on his feet at once, crouched and ready to do battle with whomever it was—debt collectors after his father or an undesirable suitor after his sisters.

"Mr. Thatcher." The voice on the other side of the door sounded familiar, and when it came again a second time, Christopher's surroundings and circumstances rushed back as he came fully awake. He stumbled through the darkness and pulled open the door.

Miss Abbott stood in the hall, wearing a nightgown and holding a candle in one trembling, bleeding hand.

"Lady Cosgrove and Lydia are ill," she blurted. "Find the ship's doctor and bring him to their rooms." She whirled away and took one step before he caught her arm.

"You're hurt." He stared at her injured hand and noticed her start as she did the same. He released her arm and took the candle from her, setting it on the table behind them. Gently he took her hand, turning it over so her palm faced up. She opened her fingers, and he saw a jagged line of blood running across her palm.

"The bottle," she murmured, then opened her other hand, revealing a cork stopper.

"Was the bottle this went with broken?" Christopher used the sleeve of his nightshirt to carefully wipe her palm.

Miss Abbott shook her head. "I dropped it. The glass

went everywhere." She tugged away from his grasp and retrieved the candle, holding it in front of her with care.

He followed her gaze downward to her bare ankles and feet peeking out beneath the hem of her nightgown. "Your feet are cut as well."

Her hand trembled, and the candle tilted precariously. "Bring a broom, too," she said, turning from him. "Only hurry. Lady Cosgrove and Lydia are *gravely* ill." Heedless of her injuries, she ran the length of the room to their cabin. Christopher did not follow but strode to the captain's quarters and pounded upon his door.

When it opened, he faced a bleary-eyed captain. "Lady and Miss Cosgrove are both very ill. Is there a ship's doctor?"

"Tenney, the cook, does our doctoring." The captain rubbed at his eyes. "But there isn't anything to be done for seasickness, aside from reaching land, that is. And even we're not that fast. Only been at sea four days," he muttered. "Can't expect—"

"Miss Abbott seems to think their illness quite serious," Christopher interrupted. "But I am sorry to have disturbed you. I simply guessed that your two wealthiest, more prominent passengers being ill might be of concern."

"It is. It is." The captain ran a hand through his thinning hair, already standing on end. "I'll come with you to get Tenney. He'll not take well to be awoken in the dead of night either. Just a moment." Captain Gower withdrew into his cabin and shut the door. Christopher paced in front of it, glancing repeatedly down the length of the saloon toward the faint light coming from the doorway at the far end.

Are they only seasick? If so, Miss Abbott seemed to be overreacting. And she didn't seem the type prone to overreacting about anything. She was perhaps the most levelheaded female he'd ever become acquainted with. She'd dealt with whatever circumstances had prevented her from arriving at the ship on time, and she'd endured the captain's rebuke, Lady Cosgrove's censure, and the criticism of the medical inspector with checked emotions. Even when receiving news about the perilous circumstances awaiting her, she had remained calm and had not been given to hysterics or anything resembling such, as many other women would have been.

But tonight, something has shaken her. Miss Abbott had not even realized she was hurt until he'd pointed it out. *And the way she was trembling . . .*

Captain Gower's door opened once more, and he emerged from his cabin. Together they went to the kitchen and approached the cook, who was snoring deeply in his hammock.

"Get up, Tenney. We've need of your doctoring."

Tenney grunted and turned his face aside.

The captain gave his hammock a hard push. "Up, you lout. That was an order. Come tend to the passengers, or I'll have you keelhauled."

One of Tenney's eyes opened slowly. "You'd sooner cut your arm off and feed it to sharks than punish one of us like that. What gives, Captain?"

"Lady Cosgrove and her daughter are ill. Miss Abbott and Mr. Thatcher seem to think it's serious."

Christopher nodded his agreement, trusting Miss Abbott's judgment.

"Be a good medical officer and have a look at our patients, will you?" the captain cajoled.

Tenney sat up and swung his legs over the side of hammock. "All ye had to do was ask." He yawned as he jumped down. "That lot's been trouble since they set foot on this ship. If seasickness has rendered them unable to speak or leave their beds, I can only think it a blessing for the rest of us."

"You'll not think it good when our highest-paying passengers tell their friends what a miserable voyage they had and we're both without a ship and employment." Captain Gower led the way from the kitchen to the saloon.

"Like them or not, we've got to see that they are as comfortable as possible."

"Aye, Cap'n." Tenney stopped long enough to locate a beat-up black leather bag that looked like it might once have belonged to a physician—decades ago. Christopher grabbed a broom and followed them out of the kitchen and down to Lady Cosgrove's cabin, though he supposed there wasn't much he could do for the ladies and might have gone back to bed.

But if the Captain and Mr. Tenney were to be busy attending Lady Cosgrove and her daughter, who would see to Miss Abbott's injuries? Christopher's concern was for her.

The smell hit him before they reached the room, and Christopher wondered that he'd not noticed it earlier today. Tenney swore under his breath, and the captain added similar sentiments. Christopher held his shirtsleeve to his nose as he entered the room behind them.

Miss Abbott sat at Miss Cosgrove's side, whispering soothing words and holding Miss Cosgrove's hair while the young woman leaned over the side of the bed attempting to empty even more contents from her stomach into an already filled bucket.

"Seasickness. Nothing to be done for them." Tenney took a step back, his heel pressing onto Christopher's toe.

"It's not just seasickness." Miss Abbott stood and faced them. "I've reason to believe it's worse. There was a bottle—a tonic they'd been taking."

"Go on," the captain said. Christopher couldn't be certain, but he thought he saw the briefest look of alarm flit across the captain's usually composed features.

Miss Abbott held out the cork. "Smell it."

Tenney took it and passed it beneath his nose before handing it to the captain. "Garlic. So what? Lots of folks think that's a cure for many ailments."

"I can't smell it," the captain said. "It's a wonder either of you can with the stench in here." His frown grew severe as his gaze traveled the room. Christopher could almost imagine the thoughts going through the captain's mind about any part of his beloved ship being treated thusly.

"It's not strong enough to be pure garlic," Miss Abbott said. "But *arsenic,* when it has been heated—as when it is mixed into a liquid—gives off a similar aroma." She took the stopper from the captain. "This was in a bottle in Lady Cosgrove's room. Lydia said a peddler at the wharf sold it to them and promised it would cure seasickness. I think it has done the opposite and made them ill—to the point that—" she lowered her voice—"Lady Cosgrove may be near death."

"Where at the wharf, exactly?" Captain Gower asked. Christopher was certain he wasn't mistaking the alarm on the captain's face.

"Near the largest shops. A man outside told us we would need it on your ship." Miss Cosgrove's voice was hoarse. Captain Gower stepped farther into the room and came near her bedside.

"Which shops? Do you remember their names? When did you purchase it?"

"Six—" Miss Cosgrove attempted to hold up the right number of fingers—"days ago. Just before we boarded. The peddler said you'd encouraged him to sell the tonic. Said to tell you Littleton was the best, and the rest—"

"Are not long for this world." Captain Gower swore. "Littleton. I might have known."

"Who is Littleton?" Christopher asked.

"Our competition. He runs the Liverpool office of the Black Ball shipping line." Captain Gower ran a hand through his hair once more, so that it stood up even straighter. His eyes were no longer bleary with sleep but wide and alarmed. "He threatened to do something to ruin our chances of success, but I didn't think he'd go so far as to poison passengers."

"Don't be so certain about all that yet, Cap'n. It could be the ladies just don't take to the sea. Or it could be someone else has harmed them." Tenney marched over to Miss Abbott. "Where is this bottle now, and how would you be knowing so much about arsenic?"

"She dropped it and it broke," Christopher said, not liking Tenney's accusatory tone. "Miss Abbott needs tending to as well. Both her hand and her feet are cut."

Captain Gower and Mr. Tenney appeared to take note of this as Miss Cosgrove began another round of retching and Miss Abbott returned to her side to assist her.

"It hurts so. Make it stop." Miss Cosgrove began thrashing about in her bed, one bare leg kicking the covers aside and her arms flung wide as her head whipped back and forth on the pillow.

"This *reaction* is not something caused by an aversion to the sea," Miss Abbott insisted as she leaned over the bed, trying to control and comfort Miss Cosgrove.

Christopher pushed past the other men and went to her side. He covered Miss Cosgrove and held the blanket down.

Miss Abbott turned back to the captain and Mr. Tenney, her eyes pleading. "You must help them. Please."

"You've not answered my question." Tenney stood with arms crossed, his battered bag dangling from one hand. "Why might you be familiar with arsenic? And if that is what they've taken, who's to say it wasn't you who gave it to them?"

"That's enough." Captain Gower's voice was sharp.

Christopher noticed Miss Abbott's hands trembling again.

"I am familiar with arsenic and its effects—" she drew in a shaky breath as she looked up at them—"because my mother died from taking it."

CHAPTER 15

"I think all of the glass is out now." Mr. Thatcher brushed his fingers over Marsali's upturned palm as it rested on the table.

"Thank you," she murmured, feeling strangely calm and almost mesmerized by his gentle touch.

"Don't thank me yet," he warned, reaching for a bottle and a rag, also on the table. "This part is going to hurt."

Marsali watched as he poured alcohol onto the cloth.

"My sister's husband studied medicine—and used this treatment on me when I had an accident with an ax a few months back. It hurt like the devil, but as Samuel said, 'A bit of fire up front, and you won't have any later on.' Ready?"

She nodded. "Go ahead."

Still he hesitated. "I'm sorry."

"Don't be. Just please hurry." She glanced over her shoulder. "I shouldn't be gone long. Lydia may wake and need me."

"You've been tending her for over three hours—three of the longest hours of my life, and I wasn't doing much good at all."

"Nonsense," Marsali said. "You swept and cleaned the room and helped Miss Cosgrove through the worst of her convulsions." *And kept me company through it all.* Marsali hadn't expected him to stay with her but had somehow known that he would. Even Mr. Tenney had returned to bed after an hour or so, declaring that there was nothing more to be done but to wait it out.

"Ready?" Mr. Thatcher asked once more.

"Yes."

He pressed the cloth to her hand, and Marsali sucked in a breath at the sting that followed. "I think the glass felt better."

He gave her a lopsided grin. "I warned you."

She nodded and looked away lest he catch her eyes watering.

"Following such torturous treatment, *this* doctor's orders are for you to get some rest and let Murphy care for Miss Cosgrove." Mr. Thatcher used his free hand to reach for some strips of cloth. "Between my keeping you up late to look at the stars and then Miss Cosgrove summoning you, you can't have had more than an hour or two of sleep."

"But think of poor Mr. Murphy." Marsali sighed. "I cannot ask him to stay with the ladies a moment longer than necessary. I do not imagine he is particularly enjoying that duty."

"He might be." Mr. Thatcher's mouth quirked. "Who's to say he's not using the time to clean out his ears or scrub between his toes? He seemed rather fastidious about his grooming the other night while keeping an eye on you. And didn't you say he'd been cleaning his teeth during last night's watch?"

"So he was." In spite of her weariness, the pain in her hand, and the gravity of the situation, she felt herself returning Mr. Thatcher's smile. Each time she was with him he had a way of making her feel better, no matter what her difficulty. "But I *should* hurry. Aside from Mr. Murphy and me, there's no one else *to* tend Lydia and her mother. And Mr. Murphy has other duties. Mr. Tenney has to be in the kitchen—the crew must eat if they are to keep this ship going—and besides, there are no other women. In their present states, Lady Cosgrove and Lydia should not be seen by anyone but me."

"I doubt very much that it matters—in their present state," Mr. Thatcher said. "And you've forgotten one other person who is and will continue to be able to help—me."

Their eyes met, and she read the sincerity of his offer.

"I shall help you," he said. "I'll watch over them while you rest. Now that we've the soiled bedding out of their cabin, and the buckets and chamber pots emptied, it isn't so bad inside."

"Lydia shall be thoroughly mortified when she discovers you've seen her in such a poor condition."

"Why should she care?" Mr. Thatcher asked, his brows furrowed.

Marsali found the look endearing. "Because she is enamored of you, that's why. You cannot say that you haven't noticed."

"But I haven't," he said. "All her talk is of her fiancé— Mr. Vancer this, Mr. Vancer that. I thought it was meant to keep me in my humble place."

"And a fine place that is," Marsali said, smiling at him and half sorrowful as he removed the stinging cloth and ceased touching her. "You are not so high as to be above helping a sick lady and her daughter—or bandaging the cut of a clumsy girl."

"You're not clumsy." He lifted her hand and began wrapping fabric around it. "I daresay there was a good reason you dropped that bottle."

Marsali cast her eyes down and saw that her free hand still shook slightly.

"Is it prying if I ask about your mother?" Mr. Thatcher asked.

"No more prying than I was when I inquired about your sisters." But Marsali did not elaborate further. How did one go about explaining something like this—like the loss of her mother and the horrid and mysterious circumstances surrounding her death?

Yet Marsali found she wanted to tell him. She wanted him to understand.

"They said my mother killed herself," she began. "By taking arsenic." She looked up at Mr. Thatcher to gauge his reaction.

"But she didn't." He held her gaze. "She loved you and would never have done something like that. She would not have left you alone."

Marsali's breath caught, and she felt a bit of weight lift from her chest. "Yes." How could he have known what to say, an admission she had longed to hear for over two years—from anyone? She'd tried explaining that very thing to at least a dozen different people during that time, but none of them had ever listened to or believed her.

And here I have not explained a word of it to Mr. Thatcher, and yet, he knows. It felt like the sweetest balm on a wound that had festered a long time.

"It wasn't suicide." Tears stung her eyes. Marsali told herself it was just because she was tired. She'd been up most of the night, after all. But the truth was, she felt so relieved that someone believed her—finally. She wanted to hug him. Instead, she fought to quell her emotions and tell him the whole of it, a task that seemed suddenly easier.

"After my father died, Mother and I had to go live with his sister, my aunt Ada. She didn't care for us one bit and made that quite clear at the beginning. We'd only been there a few months when Mother became ill. My aunt said I was too young to look after Mother, and I wasn't allowed in to see her much. Aunt Ada cared for her, while everyone whispered about what a charitable woman she was and what a burden Mother and I were upon her.

"I was kept away from Mother—until the end, when she was too ill and my aunt declared there was nothing more to be done. Mother's body had ceased to function properly, and my aunt was too disgusted to be near her."

"Was she as you discovered Lady Cosgrove to be last night?" Mr. Thatcher asked.

"Just as she was." Marsali nodded. "The bottle of medicine on Mother's dresser was empty, so I took it to town, to the apothecary, to see if he might refill it for me, just this once. I hadn't any money to pay for it, but I was desperate for anything to help Mother. My aunt had been giving her small doses of that medicine for months, and I believed—wrongly—that it was the only thing keeping Mother alive."

"When, really, it was killing her." Mr. Thatcher had finished bandaging Marsali's hand but still held it in his own, his fingers folded over hers in a gesture of comfort.

"Yes." It was as if she had told him this story already. If only someone else, someone at her aunt's house or in Manchester, had believed her like this.

"The apothecary took the bottle from me and smelled it, much as I did tonight when I found the one on Lady Cosgrove's washstand. His face turned ashen, and he leaned over the counter and stared down at me, demanding to know where I'd found the bottle. I told him it was my mother's medicine, that she'd been taking it for months.

"'It's arsenic, you fool girl,' he said. 'The only way it will cure her is to take her from this life.'" Marsali closed her eyes, remembering her horror at hearing those words. "He left his shop with me, turned the sign, and closed it, marching me right back to my aunt's house and Mother—dead.

"Aunt Ada denied ever having given anything to Mother, and in front of the apothecary she accused *me* of poisoning her—my own mother. He believed my aunt, and he wanted to take me away and have me locked up, or worse.

But my aunt persuaded him to let me stay on with her. Said she'd see to my punishment most thoroughly."

"And she did," Mr. Thatcher finished in a quiet voice.

"Yes." Marsali took a deep breath, willing away the memories to the farthest recesses of her mind. "What happened after that doesn't bear talking about. All the hatred and anger I felt—all the abuse I suffered—it's over now. You are the first person to believe me. No one else ever did, and my aunt and uncle were too well respected in Manchester for me to have hope of any sort of justice. Leaving was the only thing I could do."

Mr. Thatcher's free hand rubbed his brow as if it pained him. "And now you are headed to an equally perilous situation."

"Perhaps." *Mr. Thomas cannot be as bad. He will not be.* She must keep telling herself this or fall victim to despair. "But you see why I don't fear Mr. Thomas as much as I might. I have already lived a life in constant danger and survived. I've no doubt I can do the same in America."

"I do not doubt your capabilities either," Mr. Thatcher said, his voice troubled. "But simply because you are able to endure something does not mean you must."

Marsali waved her free hand dismissively. "With no other option available to me, I *shall* have to. But please, I do not wish to speak of it anymore. Worrying about Mr. Thomas will only deprive me of these remaining few weeks of freedom, and I should like to enjoy them to the fullest. Their memory will have to last me for quite some time."

"For years to come," Mr. Thatcher muttered beneath his breath. Marsali felt strangely comforted that he should feel indignant on her behalf.

Not that it will change my circumstances in the least. But she supposed that when she had a difficult day or had to endure an injustice from Mr. Thomas, she would have this memory to look back on and draw strength from. She would be able to remember that once someone had cared what became of her and how she was treated.

Mr. Thatcher released her hand and set about picking up the items he had used to tend her cuts. "Was it the smell that so upset you tonight? The shock of it?"

"I think so," Marsali said. "It certainly brought back that day, the realization of what had happened to Mother—that she probably hadn't been ill at all but had been slowly poisoned by my aunt. If I had only known, I could have saved Mother, and she might still be here with me." She closed her eyes briefly, imagining her mother as she had been before they'd come to England—smiling and full of life.

"When I saw Lady Cosgrove looking so like Mother did at the end, and when I realized that Lydia had taken the same *tonic*—only a larger dosage at once—I became frightened for them. As I am still." Reluctantly Marsali used her good hand to push up from the table. "I must stay with Lydia, at least. She needs a friend right now."

"She has a true one in you," Mr. Thatcher said. "I'll be in to check on you later this morning. I think I'll sleep a bit now so that I may relieve you tonight."

"Thank you," Marsali said. "You continue to prove yourself a gentleman at every turn."

Mr. Thatcher pretended to pout. "Which was entirely *not* my intention for this voyage and beyond. No fancy clothes and stuffy ballrooms for me, thank you. Instead I should like a horse and a plow and a bit of my own land. I should like to bring that land to life and to make for myself a life upon it."

"An admirable dream," Marsali said as she stood. "I must say I envy you such. Perhaps someday I will be free to plan a life like that as well."

His half smile reappeared. "Indeed? I should like to see you behind a horse and plow. It would have to be a pony for certain, with your small stature, and I should think the ground would have to already be broken in."

"Go get some sleep," Marsali called over her shoulder, ignoring his teasing and the desire she had to stay in the common room, conversing with him. Mr. Thatcher was easy to talk with—both in jest and regarding serious matters. He was unlike any man she had ever become acquainted with . . . not that she'd been truly acquainted with any while living at her aunt's home. But she had observed many gentlemen. She had learned that those who dressed finely often did not treat others that way, especially those less fortunate than they and those under their care. She suppressed a shudder and cursed other memories to be gone from her head.

CHAPTER 16

"Two days after the initial middle-of-the-night incident, Miss Abbott still had not appeared at the table for a meal, and Christopher found himself missing her presence. Even if it had meant the annoying Miss Cosgrove accompanying her and dominating the conversation, he would have preferred to have their company. The captain's speeches were interesting enough—centered around how far they'd traveled and at what speed, the amount of coal it had required, and the general state of affairs in the engine room below—but Christopher missed conversing with Miss Abbott.

He preferred their lighthearted conversations, their jesting, and even their short, serious discussions of "things best left in the past," as she put it.

Aside from missing her, he continued to be concerned for her welfare. She was doing an admirable job of caring for Lady Cosgrove and her daughter. *But who is caring for Miss Abbott?* Christopher wondered, and he worried that she might fall ill herself. Especially if what Mr. Tenney had told him was true. He believed the cause of Lady and Miss Cosgrove's illness might well be foul water.

"Giving someone a bottle of foul water is as good as poisoning him," he'd said. "Saw it myself in India when the sewage leaked into the river they drank from. People moaning and thrashing about, losing their minds and innards, just like the ladies. Bad water kills. And it spreads quickly to others—whether they've had the same drink or not."

Christopher still felt inclined to trust Miss Abbott's opinion about what ailed the Cosgroves, and Captain Gower had seemed to think it plausible as well, angry as he had made one Mr. Littleton of the Black Ball Line.

Regardless of the cause, it stood to reason that Miss Abbott might fall ill herself if she became overly exhausted and did not allow herself time to eat or sleep. And as far as Christopher could ascertain, she was doing neither. She kept a round-the-clock vigil at Miss Cosgrove's bedside and refused much help from anyone. She ate very little, only accepting a small portion of the food he brought her after each meal.

Tonight I will insist that she eat more—and that she sleep. Christopher ladled a bowl of stew and took two biscuits from the basket on the table to go with it.

"Off to relieve Miss Abbott?" Captain Gower asked, lowering his spectacles and giving Christopher an appraising look.

"If she will allow me to," Christopher said, knowing, in truth, that if Miss Abbott declined his offering or shooed him from the room, there was little he could do. Insist he might, but he could not argue with her or bully her to acquiesce when she stood up to him. She might be petite, but her stubbornness was solid.

"Admirable of you," the captain said.

"*She* is admirable." Carrying the bowl of stew carefully, Christopher made his way down the corridor. He felt the captain's eyes following him as he walked, but he did not turn around. *Let him think what he will.* Someone had to look out for Miss Abbott. For one who had seemed so concerned with her late arrival and the possibility that Mr. Thomas would not get his servant, the captain appeared to give little thought to her health now.

Christopher crossed over to the other side of the saloon, to Miss Cosgrove's door. It was partially open, but he knocked anyway before proceeding to enter.

The cabin was dark, and he stood in the doorway for a moment, waiting for his eyes to adjust. When they did, what he saw made his heart lurch. Setting the bowl and biscuits on top of a trunk near the door, he crossed to the bed and Miss Abbott, draped across the foot of it.

"Miss Abbott, are you all right?" He touched her shoulder, but she did not stir. Christopher knelt beside her and felt relief as he heard her soft intake of breath. *Just fallen asleep—little wonder with the nights she's stayed awake, watching over her patients.* Lady Cosgrove seemed to have turned a corner and moved past the critical point. It was her daughter who had Miss Abbott most concerned now, for after Miss Cosgrove's initial night of sickness and fits, she had largely failed to respond.

But Miss Abbott falling ill as well will not help.

Christopher stood once more, then bent over and carefully picked her up, cradling her in his arms. She weighed far less than it seemed she ought to, and she promptly turned her head to his chest, letting out an almost delicate snore.

Christopher grinned and tucked away the moment to tease her about later. He glanced down at Miss Abbott's slightly parted lips, and a rush of desire caught him off guard. *What would it be like to kiss her?*

He banished the thought and looked elsewhere, to the long lashes that curved over her closed eyes—*the prettiest I've ever seen*—to the wispy curls always escaping her bun.

Reaching his hand around, he touched one. *So soft.* He thought of the cruel aunt who had shorn Miss Abbott's hair and felt a surge of protectiveness—and something more. He had to make certain Miss Abbott never suffered such indignities again. He needed to know she would be both safe and cared for.

Christopher tightened his grip, holding her closer. *Take her to her room.* His feet refused to move, and he could not tear his eyes from her. Every rise and fall of her chest equally reassured and frightened him. *She is well enough now. Will she continue to be? Why do I care so much?*

He was more than losing the battle to remain unattached, unconcerned. *Free.* Had the constant worry over his sisters not left him physically and emotionally depleted? And here he had become entrapped in it once again.

But this time it felt different.

Forcing his feet to move, Christopher left the room and carried her easily from Miss Cosgrove's cabin to her own at the opposite end of the saloon.

Captain Gower looked up from the documents he was reading and, seeing Christopher's need, jumped up to open Miss Abbott's door for him.

"She'd fallen asleep by the side of Miss Cosgrove's bed," Christopher explained.

"She deserves a good rest, I'd say," Captain Gower said with what Christopher suspected was a hint of affection in his tone.

"I'll sit outside Miss Cosgrove's door tonight," Christopher offered, "if you're worried about leaving her alone." He entered Miss Abbott's cabin—smaller than Miss Cosgrove's and sparse in belongings. The captain hurried ahead to pull back the bedcovers, and Christopher laid Miss Abbott down, then reached for the quilt to cover her, though she was fully clothed.

The blanket caught on her shoe, and Christopher cast

an uncertain glance at the captain, grateful he was in the room.

"No good sleeping with shoes on." Captain Gower inclined his head toward Miss Abbott's feet. "Best take them off for her."

Christopher stared at him, uncertain he'd heard correctly and wary of the amused expression on the captain's face.

"Go on." Captain Gower folded his arms and fixed Christopher with a pointed look.

If my sisters could see me now. Gritting his teeth, he lifted Miss Abbott's right heel and tried to wriggle the slipper off. *Grace would laugh.* The slipper would not budge but appeared almost molded to Miss Abbott's foot, so Christopher set about untying the ribbon. *And Helen would be appalled at such brazenness.* Like the slipper it was attached to, the ribbon was a much-faded blue, the edges frayed, the top stained. Once untied, the shoe came off easily. Christopher set it aside on the floor but not before noting what poor condition it was in, with holes near both the toe and the heel.

Until now he'd not paid any attention to Miss Abbott's footwear, but he now recalled her explanation for her slow, pained walk that first late evening of her arrival. No doubt these were the slippers that had trod the cobbled streets for over two hours.

Quickly he untied the second slipper and removed it, grateful the moment his hands were no longer on Miss Abbott's ankle. He stood and stepped back, eager to exit the overly warm room.

"Don't you think you ought to put the quilt over her?" the captain asked. "The nights can get cool."

Christopher knew the captain to be right, but at the moment he couldn't imagine this stifling room becoming chilled. He didn't dare touch his forehead, lest the captain suspect the difficulty he was experiencing, but he felt beads of sweat forming there all the same.

Stepping forward once more, Christopher took the top of the quilt and pulled it up to Miss Abbott's shoulders. Then, instead of leaving as he ought to have done, he watched her for a brief moment, his yearning frightening in its intensity. He appreciated her beauty, yes. And he admired her strength of character, but seeing her asleep like this stirred something deep within him, a desire so powerful it felt almost like a need. He wanted suddenly, very much, to touch her, to smooth the hair back from her face, perhaps even to place his lips on hers.

I've gone mad.

He hurriedly straightened and stepped back, then fled the room, feeling vast relief—and the tiniest regret—when Captain Gower also exited and closed the door behind him.

"No need to watch over Lady Cosgrove and her daughter tonight," the captain said congenially. "I'll get Tenney to check in on them, and I'll ask Murphy to make his bed outside their door. He can alert me if he hears anything unusual."

"Thank you, sir," Christopher said. "Good eve to you, then." He nodded, then strode away, around the tables and toward his own cabin.

Behind him the captain chuckled. "Cannot ask you to watch out for Miss Cosgrove when you've more than you can handle with Miss Abbott."

"Captain?" Christopher pivoted to face him, but Captain Gower had just exited the saloon through the doorway to the kitchen.

Christopher entered his cabin and closed the door behind him, then crossed to the bed and sat alone in the darkness.

Helping a woman, admiring her, enjoying her company, and even befriending her were all acceptable actions for a man in his position—or at least he had managed to convince himself they were. But feeling as he had a minute ago was entirely different. Entirely *un*acceptable.

Yet he could not seem to rid his mind of Miss Abbott, of how it had felt to hold her in his arms and the ache he had experienced in leaving her. Christopher leaned forward, head in his hands. *At this rate, I'll be as besotted as my brothers-in-law by the time we reach New York.*

And that would never do. Grace and Helen had as much power over Nicholas and Samuel as if they were connected by a string. Christopher had witnessed the process firsthand—the not-so-covert glances exchanged between Helen and Samuel, the conversations that hinted at their attraction to one another, Helen's blushing and Samuel's clearing his throat as if he'd gotten something stuck in it. Almost overnight those seemingly harmless actions had turned to an obvious and shared affection that made an otherwise sensible man do rather nonsensical things, like carrying his wife out of doors in only her nightdress so he could show her the hundreds of roses he'd spent weeks planting for her.

Nicholas was no better. He followed Grace around like a lovesick puppy, running ahead of her to pull out her chair, offering her bites of his own meal from his fork, constantly staring at her, even in public, as if to reassure himself that she was well and his.

Such fanatical behavior is not for me. Christopher sat up and ran a hand through his hair, exasperated with himself for his wayward thoughts. Yet he knew he had no one but himself to blame. He was the one who had first reached out to Miss Abbott. He had joined her on deck and asked her to dance. He'd lent her books and invited her to walk with him. *I am my own worst enemy.*

Instead of doing a jig on deck when they'd danced, he should have been doing a jig that he was free of worrying over anyone other than himself. But he did not see how that was possible now, not when he knew Miss Abbott and, worse, knew of the trouble awaiting her.

He groaned. *I am a bigger fool than both Nicholas and Samuel combined.*

At least they had seen a future ahead of them. Marrying his sisters had made sense for each man, had led them down a path of happiness, albeit one where each had turned rather soft and acted somewhat ridiculous.

But there could be no ending like that for Christopher and Miss Abbott. He could not afford to entertain any thoughts about her as more than a friend—more than an acquaintance, really, as they would part ways in another two weeks' time. So he had best start acting like that acquaintance now.

Instead of imagining what it would feel like to kiss her. Christopher fell back on the bed, grabbed the pillow, and clamped it over his face.

As if that could somehow block out the thoughts running through his mind and the feelings pulsing through his heart.

CHAPTER  17

*M*arsali left her cabin with both the star chart and lantern in hand and walked the length of the saloon with deliberate noise, allowing the parchment to crinkle and stomping her feet in exaggerated steps. She opened the door and shut it soundly behind her, then waited a moment, hopeful that Mr. Thatcher might join her. When he did not, she held back a sigh of disappointment and resolutely took up her place on deck, determined to enjoy the night anyway. Mr. Murphy was nowhere to be seen, but First Officer Luke strode over and greeted her heartily, his mustache curving upward and twitching in a way that almost made it appear he had a small creature residing on his lip.

"Captain Gower has told me of your affinity for the stars." He gazed heavenward as he spoke, hands clasped behind his back. "I, too, find them fascinating."

"Indeed." Marsali had learned through previous unfortunate experience that First Officer Luke took his position a bit too seriously. His rank had obviously gone to his head, enlarging it to the point that it was a wonder it did not tip precariously off his bony neck. "Are you a particular fan of Greek mythology as well?" she asked politely. *This must be how Mr. Thatcher feels whenever Lydia accosts him.*

Officer Luke appeared somewhat taken aback by her question. "If you mean all that nonsense about gods and demigods, the underworld and the like, then no. I have to say that I am not."

The stories of ancient Greece were not necessarily her favorite reading material either, but Marsali at least recognized that the constellations and the myths went hand in hand.

She sat and unrolled the chart, holding the lantern above it while she tried to determine which constellations she might be able to find now that she must deal with the waxing moon's interference. Aside from that first night of the new moon—the same that Lydia had become so ill— Marsali had not been out to stargaze again and had missed the best opportunities, when their view of the moon was slight.

Mr. Luke raised a straightened arm to the sky, his fist directed at the North Star. "Just checking our latitude," he said importantly as he tilted his head back and squinted in the direction of his extended arm.

He does not actually expect to impress me, does he? Any fool knew latitude could be gauged using the North Star as a guide. She certainly hoped the first officer did as well. "Isn't a sextant usually employed for that task?"

"Well, yes." He lowered his hands. "But it's late, and this will do."

"Let us hope so." If he wished to risk the captain's wrath if they went off course and were delayed, so be it. She was in no hurry to arrive in New York. Still, she glanced toward the wheel and felt relieved to see the helmsman stationed there.

"Besides, I am not officially on duty tonight."

"Oh?" Marsali cringed inwardly, guessing what was coming next.

He lowered his hand. "Would you care to accompany me on a moonlit stroll around the deck, Miss Abbott?"

I would not. The airs with which he spoke suggested it really wasn't a question at all so much as a generous offering of time to be spent with him, of which she would be a fool to refuse.

She glanced up and caught him preening that ridiculous mustache of his, curling one end around his finger, then patting it in place. She supposed she would have to walk with him. The ship was small enough that they encountered each other at least once a day and had to endure each other's company at dinner every other night. There was no point in making a situation awkward. *Better I am annoyed and he is oblivious.* The moon seemed too bright for stargazing anyway.

"Let me put this chart away." She rolled it up, then extinguished the lantern and stowed both safely beside a folded sail.

Mr. Luke did not offer a hand to help her up as Mr. Thatcher had but continued swirling the other side of his mustache. *So much for gentlemanly behavior.* She stood on her own, and only then did his elbow jut out as if awaiting her hand. Marsali pretended not to notice and instead folded her arms across her middle and focused her gaze upon the sky as they began to walk. "Are you familiar with the tales associated with the constellations, Mr. Luke?"

"A sailor has little use for stories, Miss Abbott. The stars are not something men gaze upon with fondness. They are a tool of navigation. Why, I could safely guide us to any point on this ocean using only the stars as my compass."

New York will do fine. "No doubt such skill is why Captain Gower hired you."

"And a wise choice it was." Mr. Luke's chest puffed out. "While he is busy playing with his steam engine and other inventions, I am steering this ship across the Atlantic and into port."

Marsali could think of no comment to this, so she made none but did not doubt Captain Gower would have had plenty to say had he heard such claims from his first officer.

They reached the stairs leading to the lower deck, and she glimpsed a familiar figure darting toward the saloon door.

"Mr. Thatcher," she called before stopping to consider what she was doing.

He paused, stiffened, and turned toward them.

"What is *he* doing about at this time of night?" Mr. Luke grumbled.

"Mr. Thatcher enjoys stargazing as well, don't you?" She looked directly at him as she hurried down the stairs, silently begging him to stay and save her from further enduring the company of the insufferable officer.

"I have in the past." Mr. Thatcher's voice was not quite curt, yet neither was it as friendly as she was accustomed to. Marsali supposed she had Mr. Luke's presence to blame for that.

"However," Mr. Thatcher continued, "tonight I find that the moon is too bright for any serious study of the constellations." His tone seemed almost accusatory as his gaze flitted between Marsali and Mr. Luke. "Good evening, Miss Abbott, Mr. Luke."

He nodded briefly, opened the door to the saloon, entered, and was gone, leaving Marsali feeling bewildered and strangely bereft as well.

Beside her, Mr. Luke prattled on as they walked the circumference of the ship, all the while her thoughts circling back to Mr. Thatcher and what she might have done to earn his displeasure.

CHAPTER 18

The sun momentarily disappeared behind a cloud overhead as Christopher closed the book he had just finished—another from the captain's library, this one a volume about the various inventions of the early nineteenth century. He'd enjoyed it immensely and wondered, when subsequent editions were printed, what additional machines and contraptions would be found between those pages.

Clasping his hands behind his head, he lay back on the deck and allowed his mind to wander, imagining a plow that might dig furrows without a horse pulling it or a wagon that might propel itself, much as Captain Gower's marvelous steamship this very moment.

The sea was calm today, almost still, yet the great wheel of the *Amanda May* was turning while steam poured from her stack as she made steady progress toward America.

"Eight knots this morning," Captain Gower had announced proudly at the noon meal. "We've made up the day we lost to those fools at Liverpool."

"Splendid," Lady Cosgrove said. She was well enough to join them for brief periods, though her daughter remained in her sickbed. "The sooner I am off this wretched ship, the better."

"I quite agree with you," Captain Gower replied, at which Christopher had happened to catch Miss Abbott's eye and exchange an amused glance with her, causing her to choke on her biscuit.

Fortunately, Lady Cosgrove—most often oblivious to others—didn't catch the good captain's barb.

And fortunately Miss Abbott's biscuit caused no serious harm.

Christopher's thoughts slid from inventions to Miss Abbott and the troubling idea of her being harmed by a biscuit or anything else. Her situation continued to weigh upon his mind, though he had managed, somewhat, to force other thoughts regarding Miss Abbott from it. Seeing her out strolling with Mr. Luke should have helped, but instead he had felt only annoyed. Christopher had been avoiding her as much as possible—difficult when on a ship together—and he ought to have felt relieved that she had found other companionship in his absence.

He wondered if she had been thinking at all about what awaited her, though he had not heard her mention it since their brief conversation the morning he had tended her cut. *Perhaps she has shared her troubles with Mr. Luke.* The idea bothered him. *Likely she wishes the ship to slow down.* Even caring for fussy Lady Cosgrove had to be better than what Miss Abbott would be facing once they reached America.

While he pondered her situation, the sun made its appearance again, already heading toward its spot on the western horizon, soon to mark the end of another day. *One day closer to New York.* The thought still excited him, but not as it had when he'd first boarded the ship—before he'd met Miss Abbott. The end of their voyage would not mark happiness for her, and he could no longer think of his own adventures without worrying over hers. He was doing his best to think of a way he might help her, a way he might protect her from Mr. Thomas and his cruel, if not deadly, practices.

It was disheartening, though not surprising, to learn that such cruelty existed in America, just as it did in England. Christopher had hoped for better in the new world, but it seemed the fledging country had not yet perfected the liberties and rights its constitution so boldly promised.

"Been doing a bit of reading, have you?" Captain Gower's shadow fell across Christopher, and he rose to his feet, the book still clutched in his hands.

The captain ran a hand over his chin. "I suppose I ought to set a chair or two out here for passengers when the weather is nice, as it is today."

"I was quite comfortable," Christopher assured him.

"Maybe . . ." The captain's look was far off. "I envision a time when traveling on a steamship won't be just for those immigrating. Maybe folks will take to the sea simply because they enjoy it or they want a holiday somewhere far off."

Christopher did not want to dash the captain's hopes, but he had a difficult time imagining such a scenario. Satisfactory though his accommodations were, there was little for a passenger to do on board a ship, and it had taken less than a week before his restlessness had set in. "Those passengers would need to have stronger constitutions than Lady Cosgrove."

"True enough," Captain Gower said. Seeming to come back to the present, he withdrew his pipe from his pocket and proceeded to fill it. "But what have you been reading today?"

"Quite a fascinating volume." Christopher turned the book so the captain might view the title. "I should like to see a demonstration of that machine in your quarters, the one that can make the likeness of a person." *If I had such a portrait of Grace and Helen, would it lessen how much I miss them, or would it make my longing to see them just that much worse?* "I was thinking that if I was able to get such an image made, I might send it to my sisters."

"Ah," Captain Gower said knowingly. "Thinking of home again, are you?"

"Not too much," Christopher assured him. "I think more about America and what awaits us there." Being around Miss Abbott had lessened his longing for Grace and Helen—until he had recognized the danger in that. *I will not be with her much longer, and I do not need another bitter parting, this one on America's shores.* But in spite of his efforts to lessen their interactions throughout the day, he was beginning to fear it was too late to avoid a difficult parting.

Samuel would say it was worth it. Christopher brushed the thought aside.

Captain Gower lit his pipe. "If you'd like, you can come with me when I show Joseph's invention to those wealthy American investors he is so hopeful about. It will be interesting to see what comes of it, though I still cannot believe that making images is the way of the future, not more so than steam engines, anyway."

"Time will tell," Christopher said noncommittally, feeling rather fascinated with both the heliograph and camera obscura. Steam travel was important, yes. But it was not an invention that might apply to all. Very few people traveled across the ocean or a continent, and for those who did not, a faster ship or a self-propelled wagon was of little use.

But a contraption that could preserve an image . . . that was something that could be important to all of humankind. What family would not benefit from preserving time, as it were, in a portrait that was not painted? *Or having the ability to look upon a loved one's face when far away?*

Secretly, Christopher thought that perhaps Mr. Niépce might be correct in his assumption that the heliograph was an invention of great importance.

"And have you been conjuring inventions of your own?" Captain Gower asked, his gaze direct.

"Not exactly." Christopher had considered—on several occasions since reading Miss Abbott's letter—of telling Captain Gower of her predicament. Each time, he had decided against it, but they were now halfway through their voyage, and Christopher had yet to come up with a solution to help her. Perhaps the captain, knowing Mr. Thomas as he did, might be able to offer a suggestion. "Rather, I have been wishing I might invent a way to help Miss Abbott with a particularly worrisome problem."

"With Lady Cosgrove?" The captain waved his hand dismissively. "It's not as much of a problem as you think. Miss Abbott knows her place. She was born to servitude. It's in her blood, whether she wishes it or not. Lady Cosgrove has sensed that and taken advantage of it, is all."

"I disagree," Christopher said. Miss Abbott's demeanor and upbringing did not seem at all like that of a servant. "Miss Abbott was born to wealthy parents. She was educated and led to expect far more from life than what it has given her."

"She has adapted well, then," the captain said. "And anyway, she has but another two weeks at most to put up with Lady Cosgrove." He glanced around furtively, as if to make sure the woman herself was not about. "And then we shall *all* be rid of her."

"And it is then that Miss Abbott's real trouble will begin," Christopher said. "Just before leaving England she received a letter from her sister in Virginia."

"And?" The captain blew out a puff of smoke.

"Perhaps we should walk," Christopher suggested, as much to avoid a face full of the captain's smoke as to avoid being overheard.

Captain Gower's brows rose as he appraised him. "This sounds serious."

Christopher nodded. "I believe it is." They walked to the edge of the ship and began to follow the rail around to the stern. "How well do you know Mr. Thomas?"

The captain shrugged. "How well does one know any man? I know Thomas for my purposes. He is wealthy, and he is often right in the business risks he assumes—two requirements I sought in my investors."

"But on a personal level?" Christopher asked. "Have you any knowledge of him or his family? Have you ever been to his home?"

The captain shook his head. "Our meetings have taken place elsewhere—at shipyards, mostly, as we discussed what materials were to be used and who was to manufacture the various parts of our ship."

Christopher had never heard Captain Gower refer to the *Amanda May* in terms of "our" before. She was named after his wife, and he often spoke of the ship as if he were married to her. But though he might be the one behind her wheel, it was Thomas who had paid for that wheel, Thomas who owned nearly the entire ship, from bow to stern.

The captain is in no position to help Miss Abbott, Christopher realized. But he also saw no harm in telling him what awaited her.

"The last three lady's maids employed in the Thomas household have all suffered untimely deaths—shortly before their terms of indenture were to be over."

"An odd coincidence, surely," Captain Gower said, puffing away on his pipe.

"So Miss Abbott's sister also believed, until she and her husband undertook an investigation and discovered that the deaths were not the only ones among servants at the Thomas household. In addition to this, Mr. Thomas is known for his cruelty and ill treatment of those in his employ."

Captain Gower made no immediate response to this but appeared thoughtful as they continued to walk the ship's perimeter.

A long minute passed before he spoke again. "I would like to say that this surprises me and that I am sure you must be mistaken."

"But you are not—and cannot?" Christopher prodded.

The captain shook his head. "There was an occasion when Thomas and I were to meet, and he had purchased a slave that same morning shortly before I arrived at the agreed-upon location. The slave was still with Thomas, chained to his wagon like an animal. He happened to fall asleep sitting beside the wheel while we had our meeting. When Thomas discovered this, he beat the man for it." Captain Gower shook his head as if to rid himself of the memory, or possibly the guilt he felt for having done nothing.

"Of course I could not say anything. Slavery is allowed in Virginia, and I was there to gain Mr. Thomas's favor, to procure the funds for this ship. And so I did my best to dismiss the memory—until now."

"He beat a male slave in front of you?" Christopher asked.

"Myself and several others," Gower said. "And if Thomas is able to treat a man as I saw him treat one that day, I shudder to think how he must handle his female slaves— and servants."

"I am even more worried for Miss Abbott's safety now." Christopher waited for the captain to ascend the short flight of stairs ahead of him.

The captain looked back. "You have grown fond of her," he observed.

"I have," Christopher admitted. *Too fond.* He still wasn't exactly certain how that fondness had developed in such a short period of time, but knew he had only himself to blame. *Because I was homesick and sought out her company for solace.* He stomped up the stairs behind the captain, his frustration showing in his heavy steps.

"Would it be possible for you to purchase her term of indenture?" the captain asked. "To buy out her contract from Mr. Thomas?"

"No, unfortunately." Christopher had considered that option at length. He would not be able to do so anytime soon given what was left of the limited funds from his small inheritance. The only options available to him were selling his grandfather's ring—and breaking a promise in the process—or writing to his sisters and securing a loan from one of his brothers-in-law. No doubt they would give it to him, but with the time it took a letter to travel across the Atlantic, to Yorkshire, then back again, it could easily be months before he could secure those funds. He was loath to make such a request but would do so for Miss Abbott, though it would not solve the immediate problem of her being at Mr. Thomas's mercy as soon as they reached New York.

"I would happily contribute all of my savings to her cause," Christopher said, "but the amount would still fall short. I've only two pounds to my name with which to begin in America, and as this passage was nearly four pounds, I would still owe half to Mr. Thomas."

"You would owe more than that," Captain Gower said. "Thomas values passage on the *Amanda May* at eight pounds. I offered the reduced fare hoping to entice passengers. But he will hold Miss Abbott to the contract she signed—for the full amount."

"That is quite a bit more than the other lines are charging to cross," Christopher said, his hopes dashed even more.

"Because this ship is far more sophisticated. In addition to a faster crossing, passengers enjoy individual cabins instead of crammed berths below deck in steerage. The meals are provided and the food far better. The coal must be purchased to run the engine, and—" he paused at the stern and stared out across the sea before them before thumping the book in Christopher's hand—"passengers even have a library at their disposal."

"In that light, the price is more than fair," Christopher agreed, taking a place at the rail beside the captain. "And I was most fortuitous in securing passage."

"That you were." Captain Gower bit down on his pipe with a thoughtful expression. "Please make certain to spread the tale of your delightful excursion on the *Amanda May* far and wide once we reach New York."

"I shall indeed," Christopher promised. "Though that will not solve the problem of Miss Abbott's indenture."

"Have you considered asking Lady Cosgrove if she might be willing to help?" the captain asked. "After all, she has benefitted greatly from Miss Abbott's service throughout this voyage. Perhaps she might even consider taking the girl on permanently. I understand that well-to-do women residing in New York employ lady's maids as well."

"A sound idea," Christopher said. Annoying though Lady Cosgrove was, she posed no real threat—that he could tell—to Miss Abbott. And Lady Cosgrove was certainly in Miss Abbott's debt. "Thank you for the suggestion."

"You realize that if she agrees," Captain Gower began walking once more, up the opposite side of the ship, "it will put me in a bit of pickle with Mr. Thomas."

"I do," Christopher said, following him and only just considering the repercussions and remembering how the captain had been willing to delay their departure for Miss Abbott. *All so he could keep his promise and deliver her to Mr. Thomas.* "Will it cause you great difficulty, do you think?"

Captain Gower shrugged. "You'll have noticed that Mr. Jones and the other men working in the engine room each have a turn on deck throughout the day?"

Christopher nodded.

"And you'll have seen how I regard each of the crew? That I show them respect and rarely have to stoop to threatening behavior to get them to do their jobs."

"You're a fair man, Captain."

"Because I've been on the other side of fair—of mistreatment. And I don't hold with it. Servant or no, there's no reason to abuse another human being. If what you've told me about Thomas is true—and based on what I've seen, I have to believe that it is—then I've a lot more difficulties ahead of me than the situation with Miss Abbott."

"I'm sorry," Christopher said. "I don't want to do something that brings you trouble."

Captain Gower extinguished his pipe, and Christopher could see that his good mood was gone.

"I have no intention of letting Thomas bully me—or anyone else, particularly the most delightful passenger I have ever transported. No." Captain Gower shook his head. "That day with the slave, I ignored what I should have stood up against, and I cannot continue to do that, not if I profess to be someone else. I was weak that day—and selfish. I wanted this ship so badly, and Thomas was one of my last hopes, you see."

"And what now?" Christopher asked. "What will he do when you arrive with only a handful of passengers and you fail to deliver the one he paid for?"

A grim smile lit the captain's face. "Negotiation."

"Pardon?" Christopher didn't see what there would be to negotiate. Captain Gower seemed a good captain, but no doubt Mr. Thomas could hire another to pilot his ship easily enough.

"Simply because I sail without a full docket of passengers, it does not signify that this voyage will not be profitable." The corners of the captain's eyes crinkled, and an almost merry twinkle came to them. "I may be a bit soft when it comes to some things, but that doesn't make me stupid."

"What else are we carrying?" Christopher asked, recalling the vast hold below and the way the captain had been vague about its cargo.

Captain Gower answered his question with one of his own. "Have you ever heard of the Black Ball Line?"

"Your competitor?" Christopher said. "You mentioned it in connection with that scoundrel, Littleton, though I profess to being unfamiliar with ships and seagoing in general before undertaking this voyage."

Captain Gower nodded as if he had expected as much. "The Black Ball runs a group of packet ships to and from America. They are known for keeping a tight schedule—and costing a sailor or two his life each voyage in the process. Mr. Murphy's sailed with them before—says the seamen call the Black Ball packets 'blood boats.' You'll not find a captain among them who'll allow those working below a rotation on deck—or much of anything else, including basic food and rest. But the pay is good, so desperate men continue to sign on."

"What has that to do with your ship?" Christopher asked, not certain how any of it stood to help the *Amanda May* turn a profit.

"The Black Ball Line owns the right to mail delivery between Liverpool and New York—or it did until last month." Captain Gower rubbed his hands together almost gleefully. "I negotiated a new contract. It's temporary for now, but if we make land in twenty-five days or better, we'll be the ones delivering the mail between America and England, and that's a cargo that never runs out. Neither does it require an initial investment or purchase."

"Ingenious," Christopher said, feeling a sudden urge to applaud the captain's ingenuity. "But even at her faster speeds, how can the *Amanda May* possibly compete with an entire fleet of packet ships?"

"She can't," the captain said. "But the *Amanda May* is only the beginning. When Mr. Thomas learns of her potential with this contract, I am certain he will be interested in funding additional steamships. They're the way of the future, I tell you."

"And this Mr. Littleton, whom you believed might have sold the tonic to Lady Cosgrove, what does he have to do with all this?" Christopher asked.

Captain Gower scowled. "Littleton runs the Liverpool office for the Black Ball Line. No doubt he feels I cheated him, swooping in and securing at least a portion of his business."

"Offering a better product or service is not cheating. It's competition," Christopher said. He, if anyone, should know the difference. Cheating had been what his father did best—from using a trick deck of cards when playing poker with drunk men to lying to good, honest men, taking their money for business ventures that didn't exist.

"It's basic economics, is what it is," Captain Gower said. "Supply and demand. There is an endless supply of mail needing to be delivered between the continents and the demand for it to do so as quickly as possible. I've found a faster, better way. Nothing illegal about that."

"Not at all," Christopher concurred once more, appreciating the captain's good business sense. He would do well to listen to Captain Gower and glean as much information and knowledge as he could from him during the remainder of their voyage. Christopher knew he'd be on his own soon enough, in a foreign land and with little real-world experience.

Though growing up with Father at least taught me what to be wary of.

But time spent with Captain Gower might replace the time he had spent with Miss Abbott, and perhaps the days would not seem so long and tedious as they had the past week without her company. *And if I am assured of her safety when we reach America, I can cease thinking of her at all.*

The latter was easier said than done, he suspected.

"I thank you for your good advice, sir." Christopher paused as they reached midship once more. "As it seems you have sufficient leverage with Mr. Thomas, I will seek an audience with Lady Cosgrove immediately."

"Good luck to you." Captain Gower said. "I'll look forward to hearing the results of your conversation at dinner, if not sooner. I, too, have grown somewhat fond of Miss Abbott and encourage you to do what you can to procure a different situation for her."

"I intend to," Christopher assured him, feeling the first real hope since reading Miss Abbott's letter.

CHAPTER  19

Marsali set a bowl of broth on Lady Cosgrove's bedside table and began picking up the clothing strewn about the cabin. For one supposedly still so ill, Lady Cosgrove managed to make quite a mess each day. Over the past week, as she'd left her bed for longer periods each day, her temper and discontent seemed to have increased as well.

"What have you brought me to eat?" she asked in a falsely feeble voice as she made a show of trying to lift her head from the pillow.

With her back to Lady Cosgrove, Marsali rolled her eyes at the woman's dramatics. *She would have done well on stage.* "I've some fine chicken stock and a few crackers to go with it." Marsali withdrew the crackers from her apron pocket. Mr. Tenney had loaned her the apron the previous week, and Marsali had scarcely taken it off since.

"Broth again?" Lady Cosgrove's tone changed to whining.

"It is best while your stomach heals." Marsali set the

crackers beside the bowl and took a used cloth from the basin and began ringing it out.

"Aren't you going to help me eat it?" Lady Cosgrove asked.

"I think not," Marsali said pleasantly. *No more of that, at least.* Sitting by Lady Cosgrove's side for hours, helping her to eat, had been perhaps the worst of the tasks associated with their care. Marsali tossed the cloth in a basket near the door. "But I'm happy to help you sit up." She returned to Lady Cosgrove's bedside and helped her lean forward, then plumped the pillows behind her.

"There. That's better." Marsali smiled as she held out the bowl.

"Must you always be so cheerful?" Lady Cosgrove said, snatching the bowl so quickly that some of the broth spilled onto the quilt. "Clumsy girl."

"That was not my doing, and you know it." Marsali turned away without offering to assist in cleaning up the mess. "And I *do* prefer being cheerful to being sour, as *some* people on this voyage seem wont to be."

The second the words were out of her mouth, she realized she'd gone too far in standing up to Lady Cosgrove. *I am not her servant,* Marsali reminded herself as she cringed, waiting for the stinging rebuke that was sure to come, yet wondering at the same time why she cared—why she continued to help the woman at all.

"You think yourself so clever." Lady Cosgrove's voice held none of the feebleness that had been there but a moment ago. Instead Marsali sensed a bitterness and a dislike that surely bordered on hatred.

Marsali turned to face her once more. "I apologize. I should not have said what I did. Feeling ill as you have been is reason enough for behaving poorly."

Lady Cosgrove gasped but did not further disagree with Marsali's assessment.

It is true enough. Marsali well remembered those few occasions she had been allowed to visit her mother before she'd died. Instead of the sweet-tempered and loving woman she had grown up with, Marsali had found her shriveled and bitter, short of temper and disinterested in her own daughter. *Because she was in such agony.*

Pain, she had learned through unfortunate experience, changed people's behavior. Even those with usually good dispositions could be made cruel when enough misery was inflicted upon them.

"And I do not think myself overly clever," Marsali continued. "But this morning I am feeling particularly grateful. Lydia's color is better, and her breathing has improved as well. I have hope that she may yet fully return to us."

"Do not try to soften me with a reminder of what you have done for my daughter."

"I wasn't." Marsali held her head high but chose her words more carefully this time. "I am not so foolish as to expect gratitude from someone who hasn't experience with such—both giving *and accepting,* if I am correct." *Another insult, but certainly a true one.* "I am grateful Lydia is improving because I genuinely care for your daughter, and I want her to be well."

"As do I," Lady Cosgrove said, a bit of softening to her tone. "And I . . . thank you. For your part in it."

"You are most welcome," Marsali said, recognizing the difficulty it had to have caused Lady Cosgrove to say such words.

One does not thank a servant, Aunt Ada had instructed her children shortly after Marsali had come to live with them. *One uses her as one might a plaything or a piece of furniture. A servant is for your benefit, for you to avail yourself of whenever you need her*—not *the other way around. And if she does anything amiss, she is to be punished— severely. It is the only way she will learn.*

"If Lydia does not come round, I am not certain what will become of us," Lady Cosgrove admitted, sounding frightened now.

"She will be whole again." *She must.* Marsali could not imagine a young life with so much promise being snuffed out. *And yet she has wavered on the brink of death these many days.*

"So you say," Lady Cosgrove said. "But you have youth on your side, and ignorance. It is a blissful combination that has provided you, for the time being, with an optimistic outlook and a rash independence. I rather envy you that."

"If ignorance is found in watching one's mother waste away from illness, dying a piece at a time, little by little, day after day, then you are correct." Marsali added more laundry to the overflowing pile by the door. "Or perhaps it is knowing that my future is bound to a man reputed for cruelty and who has, quite probably, ended the lives of those previously indentured to him. If this is what you envy, Lady Cosgrove, then I pity you indeed."

"Ignorance may have been the wrong word," she conceded in a rare moment of admitting to anything less than perfection. "Nevertheless, I find myself wishing I was in possession of your willpower and determination."

"You are." Marsali opened the door, carrying the basket of used rags with her. "You've more strength than you give yourself credit for. And when the need for it arises, I've no doubt you'll reach inside and find it."

Christopher adjusted his cravat and tugged down his vest before approaching Lady Cosgrove as she sat in one of the chairs Captain Gower had brought up on deck. Instead of leaning against the back of the chair, she sat perched on the edge, her spine unnaturally straight, one hand tightly gripping the handle of the white parasol held loftily over her head.

"Good afternoon, Lady Cosgrove." Christopher removed his hat and settled in another of the chairs, leaving the one between them empty.

"What do you find good about it?" she asked, her tone icy.

"The weather is quite fine," Christopher said. "We've encountered very little storminess, in this time of year known to be most vulnerable to that sort of thing."

"Hmph."

"The breeze is light. We are making good headway. The sea is calm and beautiful."

"*That* is a matter of opinion."

"True," Christopher conceded while wondering how anyone could dispute its beauty. Both the blue sky and ocean provided an endless horizon. The air was clear and clean, the scent of the ocean so much more pleasant than that of the city they'd left behind. Out here a man could imagine and dream any possibility and believe he would achieve such.

"But you are well and your daughter nearly so," Christopher said. "Surely you cannot argue against that happy news."

"I cannot," Lady Cosgrove said stiffly.

A tiny step in the right direction. "Miss Abbott has worked a miracle if I've ever seen one. You would think she and your daughter were sisters or longtime friends, at least, with the way she has so lovingly cared for her."

Lady Cosgrove looked at him sideways. "*Lovingly* does not seem to be a word I would have thought to be in your vocabulary, Mr. Thatcher."

Tread carefully. "Only occasionally will you find it." Christopher smiled. "For example, when I am referring to the care given me by our faithful servants. And, as Miss Abbott has been like a faithful servant to your daughter, that term seems most appropriate."

Lady Cosgrove faced forward, her nose tilted upward. "I

have yet to witness Miss Abbott acting the part of a faithful servant."

Christopher nodded, pretending to agree. "I believe that is because she was not raised as a servant but rather brought up in a home with servants herself. Her father was quite wealthy and well connected in France."

"Not so well. Look what the girl has become—an indentured servant is less respectable than those who have served for years, who have remained loyal to one family and dwelt at the same estate for decades."

"So society tells us, but one cannot fault Miss Abbott for seeking a better life." He recalled his grandfather having explained the principle of longtime servitude to him once, when telling him that Harrison's family, his ancestors, had been serving at his estate as far back as the dukedom existed. "I believe Miss Abbott shows much promise. Whomever she serves will be fortunate to have her. Miss Abbott will be loyal to a fault. In addition, she has lived both in England and on the Continent, and that experience will, no doubt, prove valuable in less-civilized America."

"What is your point, Mr. Thatcher?" Lady Cosgrove somehow managed to peer down her nose at him, though he was clearly taller, even seated as they were. "All this talk of Miss Abbott grows tedious."

He decided to change tactics. *Honesty is not the best policy. It is the* only *policy*, Grandfather had said. Christopher very much hoped Lady Cosgrove felt the same. "I would like you to consider hiring Miss Abbott to be your daughter's lady's maid. Once we reach New York, it would require an upfront payment to the man she is indentured to, but then she would be your faithful servant for a period of four years. And, as she appears to be quite fond of your daughter, I've no doubt she could be persuaded to stay on beyond that term."

Lady Cosgrove's mouth opened widely, then closed,

bringing to mind a few of the unusual fish Christopher had seen on this voyage.

"How very audacious of you to presume to tell me whom I should hire as a servant—when it appears you are little better than a servant yourself."

"There is no shame in serving others," Christopher said evenly, "and I have spent a portion of my life doing that. Just as I've spent a number of years living with my grandfather, who was the seventh duke in a rather long and prestigious line."

"Was," Lady Cosgrove said. "He is dead now. And once more you are no one."

"If you view my connection to him as the definition of who I am—or was," Christopher said. Her attitude annoyed him, but it did not come as a surprise. "He was my mother's father, so I remain untitled—unworthy of company such as yourself." He made to leave, believing his cause to be lost, when she spoke again.

"I am sorry for your loss. And I understand your plight more than you may think."

"I have no plight," Christopher said. "I am my own man, responsible for my own future. It is likely that—even had a dukedom been offered me—I would have refused it in favor of this journey and the subsequent opportunities."

"Then you would have been most foolish," Lady Cosgrove said. "For a man, at least, may be secure in the knowledge that he will have an income for the duration of his life. But a woman is not so fortunate. I have buried two husbands—both men I cared for deeply. And upon the deaths of each, I found myself to be virtually penniless, without home or income."

"And with a daughter to support," Christopher added quietly.

Lady Cosgrove gave a brief nod, then immediately resumed her straight-backed posture. "In truth, I am powerless to choose so much as a servant or a gown or a cup of tea. Beyond the clothing that Lydia and I have brought in our trunks, we have nothing. Much of our jewelry was sold to sustain us these past months, until we received the offer from Mr. Vancer. From this point on, it is he upon whom we are both completely reliant. I can only hope that Lydia's being forced to a marriage of convenience turns out as fortunate as my marriage did."

"For both your sakes, I hope so as well." Christopher rose from his chair, the optimism he'd felt at the beginning of their meeting having completely vanished. *Are there any ladies who are* not *misfortunate?*

"Good day to you, Lady Cosgrove." He tipped his hat.

"And to you. I am sorry I cannot help with your request."

"As am I," Christopher said, feeling that her admission was something at least. Though it would not help Miss Abbott at all.

CHAPTER 20

Marsali watched as Mr. Tenney poured champagne into her glass, then proceeded around the table. Beside her, Mr. Luke swirled the amber liquid appreciatively before taking a drink. On her other side, Mr. Jones—ever seeming uncomfortable when away from his engine room—covered his glass with his hand.

"None for me, thank you. I've got to be clearheaded to see to things below deck." To Marsali, he said, "Never could hold my liquor well."

"I do not believe there are many men who can," she said, thinking of her uncle. "But it is an admirable one who admits it."

In answer to her compliment, Mr. Jones stared at his place setting, his face flushing red to match his hair.

Marsali leaned closer. "Please do not be flustered by all this unexpected formality," she whispered. "In truth, I am not at all certain anymore which fork is to be used first either."

He braved a glance at her, an appreciative smile lighting his face. "I'll not tell if you don't."

"Our secret," Marsali whispered, bringing a finger to her lips. "We must only watch Lady Cosgrove for our example, and all will be well."

Their *example* sat on the other side of the table between Captain Gower and Mr. Thatcher, directly opposite them. As Marsali looked up from her whispered conversation, she found Mr. Thatcher watching her, a most peculiar look—one she could not quite decipher—upon his face.

"Here, here." Captain Gower tapped the side of his glass with his spoon. "I know at the start of our voyage I said there was to be none of the fancy and formal found aboard my ship, but tonight I'm breaking my own rules. Why, you may ask. Because today the *Amanda May* clocked a record nine knots per hour—for *six consecutive* hours. We have now shaved an additional day off this voyage and will be arriving in New York one day earlier than planned, though we left England a day late." He glanced at Lady Cosgrove. "Most of you should be very pleased to hear this."

Most. But not me. Marsali turned her head from the captain and caught Mr. Thatcher watching her once more. His brows rose in question, as if to ask if she was all right. Instead of sending him a reassuring smile, Marsali gave a slight nod and directed her attention elsewhere, not trusting herself to contain her emotions.

She was *not* all right, and the reason had very little to do with their imminent arrival in New York and everything to do with the way Mr. Thatcher had been avoiding her. It was as if he could tolerate her company no more than Miss Cosgrove's. Marsali didn't understand this change in him, and it pained her. And when, occasionally—as at breakfast the other morning and again just now—he glanced at her in his old friendly and concerned manner, she experienced an unsteady swell of feelings she did not know what to do about.

Mr. Thatcher had seemed so sympathetic at the beginning of their voyage. Indeed, his concern had so touched her that she'd confided in him as she had to no one before. But something had changed during the week of Lydia's sickness. And when Marsali had at last felt she might take strolls around the deck once more or join Mr. Thatcher in a lively conversation about a book each had read, he was nowhere to be found. Instead, it had become apparent that he did not wish to see or converse with her. More than a time or two, she had caught him hurrying to his room or up on deck the moment she appeared in the saloon.

And though she had purposely lingered on deck—under Mr. Murphy's watchful eye—for the past few nights, Mr. Thatcher had not resumed his nighttime habit of observing the stars with her.

It is probably for the best, she told herself. *We will be parting ways in less than two weeks.* Perhaps several days less, if Captain Gower's ship continued to exceed expectations.

The captain raised his wineglass, and the others at the table followed suit. Even the flustered Mr. Jones lifted his water cup.

"To the *Amanda May* and our safe and speedy voyage to America," Captain Gower said.

"To the *Amanda May*." Glasses clinked together as everyone joined in the toast.

Marsali took a sip of champagne and felt a tickle as it hit her throat. She placed her glass on the table, thinking she would do well to follow Mr. Jones's example.

Two of the kitchen crew entered the saloon, arms laden with platters and bowls. As they started service at the head of the table, Marsali turned her attention to Mr. Luke. Painful though he was to converse with, he did not dredge up any feelings of uncertainty or loss as simply glancing at Mr. Thatcher did.

"Making the crossing quickly as we are, this is one of the most exciting voyages you've made," she said.

Mr. Luke gave a polite laugh, giving Marsali the impression that her statement had offended him.

"Not quite," he said. "The *Amanda May* has speed, but

our route has been most ordinary. This voyage lacks the excitement that comes with trying to outrun a pirate ship."

"Something we should all be grateful for," Lady Cosgrove said.

"True enough," Captain Gower agreed, raising his glass once more. Lady Cosgrove did the same, finishing what was left of her drink.

"Have you had many encounters with pirates?" Marsali asked Mr. Luke, more for a good tale to share with Lydia later than out of real interest. No doubt he had enjoyed several grand adventures, and it seemed likely he would be quite animated in telling them.

"I have had more altercations with pirates than I have fingers and toes on which to count."

Marsali worked to keep her smile from growing too stiff. From the corner of her eye, she caught Mr. Thatcher watching them, an almost bored expression upon his face.

"Just last year, before I had the good fortune to make acquaintance with Captain Gower, I was sailing with the East India Company. We had a shipment of costly rugs, and rolled inside these rugs we'd hidden even more valuable goods." Mr. Luke placed his elbows on the table and leaned forward, warming to his topic and frustrating the kitchen crew member attempting to ladle soup into his bowl.

"What sort of goods were you transporting?" Lady Cosgrove asked.

"The usual—tea and silks, porcelain. And, of course, opium."

"Of course," Captain Gower muttered. "Dastardly business, that trading company. Be glad you got out when you did."

"I am," Mr. Luke said. "Though, as you've sailed with them as well, you must admit there was a bit more excitement to a trading voyage than there is in transporting passengers across the Atlantic."

"I am happy to leave the *excitement* behind," Captain

Gower said, sounding rather exasperated with the direction of their conversation. "I prefer remaining in possession of all my limbs and, most particularly, my *life*."

"As do I," Officer Luke said, taking up a roll and preparing to butter it. "And on that particular voyage, with the rugs, I came as close to losing mine as I ever have—ever care to."

"Do tell us what happened," Marsali said when it appeared he would not but had transferred his interest to the food in front of him.

"We were boarded, of course. Several men were cut down at once. Other pirates went straight to the hold and began searching out the treasure and bringing it up. We offered very little resistance—or so it appeared. But three other officers and myself were barricaded in a room below, with two hidden cannons, primed and aimed at the other ship. One of the officers was killed when the pirates shot through our door. But I held my position, and we fended them off, silencing those who had found us and remaining hidden until most of the blackguards were back on their ship. Then we took aim and fired langrage—bits of scrap iron, nails, bolts and the like—at their deck."

"Most often such a move is intended to tear a ship's sails, disabling it," Captain Gower added.

"But it is equally as effective at clearing a deck of the men upon it," Officer Luke said. "As was the circumstance that day. Those of us left on board were able to fight with and defeat the pirates who hadn't yet returned to their ship, and those who had—and were laboring under the weight of the rugs—were caught unaware and dispatched through our cannon fire."

"Brilliant." Lady Cosgrove clapped her hands, or attempted to, though they weren't meeting up quite as well as they had a few moments earlier. Marsali caught the captain's nod and saw the cabin boy fill Lady Cosgrove's glass once more, though this time only halfway. It was becoming apparent she couldn't hold her liquor any better than Mr. Jones.

"It was dangerous but also exciting. Nine times out of ten the company could best a pirate ship," Mr. Luke boasted.

"Really?" Mr. Thatcher asked. "The odds were that good? Must be a lot of inept pirates at sea these days."

Marsali had been thinking the same thing but still found it somewhat audacious of Mr. Thatcher to question the first officer that way.

"The odds were never *that* good," Captain Gower said, answering before Mr. Luke could. "Particularly with one pirate."

"Sir Edmund Crayton?" Mr. Thatcher suggested to Marsali's surprise, and it appeared everyone else's as well.

"You know of him?" Captain Gower asked.

"Yes. You could say that." A troubled expression flickered briefly over Mr. Thatcher's face.

"You may have heard of Crayton," Mr. Luke said. "But meeting him is something else entirely."

"You don't say." Mr. Thatcher flexed one of his hands and held it in front of him, studying it almost as if reminiscing. Marsali followed his gaze and noticed for the first time that his index finger was bent unnaturally, as if something had happened to it and it hadn't healed entirely right.

"When Crayton and his men boarded a ship, few would return to tell about it," Mr. Luke said. "But there was one time when he intercepted an East India ship en route from China. Her hold was full of pepper, and when the men saw it was apparent they were going to be boarded, the crew went into hiding below, each reaching into a barrel of pepper and grabbing a fistful before they hid."

"Pepper?" Lady Cosgrove asked as she hiccupped, then brought a hand to her mouth.

"They had guns and knives, too," Mr. Luke said. "But Crayton and his men weren't expecting the pepper. Many got a face full when they went below looking to take men and treasure. In the time it took for them to recover, the East India men were able to gain the advantage. I was not personally aboard that ship, but I have heard tell of it many times."

"Indeed," Captain Gower said, appraising his first officer skeptically.

"Have you ever met a pirate, Mr. Thatcher?" Marsali asked, giving in to the desire she'd had all evening to engage in conversation with him.

"Just one," he said. "That I know of anyway. Though with the company my father kept, that is questionable."

"Do tell us." Lady Cosgrove placed her hand on his arm and leaned far closer than was appropriate.

"Perhaps another time," Mr. Thatcher said. His lips pressed together as if to suggest to all that he would not be speaking on the topic.

Marsali felt disappointed and wished he would tell the story. But then, she wished he would say anything, that he would simply talk to her as he had at the start of their voyage.

It would have been most pleasant to spend the days she had left as she wished to spend them—with Mr. Thatcher.

CHAPTER 21

*C*hristopher brooded as he stared out at the ocean and began his second turn about the deck. His hands were clasped behind him, and his brow furrowed at the two warring thoughts running through his mind. *I've done all I can to assist Miss Abbott, and now I must forget about her. Only a coward walks away.* At the moment he felt the part of a coward all too well, yet he did not see what more he could do with regard to Miss Abbott's perilous situation.

"And how is the young Mr. Thatcher this morning?" Captain Gower took up pace beside him.

"Young. And that is about all I am," Christopher said, wishing not for the first time that he were a bit older. He'd yearned for that increase in age—to be older than Grace and better able to protect both her and Helen—for most of his growing-up years. To find himself with a similar desire now, when, at the start of this journey he'd had thoughts only of his youth and the time on his side for adventures, seemed almost a cruel trick of nature.

"Do not wish such a gift away," Captain Gower advised. "The years will be upon you soon enough. Happens to all of us."

"It was not age, precisely, that I was wishing for," Christopher said. "Rather, I am in need of either means—which often come with age and a lifetime of work—or wisdom regarding a solution for this vexing problem with Miss Abbott."

"Vexing now, is she?" Captain Gower's grin further annoyed Christopher.

"Not she, precisely, but this bloody business with Thomas."

"We don't know for certain yet that it will be bloody," the captain gently reminded him.

"Neither do we know that it will *not*," Christopher said. "And given the facts and circumstances . . ." He didn't bother finishing his sentence. It was the thought—Miss Abbott at the mercy of a cruel man—that had haunted him beyond distraction the past several nights.

"I take it your interview with Lady Cosgrove did not go well," Captain Gower said.

"Not in the least." Christopher sighed wearily. "She is not in a position to hire Miss Abbott or to pay for her passage. And even if she were, I am not certain there is enough . . . substance . . . in that woman to do something so charitable."

"Ah." Captain Gower clasped his hands behind his back in a manner similar to Christopher's as they reached the stern and changed direction.

"It seems Lady Cosgrove is also at the mercy of a man," Christopher said. "Her last monies were spent securing this passage, and she and Miss Cosgrove are now reliant upon the good graces of Mr. William Vancer, Miss Cosgrove's intended, for their future well-being."

"I suppose that explains, in part at least, why she was so eager to imbibe at dinner last night," the captain said. "More often than not, the temptation of drink is the temptation of forgetting one's troubles for a while."

"I have seen it often enough myself." Christopher recalled that the evenings his father had come home most drunk were often the evenings he had done poorly at the tables and when the debt collectors were most insistent.

"Let us pray—for Lady Cosgrove's sake and her daughter's—that Mr. Vancer has many good graces indeed," Captain Gower said.

Christopher nodded. "The greatest of which had best be patience."

"And longsuffering," the captain added with a chuckle, referring to the brief Sunday service that had been held on deck that morning. "How old did you say the man is? Might he perhaps be blessed with a shortness of hearing?"

Christopher laughed. "I doubt he is that fortunate. Though at any rate," his tone sobered, "he is more fortunate than Miss Abbott."

"So my suggestion did not work," Captain Gower said. "What do you propose to do now?"

"I am out of ideas," Christopher admitted. "After Lady Cosgrove rejected my request, I had the thought that, collectively, myself and the crew might come up with enough funds to pay off Miss Abbott's debt. I offered up my two pounds for the cause and marshaled Mr. Murphy into helping me speak to each of the men. Quite a few have become acquainted with Miss Abbott." Of late, Mr. Luke had seemed more than acquainted with her, a situation Christopher found greatly annoying. "I had hoped they might be willing to throw in a shilling or two in her behalf."

"A sound idea," the captain said. "Though it is doubtful that many of the crew have more than a shilling or two in their possession."

"That's the whole of it exactly," Christopher said dismally. Though he was one of the highest-paid crew members, Mr. Luke had come up with an entire list of debts he owed and had been unable to pledge much at all—less, in fact, than most of the other men. Mr. Jones had pledged twice as much as Christopher, and that had annoyed Christopher as well, though he should have felt thankful. "And so I have told myself that I must forget about Miss Abbott and her troubles. I have no means by which to assist her, and dwelling on it will surely lead to madness."

A brief smile crossed Captain Gower's face. "Women do tend to have that effect on a man, don't they? Especially *particular* women, and I am not speaking of Miss Cosgrove or those like her. I'm speaking of those, like your Miss Abbott, who get under a man's skin in such a way that he cannot forget her."

"I am not certain what you mean, Captain," Christopher said a little too quickly. "It is Miss Abbott's troubling situation I am unable to forget or find the means to remedy."

"Of course, of course." Captain Gower stopped at the door to the saloon and gestured for Christopher to go inside. They both entered and walked the length of the room to the captain's quarters. Captain Gower opened his door and again motioned for Christopher to go ahead of him.

He entered the captain's private room for only the second time on this voyage and remembered the previous occasion, that first night aboard when he had been feeling slightly annoyed that Miss Abbott's absence might delay their departure. How blissfully carefree he'd been that night with nothing to concern him aside from the sorrow he felt at taking leave of his sisters.

Captain Gower closed the door behind them and turned to Christopher, a far more serious expression on his face than a moment earlier. "You are wrong. About a few things. The first being that it isn't simply Miss Abbott's welfare you cannot stop thinking of. I've no way to prove this to you, of course. But mark my words, were you to find a solution for her situation, you would still be faced with a difficult parting at the end of this voyage. And wherever your travels take you in America or beyond, you would be unable to forget her."

Christopher made no argument to this. He wished to but recognized the truth in the captain's words, troubling though it was.

"The second thing about which you are incorrect," Captain Gower continued, "is that you do not have the means to assist Miss Abbott, to protect her from harm, as it were."

"Tell me, please, where I am to find these means?" Christopher spread his hands before him, palms up. He wanted to believe the captain but felt little hope from his words. But little was better than none. He might always remember Miss Abbott, but at least if he helped her he wouldn't have to worry about her well-being or feel guilt that he had abandoned her to a terrible fate.

"To this point you have considered only a monetary solution." Captain Gower crossed to his tables of inventions and began fiddling with the closest one. "When there is another, quite obvious one available to you."

"Continue," Christopher said, curious as to what the captain had in mind.

"You must marry Miss Abbott."

"Oh no." Christopher took a step back as he shook his head. "Marriage and family are not for me, at least not for many years to come."

"Family . . . hmm." Captain Gower stroked his beard thoughtfully and continued as if he had not heard Christopher's objections. "I am fairly certain that indentured servants are not permitted to have children, so it would be best to avoid any action that might . . . ah, lead to that for the next few years."

"Did you not hear me?" Christopher asked, feeling his ire rise. *He wishes me to marry Miss Thatcher, but in name only? What good will that do?* "I have *no* plans to marry for quite some time—many years hence, if even then."

"A man never plans these things," Captain Gower said, a broad smile lighting his face. "They simply happen to him, most often when he least expects them and frequently at great inconvenience to him. Take my *Amanda May*. I had just received my first commission when she came into my life. Timing couldn't have been worse."

"Nevertheless, you had a commission," Christopher pointed out. "You had a career, a means of income, something to offer the lady and a way to provide a roof over her head. I have none of those."

"Bah." Captain Gower waved a hand dismissively. "It isn't what you don't have that matters here. It's what you do. Marry Miss Abbott, and go with her to Mr. Thomas's. He can either put you to work as well and reduce Miss Abbott's term of indenture by half, or you can find work nearby but stay at Thomas's place with your wife. The point is that you will be close by, and Mr. Thomas will have someone to whom he is accountable for her welfare."

"She is to be a lady's maid," Christopher reminded him. *Stay . . . with your wife.* "I very much doubt there is room for an additional manservant in that arena of responsibility."

The captain shrugged. "Not likely, unless they do things quite different in Virginia, but Thomas runs a big plantation. There is a strong possibility he would hire an extra pair of hands, particularly if I recommend it. Didn't you say you wanted to learn about farming? This could work well to your advantage."

"Or it could not," Christopher said shortly. He turned away from the captain and stood at the large, paned window as he stared across the sea. *Less than a week, and we shall be in America.*

"I cannot marry Miss Abbott," he said once more, as much to himself as to the captain, for he could not deny the appeal the idea held. *I would not have to bid her farewell. I could see that she remains safe. I could see her every day.*

I've gone mad.

"Why can you not marry her?" Captain Gower demanded. "Do you find her repulsive?"

"Of course not." She was anything but. From the moment that first night aboard ship when Miss Abbott had let the hood of her cape fall back and he'd glimpsed her face, he had thought her extraordinarily beautiful.

"Do her mannerisms bother or offend you?"

"No." *She makes me smile and eases the ache of missing my sisters.* "I enjoy her company well enough."

"Is she pushy and nagging?" the captain persisted. "Does she make insufferable noises? Do her feet smell?"

"No . . . How should I know about her feet?" Actually, he did know about her feet. He'd touched them briefly the night he'd removed her slippers and tucked her into bed. "Those are all most absurd questions and undoubtedly have very little to do with the union of marriage."

"True enough," Captain Gower said. "Though you must admit that any of those traits in a woman might be cause for a man to have second thoughts."

"I have not even had *first* thoughts on this matter," Christopher assured him. *Not until you mentioned it, in any case.* "I am not in a position to support a wife. Furthermore, I do not wish to be tied to one location. I've yet to see America and should like to thoroughly investigate the country before deciding where I shall settle. I do not wish to be another man's servant, and most importantly, I am simply not ready to be married."

With that, he turned away, intending to retreat to his cabin and perhaps stay there until the voyage was over.

"It was merely a suggestion," Captain Gower said. "One that would put your mind at ease regarding Miss Abbott's welfare. And I note that you said you did not wish to be tied to one location. But you mentioned nothing about not wanting to be tied to *Miss Abbott.* Be honest with yourself, Mr. Thatcher. You have come to care for the girl. I have witnessed it myself."

"She is little more than a girl." *As I am little more than a boy.* Twenty-one was far too young for a man to marry—wasn't it? Christopher did not want to be honest about his feelings regarding Miss Abbott, most especially with himself. Allowing his thoughts to venture that direction was surely the path of danger.

You must marry Miss Abbott. It had been anything but a suggestion, given here in the privacy of the captain's quarters, and the captain well knew it. As did Christopher. He shut his eyes and muttered a few words his grandfather would have had him whipped for.

When he had composed himself once more, checked his anger, and thrust panic firmly to the back of his mind, he faced the captain once more. "You are that concerned for Miss Abbott as well, that you would suggest something as ludicrous as our marriage."

Captain Gower nodded. "I am. The more I have thought upon my past interactions with Thomas, the more I must admit to seeing the signs of a cruel man, one who has little regard for the sanctity of life. There was another instance . . ." The captain's brow drew together in a pained expression. "We were at a tavern, and the serving girl accidentally filled a glass to overflowing. Thomas had papers on the table, the plans for this ship, to be exact, and though we moved them quickly enough, he stood and struck the girl and sent her reeling. She fell and hit her head on a table corner."

"Did the tavern owner not say anything to him?" Christopher asked.

"He yelled—at the girl. Thomas is too well known, you see. His coin is too well spent in many places for anyone to complain against him."

My aunt and uncle were too well respected in Manchester for me to have hope of any sort of justice.

Christopher ran his fingers through his hair as Marsali's

words rang through his mind. She was headed to the same type of situation—or perhaps one even more dangerous.

Leaving was the only thing I could do.

Was marrying her the only thing that could be done now? "Thomas's wealth and business reputation are why no one has taken up a case against him regarding the misfortunes of his servants."

"Aye," Captain Gower agreed. "I am certain you are correct."

"Then why should we not simply whisk Miss Abbott away to safety elsewhere?" Christopher asked. "Pretend she did not show up in Liverpool or make this voyage at all."

"The ship's logs, the crew, even the inspector's record in Liverpool all tell of her. Thomas may discover our deception. It's too risky."

For whom? "And my marrying her isn't?" Christopher felt his face heat with anger. "Maybe Thomas will simply kill us both. Have you considered that?"

"Yes, actually," Captain Gower said. "It is always a possibility, but doubtful, I would say. He is an older man and not in particularly good health. I cannot imagine that he would challenge you. If Miss Abbott goes to him alone, the outcome could very well be different. But you seem well able to defend yourself—and her."

Goes to him. Alone. Christopher's stomach churned at the image those words dredged up.

"No one will force you to this decision, of course." The captain's gaze left Christopher and returned to the inventions cluttering his tables.

No one but myself.

"For that matter, no one will force Miss Abbott to marry you. And now that I think on it, I believe it's highly probable she will refuse."

At least one of us will exhibit common sense, then. "Thank you for that vote of confidence." Christopher had not believed his mood could worsen, but the thought of Miss

Abbott refusing such a generous offer on his part rankled him. *No doubt she would accept a similar offer from Mr. Luke.*

Captain Gower began searching his pockets, presumably for his pipe. "Not to say that she couldn't be persuaded. But does Miss Abbott strike you as the sort of female who would accept just any offer of marriage? Do you imagine she will swoon with relief when you propose?"

"No." Christopher doubted she'd ever swooned at anything. But it wouldn't be just any offer. It would be for her safety.

"Or does she seem the sort used to self-reliance and who would have to feel strongly about giving up her independence?"

"Staying alive seems reason enough to me," Christopher said. "And going to work for Mr. Thomas is certainly going to be restrictive of her freedom." *And mine. I am mad to even consider this, to be continuing this conversation.*

"True, yet certain decisions will still be her own. But when one marries . . . never again does he or she consider himself or herself first, or alone."

Unless he is like my father. The unbidden thought was disconcerting. *I am* not *like my father.* But Christopher's arguments against marrying Miss Abbott ran through his mind, every last one of them self-centered. *As my father was to his dying day.*

It had taken his grandfather to point this out to Christopher, to help him realize that the root of his father's problems lay in selfishness.

"There are times in your life when you must think of others above yourself," Grandfather said.

"Times?" Christopher rose from his chair and stood before him defiantly. *"My whole life has been about that, about watching out for Grace and Helen."*

"And a good thing too." Grandfather wheeled his chair around the desk, closer to Christopher, as if to let him know he

was not in the least intimidated by his strapping, fifteen-year-old grandson. "Your sisters' gentleness has likely saved you from a wasted life. By thinking of their safety and well-being, you were forced to become responsible, hardworking, clever, and quick thinking. You learned what it was to care for someone, to love them so completely that you would do anything to see them safe and happy. If only your father had learned even one of those lessons, if he'd had just one thought of your mother instead of himself . . ."

Echoes of that conversation with his grandfather—a conversation that had brought Christopher to his knees in a realization of regret for his desire to be free of responsibility, and gratitude for his sisters and even the hardships they had endured—filtered through Christopher's mind now. *I have Grace and Helen to thank for my happiness, for much that I know, for what I value.*

And what he valued most was his relationship with his sisters. *And my freedom.* He wanted to value his name but could not yet. To this point in his life it had largely shamed him. It was what had most motivated him to travel to America, to start anew.

"You have begun well, then. For when I think of the name Thatcher, forevermore it will bring to mind a kind, generous man." Miss Abbott had said that to him nearly the first day of their voyage. It had meant something; it still did. *And she does too.*

And there it was, the admission he'd fought so hard against. If he *was* being honest, he did care for her. A great deal. Enough that marrying her held a definite appeal. Enough that his concern for her outweighed the plans he had made for himself. Those, he realized, could be changed. They could be postponed or altered. His affection for Miss Abbott could not—not without the potential cost of harm to her. A risk he was not willing to take.

"I'll do it. I will marry her." He spoke the words quietly but with conviction. The panic he'd felt moments earlier was gone, and in its place a resolute calm took hold of his mind and settled in his heart. He'd never gone wrong watching out for his sisters. He would not be wrong in doing this. Instead, a great many things could be very right about it. A brief image flashed in his mind, of Miss Abbott at his side, her arm linked easily through his and her head tilted upward as she bestowed one of her charming smiles upon him.

He recalled the night he had carried her to her bed. *How right it felt to hold her, and how I wished to never let her go.* If he married her, he wouldn't have to let her go. The happy thought drifted down, covering his melancholy with enough light that he felt suddenly encouraged. Enthusiastic, even, about this new possibility.

"There's a good lad," Captain Gower said, as if Christopher was a little boy who had just fetched his paper or slippers. While Christopher had been lost in thought, the captain had located his pipe, lit it, and stood puffing away, sending ringlets of smoke into the air. "Now all you've got to do is persuade Miss Abbott that this is the right course. Though I doubt she'll be as easy to convince as you were."

Christopher's mouth twisted in a wry grin at the captain's audacity. "*Now* you remind me that I'm a bad catch?"

"Not at all, but I believe Miss Abbott will not be in favor of a marriage of convenience—even if it is for her safety. Have you not heard her tell of her family? Her sister married for love, her parents did the same, as did her grandparents. It's in the girl's blood to expect romance. You've got your work cut out for you, and with very few days remaining until we reach New York. Have you any experience courting?"

"Personally, no." A burst of laughter escaped his mouth, followed quickly by another. *If my sisters could see me now.* They would be laughing harder than he was. And he could not seem to stop.

"I beg your pardon?" The captain's brow furrowed with worry. "What is amusing about this? You haven't even begun an official courtship yet, so you cannot claim to have lost your mind already. That comes much later—after you are married." A devilish grin curved his mouth.

"I assure you I am still in possession of my senses." *Most of them, anyway.* Christopher wiped at the corners of his eyes and pressed his lips together in an attempt to hold in his laughter. But he could not cease grinning as he thought of Grace and Helen and their reaction when they received a letter telling them of his marriage. "I have no personal experience with courting, but I have had ample opportunities to both arrange and witness it for and from others. I promise you, Captain, I am up to the challenge."

CHAPTER  22

Marsali wrinkled her nose in dismay as she looked at the enormous pile of Lydia's laundry. She'd avoided the task as long as possible, using the excuse that Lydia was still too sick for her to spend an entire afternoon away from her. And when that was no longer true—with Lady Cosgrove out of bed and able to watch over her daughter—Marsali had reluctantly bundled the garments in the bedding also needing to be washed, then hauled the lot up to the deck. Delaying the dreaded chore even longer, she'd decided to wash her own few articles of clothing first and had just finished hanging them out to dry on the clothesline Mr. Tenney had kindly strung up for her on deck, outside the kitchen.

Perhaps my duties below stairs were not so bad after all, she mused as she picked up the first of Lydia's nightgowns. Pinching the fabric between her finger and thumb and holding it as far away from her as possible, she carried it to the washtub, then dropped the gown in the water, where it merely floated on the surface. Marsali frowned as she watched the garment, willing it to submerse of its own accord. When after a long minute it became apparent the nightgown would do no such thing, Marsali used both hands and quickly plunged the fabric beneath the surface with a heavy sigh and great reluctance. Then, using only her thumb and finger once more, she picked up a section of the gown and lay it across the washboard. She retrieved the lye soap from the deck and bent over the tub to begin the scrubbing.

"You've not much experience laundering clothes, have you?" Mr. Thatcher leaned casually against the frame of the open kitchen door, his arms folded and a rather smug look upon his face.

"More so than you," Marsali snapped, her mood soured by his untimely arrival, surrounded as she was by the pile of foul-smelling bedsheets and clothing. She had wished for his company for days but did not wish for him to see her now— at her worst. She felt entirely unappreciated this afternoon— friendless and tired and overworked, when really, it was not her duty to do any of this work at all. It had not helped matters that, as Lady Cosgrove's health had improved, so had her demands—including her insistence that Marsali wash all of all Lydia's dirty clothing.

"What will Mr. Vancer think should Lydia arrive looking like a wilted flower? It is bad enough she is so pale and fragile. We must have her looking her best if he is to accept her as his bride. You wouldn't wish it otherwise, would you?" Lady Cosgrove had asked with that falsely innocent air of hers.

She had known, no doubt, that Marsali would not disagree, fond as she was of Lydia. She wanted her friend to have as easy a time as possible adjusting to her new life, and if clean gowns helped, then Marsali would see to it she had them.

She wished she might fix the problem with Mr. Thatcher as easily, but she still didn't know what she had done to upset him, to cause him to withdraw. And she felt cross with herself for even noting his absence these past days and caring about it. *About him.*

"If only Lydia wore more sensible dresses instead of these," Marsali grumbled, inclining her head toward the towering pile of petticoats and frills. "Even this sleeping gown is not made from practical fabric. However, I daresay I know more about washing it than you."

She cringed inwardly, hating her harsh tone. It wasn't in her nature, yet her feelings this afternoon were raw and fragile. She had missed his friendship and felt ridiculously hurt by his neglect. *And being put out with him will certainly encourage his attentions again.* She sighed at herself and tried to appear more approachable.

"You are saying you can do wash better than me?" Mr. Thatcher's brows rose, and his mouth twisted in a look of challenge. "I wouldn't be so sure." He pushed off the doorframe and strode toward her, rolling up his sleeves as he came.

Feeling something between disbelief and anticipation, Marsali watched him approach. "In your other, pre-avoiding-being-a-gentleman life, you were a laundry boy? Is there even such a thing? I've never heard of a man washing clothes."

He held out his hand, and she gladly surrendered the soap.

"A bar like this is especially hard on your skin," he said. "It's better if you grate it and boil it with your water—better for the clothing as well. But, since you've already begun . . ." He moved aside the portion of the gown she had been preparing to wash, then ran the soap over the washboard, covering it thoroughly. Only then did he spread a section of the gown flat across it. His hands moved up and down over the fabric. "You have to use a certain technique when washing a garment such as this. A plain shirt, such as mine, can be rubbed back and forth over the board, but a delicate fabric may snag or tear if you do that, so your hands must move over the fabric instead."

Marsali was speechless. She was sorry for having been peevish, and she was impressed, and humbled, to see him doing woman's work, and doing it well. Every five strokes he turned the gown so that the next section lay on the board. His movements were quick, efficient—and practiced. "So you *were* a wash boy?"

He grinned as he looked up at her. "My sister Grace supported us by taking in laundry, mostly for women who wore ridiculous dresses like these. By the time I was six I was helping her. And may I say, Miss Abbott, that I vastly prefer your more sensible, simpler gowns for many reasons." He winked, or at least Marsali thought he did.

"Thank you—I think." Feeling suddenly uncomfortable and worried that she was blushing, Marsali glanced at her feet. "I am sorry for my rude words and wrong assumptions."

"No harm done," Mr. Thatcher said in his usual, easy way. "It appears you are not the only one surprised by my abilities."

Marsali followed his gaze and saw Mr. Tenney and two of his assistants standing in the kitchen doorway, clearly gawking at the scene before them.

"I've seen it all now," one exclaimed, shaking his head. "A *man* washing a woman's petticoats."

Mr. Thatcher had finished with the gown, placed it in the tub of rinse water, and started on one of Lydia's underskirts.

"It's no different than you peeling a potato for a woman's supper," he said loudly, though his tone was light, giving Marsali the impression that the teasing didn't bother him.

"'Course it is," Mr. Tenney said, appearing downright insulted, a scowl upon his face. "A potato isn't a lady's possession, it's simply a potato, and cooking on board a ship is a man's job. Laundry—especially a woman's—is in no way, no how, a task for a man."

"Maybe not," Mr. Thatcher said, a smile playing at the corners of his mouth, "but we shall see whose company Miss Abbott prefers near the end of this voyage—yours, in your month-old shirts, or mine, smelling and looking fresh and clean."

"No washing for me." Mr. Tenney waved a hand in the air, apparently dismissing the notion that clean clothes mattered, then retreated into his kitchen.

Feeling guilty that Mr. Thatcher was doing all the work, Marsali returned to the tubs and began the far less distasteful task of rinsing and wringing out the clean garments. As she carried the gown over to the line, she caught sight of five other crew members, Mr. Murphy included, all watching and pointing at Mr. Thatcher with keen interest.

This will never do. She might not wish to do this task, but Marsali found she wished Mr. Thatcher to be ridiculed even less.

She returned to the tubs and searched the deck for the soap, intending to take it from him, only to see that he had placed it on the top ledge of the board.

No wonder he asked if I'd had much experience. I didn't even know where to put the soap. Her former tasks—the emptying of chamber pots and fireplace ashes—had not required much skill at all. "Thank you for showing me how to properly wash clothes."

"Anytime." He continued scrubbing.

"I can do it now," Marsali said, uncomfortably aware of the growing crowd.

"I am certain you can, but why hurt your hands? You rinse the gowns and hang them out, and I'll finish the washing."

It was a tempting offer, but she couldn't allow it. "That's very kind, but—"

"If you're worried about what the crew will think of me, don't be." He glanced at her.

"It isn't that," Marsali hurried to say, though that was precisely her worry. She viewed Mr. Thatcher as a gentleman, though not one who wore gloves and stood around in elegant sitting rooms smoking cigars. He was more *man* than that, and an equal at least to the ship's crew. It seemed important that they not see him as anything less. She scrambled for another excuse as to why he should allow her to finish laundering the clothes.

"In my new position as a lady's maid, it may be that I am required to care for delicate gowns such as this. I should practice so it will at least appear to my new employer that I am familiar with the task." From the sideways, skeptical look he gave her, Marsali very much doubted he believed this excuse. Nevertheless, he stepped aside.

"If you insist."

"I do." Marsali stepped up to the tub and began running her hands over the fabric as Mr. Thatcher had done. When she felt she'd sufficiently covered the entire piece, she picked it up to move it aside, but it would not move, instead clinging to the board.

"Slip your finger beneath the top like this." He leaned close, putting his hand in the water again. "Board needs more soap," he observed after freeing the fabric.

She picked up the lye and rubbed it generously over the board, then placed another section of the dress across it.

"That's the piece you just washed," Mr. Thatcher said, a hint of amusement in his voice.

Without a word, Marsali pulled it up again—it *was* easier this time; apparently the amount of soap on the washboard did make a difference—and arranged the section beside it.

"That piece has already been scrubbed as well." He was suddenly right behind her, leaning close, his arms on either side of her as they reached into the tub. "You don't have to do it this way, but I always turn the fabric in the direction of the tub of rinse water. I start with the back seam and work my way around. That way I know I've done it all." With deft movements, he adjusted the skirt on the board once more. "Watch my hands, and follow them. How well the garment becomes washed depends upon how you move your fingers."

He placed his hands on either side of hers and began scrubbing. "Move the fabric so that it goes into the grooves of the board and collects the soap, then back, so the soap doesn't simply sit there but becomes agitated over the garment and does its work."

"I didn't realize there was so much to washing clothes," Marsali said, feeling a bit overwhelmed, and not from the many instructions he'd given her. *I didn't realize that having a man so close to me would feel so . . . pleasantly unsettling.*

Various members of the crew still milled about the deck, and she knew she ought to scold Mr. Thatcher for standing thus. *At the least, I should feel embarrassed. A woman in polite society would never stand so close to a man.* But she was not in polite society, and she could not bring herself to ask him to move.

"Try this." Mr. Thatcher placed his hands over hers and moved them over the fabric. "When you know how to use it correctly, the board does much of the work."

"Mmm." Marsali didn't trust herself to say more than that, and she was having great difficulty concentrating on the washing itself, the clothing—much of anything but Mr. Thatcher's nearness. His face was pressed close to hers, his arms around her, his hands gentle but firm as they moved over hers on the fabric. The combination had aroused some new, unfamiliar sensation—overpowering to the point she felt she might wilt right there on the deck.

When they had danced together that second night—not more than two weeks ago—she had held Mr. Thatcher's hand, but their mood had been jovial and their movements quick. She had enjoyed the light touch of his hand on hers, the music, and having someone to be merry with. But now, **this** seemed different. *Intimate.*

Ridiculous. He is showing me how to wash clothing. Nothing more.

When, after another minute, he released her hands and stepped back, she felt vast relief, yet keen disappointment. Wiping the back of her wet hand across her brow, Marsali told herself that her weak knees were nothing more than the result of several nights' lost sleep from staying up with Lydia. But when she turned to look at Mr. Thatcher and caught him stripping off his shirt, her racing heart indicated otherwise.

He wasn't a man used to idle days spent in clubs or in other such gentlemanly pursuits. His chest and arms were broad and muscled, as if he was used to a life of physical labor. *No mere washboard did that,* she thought and felt herself blushing again.

A grin appeared on his face as he caught her staring. "Before I joined you outside, I asked Mr. Tenney to heat another pail of water. It should be just about ready. With the amount of clothing to be washed, I knew you'd need fresh water at least a time or two. And since I'm here, I might as well clean my clothes as well."

"Of course." Marsali grabbed another petticoat from the stack and tossed it into the tub. She soaped the board, then began scrubbing with fervor. *He has sisters,* she reminded herself. And they had grown up together in unusual circumstances. No doubt he was used to removing his shirt in front of them. *Does that mean he thinks of me as his sister?*

"You've got the hang of it now," he said, stepping into her line of view once more.

Marsali bent her head lower, determined to dismiss her errant thoughts and regain control of her senses.

"You'll find that it isn't a difficult chore so much as it is tedious," he continued. "Grace and I would wash gown after gown, for hours and days on end. I think that is perhaps one reason I have been loath to attend balls—the sight of so many dresses is likely to give me nightmares."

"Do not let Mr. Tenney overhear that you've nightmares about women's ball gowns, or he will think you even more peculiar," Marsali advised.

"I'm not particularly concerned with what he thinks of me," Mr. Thatcher said. "When I bid farewell to my sisters in Yorkshire, I made up my mind; from that moment on, I would only undertake to do something if I wanted to do it. Too much of my life to that point had been spent in doing the opposite." He grimaced as if recalling unfortunate times. "This morning I wished to assist you; what others may think of my choices does not concern me."

What of me? Marsali wondered. *Does he care what I think of him? I am thinking too much of him.* "It was very kind of you," Marsali said in a voice that sounded strangely choked to her own ears.

Whatever Mr. Tenney and the other crew members might think of Mr. Thatcher, there was no doubt in her mind he was manly in every sense of the word. And a gentleman as well.

CHAPTER 23

Wearing his freshly laundered shirt, Christopher strolled the length of the deck as he considered what options he had available for courting Miss Abbott. Yesterday afternoon's discovery—finding her busy with the wash—had been most fortuitous, though not at all how he would have thought to begin a courtship. But it had worked, or at least he believed it had. He'd helped her with an unpleasant chore and found it to be almost enjoyable. Having his arms around Miss Abbott as they stood at the washtub had certainly affected him, and by the blush that crept up her cheeks, he guessed she'd been affected by their nearness as well.

Not to mention that he'd impressed her with the skill he was least fond of. *But one must use the resources given him.*

He and Grace and Helen had become expert at that very thing over the years, and he laughed that he was counting on those skills to serve him well now.

But what to do next? He could not take Miss Abbott on a drive. They had already read and discussed several of the books available to them on the ship. He could not even join her for stargazing again, as that pompous Mr. Luke had taken to accompanying her each night. On three different occasions, Christopher had gone up on deck at night, only to find Mr. Luke already monopolizing Miss Abbott's attention.

No more, Christopher vowed. *Not tonight or any other night.* He would speak to the captain about finding other occupations for the first officer's time. Mr. Luke, who had scarcely offered more than a penny for Miss Abbott's protection, did not deserve to be on the same ship with her, let alone to spend pleasant evenings in her company.

The sun disappeared behind a cloud, and Christopher lifted his gaze skyward, noting that the ocean was not as calm today. As they neared America's shores, the sea was apt to become more turbulent, Captain Gower had said. He'd also mentioned that hurricanes were not uncommon this time of year and had put them all on alert that the pleasant days of their voyage might well be behind them.

Nearly all the days of this voyage—pleasant or other-wise—are behind us. With their increased speed, Captain Gower was estimating they would arrive in New York this Friday, a mere twenty-two days after their departure. Which left Christopher with only three days in which to both woo Miss Abbott and win her over to the idea of marriage.

Three days, and I haven't a clue what to do next. He was discovering that arranging for his sisters' happiness had been far easier than orchestrating his own. If only he had more time.

The sun reappeared, and Christopher searched the sky, hoping to see more clouds or a storm that might bring a strong headwind to slow the ship.

However, it was not clouds that caught his attention but a faded piece of ribbon fluttering in and out of sight above him. Stepping closer, Christopher saw that it was attached to something inside one of the lifeboats hoisted above the deck.

Could it be? The ribbon fluttered out of sight once more, then back into his line of vision, and this time Christopher felt almost certain it was the same ribbon he'd seen tied in Miss Abbott's hair at breakfast. He'd noted the faded color then and wished he might purchase a new one for her—and promised himself that someday soon he would.

But for that ribbon to be inside the lifeboat now would mean . . . *Miss Abbott is inside that boat.* And to get up there she would have had to climb . . . *those crates, a barrel . . . that edge of the rigging.*

With a quick glance around him to see if the captain or any senior crew members were about or watching him, Christopher stepped up onto a crate and peered over the edge of the boat, where a glimpse confirmed his theory. Miss Abbott lay on her back, a partially eaten apple in one hand, a book in the other held open before her and covering her face from his view. Her ankles were crossed and peeking from beneath the hem of her skirt, which was spread over the floor of the boat. She'd removed her shoes, and her hair appeared to have escaped its bun. Wisps of brown, along with the ribbon, lifted and fell in the breeze.

She had not noticed him yet, and Christopher ducked out of sight before she could. He climbed down, stepping quietly onto the deck below.

Smiling, he moved away lest anyone see him lingering in this spot and discover Miss Abbott's hiding place. He was certain that was what it was—a refuge where she might find a few moments' peace from Lady Cosgrove's demands and Miss Cosgrove's chatter.

Captain Gower had pegged Miss Abbott as resourceful and independent. Christopher found her solution more than that. He thought it ingenious and plucky—especially given the captain's edict about not climbing—and wished he had thought of it himself. Not only was Miss Abbott clever, but she wasn't afraid of taking chances. A very good quality, Christopher supposed, given that a marriage between them would involve a considerable amount of risk on several fronts.

He was willing to take those. But he did not know at all when or if Miss Abbott would be in agreement.

If only I might convince her to give me a chance.

It was Marsali's good fortune that Mr. Luke was on duty during the dinner hour. He had been strangely absent this evening, for which she felt grateful. With Lydia returned to the table for the first time since her illness, there was no lull in the conversation, though neither could a person get a word in edgewise, preventing Marsali from engaging in conversation with Mr. Thatcher—the very thing she had looked forward to this evening.

He had been so generous yesterday, helping her with laundry, of all things. She could only hope that whatever rift had occurred between them, that had kept him both silent and away, had been mended and that he would be her friend once more. But it was difficult to tell when neither was able to speak even a word with Lydia's constant stream of chatter.

She has two weeks of lost conversations to make up for, Marsali told herself as she listened good-naturedly while she ate.

"Mother bought the tonic from that horrid man with the red hair—no offense to you, Mr. Jones." Lydia paused long enough to send an apologetic glance his way.

"None taken." Mr. Jones, looking increasingly uncomfortable, consulted his watch for perhaps the tenth time in the past half hour.

Counting the minutes until he can return to his engine room? Normally Marsali felt sorry for his apparent anxiety and the need for him to be below deck so often. But just now she could not entirely blame him for wanting to leave. Even the stifling heat of the engine room might be preferable to another hour of this same story. Lydia was already telling them—for the third time—every detail she could recall about the night her mother had purchased the tonic from the man at the wharf.

"And to think he told us that *you* had authorized such a sale." Lydia cast a doleful look toward the captain. "And do you know how much that cost? It took the very last of our money, plus one of Mother's—"

"That's enough, Lydia," Lady Cosgrove cut in sharply. "There is nothing to be done about it now, and we needn't continue recounting our folly to the captain."

Lydia appeared to wither in her chair. "Yes, Mother." She slouched lower, looking—for the first time all night— quite as ill as she had been.

"What have you been reading lately, Miss Abbott?" Mr. Thatcher asked, both changing the topic and kindly drawing everyone's attention from Lydia. "I believe we are each nearing the end of the captain's library."

"She has been reciting poetry to me," Lydia said, answering before Marsali could. "I adore listening to her. Today she recited some of Mr. Burns's poems with a perfect Scottish accent."

"As my grandmother used to recite them to me," Marsali said. She cherished her memories of her grandmother nearly as much as she cherished those of her father.

Lady Cosgrove made a *tsking* noise in the back of her throat and shook her head as if Marsali had just announced she had been reading the most scandalous gothic romance novel.

"I should like to hear Mr. Burns's poems myself sometime," Mr. Thatcher said, causing Marsali's heart to give a joyful leap, for which she swiftly and silently scolded herself.

Don't be a ninny. But it was impossible not to feel happy at the hint that he wished to spend more time with her.

"Have you perhaps had some time *alone* in which to read?" Mr. Thatcher asked.

She puzzled over his emphasis of the word *alone*, though she had stolen a few minutes to herself. And it had been heavenly. "Just today I finished *The Last of the Mohicans*."

"And did you find the story uplifting?" Mr. Thatcher's brows rose, and his eyes shifted upward.

Lydia giggled. "Oh, you can't have read Mr. Cooper's book or you would not have asked such a silly question. It is a most tragic story."

Marsali had the feeling that Mr. Thatcher still would have asked and that they were no longer discussing the book.

"But I have read it," he said. "Last year—in my quest to learn everything possible about America."

"Do not let fiction be your guide," Captain Gower cautioned.

"It is not at all an uplifting story," Lydia continued. "Poor Cora is killed, after all."

"I see your point," Mr. Thatcher said. "Though for some reason I believed the book might make Miss Abbott feel as if she had . . . *attained new heights*."

He knows. At once she understood the direction of his hints. *He knows I was up in that boat.* Marsali narrowed her eyes at him, and he answered her with a roguish grin.

Insufferable man. But it was with some difficulty that she held back her own smile.

"Are there not times, Miss Abbott, when we find literature boosts us *aloft* in this world?" He reclined in his chair, and his grin turned lazy, as if he had all the time in the world to watch her squirm.

And she was beginning to. Did Mr. Thatcher *wish* her to be in trouble? Usually she did not mind his teasing, but if the captain discovered what she had been up to—quite literally— he might well be upset with her.

With the toe of her slipper, she nudged Mr. Thatcher's shin beneath the table and sent him a silent plea to cease speaking of her respite above the deck.

He winked at her as he had yesterday when they were washing Lydia's gowns. *What is he about?* Marsali dared not look at him again but took a few seconds to compose herself as she cut a piece of her meat. Perhaps he *was* still upset with her and had only pretended kindness yesterday and was now intending revenge. But Mr. Thatcher did not seem the type, and he *had* helped her, staying with her and assisting until every last article of clothing had been washed and hung out to dry.

Maybe she was simply reading more into his words. *My own guilt is sabotaging me.* Yet she had not felt guilty about her slight break of the rules until now. At the time, whatever action was required to escape Mr. Luke's company had seemed more than justified.

And she had taken great care when climbing into that boat, both with her steps and to make certain she was not seen. She'd waited several minutes—until the time the crew had changed shifts and no one was near to observe her.

Unless Mr. Thatcher was spying on me.

While Marsali had been thinking, Lydia had been retelling the story of *The Last of the Mohicans* to Mr. Jones and her mother, the only two at the table who had not read the novel. "It is good you have not read it, Mother," Lydia exclaimed at the end of her long summary. The horrors those two women endured would give you nightmares. You would never have agreed to sail to America."

"I shall have nightmares now, thanks to you." Lady Cosgrove looked longingly at her glass as if wishing that something other than water would appear in it. "And I did not exactly agree to come to America. It was the only option left open to us."

"A difficult position to be in," Captain Gower said sympathetically.

"Tell us, Miss Abbott, what were your thoughts while reading the novel?" Mr. Thatcher persisted. "Did it almost seem as if the story took you from the ship to another place . . . high above the ground?"

You go too far. He *was* attempting to get her into trouble with the captain. She could see no other reason for Mr. Thatcher's continued line of questioning and his not-so-subtle hints.

"I was quite caught up in the story," Marsali admitted. "As with any good novel one enjoys, I did feel transported to another time and place." *So there*, she finished silently.

From the corner of her eye Marsali glanced at Captain Gower and found, to her concern, that he appeared to be paying close attention to this exchange. Lydia, on the other hand, was openly pouting, nonplussed, no doubt, about the sudden turn in the conversation.

Internally Marsali prepared for the next onslaught of battle, her mind searching for possible retorts to anything else Mr. Thatcher might imply or hints he might drop that she had gone where she was not supposed to.

He is only jealous that I thought of it first. But if Captain Gower discovered what she had done, he might decide to have her chaperoned during the day as well. To this point the captain had been quite liberal in allowing the passengers to move about as they pleased. Surely Mr. Thatcher realized that such freedom—or hers, at least—would be in jeopardy if he tattled on her.

Their eyes met over the rim of his glass as he spoke again. "I am glad to know the story elevated you to a place you had not previously imagined."

She was imagining herself punching him, yet having difficulty holding back laughter, as that would surely give her away. But, oh, she could tell he thought himself clever.

And full of mischief tonight.

"All good literature is uplifting in one regard or another," Marsali said as she raised her chin and met his gaze head-on. "We see the *beastly* behavior of characters and learn that we must hold ourselves to a higher standard. Or we read of a story where much happiness is found, and it gives us hope that our own may yet come to pass, in spite of those who would stand in our way of finding it." *Do not ruin this one thing for me. Allow me a few pleasures in the time I have left. And join me in them, if you will.* There was plenty of room in the boat for Mr. Thatcher to read as well, should he wish to escape Miss Cosgrove's attention, which, now that she was up and about again, would likely be directed at him.

"Well said," Captain Gower raised his glass to Marsali.

"Agreed." Mr. Thatcher inclined his head toward her in a gesture of surrender. "To Miss Abbott, her love of literature, and her ingenuity in finding clever solutions to her problems."

"What solutions? What problems?" Lydia glanced back and forth across the table from one to another. "*What* are we speaking of?"

"An important and somewhat private matter," Captain Gower said, surprising Marsali. "Miss Abbott, Mr. Thatcher, I would like to see both of you in my quarters in *one* hour." He exchanged a pointed look with Mr. Thatcher, making Marsali feel slightly ill. *The captain already knows I was in that boat.*

She felt the sting of Mr. Thatcher's betrayal and cast her eyes down at her plate, lest he notice her hurt.

Which is entirely absurd. She had been in trouble before and would no doubt be in it again at Mr. Thomas's. And surely the captain would do little more than reprimand her and have her activities more closely watched. It was the thought that Mr. Thatcher was responsible for putting her in this tight spot that wounded her. She would never have done the same to him.

But then she cared for him—far more than she should have—and it was at once apparent that his feelings for her were not the same.

CHAPTER 24

*P*recisely one hour later, Marsali knocked upon the captain's door. It opened at once, and Captain Gower beckoned her inside. Marsali stepped into his cabin, her worry momentarily forgotten as she took in the vast array of unusual objects on the tables lining the walls. She had not been sure what a captain's quarters would look like, but she had definitely not expected this.

The crammed tabletops explained why he always ate with the passengers and never in his private quarters. There was nowhere in here *to* eat, no surface over which to spread a map or even write a letter.

"Are these all your inventions?" Curiosity momentarily overtook her concerns as she moved closer to the nearest table and bent over to peer at a glass globe resting in a wooden stand. A wire was coiled around a metal piece at the bottom of the globe, and a second wire, connected to another contraption, lay beside it.

"Not mine alone," Captain Gower said. "I have collected many of these. Often they were projects well begun but, for one reason or another, could go no further. I find it interesting to study them and to learn from their potential. Occasionally, I am able to improve upon them." He picked up the second wire and touched it to the one coiled around the globe. It sizzled, and Marsali jumped back.

"Not to worry," Captain Gower assured her. A second later the glass globe flared, then lit as a wick inside a lantern would.

She clapped her hands. "How marvelous. But there is no flame or fire?"

Captain Gower shook his head. "Not in the sense you are thinking of. It is a *quantity of electricity*." He pulled the wires apart, and the light died.

Not very practical, Marsali thought. A lantern might not be as bright, but at least one did not have to hold it the entire time it was lit.

The captain had picked up another item with a small keyboard similar to that of a pianoforte. The object was awkward and bulky, with folds or wrinkles of some type of material making up much of it. Taking each side in one hand, he pushed the folds together, and a screeching sound came out. When he pulled it apart, a similar yet different sound was made.

Marsali watched and listened, fascinated, as the captain repeated the process, pressing on various keys so that it began to sound almost musical.

"It's an instrument?" She stepped closer, wishing he would allow her a turn.

"It is called an accordion," Captain Gower said, "though I am no musician and cannot do it justice."

After a few more pulls and pushes, he set the accordion back on the table and was about to move on to showing her the next object when the sound of someone clearing his throat stopped them both.

Marsali turned around and was startled to discover Mr. Thatcher sitting in a window seat on the other side of the room. Tucked into the alcove as he was, she had not noticed him upon entering.

"Good evening, Miss Abbott." He rose from the seat and stepped forward, quickly closing the space between them so they stood very near to one another. Marsali glanced over her shoulder at Captain Gower, but he was not looking at them as if anything was amiss. Instead, he nodded his head as if he had been expecting this very scenario and was now encouraging Mr. Thatcher in something.

An apology? She very much doubted that, as Captain Gower was present and, no doubt, upset with her . . . though he had not seemed so in the past few minutes since her arrival.

Mr. Thatcher cleared his throat again. "You've been troubled." He directed the question at her.

Kind of you to notice, as my trouble *is of your doing.* "I have been." She did not deny it, having spent the last hour reevaluating her actions and feeling guilty that she had disregarded one of the few rules the captain had given them. She realized Mr. Thatcher had said nothing about her being *in* trouble.

"The captain has . . . I have . . . *we* have come up with a possible solution." Mr. Thatcher did not sound like his usual, confident self.

Perhaps his conscience had awakened, and he felt guilty for telling on her.

"A solution?" *Instead of a consequence or punishment?* Perplexed, she glanced from one man to the other.

"To the situation regarding your term of indenture," Mr. Thatcher clarified. "A way to provide for your safety."

"*That* is what this meeting is for?" Perhaps Captain Gower was not upset with her after all. She let out a slight breath of relief.

"In a manner of speaking," Captain Gower said. "But there is more to it as well." He strode closer, standing before them.

Feeling suddenly wary and vulnerable, though she had no reason for distrusting either man, Marsali stepped backward, away from both.

"Mr. Thatcher assured me he had the matter well at hand, and I believed him—until I witnessed his somewhat clumsy attempts at dinner this evening." Captain Gower's mouth twisted in a grimace as a look of chagrin appeared on Mr. Thatcher's face.

He is in trouble instead of me? Marsali felt as perplexed as Lydia must have during the enigmatic conversation they had engaged in throughout dinner. "What has he done?" she asked Captain Gower. To Mr. Thatcher, she asked, "What have you done?"

"Teased you to the point that you became upset."

"Oh." *Is that all? And what has that to do with my indenture?* She could not imagine, neither could she consider that at the moment, in light of the changed circumstances. If Mr. Thatcher truly had not told the captain about her climb to the lifeboat, then she saw nothing to be upset about. *Nothing to be hurt by.* It seemed she had read both him and the situation incorrectly. "I am no longer bothered. But I thank you for your concern." She smiled brightly at both men and turned to go, eager to leave before the boat incident could be revisited.

Mr. Thatcher's hand on her arm stopped her. "Does the thought of going to work for Mr. Thomas not trouble you?" he asked.

"It does." *Not nearly as much as your touch.* Marsali's heart raced, and she worked to hide her reaction—one that seemed to grow stronger the more they were together. If she was being truthful, she had wanted an afternoon to herself to daydream and reflect on the time she had spent with Mr. Thatcher as much or more than she had wanted the time alone to read. She faced him once more, and he dropped his hand. Though the breathlessness caused by his touch had not been unpleasant, she felt grateful for its removal, so that she might think clearly—a task made more difficult by his proximity. She forced her thoughts from his concerned gaze to the question he had posed.

She *was* worried about Mr. Thomas—a little more each day as America's shores grew near, but as they had previously discussed, there was no help for her situation. "I have already told you my feelings about my circumstances," Marsali said. "I refuse to let future troubles disturb present joys. I shall do my best to overcome whatever difficulties lie ahead *when* I encounter them. In the meantime, I don't wish them to hinder an otherwise pleasant existence."

"What if you did not have to face Mr. Thomas alone?" Mr. Thatcher asked. "What if I was to come with you, and to work for him as well, to shorten your term?"

"You would do that?" Marsali felt a catch in her heart.

"If you will allow me to." He took both of her hands in his, surprising her and bringing instant heat to her face, even as she also felt comforted.

"I will both go with you and stay with you throughout your term—and beyond," Mr. Thatcher promised.

She could not have heard him correctly, but the way he exhaled after speaking the rushed words, and the genuinely hopeful expression he wore, told her she had.

"That is the most noble, gallant, *gentlemanly* offer I have ever received." Her smile wobbled. Oh, how she wished to take it, to have him work where she was, to be able to see him beyond the remaining days of their journey. It was about so much more to her than simply having his protection. It would mean friendship and possibly . . .

She shook her head and fought back the emotion that had risen in her throat. "I cannot allow you to make such a sacrifice. You are going to have your own farm, remember?" She squeezed his hands excitedly as she forced her enthusiasm for his plans—plans that did not include her. "With a horse and a plow and a home you build yourself." She could picture it just as he had described. And inside that house he'd built, there would be another person—people—his wife and their children. Marsali suddenly wanted nothing more than to flee this room to the privacy of her cabin where she might cry.

"My plans for those things have not changed," Mr. Thatcher said, holding tightly to her hands when she tried to pull away. "Only the timing is perhaps a bit different. And, as Captain Gower so kindly pointed out to me following dinner—I am but a foolish young man with much time on my hands."

Marsali glanced at the captain, who still stood beside them, watching their exchange. If she could not have her wish for the privacy of her cabin, she wished that Captain Gower, at least, might give them a moment alone. But she did not suppose that likely, considering they were in his quarters.

"I may have been a bit harsh," Captain Gower conceded. "But you *are* young, and so obviously in-experienced at courting. I hated to see Miss Abbott ill used for your attempts."

Courting? Could it be that Mr. Thatcher's offer was about more than keeping her safe?

"I have hope that I would be better," Mr. Thatcher said, a slight note of defense in his tone as he looked at Captain Gower, "had we the time and resources available to us that were allowed my sisters and their beaus. Young though I am, I find myself with very little of either at present." He returned his attention to Marsali, and his voice grew tender. "Four weeks is not ample time in which to become acquainted with and court someone. Three days is nearly impossible."

Marsali's hands began to sweat where he held them, and the fluttery feeling she'd had when being near him at the washtub returned. *What are you trying to say to me? If you are teasing again . . .*

"*Nearly* impossible," he said. "But not entirely." His

mouth quirked, and the light of challenge flickered in the deep blue of his eyes.

"In his defense," the captain continued, "I must tell you what your young Mr. Thatcher has been up to this past week."

My *Mr. Thatcher*? She felt suddenly shy and completely uncertain—about everything. Why should Captain Gower and Mr. Thatcher be so concerned over her future? It wasn't as if either of them had any obligation toward her. Yet they appeared to be taking the situation far more seriously than she had. *Or than I have allowed myself to.*

It had taken effort, but she had managed to put Charlotte's letter and the news it contained firmly from her mind the past couple of weeks. Caring for Lady Cosgrove and Lydia had proved most helpful in that endeavor, particularly when Lydia was so very ill at first, and concern for her had outweighed all else in Marsali's mind. By the time Lydia was on her way to being well again, it had been easier for Marsali to continue avoiding thoughts of her future. Especially when a certain gentleman kept intruding on them day and night.

The captain left their sides and began pacing in a circle around them. Marsali followed his movement, though she noticed Mr. Thatcher did not. Instead, he released her hands and shoved his own in his pockets in a poorly disguised attempt at acting as if he did not care what was about to be said of him—though she suspected, from his covert glances, that he was eager to gauge her reaction to the captain's words.

"Mr. Thatcher has considered and attempted every means at his disposal to find a way to see to your safety. He petitioned Lady Cosgrove and the entire crew for monies on your behalf," Captain Gower explained. "But before doing that, he first pledged his entire savings to your cause, hoping to come up with enough to pay your passage and thus free you from your contract with Mr. Thomas."

"You did?" Tears of astonishment sprang to her eyes, and this time she could not hold them back.

"I was not successful," Mr. Thatcher said.

She knew that—had known that it had to be if he was offering to accompany her instead. But somehow it didn't matter. Her heart soared because he had cared enough for her to offer all he had—both his time *and* his means. That his savings were meager meant all the more.

"Lady Cosgrove spent the last of her income on this passage and is heretofore dependent upon her daughter's intended for their support." Captain Gower stopped before them, turned on his heel, and began walking in the opposite direction. "And many of the crew are little more than paupers themselves. Though it is my hope the success of this ship will change that."

"But, collectively, we were not able to come up with enough to pay your passage," Mr. Thatcher added.

"I myself am heavily in debt from building this ship," Captain Gower said almost apologetically.

"I am touched by your efforts, Mr. Thatcher. And by yours, Captain, in helping him." Marsali brushed aside her disappointment. Indeed it was difficult to feel any, so full was her heart from learning of all they had done, or attempted to do, on her behalf.

"I am sorry we have fallen short," Mr. Thatcher said.

"You've not fallen short in anything," Marsali assured him as she looked up through lashes wet with tears. "No one has ever shown me such kindness; no one has ever cared so much for me as you have on this journey. I shall remember it always." Heedless of the captain's presence behind her or of how appropriate or inappropriate her actions were, Marsali stepped forward, taking Mr. Thatcher's hand in hers and bringing it to her lips in a gesture of profound gratitude.

Let each of them think her a forward woman if they would; she did not care and wanted only for him to realize how much the extent of his concern meant. Her tears fell freely. She'd succeeded in keeping them at bay these three and half weeks but shed them now—not from fear or regret that his attempts had not worked but because he *did* care for her. Because he had touched her soul so deeply.

Behind her she heard the click of the door and realized the captain had at last left them alone.

Mr. Thatcher pulled her closer, and his arms came around her with a strength and certainty that seemed natural and felt so right. She laid her head against his shirt and took comfort in the quick, steady beating of his heart. He was her knight in shining armor, and though she knew she could not allow him to go to battle for her, for this moment alone it felt good to imagine he might. And that he could really stay with her. That they would continue on as they had been. *That he could court me.*

His arms tightened around her as if he was feeling the same as she and wanted to hold on to this moment as long as he could. His chin came down to rest upon her head, and Marsali sighed with a contentment she had never known, feeling safe and secure and cared for.

"Do not cry." Mr. Thatcher's hand found her cheek and brushed her tears away. "There is yet hope, if you will but allow me to accompany you."

He misunderstood her tears. Marsali wasn't quite certain that *she* understood them. She felt happy and yet terribly, terribly sad—a sense of loss—though they had not yet parted. He pulled back, holding her at arm's length.

"Allow me to accompany you, Marsali."

He hadn't asked permission to use her Christian name, but it fell from his lips as if it was meant to be spoken by him and they had long been on such intimate terms.

"What if Virginia is not the place for you? What if you are unable to find work?" She could not let him do this, no matter how much she wished it.

"I am always able to find work—have been since I was a

boy." A corner of his mouth quirked in a smile. "I can always do laundry."

She laughed and shook her head. "No, you cannot, Mr. Thatcher. You must find employment where you can learn about farming and where you can save enough for your own property."

He shrugged. "If you insist. Captain Gower tells me Virginia is quite a fertile land, and I am optimistic about the possibilities for work there."

"Maybe you can find employment nearby," Marsali said, allowing a faint hope to begin to grow. "And we could see each other sometime."

"Nearby is not good enough, neither is *sometime* sufficient—not when I find that I have grown accustomed to our interactions each day. Last week, during my failed attempts to avoid you and thus cure my yearning to be with you, I learned that being apart is most unsatisfactory." Mr. Thatcher pulled her over to the window seat, where they sat facing one another and staring out at the dark sea.

"While I was waiting for you this evening, I sat at this window, looking out at the ocean and imagining that I was elsewhere, that I had a large window like this in my home in America."

"Your home will have to be grand to have a window as large as this," Marsali observed.

"Perhaps," he said vaguely. "My window overlooked a garden where there were children playing. As I was watching them, I noticed something about each." His gaze left the window and drifted toward her. "I had a yard full of brown haired, brown-eyed children who all looked very much like you."

Marsali gave a short laugh. "Even the boys? How terrible for them."

"Even the boys, and not so terrible at all." Mr. Thatcher scooted closer, no longer focused on the sea but looking intently at her.

With intent, Marsali thought, her heart pounding. But *what* was his intention? She felt hers well enough. They were sitting close, but she wished for more and longed for him to take her in his arms again. That was all she wished for, and to stay there forever.

"Marry me, Marsali."

His lips moved, and it was his voice she heard, but the words had to be in her imagination. It was impossible that she could be hearing them from him. Four weeks wasn't time enough to come to know someone so well, to become betrothed. He had said so himself.

"I promise to keep you safe throughout your term of indenture—and beyond." He offered her a tentative smile, the first glimpse of vulnerability she had ever seen in him. "Captain Gower can marry us here, aboard his ship, before we reach America, and he has agreed to help with the transition to Mr. Thomas's residence. I will offer to work for Mr. Thomas as well—hopefully to shorten the length of your service, but if not, to at least see you safely through it."

A fresh set of tears leaked from her eyes as Marsali brought her hand to her head, certain she'd heard him incorrectly, that there was some terrible mistake. *Am I dreaming?* She pressed her hands to her still-damp cheeks and felt that the tears there were very real and she was quite awake.

"You have . . . just asked me to marry you?" She cringed as she spoke the words, knowing they could not be true.

"I have." His smile widened to the more familiar, confident one. "You cannot be more astonished than I was when I first considered the possibility."

"I wouldn't be so certain." She offered a tremulous laugh. "But you don't wish to be married—especially not to me, not when you've your dreams and plans."

"Which include you now." He reached for her hand once more, and she allowed him to take it, savoring every second of this closeness and his touch as his fingers brushed over hers.

"Marsali?"

She loved hearing him speak her name. "Yes." *Christopher*. She was not brave enough to speak it or to quite believe this was truly happening.

He leaned forward, then stopped, his brow furrowing. "Was that yes a question, or a yes as in—"

"Yes," she whispered. "I will marry you."

"You will? You are certain?" He studied her quizzically, as if not quite believing her answer. She felt suddenly alarmed and pulled away.

"Were you not in earnest when you asked?"

"No one has ever been more earnest than I." He placed his hands upon her shoulders and looked at her directly. "It is only that Captain Gower believed you would take a great deal of convincing to accept my offer."

"What would *he* know about my feelings?" Marsali demanded with a huff.

"Not much, apparently." Mr. Thatcher's lopsided grin returned. "*Thankfully.*" His hands slid from her shoulders and down the length of her arms. "I meant every word I said, every promise I made."

"But why change your plans—for me?"

"Because it is for *you*. Because I have scarce been able to stop thinking of you since the moment you first shuffled up the ramp in that clever disguise. I was so very impressed that night. And then we danced, and you told me about the stars, and you helped Miss Cosgrove—every day I found something more to admire about you."

She blushed from his praise while beneath her dress her heart pounded.

"And then just yesterday I realized that if I did not marry you, you should suffer a lifetime without clean clothing, considering your lack of laundry skills."

"You told me I had improved," she said, sticking out her lip as if he had wounded her.

"Oh, you have," he rushed to say. "But considering what skill you began with . . ."

She folded her arms and did her best to look cross. "Be grateful that I am not in possession of a wet article of clothing right now. You might find it upon your head."

"Deserved, no doubt." He continued with his assessment. "I do believe that watching you attempting to do laundry was the deciding factor in my proposal. That, and your gumption at climbing up to the lifeboat. Oh, and Mr. Luke persuaded me as well."

"Mr. Luke?" Marsali's frown deepened and was no longer pretended. "What has he got to do with this?" One minute Mr. Thatcher spoke tenderly, and the next he teased. She could scarce keep up or believe him.

"Well . . ." He released her and stood suddenly, then began walking before her, imitating Mr. Luke's arrogant gait. "As you began to spend more and more time with the gallant first officer, it became quite apparent that if left to your own devices, you would end up with someone ostentatious like him. And I knew it would not be long before the fellow drove you completely mad, and then I began to worry not only for your safety with Thomas but your sanity with Mr. Luke, or someone like him. And so I said to myself, 'Christopher, you've got to save that woman not only from the cruelty of her employer but from herself as well.'"

"Such chivalry." Marsali rolled her eyes. "I had the matter in hand, you know. Why do you think I was hiding in that boat?"

"I thought you were avoiding Lady or Miss Cosgrove."

"I was not," Marsali said, eager to clarify the matter. "Lydia could talk to me for an entire week, and I would prefer to wash all of her dresses again over another hour spent in Mr. Luke's company."

"I am quite happy to realize that." Mr. Thatcher ceased

walking and stopped before her. "I might, perhaps, have been jealous." He helped Marsali from the window seat.

"You have no reason to be jealous," she assured him. "I have wished only for your company since that very first night."

The room grew silent as they faced one another.

"I only tease those I care for," he said quietly. "My younger sister, Helen, used to be my favorite target, and I love her dearly. But were she here with us now, I should think she would come in second to my love of sparring with you."

"I shall take that as a compliment." Marsali's tears had finally dried, so she allowed herself to look up at him. "Still, this is madness, and I cannot quite believe it."

"Believe it," he said. "I shall be haunted if you leave without me, if you knowingly go alone to face danger. That would be the only madness herein."

"What if Mr. Thomas is a danger to you as well?" Marsali asked, worrying suddenly that he would be.

Mr. Thatcher shrugged. "As a wise young woman recently once told me—" he brought a hand to his chin as if speculating—"there is little point in letting the possibility of tomorrow's troubles interfere with today. When they come, *if* they do, we shall face them together—as husband and wife. Marry me, Marsali."

She attempted to mirror his casual smile. "I already said yes."

His eyes grew dark with intent once more. "Perhaps something more, then, to seal the bargain."

She stuck her hand out in the manner of a business agreement. He took it and pulled her to him, slipping his other arm around her waist, then whispered in her ear.

"Am I truly as bad at courting as the captain says?"

"Worse." Her hair caught on the evening stubble along his jawline. "I had no idea you *were* courting me until a few minutes ago."

"Ah," he said. "My subtlety worked, then."

"It did," she conceded, thinking it seemed days ago—not within the last hour—that she had come to this room, believing a reprimand from the captain awaited her. "But do not think that tactic will continue to work for you. From now on I should like more direct communication, so as to not be confused about your objectives."

"I've only one at the moment." He leaned in closer. "My objective is to kiss you."

"You are too bold, Mr. Thatcher." *Delightfully so.*

"My name is Christopher. I should like to hear you say it."

"You are too bold, *Christopher.*"

He grinned rakishly. "Get used to it." He kissed the bridge of her nose.

Marsali sighed with disappointment when he pulled back. "*That* was your objective?"

"Hardly," he said, "but the captain's quarters are no place for a first kiss between us."

"Why not?" She glanced about the room again. *It is pleasant enough, and we are alone.* Instead of being frightened by the prospect of kissing him, she felt exhilarated.

"Trust me." Christopher pulled her close briefly, then kissed her forehead and set her away from him. "If I have learned one thing from my brother-in-law, it is that a first kiss must be done right."

She tilted her face up toward him. "There is a wrong way to kiss?"

"No," he said. "At least there won't be when we do it—tomorrow."

CHAPTER 25

Christopher knew the second Marsali entered the room. Before he heard the click of her door or caught a glimpse of the fabric of her dress as she sat across from him, he felt her presence and the quantity of electricity that came with it. It stretched between them, an invisible force that seemed almost tangible. He felt pulled toward her, aware of her every movement, conscious of her expressions, the slightest change in her delicate features, every breath she drew.

It was driving him mad—in a pleasantly torturous sort of way.

If one could only patent this feeling, he would surely make a fortune.

"Good morning, Miss Abbott." He handed her the dish of berry jam, knowing—from days of studying her habits—what she would choose to spread across her biscuit.

"Good morning, Mr. Thatcher." Their fingers touched briefly, and color flooded her cheeks. She avoided his gaze, but he caught her biting her lip in an attempt to hold back a smile.

He didn't bother holding his back—probably couldn't have if he'd wanted to. He'd woken with two thoughts this morning: that Marsali was to be his wife; and that they would soon be in America. With both of these events to happen within the next two days, he'd never felt happier or more alive.

"Enchanted morning, everyone," Miss Cosgrove called as she wrestled her wide gown through the doorway, then sailed down the corridor toward them, flamboyant layers of lavender preceding her.

Enchanted. *A fine word. I am enchanted with my soon-to-be wife.* Marsali wore a pale green gown today, simple in adornment compared to Miss Cosgrove's, but he thought it very pretty on her. She needed no frills or frippery to assist her beauty.

"Green becomes you," Christopher said as he handed her the milk before she could request it.

"Thank you. My father used to tell me the same thing." She pulled at the pitcher, but he refused to release it, preferring to maintain their eye contact across the table and having her hand so near to his.

"He was a very wise man."

"As are you. Feel free to compliment me often." Marsali leaned forward. "However, you must share the milk if this courtship is going to come to fruition."

He laughed and let her have the pitcher just as Miss Cosgrove joined them.

"Good morning," Marsali said with far more enthusiasm than Christopher felt about Miss Cosgrove's arrival, though even her chatter could not dampen his spirits this morning.

Miss Cosgrove returned Marsali's greeting and followed it with what sounded strangely like an order. "Do be a dear and slide down so I may sit across from Mr. Thatcher this morning." She held her skirts and waited expectantly.

"Of course." Marsali slid to the end of the bench, stood,

and walked around the head of the table, past Captain Gower's as-yet vacant chair, to the other side.

Feeling inordinately pleased at her bold move, Christopher made room for her next to him and reached across the table to pull her dishes to his side. Miss Cosgrove still stood, squinting at them, her brow furrowed, a look of perplexity mingled with a dash of annoyance. She gave a forced laugh as she clapped her hands together.

"Well, I did not mean *that* far, but I suppose it shall do. Now I can look at both of you."

"And we you," Marsali said pleasantly.

Christopher silently admired both her assertiveness in staking her claim and her apparent lack of a grudge against Miss Cosgrove. He doubted he would have been so generous had Mr. Luke requested to sit near Marsali.

Miss Cosgrove poured herself a cup of tea. "Since we've only three days left for amusement, I thought we might stroll the deck this morning. The captain says we shall begin to see signs of land soon—birds and such. After being inside that dreary cabin so long, the sea air will be most refreshing. Though I dare not go walking on my own, weak as I still am."

Her tongue has not weakened with her illness. Christopher took a larger bite of his roll than necessary, ensuring his mouth was too full to respond to anything Miss Cosgrove said.

"I will accompany you," Marsali offered.

Christopher hurriedly chewed, then swallowed too quickly, the dry bread scratching his throat as it went down. "Will you not have other matters to attend to today?" he asked, giving her a sideways glance as he reached for his cup. He had assumed—wrongly, perhaps—that their remaining time on the ship would be spent together. At the least, they were to be married today. And though they could not have a traditional wedding night, he wished to spend the time talking with Marsali and enjoying her company.

"Actually," Miss Cosgrove cut in, "I was hoping you would walk with me, Mr. Thatcher. You're much taller and will be good for me to lean upon, should the need arise."

"I am afraid that will be quite impossible." Christopher tried not to sound too smug. He had not considered the immediate benefits of his betrothal, but this one he intended to make use of at once. "I'm afraid that it would not be appropriate for me to walk with you when I am betrothed to another woman."

"*Betrothed.*" Miss Cosgrove's mouth opened nearly as wide as some of the pelicans he had viewed at the Liverpool docks.

"Miss Abbott and I are to marry before the end of our voyage."

"It was a very sudden decision—arrived at just last night," Marsali added in a tone likely meant to soften any hurt Miss Cosgrove might feel. "Mr. Thatcher is marrying me to keep me safe from Mr. Thomas, the man my sister warned me about and the one to whom I am indentured. You'll remember her letter?"

Miss Cosgrove nodded and managed to close her mouth.

"I am marrying you because I wish to." Christopher placed his hand over Marsali's on the table. The urgency of her situation may have prodded him down this path, but he now embraced it wholeheartedly. To arrive on America's shores, not alone as he had imagined but with someone at his side, with whom he might build a life, was now infinitely appealing—on many counts. That this someone would be Marsali filled him with a joy he had not anticipated. No longer did the actions of his brothers-in-law seem so absurd or shameful. If anything, Christopher felt his behavior had been shameful, silently ridiculing them as he had. Really, they had been confident and mature enough to show their affection for his sisters, the women they loved.

He sought that same confidence and maturity now as he

leaned closer, brushing an imagined crumb from the corner of Marsali's mouth. "Remember my policy never to do anything that I do not wish. I *wish* to marry you."

"You make it impossible to forget." Her gaze flickered to his lips as she wet her own. She turned her hand beneath his and entwined their fingers together.

A look of great consternation had crossed over Miss Cosgrove's face as she witnessed this exchange. Christopher could see that she was wrestling with her feelings, and he recalled suddenly what Marsali had told him weeks ago— that Miss Cosgrove fancied him, though she herself was engaged to be married.

"You are to be married *here*, on the ship, before we reach America?" she asked, looking from one to the other.

"That is what the plan is, yes." Captain Gower's door opened, and he stepped into the saloon and took his place at the head of the table. Before this morning he had never been late to a meal, that Christopher could recall.

"If Miss Abbott is not married before meeting up with Mr. Thomas, it is not likely to happen," Captain Gower said. He directed his attention to Christopher and Marsali. "However, I am afraid the situation is not as simple as I believed it to be. While it is clearly in my authority while on this ship to do as I see fit regarding matters of importance— including marriage—having that authority recognized elsewhere may prove a difficulty." He dished porridge into his bowl and began spooning sugar over it.

"If it will not be recognized, then why go through with it?" Miss Cosgrove asked. "Why—"

"Because I believe we still have a good chance of pulling this off," Captain Gower said, cutting her off before she could entirely launch into a monologue of questions. "I must ask you to please enjoy your breakfast, Miss Cosgrove, and allow me to speak. There is much that needs to be decided, and Miss Abbott and Mr. Thatcher have little time in which to make those decisions."

Christopher and Marsali exchanged an uneasy glance. He wished he knew what she was thinking.

"I've been reading up on American law this morning," Captain Gower said. "It is vastly important that you are recorded as a married couple before you leave for Virginia. New York recognizes common-law marriages, which is what yours shall be, as I am not authorized clergy, as there were no banns posted, and all of that. New York will recognize your marriage, but Virginia will not—unless, possibly, it is initially recorded in another state."

"Does that mean that Mr. Thomas will not believe us to be married?" Marsali asked, coming to the same conclusion Christopher had.

"It is possible," Captain Gower said. "But you must remember, Thomas is a businessman, first and foremost. In essence, I am offering him a gift in you, Mr. Thatcher. I have to believe that the offer of your free labor for a period of two years will be difficult for him to refuse. No doubt, Miss Abbott, you are a valuable commodity as a lady's maid, but Mr. Thatcher's ability to labor will be far beyond yours, and if Thomas is half as intelligent as I have known him to be, he will see what a bargain he will be getting."

"This isn't right," Marsali said anxiously. Hair had escaped her bun—a frequent occurrence, Christopher had noted—and she began winding the strands around her finger as she worried her lip. He had not seen her doing either of these things since the day she'd first read her sister's letter, and he attributed the habits to the seriousness of her concerns.

"I cannot allow you to go through with this." She tipped her face up to his, and he read the agony in her eyes.

"You already told me yes," he reminded her gently. "It would be most unkind of you to withdraw from our agreement now."

"Do not lose hope as of yet," Captain Gower advised. "I have one other idea in addition to having your marriage recorded when we arrive. It is likely that Mr. Thomas will not be there to greet us in port, as we are arriving a full two days earlier than expected. If that is our good fortune, I suggest you use that time to seek out an official clergyman and have a second ceremony. That way there could be no question as to the validity of your marriage."

"Thank you for the suggestions, Captain." Christopher planned to take both of them, though he worried whether the two pounds in his possession would be enough for the license and any other fees associated with a marriage ceremony.

"In the meantime, I am ready when you are to perform your shipboard wedding."

"After breakfast will be fine," Christopher said, giving Marsali's hand a gentle squeeze. He could not allow her to change her mind. Last night had been the best sleep he'd had since learning of what awaited her in America.

"Having your wedding after breakfast will not be *fine*." Miss Cosgrove jumped back into the conversation with a voice that rose to an unnaturally high pitch. She slapped her palms on the table and stood, fixing a glare upon him.

"We did not mean to pain you, Lydia." Marsali attempted to wriggle her fingers from his, but Christopher held them fast.

He could not allow regret—of any kind—to change her mind. He had never encouraged Miss Cosgrove's attention, and if she had somehow misconstrued the forced kindness he had shown her, the wrongdoing was certainly not Marsali's.

"*I* am not the one who will be pained by this," Miss Cosgrove said, astonishing him—and Marsali, too, given the look on her face.

"It will be you who is pained, Marsali, with this rushed, shipboard ceremony." Miss Cosgrove's eyes narrowed on Christopher once more. "You are speaking of a wedding, a most sacred event, one many girls dream of their entire lives.

Marsali needs a special gown. She ought to have a church and someone to give her away. She should have a posy of flowers. And *after breakfast* will never do. Do you not know that there should *be* a breakfast following the wedding?"

"Miss Cosgrove, perhaps you are unaware that the circumstances are somewhat different than usual," Captain Gower said patiently. "It came to Mr. Thatcher's attention near the start of our voyage that Miss Abbott's life could very well be in danger when she reaches America and joins her new employer. A rushed marriage is her best chance at protection."

"There need be no special preparations," Marsali concurred, rather sensibly, Christopher thought, though he heard the faintest hint of wistfulness in her voice and caught a glimpse of stoic bravery in her smile.

"Nonsense." In a huff of skirts and petticoats, Miss Cosgrove removed herself from the bench and her untouched breakfast. "Mr. Thatcher, if you care for Marsali as much as you profess, will you not then see that she has a proper wedding?"

"I care for her a great deal," Christopher said. "Your definition of proper merely differs from ours." *Or mine.* Marsali was looking down at her lap, and her features had taken on a definite expression of melancholy.

"I beg of you to consider your bride in this." Miss Cosgrove clasped her hands before her as if preparing to offer a most earnest prayer. "You simply cannot marry this morning. Marsali must at least have enough time to get a proper dress ready. She cannot wear that to her wedding."

Marsali flinched. "I haven't any gowns better than this. It is my best, and I wore it purposely this morning."

"There. You see. All is well." Christopher attempted to steer the conversation away from the subject causing his fiancée discomfort. Along with new hair ribbons, he would buy her a new gown as well. Soon. Somehow. "We have what is most important—each other and one with the authority to marry us." He had the ring from Grandfather as well, but he did not wish Marsali to know it just yet. It would be nice to surprise her with something of meaning.

"I must disagree." Lady Cosgrove's voice echoed the length of the saloon. She walked resolutely toward them, head held high, spine rigid. "My daughter is correct. Marriage of convenience or not, it should be done properly. I ought to know, having had two of them myself. Captain Gower, we shall help with the arrangements. It will give Lydia and me something to do these last miserable days aboard your ship."

Captain Gower's lips pressed together in a flat line. No doubt he was offended at hearing the words *miserable* and *your ship* in the same sentence. "My lady, you do not realize what an easy, pleasant voyage we have enjoyed. I pray it will continue a few days more, and I beg of you—when you speak to others of your crossing on the *Amanda May*—that you do so in a complimentary matter. The crew, and even the passengers—" the captain's gaze flitted to Marsali—"have done all they can to ensure your comfort on this voyage. And of course, we shall happily indulge your wishes once more. Do what you will with regard to a wardrobe for Miss Abbott. I shall perform the wedding *tomorrow* morning, and we shall breakfast after. I shall request that Mr. Tenney and his staff prepare something special for the occasion. Is that satisfactory to all here?"

"Oh yes. It's perfect." Miss Cosgrove flung her hands wide and, in her excitement, knocked over her teacup, sending tea splashing all over the front of Lady Cosgrove's gown.

"Lydia!" she screeched. "Look what you've done. Will you never learn to control yourself? Even Miss Abbott's behavior is more civilized—little wonder it was she and not you who was able to attract Mr. Thatcher's interest."

At this Miss Cosgrove burst into tears and ran past her

mother, down the length of the saloon, and into her cabin. Awkward silence descended upon the room.

"That was entirely unnecessary," Christopher said, not much caring what Lady Cosgrove thought of him or his opinions. He held very little regard for hers.

Captain Gower cleared his throat uncomfortably.

"You oughtn't have been so hard on Lydia," Marsali added. "She meant well and was only showing her enthusiasm." Sighing heavily, Marsali turned her gaze on Christopher. "And she *did* fancy you."

"But I did not encourage her," Christopher said defensively, wondering how it was that he had earned a reprimand. He had not spilled the tea or exhibited an inappropriate display of emotion, as he felt both mother and daughter had done. "Is Miss Cosgrove herself not betrothed, to this Mr. Vancer she is forever speaking of?"

"She is, but she will not be much longer if she does not learn to exhibit a bit of decorum," Lady Cosgrove said. "Lydia is *always* showing her enthusiasm, and it is high time she learned to control herself and to curb her tongue. If she continues to act like she has on this ship, I fear Mr. Vancer will soon send us packing."

"Lydia has fears, too," Marsali said. "She is afraid of marriage. Can you not find it in you to comfort her?"

Lady Cosgrove's spine stiffened even more, were that possible. She stood rigidly, the only part of her not perfectly straight being the slope of her nose, from which she stared down at them.

"The only thing that would comfort her would be a change in our situation—an improbability at best. No one comforted me when I lost each of my husbands and had to fend for myself. Lydia must learn to do the same. All women must if they are to survive in this world."

Fending for oneself need not be synonymous with unkindness, Christopher thought. Marsali was proof of that. But he held his tongue, not wishing to cause any more problems between the women, especially not when Lady Cosgrove had offered to help Marsali with a gown to be married in.

"Now, are you going to accompany me or not?" Lady Cosgrove demanded. "We've but one day, and I am not a seamstress."

"I am," Marsali said, surprising Christopher. *How much I still do not know about her.* He was excited for each discovery that lay ahead.

"Go," he said, leaning into her, nudging her with his shoulder. Their hands were still entwined, and he withdrew his now, reluctant to end their touch but wanting her to have as much happiness as possible at their wedding. He did care for her and wanted to make everything about their day as good as it could be. His sisters would be disappointed in him if they learned he had not.

"Are you certain you do not mind waiting until tomorrow?" she asked.

"I would wait much longer to be with you."

She reached up, touching his cheek. "Thank you. But if you change your mind before then, I shall understand entirely."

"I will not," he promised, covering her hand with his.

"Then I shall attempt to come up with something worthy of your fine suit." Marsali stood, leaving the table and the room with Lady Cosgrove and leaving him feeling oddly vacant.

"See what I mean about a woman getting under your skin," Captain Gower said as he reached for a roll and took up his knife.

"Does it ever get better?" Christopher asked. *Will I ever be able to cease thinking of her every minute, worrying over her, wishing she were near?*

"Not if you are lucky." Captain Gower sliced his roll open. "Not if you are very lucky."

CHAPTER

$\mathcal{T}$he atmosphere in the Cosgroves' cabin was stilted at best. When they entered, Lydia looked up from her bed, her eyes puffy from crying. Heedless of what Lady Cosgrove might think of her, Marsali quickly crossed the room, sat, and embraced Lydia.

"You are perfect the way you are," she whispered. "Do not change for anyone, especially not Mr. Vancer. If he does not simply adore you, I shall come to New York myself and help him to realize his good fortune."

Marsali pulled back, and Lydia gave her a tearful smile. "Thank you for being my friend."

"Thank *you* for being mine. Aside from my sister, I have never had a friend before you. We must write to each other when we are in America. And perhaps someday, when we have finished working for Mr. Thomas, Mr. Thatcher and I shall come to one of your fancy masquerade balls."

"You shall both be my guests of honor," Lydia promised, squeezing Marsali's hands. "I am happy for you— truly. Please do not think me envious. I *would* have liked it had Mr. Thatcher fancied me, but Mother would not have cared for it at all, as he has no wealth to recommend him."

"Do you wish to spend the day in sentimental expression, or are we going to select a gown for Miss Abbott?" Lady Cosgrove's tone held no sympathy, and—as she had been earlier at breakfast—Marsali was left puzzled that she had offered to help at all.

"I know just the one." Lydia bounded from the bed, her previous enthusiasm restored in spite of her mother's harshness. She crossed to the trunks lining the wall and raised the lid of the third. "These gowns have not been worn for quite some time," she explained. "We had only just come out of mourning at the start of this journey, and we haven't been to a party or a ball in ever so long."

She bent over, digging through the prettiest fabrics Marsali had ever seen. Anything from that trunk—*any* of Lydia's gowns, even her morning frocks—would be better than Marsali's long-outdated but best green chintz, a hand-me-down from one of the maids at her aunt's house.

"This one," Lydia declared, pulling an exquisite silver-grey gown from the very bottom of the trunk. "I wore this at the second ball of my coming-out season. It was one of my favorites."

"A good choice." Lady Cosgrove nodded her approval. Marsali stepped forward and tentatively touched the lovely gown.

"It won't bite you." Lydia thrust it at her, and Marsali took it, surprised at both its heaviness and how smooth the fabric was.

"It is satin," Lydia said as if sensing Marsali's astonishment.

"The lace was imported from Paris," Lady Cosgrove said. "And all that pleating cost a fine penny. My husband was much astonished when the bill arrived. But Lydia was the envy of every woman in attendance the night she wore that gown."

Marsali had no words. She had never seen or held a gown so beautiful, let alone worn one. Her father's active lifestyle and their frequent outdoor excursions had required that most of her childhood clothing be simple. As she'd grown older, her gowns had changed to the more traditional wear of the upper class. A modiste had come from Lyon twice a year, and Marsali had a vague recollection of being allowed to choose some of the fabrics for her gowns. But she had still been young when they'd moved to England, and many of the luxuries they had become accustomed to—including having fine clothing made—had ended with that move.

Now she was used to practical fabrics with little adornment, and it was not often she thought of or pined for anything else. But holding this gown changed all of that.

She longed to wear it, longed to be beautiful and to have all of the extravagances for her wedding day that Lydia had described at breakfast.

Charlotte's wedding had been simple but lovely. *Because she and Matthew* were *in love.* Marsali did not know if she could make that claim yet—either for herself or Mr. Thatcher, though they each cared a great deal for one another. But to have their day be made special—regardless of their reasons for marrying—suddenly held great appeal.

"Will you really allow me to wear it?" It was all Marsali could do not to hug the dress to her chest or rub her cheek against the soft fabric.

"Of course I will." Lydia laughed. "Though something will have to be done to hem it. You are quite a bit shorter than I am."

"Hemming is quite simple," Marsali assured her. She laid the gown across her arms and lifted the skirt to see what she would have to work with. "I can do an invisible hem, with tiny stitches. It need only be attached to this inner layer. Then, after the wedding, I can unpick the stitches for you, and no one will ever even know it was altered."

"Try it on, then, and we shall pin it."

"Have you needle and thread?" Marsali asked, remembering that her sewing kit had been abandoned at Madame Kelner's.

"We have, though it is embroidery thread. It will have to do, I suppose." Lady Cosgrove walked through the passageway connecting her room with Lydia's. "I shall fetch what we need while Lydia helps you change."

The next hours passed in a happy blur. Once she had the regal gown on, Marsali could hardly bear to take it off. It was amazing how different a fancy gown could make one feel. She stood straighter when wearing it—and not just because of the restrictive stays beneath. She felt like a princess in a fairytale, no longer Marsali Abbott, a girl alone in the world who must work hard for her bread.

When the hem had been measured and was pinned, she reluctantly allowed Lady Cosgrove and Lydia to help her from it. Then Lady Cosgrove left to speak with Captain Gower, and Marsali and Lydia sat on the bed and visited while Marsali sewed the tiniest, neatest stitches she had ever made. She had no wish to repay Lydia's kindness by ruining her dress.

"It is doubtful it fits me any longer," Lydia remarked with a sigh after asking Marsali why she was taking such great care. "I was both shorter and thinner at sixteen than I am now."

"I should hope you were not thinner," Marsali said, her eyes going to Lydia's trim waistline. "Especially considering the week and a half of sickness you've just endured."

Marsali asked Lydia to show her the other gowns in her trunks and enjoyed the ensuing fashion parade and the layers of silks and satins and ruffles and ribbons that began piling up on the bed beside her. Near the noon hour, when the gown was at last finished, Marsali leaned back, resting her head against the wall and feeling a happy contentment.

"And this is the one I wore when I received my very first kiss." Lydia held a deep purple silk in front of her.

"Your *first* kiss?" Marsali said. "How many have you had?"

"Just two. From the same man." Lydia smiled wistfully, and her eyes drifted to the window. "I wish now that I had run away with him. Had I known what was to become my fate, I would have."

Instead of asking of whom she spoke, Marsali tried to steer Lydia's attention back to the present and the future that was shortly to be hers. "Perhaps you will feel the same about Mr. Vancer. No doubt he has been thinking of you these many weeks, anticipating your arrival."

"Do you think so?" Lydia sat on the edge of the bed, the purple dress folded over her arm, its memories temporarily forgotten.

"I do." Marsali sat up straight and scooted closer to her. "He *must* be thinking of you. And I believe that once he comes to know you, he shall care for you a great deal." It was true—or so she hoped it was. Beneath Lydia's incessant chatter was a delightful and caring woman. If Mr. Vancer would only allow for Lydia's nerves and give her time to get past them, he very well could come to love her.

"Has Mr. Thatcher kissed you?" Lydia leaned closer, her hand clutching Marsali's as if she would not release it until Marsali had spilled all of her secrets.

"He has. Right here." Marsali pointed to her nose.

Lydia giggled. "That does not count. A real kiss is given on the lips."

"Perhaps," Marsali conceded. "Nevertheless, I enjoyed it very much." Though she recalled her disappointment when he had released her and told her the captain's quarters were no place for a first kiss.

"Have you fallen in love with him?" Lydia asked. "And has he told you he loves you?"

"He has not," Marsali said, feeling a bit disappointed

with the admission, though Mr. Thatcher's actions had shown that he cared a great deal for her. "I am not certain what it is I feel for him." Had *she* fallen in love? Marsali could not be certain, having never allowed her thoughts to stray to that possibility until late last night. "I am very fond of him, and when I am with him I feel different, more alive somehow."

"Does your stomach quiver like it is made of jelly, and do you feel as if you might faint?" Lydia pressed.

"No." Marsali shook her head. "That does not sound like love. That sounds dreadful!"

"Oh, but it isn't," Lydia exclaimed. "It is wonderful. You feel as if your feet are not quite touching the ground and you are walking among clouds. You are happy for no apparent reason. Your heart seems to swell." She pressed a hand to her chest.

"I should think that would be painful." Marsali rose from the bed on the pretense of putting away the gowns. She did not wish Lydia to see the truth registering on her face, for the feelings she had described of inordinate happiness and walking among clouds rang true.

Lydia changed position to better follow Marsali's movements. "When you love a man, he is your first thought in the morning and your last at night, and you want nothing more than to be with him constantly. Parting is agony. But when he touches you . . ."

"Yes?" Marsali looked over her shoulder as she placed a peach dress in the trunk. "What happens when he touches you?"

Lydia batted her eyes coyly. "Well, if you don't know by now—if Mr. Thatcher has not affected you in any way—then I fear you've little hope of it being a love match."

Marsali did not reply but took her time folding the sleeves of the gown carefully, so they would not wrinkle. The trouble was, she *did* know. When Christopher touched her—even slightly—it was as if a flame ignited inside her. He had been her last thought before she drifted off to sleep for many nights on this voyage. And he had definitely been her first this morning. She suspected Lydia was very much wrong and that theirs *was* a love match—for her at least.

CHAPTER  27

*L*ydia fastened a string of delicate pearls around Marsali's neck and stood before her. "Oh, I wish you had a mirror to see yourself."

Marsali wished the same as she fastened matching pearl earrings in place. Lady Cosgrove had shown continued and surprising generosity, insisting that Marsali have both gloves and jewelry for the occasion and producing each for her to borrow.

"You look beautiful. Just like a princess." Lydia grasped Marsali's hands and danced her around the cabin. "If Mr. Thatcher is not madly in love with you already, he will be when he sees you this morning."

Marsali only smiled in reply. Beyond her conversation with Lydia yesterday, she had not allowed herself to dwell on the possibility of a love match. "Mr. Thatcher is marrying me to keep me safe. Had the problem with Mr. Thomas not arisen, I very much doubt we would be about to speak wedding vows." For now, she had decided it was best to remember that. She wanted to be a good wife to Christopher and strongly suspected she was half in love with him already.

But last night Captain Gower had made very clear to them the terms of their marriage and the strict discipline that they would, in all likelihood, be required to follow.

It was probable, he had explained, that she and Christopher would not be allowed to live together as husband and wife but that she would live in the main house, where she might attend to her duties as a lady's maid, and he would be required to live with the field hands, or wherever it was the servants who worked out of doors resided.

Christopher had not taken this news well. "How am I supposed to protect Marsali if I am never with her?"

"You won't be with her much," Captain Gower said. "But you will at least see each other often—hopefully every day."

The room was silent as each considered this.

"You must promise me," Christopher had said to her at last, "that you will always be honest with me. If Thomas or anyone else has threatened you or hurt you—if you feel you are in danger in any way—you must let me know."

"I will," Marsali had promised, all the while thinking that she was already in danger—or her heart was. The day before, she had believed she and Mr. Thatcher would part in New York, and that had made her sorrowful. But to that point she had guarded her feelings well and not allowed them to go where they would. But now that had all changed. She had given in to the emotion she'd been fighting these past weeks. She had believed she and Christopher were to be together, and the idea of seeing him only briefly each day made her wish to weep. How would she ever endure such an arrangement? It would be a constant torture, having him so close, yet not being allowed to be with him.

"We will make this work." Christopher had clasped her hand as they sat together in the window seat of the captain's quarters. "And appreciate what time we have together all the more for it."

"They are ready for you." Lady Cosgrove stood in the

doorway of her cabin, bringing Marsali back to the very happy present of her wedding day, which she intended to enjoy to the fullest. *No use worrying over what is to come*, she reminded herself but found the edict more difficult now that Christopher was involved.

She stepped into the hallway and found Mr. Murphy waiting for her. In addition to the usual cleaning of his nails and teeth, he appeared to have bathed and obtained a new suit of clothing that appeared suspiciously like one of Mr. Luke's uniforms. It was stretched tightly across Murphy's stomach, and the sleeves were cuffed on his shorter arms, but all in all he had cleaned up rather well.

"Mr. Murphy, how dashing you look this morning."

"And you, miss. I like them gloves."

Gloves? She wore this gorgeous dress and a string of pearls at her throat, and all he could think to comment on was her gloves? *No matter.* "Why, thank you," she said graciously. "They are Miss Cosgrove's. She has kindly shared this ensemble with me." Marsali swept her hand over the lush skirt, lest he had somehow failed to notice her gown.

"Well, now. Captain says I'm to escort you up to the deck. And then he says I'll be relieved of watching out for you for the rest of our trip—whole day and a half of it we've left."

Marsali bit back a laugh at his gruff tone. No doubt poor Mr. Murphy had been disgruntled throughout much of this voyage, having to keep an eye on her as he had. "I do appreciate your attentiveness at keeping me safe."

"Hmph. Not safe enough, it appears. There's a gentleman up top says he plans to marry you." Mr. Murphy cracked a grin—the first Marsali had seen from him this entire voyage.

She laughed along with him and took his arm when he extended it to her. "Had I known you were in the market for a husband, I would have asked first," he confided as they left the room.

"What a pity Mr. Thatcher beat you to it," Marsali said, quite enjoying their exchange and this new side to her chaperone. Lydia and Lady Cosgrove trailed behind but then called for Marsali to wait before they reached the stairs to the upper deck.

"Stay here," Lady Cosgrove instructed. "I shall call down to you when all is ready. Mr. Murphy, join me for a moment, please."

They left, and Marsali waited, puzzled at what else needed to be readied—*the groom is here, isn't he?*

A moment later Mr. Tenney came down the stairs. Looking slightly embarrassed, he thrust what appeared to be a fistful of fragile, rapidly wilting plants at her.

"Your posy. It's not much, but parsley and dill were the only things we've left growing. Everything else I've used up or has died."

"Why, thank you," Marsali said as enthusiastically as she could and hoped it was enough that she hadn't hurt his feelings. The bundled stalks were so thin that they could not support the tops of the sprouting herbs unless she held them above the ribbon tied midstem.

"It doesn't look like much, but dill is good luck on your wedding day," Mr. Tenney informed her with an air of importance.

"Oh?" Marsali's brows rose in question.

He nodded. "Give that back to me after the ceremony." He pointed to the sad bouquet. "I'll cut it up and put it in your soup tonight. It'll help with, well—you know."

She didn't, actually, but could guess well enough from his sudden discomfort. "Thank you—that is most kind." She made a mental note to eat very little soup tonight and to encourage Christopher to do the same. They had enough difficulties before them without an overabundance of dill— and its effects—added.

Mr. Tenney left her, and Mr. Murphy returned. "Ready?" he asked, offering his arm once more.

She took it, and they started up the stairs. They reached the upper deck, and Mr. Murphy paused just as the boatswain's shrill whistle of attention sounded. Lady Cosgrove and Lydia and the crew assembled on deck; all rose from the benches they had been sitting on and turned to face her.

Marsali didn't know where to look first—at the faces all smiling at her or at the cook's assistants, struggling with the captain's accordion in their attempt to create some sort of music for the occasion, or at the captain himself, standing next to the ship's large brass bell, at the top of the aisle that had been formed by the benches brought up from the saloon.

She clutched the wilting herbs tightly as tears of happiness sprang to her eyes. The music sounded awful, and the breeze was already pulling her hair from its bun. The sky looked very much like it might rain. And it was entirely possible that this marriage would not be recognized once they reached Virginia, but her heart was full, and she had never felt so loved. They had done all this for her. Even Lady Cosgrove had shown that, deep down, she cared as well.

Mr. Murphy glanced at her. "Are you well?"

"Never more so." Marsali took her first step up the makeshift aisle, which was lined with what appeared to be extra sails swathed and tied along the lengths of the rows of benches. Christopher appeared on the other side of the bell, standing straight and tall and looking almost princely in his suit with the brilliant blues of the ocean behind him. Everything and everyone else faded away as their eyes met.

Her heart pounded and felt as Lydia had described—as if it might swell and burst, or *she* might burst from sheer happiness.

Can this be real? If she could have come up with the perfect dream, this would be it. Christopher was her knight in shining armor; he really was going to save her. And, even better, she was in love with him.

256

CHAPTER  28

Christopher's experience with brides and weddings had been limited to his sisters and their double ceremony the past February. He had recalled that they were each especially beautiful that day, happy to be marrying the men they loved, and wearing the ivory gowns Grandfather had given them. He remembered that the grooms had shown little sign of nerves, save for Samuel, who had at first been unaware that he and Helen were to be married that day as well.

The ceremony had seemed to go on forever. And afterward each of his sisters had exchanged a kiss with their husbands—right there in the church—which had about sent Grace's new mother-in-law into an apoplexy. Personally, Christopher had thought it rather gutsy of his sisters, particularly Helen. Though all that kissing nonsense was not for him.

Or so he had believed.

He'd had second thoughts about that recently—a complete change of heart, to be accurate. He'd thought of little else the past two nights, other than when and where he would first kiss Marsali. It would not be at their wedding, that much was certain. He'd known for a fact that each of his sisters had been kissed prior to being married and that the occasion had been one of great importance to them. It had been a private affair for each—or so they'd believed, though he had secretly witnessed Helen and Samuel's first kiss from an upstairs window of the house.

But I have no gazebo, and it is unlikely we will find a moment alone at sunset. Christopher realized that he should have taken advantage of the moments alone with Marsali in the captain's quarters two nights ago, but the timing hadn't felt right to him. Their courtship had been almost nonexistent. Their wedding had to be rushed. Even the terms of their marriage were not to be the usual, and he would, in all likelihood, have little time with her in the weeks and months to come. Therefore it had become imperative to him that their first kiss—perhaps their only kiss for quite some time—should be special. Memorable.

We must make a memory to sustain us through what lies ahead. To help solidify what we have well begun.

He had no doubt that regardless of what they faced, he would remember. *She is the miracle of this voyage—of my life,* he thought as Marsali began her walk down the aisle toward him.

He'd professed to detesting fancy gowns, but his opinion regarding that now also changed—instantly—when he saw her floating toward him, a vision in grey satin and lace and pearls. There could never have been a more beautiful bride, anywhere, anytime, throughout history. He had no idea how he had come to be so fortunate as to be the one marrying her but knew only that he felt in awe of his good circumstance. Not only was his wife-to-be extraordinarily beautiful, but beneath that beauty was a delightful, strong, and spirited woman. They suited each other amazingly well.

He loved her, and it terrified him. He had worried over and loved his sisters, but this was infinitely worse—and better. It seemed impossible that something so earth-shattering could have happened so quickly—to him, of all people—but there was no other way to describe the feelings overwhelming him. He would have fallen to his knees in front of her and asked for her hand before all these people if that's what it had taken to convince her to take this chance. He would work for Thomas for her; he would wait for her; he would do whatever it was that needed to be done.

He wanted to protect her, to make her happy.

As happy as she has made me.

Marsali's eyes never left his throughout the entire walk across the deck to the "altar"—the ship's bell. Every step brought her closer, but neither fast enough nor close enough for his satisfaction. He wanted to touch her again, to hold her hand, to hold her close. To talk with her and hear her laughter, to learn of her hurts and heal them. He wanted hours and days and weeks in which to discover more about this woman he was pledging his life to.

But at the most they had another day at sea and perhaps one more in New York.

When Marsali had nearly reached them, Captain Gower grimaced toward the struggling musician at the back of the crowd and drew his hand quickly across his neck. He winced as the screeching notes slowed to a painful halt. Everyone seemed to breathe a collective sigh of relief as the accordion was set aside. Christopher bit back laughter and could see that Marsali was struggling to contain hers as well.

We will remember this day, without doubt, he thought as he felt the first raindrop on the back of his hand and glanced at the darkening sky. Hopefully they would be able to recall it for more reasons than the amusement provided thus far.

"Who gives this woman in marriage?" Captain Gower asked with authority as Marsali stopped before him.

"I do," Mr. Murphy said loudly.

"Is there anyone here who objects to a union between them—between this woman and *that* man?" Captain Gower inclined his head toward Christopher.

Miss Cosgrove sniffled, and there were a few coughs covering up sniggers of laughter, but there were no objections. Mr. Luke, Christopher noted, was nowhere to be seen and had likely been assigned duties that kept him elsewhere during this time.

Mr. Murphy held Marsali's hand out toward Christopher.

He stepped forward and took it, pausing long enough to bow and lift her gloved fingers to his lips before leading her to stand with him in front of the captain.

"The congregation may be seated." Captain Gower opened a large Bible, held it in front of him in both arms, cleared his throat, and began reading from a paper resting between the pages. "Marriage is ordained of God. The scriptures tell us that the twain shall be one. In Psalms we read . . ."

Another drop landed on his nose, and Christopher scooted closer to Marsali so that their shoulders were touching, as if that might somehow protect her from the impending rain. He wondered if the captain had planned to read from the Bible or if Lady Cosgrove had put him up to it. Christopher guessed it was the latter, as she had been the force behind everything from the attempted music to the arrangement of the benches and sails on deck. She'd even spoken with him last night about a wedding ring for Marsali, giving him the idea that she might have offered one of hers for the occasion had he not already had the one Grandfather had given him.

Either he had judged Lady Cosgrove wrong, or her sudden interest and generosity in Marsali was an attempt to repay her for the service rendered during Miss Cosgrove's illness.

"The purposes of marriage are as follows." Captain

Gower's head bent low as he read. "'First, for the procreation of children to be—'" He stopped suddenly and cleared his throat before sending a furtive glance at Christopher. "Never mind that one. Not now, anyway," he muttered under his breath.

Tugging at his beard with one hand, the captain buried his face in the book once more. "'Second, as a remedy against sin, to avoid forn—'" He let out a loud, exasperated breath. "Disregard that one as well." He sent an accusing glare in Lady Cosgrove's direction. "'*Third*, marriage was ordained for mutual society, help, and comfort—both in prosperity and adversity.' Well, that's better," he declared loudly.

Confident smile back in place, the captain looked up, even as beads of sweat appeared on his brow beneath his cap. "'Into which holy estate these two persons present come now to be joined.' Face one another and join hands, please."

Marsali removed her gloves and handed them, along with the sad clump of herbs she had been clutching, to Miss Cosgrove before turning to face him.

Christopher felt inordinately pleased at the laughter he saw in the depths of her eyes. He could tell she was not put off by any of the abnormality of their ceremony but amused by it, as was he. He took both of her hands in his and brought each to his lips as he held her gaze.

He heard Lady Cosgrove's cluck of disapproval but did not care. *The ceremony be damned.* He was in love with Marsali, and he wished her to know it. Vows and promises might show his commitment, but his display of affection was important as well. Christopher understood that now.

"*Finally*," he could imagine his sisters saying, were they present.

"Mr. Thatcher first—*if* you are done devouring your bride's fingers," Captain Gower said sternly. "It would be good to get this done before the rain descends in earnest."

Marsali laughed as pink tinted her cheeks.

Christopher flattened his lips and attempted an

appropriately solemn expression. He was about to be married, after all. Strange, how he was not the least concerned. He had always imagined that if such a time ever came, it would be with some reluctance that he faced it.

"'Wilt thou have this woman to be thy wedded wife?'" Captain Gower asked. "'To live together after God's ordinance in the holy estate of matrimony? Wilt thou love her, comfort her, honor, and keep her in sickness and in health; and, forsaking all others, keep only unto her, so long as you both shall live?'"

"I will," Christopher said. The words settled over him, bringing a deep contentment. *Keep unto her as long as you both shall live.* He squeezed Marsali's hands gently, again feeling the need to offer her physical proof as well as his words.

"Miss Abbott." Captain Gower leaned forward, attempting to shelter the Bible from the raindrops increasing in frequency. "'Wilt thou have this man to be thy wedded husband, to live together after God's ordinance in the holy estate of matrimony? Wilt thou obey him, and serve him, love, honor, and keep him in sickness and in health; and, forsaking all others, keep only unto him, so long as you both shall live?'"

"I will." Marsali's eyes appeared overbright, and Christopher worried she might be about to cry, until she gave him one of her radiant smiles.

"The ring, please," Captain Gower said.

Marsali looked to the captain, her mouth open, as if to remind him there was no ring, when the cabin boy stepped from behind the bell, bearing Grandfather's ring on his open palm.

"Thank you, Marc." Christopher released Marsali's hands and took the ring. The diamond had belonged to a grandmother he had never met, and now it would belong to his wife.

"Where . . . how?" Marsali looked over her shoulder at Lady Cosgrove.

"It isn't mine," Lady Cosgrove said, shaking her head. "Ask your husband."

"My grandfather gave it to me," Christopher said when she looked at him again. He held the ring up so she could better see it. "I promised him I would give it to no one but the woman I *loved*—and married. If not for that promise, I would have sold it to free you from your contract."

"There was a better solution," Captain Gower said.

"Yes," Marsali agreed. "I am relieved you didn't break your promise—for many reasons." Her voice quivered as she held her hand out. Christopher slipped the ring over her finger.

Marsali stared at the ring a moment, then clutched her hand tightly to her chest. Christopher pulled her to him, holding her close. The assembled crew members let out a cheer and clapped. The accordion started up again, screeching painfully, causing them both to laugh until a clap of thunder made Marsali jump.

"Wait. Silence!" Captain Gower bellowed. "We haven't finished yet. They haven't spoken their vows. I haven't declared them man and wife. There is more to this ceremony." He pulled the paper from between the pages of the Bible and waved it overhead.

"I think it is enough, Captain," Lady Cosgrove said approvingly. "The important parts have been said. The rest is up to them, and I believe they shall do very well."

Captain Gower placed the paper back inside the book and slammed it shut. "I've got to make it official at least. Do you her wed with that ring?" he asked Christopher.

Still holding Marsali close, Christopher answered. "I do."

"And you accept and pledge your troth to him and all that?" the captain asked Marsali.

"Yes, I do." She laid her head against Christopher's shoulder.

A flash of lightning lit the sky behind them.

"In that case I now pronounce you husband and wife. For better or worse, sickness and health, and rain and everything else."

Thunder echoed across the sky once more, as fat raindrops began to pour down upon them.

Captain Gower tucked the book beneath his arm. "Just watch out for each other, all right?"

"We will." They spoke in unison as the ship's bell began pealing and the accordion started up a third time.

"Get that thing inside," the captain bellowed. "We're done here. All hands to your stations. Storm's coming!"

"Congratulations, *Mrs. Thatcher*." Christopher placed his arm around Marsali and steered her toward the stairs.

"And to you, Mr. Thatcher." She tipped her face up to him, and a raindrop landed on her lips.

It would have been so easy to kiss it away, to hold her in his arms right here, where they could have at least a modicum of privacy with the others rushing inside to shelter or to their posts.

But the timing still wasn't right.

Patience, he told himself again as they followed Lady Cosgrove and her daughter into the saloon for the wedding breakfast. *She is your wife now. You have the rest of your life to kiss her.*

He hoped it would be a very long life but a very short servitude.

CHAPTER 29

As she had been expecting, at exactly ten o'clock Christopher knocked on Marsali's door. She opened it quietly, lest Captain Gower hear.

"Mrs. Thatcher, might I interest you in an evening stroll on deck to look at the stars?" Christopher whispered.

"I keep wondering to whom you are speaking when you say that." Marsali tied her wrap securely over her nightgown, then bent down to retrieve her shoes from the floor.

"With you attached to it, I have decided the name Thatcher is not detestable at all," Christopher said. "In fact, I am rather fond of it now."

"I *adore* it." She pulled the door closed softly behind her and followed him out into the hall. Lady Cosgrove would be entirely scandalized to see Marsali parading around in her sleeping attire, but Marsali did not particularly care what anyone thought of her tonight—except for her husband.

Marsali wrapped her hand around his arm and leaned into him as they left the saloon. "Who has the watch tonight?"

"Our favorite first officer." Christopher's lips turned down in a scowl she found endearing.

"Dear Mr. Luke." Marsali felt the tiniest bit sorry for him. The captain had assigned him so many shifts lately.

"The one and only. And you can bet he'll tell the captain we were out alone together at night." Christopher paused to look up at the sky. "No stargazing tonight. Too many clouds."

"No matter," Marsali said. There would be other nights with stars—many, many nights. "And if Mr. Luke does see us, all the better that we are outside than *in* alone together at night." Marsali felt—as she had earlier—rather perturbed about the restrictions that came with their marriage. So she could not become with child. That did not mean a husband and wife could not be alone together, did it? She only wished to spend time with Christopher, to enjoy his companionship, to converse.

And perhaps to have that kiss he's promised.

Holding back a sigh, she bent to put her shoes on now that they were outside.

"It's cooler tonight, and the air feels heavy," Christopher remarked as he lit the lantern he'd brought from his cabin.

"Fog," Marsali said grudgingly. "Just as we had in Manchester. I had hoped America would be different."

"Maybe Virginia will be." Christopher took her hand and led her out to the main deck, toward the wheel.

"Mr. Luke is not there," Marsali said, pointing to the empty post.

Christopher shrugged. "No doubt he will be shortly. But let's not waste our time worrying about him. I should like the evening to discover more about my wife—not the first officer who tried to steal her."

"He did no such thing." Marsali tugged at Christopher's hand. "This way. Hurry. And put out that lantern." She led him carefully across the deck to the side where the lifeboats were stowed. Stopping beneath the one she'd sought refuge in the other day, she asked, "What do you think?"

His mischievous grin was answer enough. "You first. I'll keep a lookout."

Marsali didn't wait to be told again but gathered a fistful of her nightgown in one hand and climbed on top of the nearest crate. From there she hopped to the top of a barrel of water, then leaned over to catch the edge of the rigging. Five squares up, and she was able to let go and hoist herself into the boat. Christopher was right behind her, and she'd barely scooted over and tugged her wrap back in place when he landed beside her. The lifeboat wobbled for a second, and she gripped the side.

"Sorry." Christopher slid forward and lowered himself between the seats, to the center of the boat. "I weigh a bit more than you. We'll have to be careful to keep it balanced."

"Why do they store them like this, anyway?" Marsali asked, sitting on the floor beside him and arranging her gown carefully.

"More room on deck, I suppose," Christopher said. "And it would be faster to launch them, as they're already hooked up to the pulleys."

She suppressed a shudder. "How terrifying that would be. I'm glad ours has been a calm crossing."

"It has been anything *but* calm." He searched for her hand in the dark and found it. "I came on this trip seeking peace, and look what happened. Now I've a wife!"

"Most fortunate, don't you think?" Marsali attempted to bat her lashes coyly, as she'd seen Lydia do, though the effort was likely lost on him in the darkness.

"*Extremely* fortunate." Christopher put his arm around her and pulled her close. She leaned her head against his shoulder and sighed contentedly. "I think I should like to stay here all night with you."

"We should have brought our pillows," Christopher lamented.

"There are some pieces of cork beneath the seats." Marsali stretched and pressed her toe against one. "I used them the other day to be more comfortable."

"You did look quite cozy when I peeked at you," Christopher said. "Ensconced as you were and lost in the book you were reading."

"I wasn't really reading," Marsali confessed. "I'd finished the book earlier that day. I was thinking."

"About Thomas?" Christopher's tone turned serious. "We should discuss him before tomorrow."

"I know we should, but not now. And no," she said, tipping her face up to him, "I was up here thinking about *you*, about how you are like Hawkeye from *Last of the Mohicans*."

Christopher snorted loudly. "My wife is blessed with a keen imagination."

Marsali placed a finger over his lips. "Shh. Do you want them to discover us here?" She paused, remembering something that had been nagging at her for the past couple of days. "How did you know I was up here the other afternoon? I wasn't making any noise."

"Your hair ribbon." Christopher turned to her. "It was floating up with the breeze, along with wisps of your pretty hair."

"My hair is not pretty," Marsali said. "When I was younger, maybe, but—"

It was Christopher who silenced her this time, his finger brushing over her lips in a soft caress. "Long or short, your hair will always be lovely to me." He reached out to touch it, then stopped. "May I?"

Her eyes closed. "Yes." He touched the side of her face, then moved to her hair. He found a pin and pulled it out, then another and another until her curls were freed and tumbled to her shoulders. Gently he ran his hand down the length of her hair, careful not to pull it. "You should wear it down more often."

"Perhaps someday," she murmured, lost in his touch—truly taken to another place, as he had teased her about previously. How was it that something so simple could seem so profound? She felt as she had that day at the washtub—as if she might simply melt into a puddle.

"In the book, Cora wore her hair down," he teased gently.

"I did not say I was like Cora," Marsali said. "And you are not like Hawkeye. Though your hair has grown enough on this voyage that it does brush your collar now." She had noticed that earlier when they were standing close and speaking their vows. She longed to touch it as he had touched hers a moment ago but still felt too shy to make such a request. "Anyway, do not compare us. Theirs was not a happy ending. Ours will be better."

"Ours will be *much* better," he agreed. "But who knows, perhaps after a year in America I will look like Hawkeye—wearing buckskin breeches and with my hair so long I must tie it back."

Marsali laughed. "What would your sisters think had become of you?"

Christopher's mischievous grin appeared. "Wouldn't it be grand if they could see me thus? I shall have to stay in touch with Captain Gower and see what becomes of the camera obscura. It may be that someday I can send them a likeness—of both of us. I suppose I will simply have to allow my hair to grow until then."

"I may hold you to that," she said, enjoying the way it curled on his neck now.

They did not speak for a while after that, but sat, content to be close, to be touching one another.

Marsali might have fallen asleep, she wasn't certain, but his arm around her was so comforting. She could have stayed here forever.

"I do not see why Captain Gower *suggested* that we not share a cabin tonight," she said sometime later, groggy with both sleepiness and from Christopher's gentle touch. "We are perfectly capable of controlling our emotions within the limits that we must."

"Speak for yourself." A low growl rumbled in Christopher's throat. "One of us is in agony."

She sat up quickly. "That is a terrible thing to say to your wife, Mr. Thatcher."

"Not when it's true. I thought you were causing me to go mad before we married, but this is far worse. To know you're mine and to not be able to—"

"Do not even say it." Marsali pressed a finger to his lips once more. She rose up on her knees before him and shook her head as she gave him her most solemn look. "I do hope this isn't a mistake." She leaned forward and pressed her lips to his in a quick, efficient kiss.

His eyes widened before she glimpsed a corner of his mouth lift. "That is what I have been waiting for."

"Good." Marsali leaned back, prepared to return to their previous position, sitting side by side.

"Oh, no you don't." Christopher caught her arms and held her in place in front of him. "I could not determine why the timing to kiss you never seemed right. Now I understand. I was waiting for *you* to kiss me first."

"And so I have." Marsali attempted to squirm from his grasp, but he would not let her go. "Please do not make any more of it," she begged. "I know a proper lady would never do such a thing, but I wanted to kiss you tonight, and we both know that I—"

His lips silenced her. Their contact was not fleeting as hers had been when she had kissed him a moment ago; his mouth lingered over hers, warm and soft. He pulled away slightly. "Do you feel it yet?"

"What?"

He kissed her again, a deeper kiss this time, as if he was searching for something within her—the fire that had flared to life at their first contact.

Marsali's heartbeat quickened, and she grasped his shoulders, fearful she would lose her balance, he was making her head spin so.

"Now?" his lips whispered over hers. He did not wait for her answer but kissed her a third time. She clung to him, and his arms came around her waist, pulling her onto his lap. He touched her face, cradling it in the palms of his hands. And still he kissed her. She was long out of breath and certain her heart would explode any minute. Their kiss was glorious. She was soaring, but there was something else . . . just beyond her reach.

"Now—" she gasped, pulling away, scrambling off his lap and practically climbing out of the boat, "I understand."

He chuckled. "Not so easy, is it?"

"No." She ran her hands through her tousled hair, then realized her nightgown and wrapper were no longer covering her ankles and tugged them down again. All the while her husband watched her, a knowing smile on his face.

"Do not be afraid of me, Marsali. I would never do anything to hurt you."

"I know." She drew in a deep breath, willing her heart to slow to normal—or as near normal as possible. She doubted it would ever be quite the same again. "It's not you I'm afraid of, but me. You make me feel—"

"Desperate and reckless?" He pulled her closer and faced her away from him, putting his arms around her once more.

"I was thinking more of exhilarated and passionate."

"Mmm. Those are good too. I'll take them."

"Not tonight you won't." *This is going to be impossible.*

"Not tonight," Christopher agreed. He rested his chin on the top of her head. "Lean against me and go to sleep, Marsali. Tomorrow will come soon enough."

"Marsali, wake up. It's raining. We're getting wet."

Christopher shook her gently, but she only snuggled closer into the crook of his arm. "Or one of us is getting wet," he said, noting that the sleeve of the arm that had been around her was soaked.

He held her away and leaned her head against a piece of cork, and still she did not awaken. *My wife can sleep through anything.* He wasn't certain whether that was a good thing or not, but it amused him. He stood carefully, pulling the heavy canvas cover from the side of the boat where it was bunched, over to them, using it to cover them the best he could. He guessed Marsali had removed it the other day and forgotten to replace it. They were lucky the morning storm had passed quickly and the boat had time to dry out before they'd climbed in.

He crawled beneath the canvas and lay beside her, listening to the even rhythm of her breathing and the steady patter of rain. The wind was picking up as well. They wouldn't be able to stay here much longer. Without the canvas properly attached at the sides, the boat would soon begin taking on water. Still, he was loath to leave. This might be the only night he had to spend with Marsali, and he wanted to cherish every moment. Even watching her sleep was a luxury.

The sky lit briefly, outlining her face and the delicate features he'd admired the first time he'd seen her. A thunderclap followed all too quickly, loud enough that the boat seemed to tremble, and Marsali woke with a start.

"Not to worry," he soothed.

"Christopher." Her hand reached for him in the dark. He took it and pressed it to his heart. He loved hearing her say his name.

"There's another storm. We need to go inside." He felt reluctant to go, though he knew it foolish to remain. "Come." He pulled her up, and they crawled toward the end of the boat nearest the rigging. "Do you wish to go first?"

"No." She shivered. "You go and then help me down, please. It was tricky last time when I wasn't in the dark."

Christopher swung his leg over the side of the boat as another bolt of lightning flashed in the sky. Marsali screeched and clambered after him. He jumped to the barrel and reached for her, catching her around the waist and holding her close as the answering thunderclap boomed overhead.

"What are you doing up there?" Captain Gower shouted, stomping toward them across the deck, his oil coat flapping behind him.

"Oh, dear," Marsali said.

Christopher kept hold of her hand and guided her from the barrel to the crate. He jumped down and had just lowered her to the deck when the captain arrived.

"What were you doing up there? And in a storm! Look at this lightning! Do you want to get her killed? I married the two of you so you'd keep her safe."

"It wasn't storming when we went up there," Marsali said meekly. "And it was my idea. We were only sleeping."

Christopher didn't see the need to make excuses. The captain had given his suggestions, but they were married now, and what they did was their own concern. "This is the only night we are to have together. What would you have done, Captain?"

Captain Gower grumbled something unintelligible. "Get inside and get out of those wet clothes—in your own cabins!" He stomped past them, shouting orders to the crew on deck to tie down the sails and make sure everything was secure.

Mr. Jones passed them as they attempted to move over the rolling deck toward the saloon.

"Captain," he called. "Mr. Luke said you want the boilers at full capacity."

"Aye," Captain Gower shouted back through the rain pelting the deck. "We're not going to ride out this storm, but maybe we'll outrun it. We're not waiting until tomorrow.

273

Take us home, Mr. Jones. Full steam ahead to New York Harbor."

Christopher reached the door of the saloon and pulled it open for Marsali to enter ahead of him just as lightning struck a third time, hitting the center mast of the ship. The air sizzled around them, and he felt his hairs stand on end. Time seemed horrifyingly suspended as the entire deck lit up as brightly as if it was midday. Everyone stood as if frozen in place, looks of terror on their faces, their heads all tilted upward, drawn toward the sky and the powerful force of nature suspended from it.

A sudden recollection came to him, of the conversation from the start of their voyage, wherein he had mentioned that a steamship was seen by some as a challenge to Mother Nature—to God. Christopher didn't think he believed that, but the power flowing through him—through his hand linked with Marsali's and to his other still on the metal doorknob—felt frighteningly real.

Marsali screamed, and time moved again. He jerked his hand from the knob and found his palm burned.

"Fire!"

"It's the mast. Get it before it reaches the wheel or the deck." Feet pounded toward the blaze already engulfing nearly the entire length of the mast. The barrel he and Marsali had just stood on was wrenched open and a bucket brigade formed.

Christopher started forward, knowing he must help, but Marsali held him back. "Don't leave me." She was crying, frightened as he had never seen her.

"I won't." His decision was made in a split second. He was a husband now. He would stay with her and leave the crew to its duties. They entered the saloon and found Lady Cosgrove near hysterics.

"Lydia is gone. She's missing. She isn't in her bed."

"What?" Marsali let go of Christopher and ran into the

Cosgroves' shared cabin. Christopher followed, verifying with her that the room was indeed empty.

"She never even put her nightgown on. I can't think where she would be. Find her," Lady Cosgrove implored, grasping Marsali's hands.

"We will," Christopher promised. "Wait inside," he said to Marsali. "Check all the other cabins. I'll learn if anyone has seen her on deck."

"Be careful." She grasped his hand and brought it to her lips.

He pulled her close and kissed her swiftly. "You as well." He pulled away and ran outside to find that the fire had reached the deck.

CHAPTER 30

*M*arsali braced both palms on the table as the ship rose sharply and pitched forward.

Beside her, Lady Cosgrove lost her grip and was flung back into the door of one of the vacant cabins.

"Are you all right?" Marsali fell to her knees and held her hand out toward Lady Cosgrove.

The saloon door banged open, and she turned toward it, hoping to see Christopher with Lydia in tow. Instead Mr. Luke stood in the open doorway, his stark figure momentarily silhouetted in the flash of lightning behind him.

"To the lifeboats, ladies." He strode toward them as Marsali stood, then helped Lady Cosgrove rise.

"We can't," Marsali said. "Lydia is missing, and Christopher has gone to find her."

"I've my orders, and they are to put you in a boat and get you away from this ship." He held his arm out as if he was about to lead them to the dance floor.

"You go with him," Marsali said to Lady Cosgrove. "I'll wait here for Lydia and Christopher and bring them when they come."

"Your daughter?" Mr. Luke paused. "Miss Cosgrove is already on the lifeboat, waiting for you."

"Why did you not tell us?" Marsali said, confused.

"I just did."

The ship pitched again, and Lady Cosgrove tottered forward, reaching her hand our to his arm while Marsali stood her ground.

"Foolish woman!" he snapped. "The ship is on fire. Do you wish to burn up with it?"

"Christopher will come back for me. And I don't believe you've found Lydia." Marsali didn't know why, but she suspected he was lying.

"Why should he lie?" Lady Cosgrove had regained her footing and had a firm grip on Mr. Luke's arm. She sent a bewildered look from one to the other. "Have you seen my daughter?"

"I have. She was—with me this evening."

Oh dear. He seemed all too truthful now, and Marsali worried some harm had come to Lydia. Before tonight Mr. Luke had treated her with a cold indifference. What had changed that he would alter his behavior the last night of their journey?

"With *you*?" Lady Cosgrove sounded distressed as well, but she allowed Mr. Luke to steer her toward the door.

"I'll be back for you," he called over his shoulder as they left the room.

Marsali braced herself as the ship pitched again, this time listing heavily to the side. *We* are *sinking.* The door to the saloon banged open and shut with the violent wind and rolling of the ship. Water poured in, streaming along the floorboards and seeping under the cabin doors. Marsali took a hesitant step forward, half regretful she hadn't gone with them. At the least maybe she should go up to the deck herself to search for Christopher.

Going outside might be her best chance at finding him quickly. *But I promised him I would wait here. If he returns and I am gone . . .* No. She would wait.

Still gripping the table edge, Marsali moved slowly away from the door, toward the opposite end of the saloon. She and Lady Cosgrove had checked all but the captain's quarters. It was doubtful Lydia was there, but she had to look just to be sure.

The door was unlocked and opened easily.

"Lydia?" Marsali peered inside then stepped into the room. She turned a circle, squinting through the dark, barely able to make out the captain's berth and window seat and the tables that had been crammed with inventions, many of which lay broken and scattered on the floor.

Poor Captain Gower.

Thunder clapped angrily outside, as if demanding to be let in. The sea answered with its own violent lashing. Waves pounded against the paned window where she and Christopher had sat together just days ago. The floor beneath her seemed to turn on its side as the icy water reached her heels and washed over her feet. Marsali slipped and landed hard on her side.

Behind her the door slammed, sealing her in almost complete darkness, with the window buried in the waves. She scrambled to her knees and crawled toward the door.

"Marsali!"

Christopher.

"In here," she cried.

The door was flung open, and then she felt his arms around her, lifting her.

She clung to him. "I was so frightened for you."

He held her away from him. "We have to go. The fire spread. I couldn't find Lydia."

A hand appeared above him, slicing through the darkness as it came down over Christopher's head. A bone-crunching thud was followed by his shudder as he fell forward, slipping from her grasp.

"Christopher!" She fell to the floor beside him, touching his face, trying to turn him over. "Christopher, can you hear me?"

"Get up." Mr. Luke stood over them, pointing a pistol at her.

She stared at him, attempting to connect the chain of events.

He bent down and used his free hand to grab her arm and haul her up beside him. Marsali's eyes were still riveted to the gun, now very near her face. She wrenched herself free of his grasp.

"You hit him." It wasn't logical, though the evidence was right in front of her. "Why?" she asked, her eyes filling with tears.

"Couldn't shoot Mr. Thatcher right there, not with you so close." Mr. Luke cocked the pistol, and his gaze flickered downward.

Marsali launched herself at him, pushing the pistol sideways and plowing into his stomach and taking him off guard, but not so much that he did not catch her hand as she swung it at his face. He jerked her toward him. "Don't be a fool. There's a space in the lifeboat for you."

"You killed my husband," she sobbed.

"It's not my fault you married him. But you're right. If he's not dead already, he will be when this ship goes down, so forget him." He shoved the pistol in his belt and began dragging her down the corridor. Marsali struggled to break free as she looked over her shoulder at Christopher's still form. "Christopher!" She screamed his name until Mr. Luke struck her across the mouth.

"Keep quiet, or I'll kill you too. And you don't need to die."

"Neither did he. There are plenty of lifeboats." The bitter taste of blood filled her mouth.

Mr. Luke gave a vile laugh. "This isn't about lifeboats." Still keeping a hold on her, he kicked the outside door open. "Bet you didn't know your husband had a price on his head of ninety pounds sterling. Too good to pass up. I told Crayton I'd take care of it, and he'll have the reward waiting for me when I return to England."

Crayton . . .

"Cheating a pirate is never a good idea." Mr. Luke thrust her out in front of him. "Humiliating one is even worse."

"Christopher wasn't involved with pirates." Their dinner conversation and her suspicions suddenly came back to her.

"Didn't know your husband as well as you thought, did you?" Mr. Luke's sinister laugh was lost in the storm. Rain pelted Marsali, and her hair stuck to her face as he dragged her toward the lifeboats. Fire had consumed the mast and the wheel. The woodwork and casings around the smokestack were burning too.

"Christopher!" she shouted, but the storm was too loud, and everyone was too busy with the fire to hear her. "Christopher!"

"Not even married a day and a widow already." Mr. Luke picked her up and dumped her into a lifeboat that had already been partially lowered.

Lady Cosgrove sat on one of the seats, keening as she rocked back and forth. "Lydia? Did you find her?"

"No." Marsali scooted next to Lady Cosgrove and wrapped her arm around her. Mr. Luke dropped into the lifeboat beside them, then reached up to the pulleys to lower the ropes.

"Where is Lydia? We can't leave without her." Lady Cosgrove leaned forward and clawed at him. He thrust her away, sending her sprawling across the seats.

One side of the boat dropped suddenly, much lower than the other, so that both Lady Cosgrove and Marsali had to cling to the side to keep from falling out.

The other side seemed to be stuck, and now that they were lower, Mr. Luke could no longer reach the pulley. He pulled out a knife and began sawing through the rope.

"Don't!" Marsali cried.

"Where is my daughter?" Lady Cosgrove crawled toward him then clutched his leg. He struck her across the face.

"Your daughter's dead—already dumped her body over the other side of the ship. You can join—"

His knife cut through the rope, and the nose of the boat plunged straight down. Mr. Luke lost his footing and pitched over the end. Lady Cosgrove screamed and slid forward, her leg catching on the bench in front of her. Marsali grabbed the back of her dress with one hand and wrapped her arm around the bench with her other.

"Help!" she screamed, lifting her face to sky.

"I'm slipping," Lady Cosgrove yelled.

"Hold on," Marsali sobbed. "Please." She couldn't bear the thought of losing Lady Cosgrove as well and being left alone.

A head appeared over the side of the boat.

"Help us!" Marsali shouted once more. The head disappeared, then reappeared a minute later, closer to the rope that was still intact. The cabin boy, Marc, pulled out a knife and began cutting.

"No. Stop! Don't do that." Marsali dared not let go of either the bench or Lady Cosgrove to wave at him.

The other end of the boat plunged downward suddenly. Marsali's scream was lost in the sound of the splash as they hit the water. They bounced, and she rose out of the boat, suspended in the air for several terrifying seconds before she landed again on the hard seat.

"Lady Cosgrove," Marsali called as soon as she found her voice again.

There was no answer, and Marsali leaned forward, frantic, as she felt around for another passenger. Her fingers found hair and then a face, and she heard faint moaning. She burst into tears, so grateful she was not alone—that Lady Cosgrove was with her and they had each other.

Marsali scooted closer, found her hand, and held on to it.

Beside them the ship was ablaze. She could see the men shouting and running to and fro across the decks. "Please, someone. Find Christopher. Find Lydia." Tears poured from her eyes, and she trembled and wept.

When Marsali looked again, the *Amanda May* had moved. Its great paddle wheel was still churning, drawing ever closer to their lifeboat.

Someone in the water shouted, and she thought she could make out hands waving for help. The cry came again, and she realized it was Mr. Luke, just beyond them, drifting ever closer to the wheel. Marsali crawled across the benches, searching the boat for the oars she had seen fastened to the sides in the boat she'd been in earlier. She couldn't find them, and the *Amanda May* had turned again.

Marsali peered through the darkness and saw the arms disappear beneath the surface right beside the wheel. She turned away, hand held to her mouth and her eyes squeezed shut tight as she imagined Mr. Luke's fate.

After a minute she forced herself to look again and saw that the ship was farther from them, a blaze of orange steaming into the night. She found Lady Cosgrove's hand again and held it, then sat on the floor of the boat beside her, curled up as tightly as she could.

The rain continued falling, and the night grew colder. But Marsali ceased to care. Christopher was gone, and nothing else mattered.

CHAPTER 31

A uniformed gentleman, logbook in hand, stopped before Marsali and Lady Cosgrove on the deck of the *Josephine*, an Irish packet ship en route from Dublin to New York. They had been picked up by the ship in the predawn hours and treated kindly—given both new clothing and warm blankets in an effort to ward off the bone-deep chill.

But the blankets had not helped, and the kindness seemed to matter little. Marsali's limbs were still stiff, and her chest hurt with every breath. Something was wrong—terribly, terribly wrong—but she was no longer certain what that was. After hours spent alone in darkness, in a tiny boat threatening to capsize at any minute, they had been rescued from the violent sea. She was safe now. At the least, it seemed, she ought to feel relieved. Instead she could not stop the tears continuously leaking from her eyes or the terrible sadness engulfing her.

The gentleman cleared his throat. "Ladies, we are nearing port, and I need to record your names for the ship's log."

Lady Cosgrove straightened and removed her arm from around Marsali's shoulders. The wool blanket she'd been holding in place slid to the floor, but Marsali did not bother to pick it up. She'd long since ceased feeling the cold or caring if she did.

"I am Lady Cornelia Cosgrove, widow of the late Earl of Aylesford."

"Spell Cornelia and Cosgrove please."

Lady Cosgrove rattled off letters while Marsali stared at the approaching shoreline. *America.* She had wanted to come here, but she couldn't seem to recall why.

"Duly noted. Thank you." The uniformed man inclined his head toward Marsali. "And your name."

"Miss Lydia Cosgrove," Lady Cosgrove said. "My daughter."

Lydia. An image of a bright dress and a smiling young lady came to mind.

I couldn't find Lydia.

The pain in her chest intensified, and another terrible image flashed before her.

"My daughter is betrothed to Mr. William Vancer, of New York. Perhaps you have heard of him," Lady Cosgrove said.

"I do not reside in New York." The man sounded annoyed. "Spell Lydia please."

"L-Y-D-I-A. Will there be transport to Mr. Vancer's estate once we have arrived at the port?"

"I'm sure something can be arranged." He closed his book and held it to his chest, then stared at them a long moment, apparently in deep contemplation. "Do either of you think you might be able to help with identifying the dead? You're the only survivors we've picked up thus far, but we've collected more than a few bodies."

Christopher.

"I'm sorry, but I do not believe we are able to help you." Lady Cosgrove put her arm around Marsali once more. "You can see that my daughter is still somewhat in shock. It has been a long, traumatic night."

"I understand. Good day, ladies. Or at least, I hope it gets better." He left them to sit in silence, watching the New York skyline come into view.

Something nagged at the back of Marsali's mind, something she felt she ought to do. "I must see Mr. Thatcher—Christopher." She attempted to stand, but Lady Cosgrove restrained her.

"You don't know that they've found him," she whispered. "And even if they have—it isn't something you wish to see. It is better to remember him as he was. Trust me. I have seen two husbands in death, and I will both remember and regret it for as long as I live." She smoothed Marsali's hair away from her face. "That life is over now. You have a new one."

"But, Lydia," Marsali turned to Lady Cosgrove. "He couldn't find her."

"Shh. All will be well. You shall see," Lady Cosgrove said, and Marsali was not sure to whom she was speaking.

She felt as if nothing would ever be well again.

"We've suffered terrible losses, but we have each other now." Lady Cosgrove held Marsali's hand. "And we can help one another. We will *have* to help one another if either of us is to survive."

"The poor miss. She's been through so much." A woman was speaking nearby.

A second female voice came from Marsali's other side, this one farther away. "Yes, but she's here now. *She survived.* She and her mother were the only ones from the whole ship."

Mother is dead. Marsali attempted to open her eyes to see whom the voices belonged to, but the effort required was too great.

"She'll be all right." The second voice spoke again. "Mr.

Vancer will take care of her. He's half in love with her already. Have you seen the way he looks at her?"

The name Vancer sounded familiar, but Marsali could not put a face with it. And she still did not know who was speaking—or, for that matter, where she was. She was going to have to open her eyes.

They didn't want to at first, heavy as they were with sleep, or possibly some medicine, but at last she forced them open and stared wide-eyed at a completely unfamiliar room and two maids she had never seen before, one seated on either side of her.

"Who are you?" Marsali asked. "This isn't my aunt's house."

The one closest to her smiled kindly. "You're in New York, miss. In Mr. Vancer's house. Your ship wrecked off the coast, but you were rescued, and he brought you here."

"Mr. Vancer?" She still had no recollection of who he was, though the events they had described were at least partially familiar. She remembered the storm and being in the lifeboat.

The second maid's mouth turned down, and she exchanged a worried look across the bed with the maid who had just spoken. "You do not know who Mr. Vancer is?"

Wasn't that obvious? She'd just asked, hadn't she? "I do not," Marsali said, trying not to panic.

"Mr. William Vancer," the first woman said, "is one of the wealthiest men in New York—and your fiancé."

CHAPTER 32

The clock downstairs struck eight times, and Marsali left the luxurious bedchamber, wondering if she had spent her last night in it. She had planned her meeting with Mr. Vancer for morning, when it was sure Lady Cosgrove would not be awake and about, for she would not approve of what Marsali was about to do and might have found some means to prevent it.

And though Lady Cosgrove's plan might have been the easier route, Marsali could not go through with it. She *would* not. No matter what the consequences. A week had passed since she had arrived at Mr. Vancer's home, and it was long past time that he learned who she really was.

Perhaps Mr. Vancer would be so put off by her deception that he would throw her out immediately—and Lady Cosgrove along with her. If so, Marsali felt regret about that, but she could continue this ruse no longer. She was not Lydia, and she had no intention of becoming so.

Even risking her life by subjecting herself to Mr.

Thomas and the terms of her indenture was better than losing herself, simply disappearing, and becoming someone else, as if she'd never existed.

Though a few servants moved about the upper hall and downstairs, no one stopped Marsali as she wandered, searching for the breakfast room, or perhaps a study, where she might locate Mr. Vancer. She'd yet to leave her chamber before today, and she'd dared not voice her request to meet with him to anyone else, lest word of it got back to Lady Cosgrove.

After peering into several rooms—a sitting room, a music room, a library—Marsali discovered what she had been searching for, along with the man she had been hoping to see. Gathering her courage, she stepped through the doorway. "Mr. Vancer."

He'd been looking down reading a newspaper, a tray of sundry breakfast items on the table in front of him, but lifted his head to look at her. She was relieved to see that it truly was he; she'd only guessed it would be but recalled his face from their earlier, brief meeting, when he had come up to her room for a few minutes to see how she was recovering. She ought to have told him the truth then, but Lady Cosgrove and two maids had also been in the room, and Marsali had been too surprised by his presence to form any kind of cohesive thought or explanation.

"Miss Cosgrove. Good to see you up and about." He pushed back his chair and rose, then held his hand out, inviting her to join him and take the seat nearest his.

Marsali strode purposefully into the room, stopping before the chair he held out. She hesitated, then sank into it, rationalizing that she might as well have a bit of breakfast while she broke the news to him.

He passed a plate of toast and a dish of marmalade to her. "Are you feeling much improved this morning?" His brows lifted as he studied her with a look of hopeful concern.

"I am well rested, thank you." She gave up all pretense

of fixing her toast and turned to face him. "But I am much troubled otherwise. There is something I must tell you."

"Go on." Neither his expression nor tone suggested any concern at her announcement. Rather, it almost seemed as if he was having difficulty containing a smile.

"I am not Lydia Cosgrove," Marsali blurted. There was no easy way to say it.

He smiled warmly. "I know."

"You do?" All of the tension and worry she'd felt over his reaction left in a rush, leaving her feeling somewhat deflated, yet much better at the same time.

"I know all about you, Miss Abbott."

Not everything, apparently. "I am no longer Miss Abbott," she corrected him. "I am a married woman. My last name is Thatcher." She showed him her hand with the wedding ring.

Mr. Vancer glanced over her head toward the doorway. Wordlessly, he rose from his chair once more, then crossed the room and slid the doors shut.

"*I* know, but much of the staff does not," he said by way of explanation. "And we don't need a lot of gossip about you spreading around New York, do we?"

She shook her head, though she had no idea what he was talking about. *Who would bother to gossip about unimportant me?*

"I can see you don't believe me," he said. "So please allow me to explain."

"Go on," Marsali said, wondering how it was that he was the one doing much of the talking when she'd planned out her long speech so carefully.

"You married a Mr. Christopher Thatcher while aboard the *Amanda May*. Is that correct?"

"It is," she said, her heart throbbing with loss at the reminder. "The captain married us."

"That would be Captain Gower, whose body was recovered from the wreckage?"

Marsali swallowed with difficulty as she nodded. She hadn't known Captain Gower long, but the thought that he had died still made her sad. He'd had a family—a wife and children—to return home to. *What must the real* Amanda May *be feeling now?*

"So the man who performed your marriage is dead," Mr. Vancer continued. "As is the man you married—Mr. Thatcher."

"That is not certain." Marsali looked at her lap as she fought back tears. *Christopher dead.* She still refused to believe it. She'd never known anyone more alive. "I have checked the papers daily, and there has been no report that his—that he—has been found."

"I do not mean to be unkind," Mr. Vancer said, compassion in his voice. "But much of the crew has not been discovered. Those who went down with the ship likely remain in it."

Marsali thought of Christopher as she had last seen him, on the floor and unmoving just inside the captain's quarters. It was not likely that he had survived. *But neither is it impossible.* She looked up at Mr. Vancer and found him gazing at her with concern.

"With the captain dead and your husband . . . missing . . . and the ship's records at the bottom of the sea, any proof that your brief marriage even happened has vanished. It is simply gone."

"I realize this." Marsali straightened and met his intense gaze with her own. "And so I am prepared to honor the terms of my indenture with Mr. Thomas."

"But why?" Mr. Vancer leaned back in his chair and brought a hand to his mouth as if puzzled. "Why should you do such a thing? Lady Cosgrove has told me about him as well. Surely you do not wish to subject yourself to his cruelty—or worse?"

"I do not see that I have a choice," Marsali said, then hurried on before he could suggest otherwise. "I am not

Lydia Cosgrove, and I do not feel it right to pretend to be. I haven't amnesia. I did not hit my head. When we arrived I might have been temporarily unsettled, but now I am perfectly aware of who I am—and what debts I have incurred that must yet be paid."

"What if I were to pay them?" Mr. Vancer asked.

"That is a very generous offer, but it is unnecessary."

"As it was unnecessary for Mr. Thatcher to marry you?"

Marsali squirmed uncomfortably in her seat. "Yes—no. That was different."

I never do anything I do not wish. How many times had Christopher told her that? He had wanted to marry her, had even mentioned love when he had given her his grandmother's ring.

There had been far more between them than the issue of her safety, though each had danced around their mutual attraction, avoiding it as long as possible. *Wasted days,* she thought with regret. "Mr. Thatcher and I had become acquainted with one another on our voyage. We felt we suited each other."

"But still, the primary reason for your hasty marriage *was* so that he could protect you from Mr. Thomas, is that not correct?"

"It is," Marsali said. "But as Mr. Thatcher is . . . missing, and possibly deceased . . ." She closed her eyes briefly, attempting to shut out the pain of that admission. "And as I am not—"

"You are now a widow," Mr. Vancer finished. "Who is recovering from a tragedy and is a guest in my house." He pushed back his chair and stood suddenly, then came around the table and seated himself in the chair directly beside hers. Leaning forward, he reached for her hand, taking it into his two as he looked at her directly.

She resisted the urge to pull away from him, all the while feeling an unfaithful wife, sitting here conversing so intimately with another man when she ought to have been out looking for her husband.

"Will you not give me that same opportunity, Miss Abbott? Allow me the same four weeks you spent with Mr. Thatcher, and let us see if we do not suit each other as well? I have lost the woman I was going to marry, and you have, in all likelihood, lost your husband. I can pay your debt, freeing you from the term of your indenture, and if—at the end of a month spent together—you do not feel a marriage between us to be in your best interest, you will be free to leave."

"That is very kind, but—"

"Kindness has little to do with it," he confessed, a smile playing at the corners of his mouth—a mouth, Marsali noticed suddenly, that was rather attractive, along with the rest of his face.

"Lady Cosgrove has not stopped singing your praises since she arrived, and I find that I am deeply curious to get to know you. To count the extraordinary young woman described to me as my friend—at least."

"I am quite flattered, but still . . ." She searched her mind for another argument and could find none. Yet staying here, with him, under any pretense, felt wrong. Disloyal—to Christopher.

"One month. That is all I ask." He was fully smiling now, as if he knew he had won.

"And, at the end of that month, if I should wish to leave—" *When I find my husband.*

"You will be free to go." He released her hands and held his up as if freeing her now.

"And Lady Cosgrove?" Marsali asked. "What would become of her if I were to go?"

"She will remain my guest indefinitely. Our families are old friends, and when I offered for her daughter, I knew it meant Lydia's mother would be coming as well."

"You are very generous," Marsali said. "How is it that a

man like yourself does so well at business if he is forever paying other's debts and supporting them with his means?"

Mr. Vancer's smile turned sly. "Fortunately, I do not conduct many business transactions with damsels in distress. Rather, it is stuffy old men with whom I barter and bargain. And for those, I show no mercy."

"You must make one deal with this damsel if she is to stay," Marsali insisted, rationalizing that what she was about to propose would make her feel better about the situation. "My true identity must be made known to all. I cannot continue on as Lydia. And second—"

"Ah." He held up a finger, stopping her. "You said *one*."

"Yes, but that is only the first part of the one." She smiled sweetly, causing him to laugh.

"*That* is exactly why I do not do business with females." He brushed his fingers down the side of her cheek, causing Marsali a sudden intake of breath.

His face grew serious. "I can see already that I will not be impervious to your smile. What is it you wish, Miss Abbott?"

"I wish to continue a search for my husband. And if I find him or if I choose to leave at the end of the month, you must allow me to repay the money of my indenture. It will take some time, but I shall be able to do it."

"Honesty, loyalty, and equity . . . you strike a hard bargain." He held out his hand. "But I'll take it." Marsali placed her hand in his and felt the pressure of his fingers closing over hers. But instead of being comforting, as Christopher's touch had been, she felt entrapped—caught by Mr. Vancer's kindness, ensnared in his generosity.

But as they returned to eating their breakfast, and she silently admired the fine china and beautiful furnishings in the elegant room, she realized she had arrived at the station in life she had only dreamed of. Just like that, she had returned to the status she'd been born to, a refined and luxurious life laid at her feet.

If she chose to start down that path—one that promised everything she might wish and included the kind Mr. Vancer at her side.

CHAPTER 33

*M*y Dears Lady Grace Sutherland and Mrs. Helen Preston,

It is my unhappy fate to tell you that your beloved brother, Christopher, has been missing since the night of 25 September, when he incurred an injury just prior to the ship, the Amanda May, *being lost at sea. Rather than share with you the details regarding the event (and revisit those myself) I must simply tell you that his probable death was a result of a price of ninety pounds sterling on his head, the sum of which was offered by a pirate named Crayton. A man whom we (all of us upon the ship* Amanda May) *believed to be a trustworthy member of the crew was, in fact, in league with Crayton.*

What I do wish for you to know is what Christopher's last weeks and days were comprised of. You may think me forward for referring to him by his Christian name, but I assure you I mean no disrespect. I loved your brother dearly and was given to believe he felt the same for me. We were wed by Captain Gower while still aboard the Amanda May, *on the morning of 25 September . . .*

Marsali walked down the hall, the sealed letter in her hands. She hated that it was to deliver such sorrowful news to two ladies she almost felt she knew, but she realized it was her duty, as Christopher's wife, to inform them that he was missing. She had been to both the hospital and the docks every day and had discovered no news of him. With each passing day, it became more difficult to hold onto hope that he was yet alive.

She passed Lady Cosgrove's open door, and a few seconds later, Lady Cosgrove herself emerged, walking briskly to keep pace with Marsali.

"What have you got there? Where are you going?" Since learning that Marsali had slipped out of her room and sought out and spoken with Mr. Vancer, Lady Cosgrove had assumed the position of Marsali's shadow—a situation Marsali found most unpleasant.

"I wish to find the butler. I have written a letter to Christopher's sisters informing them that he is missing." *That it is probable he is dead.* She had yet to say the words. Though the days stretched further between her memories with Christopher and her new future, he remained as present in her mind as if he was here with her. She would not be surprised to find him at breakfast, holding the milk captive, or waiting outside on the step, wishing to take her for a walk.

"Well, hurry, then. We mustn't miss our appointment."

Inwardly Marsali bristled at Lady Cosgrove's tone, though she had heard Lydia addressed the same way on many occasions. *But I am* not *Lydia.* At least her chat with Mr. Vancer had cleared that up. He promised to make everything right concerning Marsali's identity, and she trusted him to do it.

"We've only *three* hours. We must be prompt," Lady Cosgrove insisted. "The dressmaker will be here at precisely ten o'clock, and we mustn't waste a minute of her time. I took the liberty of arranging to have her come here, rather than going out to her shop. I thought you would prefer that."

"I do," Marsali said earnestly. As much as she had professed to Mr. Vancer that she needed to leave and fulfill her obligations to Mr. Thomas, she could not deny that she felt some measure of safety here. Now that she knew she did not have to seek employment for a few more weeks, she wished to leave the house as little as possible. She especially did not want to go out for something as frivolous as purchasing a gown.

"How am I to pay for all this clothing, which you insist I must have?" Marsali asked. For that matter, how was Lady Cosgrove to pay for hers? In the end she had arrived every bit as destitute as Marsali.

"Mr. Vancer will pay for it, of course," Lady Cosgrove said, as if that was the most logical, most appropriate thing to be done.

Marsali felt quite the opposite. It had been one thing for Mr. Vancer to take her into his home and offer her food and shelter as she recovered from her ordeal. She could even justify his loan, paying off her debt to Mr. Thomas, as she fully intended to repay every penny of it. But to spend his money on purchasing her clothes when this borrowed servant's gown was finer than any dress she had owned for quite some time seemed very wrong.

One more thing to bind me to him? She imagined a noose tightening around her neck.

She found the butler and gave him directions regarding her letter, then allowed Lady Cosgrove to steer her where she would. They returned to the second floor and ventured into a corridor Marsali had not yet visited. Lady Cosgrove led her toward a set of open double doors, through which Marsali glimpsed the finest dress makings she had ever imagined.

They stepped inside the room, and Lady Cosgrove moved forward to speak with the dressmaker and her assistants—three of them—already in place, waiting to attend to them. Marsali stood transfixed, certain her eyes were large as they took in the bolts of silk and velvet and organza in every color imaginable. *No plain muslin here.* There were open boxes of ribbon and lace, and a small, circular dais upon which she was to stand. For a moment, Marsali closed her eyes, remembering a similar scene, long ago, when she and her mother and sister had gone to visit a dressmaker in Lyon.

After her mother had selected the fabrics she wished Marsali's dresses to be made from, she had allowed Marsali to choose one additional fabric—any she wished—for a party dress. Marsali had chosen a blue silk, the color of the sky.

How I loved that dress. She realized that she had not appreciated it or the many other fine clothes she'd owned. And in the years since, she had nearly forgotten them.

"Come in, come in." The stoutest of the four women came forward, beckoning Marsali into the room.

Marsali entered, feeling as if she had stepped back in time or into a dream. She allowed the woman to guide her to the dais and then held her arms out obediently while her measurements were taken.

"Something rose-colored to start with, I believe," Lady Cosgrove was saying and pointed to a bolt of pink fabric laid out on one of several tables.

"A lovely choice." The dressmaker picked up the fabric and brought it over to Marsali, holding a swathe of it in front of her.

"Do you like it as well?" the dressmaker asked.

"It is very pretty," Marsali concurred, rubbing a piece of the fabric between her fingers. *Very soft. Like Lydia's borrowed satin.* Would she forever be reminded of that when she wore fine gowns?

"Good. We will make your first dress out of this." The dressmaker whisked the bolt away, handing it off to the third woman before marching back over to the table and Lady Cosgrove.

"I think a pale yellow next," Lady Cosgrove said. "And then a green and perhaps a lavender."

"No." Marsali left the dais and came over to the tables. "I do not have need of so many gowns. You may make me two only. And I wish one of them to be blue."

The image reflecting back at her in the mirror shocked Marsali. Disbelieving, she stepped closer, squinting at her reflection and feeling slightly better when she recognized the way her nose wrinkled. *But the rest of me . . .*

Her hair was done up in what she'd been told was the latest fashion, something called an Apollo knot. The maid who'd been sent up to fix it for her had complained heartily that Marsali hadn't long enough hair to work with for such a style, and even if she had, Marsali wasn't at all certain that she liked it. The curls hanging down on either side of her face seemed a nuisance, and the bun was pulled much too tight, not to mention the ridiculous amount of time it had taken with the curling tongs to get her short hair to curl as it should.

But the jeweled butterfly combs were quite lovely, and Marsali could not help but admire her new gown. She could hardly keep from running her fingers over the smooth blue silk.

"Mr. Vancer awaits you."

Marsali turned from the mirror to see Lady Cosgrove standing in her bedroom doorway.

"The blue was a good choice. It becomes you."

"Thank you." Marsali heard the sadness in the older woman's voice and guessed at once that she was imagining what it would have been like had Lydia been standing here—as she ought to have been—preparing to attend a dinner and be presented by Mr. Vancer.

Marsali quickly crossed the room, took Lady Cosgrove's hands in her own, and leaned forward, kissing her on the cheek. "Thank you for your kindness to me."

"You're most welcome." Lady Cosgrove blinked rapidly

and pulled away. "Forgive me. I was just thinking of when I was younger, and my first husband was courting me, and what a lovely time that was."

"You must tell me all about it tomorrow." Marsali felt her own sorrow swell, pained that Lady Cosgrove had not been thinking of her daughter but of herself. Marsali knew Lady Cosgrove had to be grieving and had heard her crying at night. But for some reason, she seemed unable to show her emotions to others.

And I am no better—attending a dinner as another man's guest when my husband has been missing but two weeks. Marsali walked down the hall, knowing she did not belong here—not in this fine house and especially not seated beside Mr. Vancer at his table, as she would soon be.

She twirled her wedding ring beneath her glove and remembered the moment Christopher had slipped it onto her finger and the promises that had come with it.

As long as we both shall live. What if he no longer does? Though they had been married but one day, a mourning period seemed appropriate just the same. He had given her all he had, and moving on so quickly felt wrong. *And impossible.* Circumstances might require her to wear a pretty gown and to pretend to enjoy another's company. But her heart and soul felt bleak.

CHAPTER 34

My Dearest Sisters,

I am writing with all urgency lest you have somehow learned that the ship I sailed upon, the Amanda May, *was sunk just outside the New York Harbor in the early morning hours of 26 September. If it seems the greatest irony to you that I made it safely across the Atlantic only to encounter disaster on the shores of this new land, know that you are not alone. Know also that I am well—in body, if not spirit.*

You will laugh to hear this, or perhaps you will believe that my injuries have caused my mind to fail (and yes, I do have some injuries, though none too serious or life-threatening), but I will attempt to share with you the adventures of my sea voyage. The journey was not at all what I had expected and would have been rather dull were it not for an acquaintance I made my first night aboard ship. One of my fellow passengers, a young woman by the name of Marsali Abbott (she is French and English and a bit Scottish, and entirely delightful), arrived late and in quite a poor condition. I could not resist helping her, neither could I cease my concerns for her welfare when she was discovered to be indentured to a man known for cruelty.

Not having the means by which to free her from her circumstance (excepting the sale of Grandfather's ring, which I had promised never to part with, save for the purpose of marriage), I chose the only action available to me. On 25 September, while still aboard the Amanda May, *I married Marsali Abbott of Manchester. It was the finest day of my life . . .*

Christopher winced as the doctor parted his newly regrown hair and probed the red, puckered scar running down the back of his head. "Your stitches are healing nicely, and you're looking more healthy each day. I predict a full recovery."

"Thank you," Christopher said without enthusiasm. He didn't feel grateful. He felt bitter. And frustrated that he had no recollection of how the cut that nearly split his scalp in two had come about.

He had recalled the scene over and over again until his head pounded as much from the effort as from his injury. He had been in the saloon speaking with Marsali. She had seemed frightened. He'd been as well. The ship was burning too quickly for the flames to be kept from spreading, storm and rain notwithstanding.

The next thing he recalled after that was waking to excruciating pain. His right side had felt as if it was on fire, though the night was chill and rain continued falling. He'd been in a lifeboat with Mr. Murphy and had drifted in and out of consciousness for a day and a half until a fishing boat had picked them up off the New Jersey coast.

"I cannot recommend you to labor for two more weeks, at the least," the doctor said. "And that is optimistic."

"It is impossible for me to remain idle so long." It vexed Christopher to have started out his new life in America *in debt*. It was the very legacy he'd come here to escape. Yet there had been no help for it. When they'd been found, he had needed a doctor—badly. And he had required food and lodging in the nearly three weeks since. He'd written his sisters just this morning—at last being able to bear moving his hand and arm enough that he *could* write—advising them of his circumstances and requesting a loan so he might pay both the doctor and the kind widow who ran the boarding house where he was staying.

"Nevertheless, I must advise against working so soon," the doctor continued. "If you wish your injuries to heal completely, that is."

Christopher glanced at his arm swathed in bandages. It hurt far worse than his head wound and worried him more. The doctor had assured Christopher that if cared for correctly—cleaned and rewrapped frequently—his burned skin would eventually heal and he would likely regain full mobility of both his arm and leg. *But if I do not . . .* He would be unable to perform the labor necessary for farming. *Any labor.* He would have to do as the doctor suggested and wait a while longer.

"I will cease seeking employment until you have given your approval," Christopher agreed. "Though I must continue to perform tasks for the widow Jensen. She has been kind enough to keep me, and I must begin to repay her as I can."

"That should be fine, so long as you are careful with that arm."

I have little choice but to be. Christopher recalled his frustration when he had injured his hand taking out Crayton some months ago. But losing mobility in much of his arm and having a leg that could not properly support him was proving far worse and more concerning to his future. How could he hope to take care of—

Christopher swallowed and quickly reached for his borrowed hat. He glanced at the clock on the wall—almost fifteen minutes had passed since he'd thought of Marsali.

Too long. And he had waited too long to find her. But she had to have survived. *And must feel equally frantic.*

"I will not seek employment yet, but I must travel. I must find my wife."

"Stunning. You look absolutely beautiful." Lady Cosgrove stood behind Marsali, adjusting her bonnet to fit over the back of her hair.

"I said *two* dresses, not seven." Marsali stared at her reflection in the long mirror and tried to find fault with the dark green gown. Delicate gold embroidery covered the bodice and the puffs of the sleeves. The fitted waist and flared skirt made her plain figure appear better than it was. The color contrasted nicely with her fair skin and dark hair and . . . She turned aside, unable to meet her own gaze in the mirror. The dress was not the problem. *She* was.

"Come now. You mustn't keep Mr. Vancer waiting. He has been looking forward to this outing, and so must you. Will it not be fine to be outside?"

Marsali did not feel that it would be fine at all. The house offered protection, a sanctuary while she attempted to heal and to determine what she must do next. Going to live and work with Charlotte seemed the most logical move, but Charlotte had yet to write that there was a position for her. *Though I have reached America, I am still parted from my sister.*

"What shall we speak of?" Marsali asked, worrying over the length of time she would be alone with Mr. Vancer.

"Whatever he wishes," Lady Cosgrove advised, bustling Marsali from the room. "You must appear interested no matter what the subject is."

Marsali was not certain which be worse— awkward silence during which neither she nor Mr. Vancer were able to think of a topic to discuss, or animated dialogue between them. Conversation with Christopher had been effortless, and she had so enjoyed his company in all circumstances. To enjoy Mr. Vancer's as well seemed disloyal. Yet he had shown nothing but kindness and courtesy to her, and she could not help but like him a little bit at least.

He met her in the foyer, a glow of approval in his eyes as he took in her ensemble. Marsali took his arm, and they exited the foyer to the front of the house, where an open-topped carriage awaited just beyond the iron gate. She had worried that the shawl Lady Cosgrove had brought her would not be enough to ward off a chill October day—not that she could have worn any sort of coat over this dress, with its somewhat ridiculous enlarged sleeves and flared skirt—but the day was mild and sunny, and, to Marsali's surprise, she felt her spirits lift the moment they left the house.

Mr. Vancer had no sooner helped her into the carriage than she was leaning back, her head tilted up, attempting to take in the tall buildings, all so closely built together, that surrounded the street on either side. When she had gone out before to visit the hospitals and the docks, she had always traveled in a closed carriage and refrained from looking outside much at all, especially when close to Mr. Vancer's residence, as she did not want any neighbors who happened to be about seeing her and speculating.

"We haven't a proper park to drive in as they do in London, but there are many lanes quite beautiful with autumn colors this time of year." Mr. Vancer wielded the reins with skill and guided the team to a brisk trot as they left the house.

Marsali had not been certain what to expect but found the fact that he was driving them himself pleasing. Her aunt and uncle had always had a coachman to drive them about, even on the smallest errand, as if exerting themselves in the slightest amount would have been too difficult a task.

"It is fascinating," she said, marveling at the strange

combination of bustling city and brilliant foliage. "I did not know what to expect of America. It is thrilling to see a bit of it at last."

He gave her a sideways smile while keeping his eyes on the road. "You may see much more than a bit. Where would you like to go?"

"To Virginia," Marsali suggested hopefully, to which he laughed.

"Perhaps not today—we should have started much earlier and been more prepared for a journey—but I promise we shall reunite you with your sister."

"Soon?" Marsali asked, still hopeful.

"Soon," he promised.

The buggy picked up speed as they left the neighborhood behind in favor of less crowded, tree-lined avenues, lush with the reds and golds of autumn. The air felt crisp and cool and fresh—more so than anywhere in Manchester—and Marsali felt as if new life was being breathed into her.

At her side Mr. Vancer chatted amiably, pointing out places of interest and telling her of the history of the region. She was neither bored nor uncomfortable but quite enjoying herself. For the next hour she allowed herself to cease thinking of the past and the voyage across the ocean that had changed her life.

"I love America, and particularly New York." Mr. Vancer waved his hand emphatically at the outline of the city as they reached a vantage point, ready to begin their return voyage.

"Do you never miss England?" Marsali asked.

He turned toward her, as they had not yet begun driving again. "Not really," he said. "Business necessitates that I return every few years, and on the last of those voyages I could hardly wait to return home—*here*," he clarified.

Mr. Vancer still travels to England and Europe every couple of years. I shall be able to accompany him . . .

Recollections of an early conversation with Lydia echoed through Marsali's mind, haunting her and bringing her back to the present and the guilt she felt at being out driving with her friend's fiancé. *Lydia should be here. Not I.*

And she should have been with Christopher, the man who had sacrificed so much for her. *The man I loved. The man I* still *love.* But she could not continue to love him while enjoying Mr. Vancer's company. It wasn't fair to either.

"When will you be traveling to England again?" Marsali asked.

His brow drew together with apparent concern. "Not thinking of leaving, are you?"

"No." Marsali shook her head and forced a smile. "I do not ever wish to go back." Her gaze dropped to her lap, and she began twisting the ring on her finger beneath her glove. "But there is something I ought to return. Perhaps, if the timing is right, you could see it safely home for me."

CHAPTER 35

*C*eaning heavily on his cane, Christopher disembarked the steam ferry in New York, on the other side of the North River. His leg was throbbing, and he still had half the distance to go to reach Mr. Vancer's estate. The journey would be worth it if only Lady Cosgrove could give him some idea as to where he might find Marsali. Had she been injured? Was she in a hospital somewhere nearby, waiting for him to come to her?

The thought of Marsali hurting and alone prodded him to walk faster. *Lady Cosgrove will know something. She must.* After all, he reasoned, she had been with Marsali that last night when he had gone in search of Lydia.

Mr. Murphy's investigation at the docks this past week had revealed that Lady Cornelia Cosgrove and her daughter Lydia had been rescued from a lifeboat at sea, picked up by the Irish packet ship *Josephine*. They had disembarked in New York on Friday, 26 September—three full weeks ago.

Perhaps Marsali had been picked up by a different ship. *Why is there no record of her?*

Murphy had been unable to locate or learn of any other survivors from the *Amanda May*. But he had been called upon to identify bodies of many of the crew, Mr. Tenney and Captain Gower among them.

But not Marsali. Because she is not dead. Christopher mourned for those who had been lost, particularly Captain Gower, but he did not allow himself to dwell on their deaths and instead held on to hope as he clumped along the sidewalk, past the immigrant districts and to the more wealthy neighborhoods.

At midafternoon, he at last came to Fifth Street and located the Vancer mansion. It appeared every bit as opulent as Miss Cosgrove had described it, and he imagined that she and her mother were both quite comfortable here.

Christopher knocked on the door and was admitted by a butler who looked at him askance, as if his clothing indicated he ought to have rung at the servant's entrance.

So much for my fine suit, Christopher thought, caring little. His two pounds were gone, as were his books, clothing, and other belongings. But he cared not a whit for any of that and would have gladly given all of it and more to find Marsali.

Hat in hand, Christopher waited in the foyer, wondering that the butler had not offered to take his hat or shown him to a room to wait. After so many hours of walking, sitting would have been a vast relief.

A few moments later, Lady Cosgrove swept into the room, appearing far better than the last time he had seen her. As he opened his mouth to greet her, Lady Cosgrove's face turned ashen, and she stumbled backward, only just managing to catch herself from falling by grabbing onto a side table.

"Lady Cosgrove, are you not well?" He stepped forward, intending to offer his good hand to her.

She shook her head and did not speak but took a step

backward, declining his assistance. "Impossible. You are dead."

"Not quite." He gave a tight-lipped smile. His leg and arm hurt enough that he might have wished for death a time or two the past weeks, had he not had Marsali to think of. "I have come to inquire about my wife's whereabouts. When last I saw you, Marsali was with you in the saloon of the *Amanda May*. Do you know what became of her?"

"She—" If possible, Lady Cosgrove's face grew more pale.

Christopher stepped closer, judging how he might be able to catch her, lest she fall. "Have you seen her? I have had no word and *must* find her."

Lady Cosgrove took several shallow breaths before meeting his eye and speaking again. And then it was not to answer his question.

"You are injured?" Her eyes flickered from his cane and bandaged arm to his closely shorn hair.

"I was," he clarified. "I will be well soon enough. Please, have you any news of Marsali?" *She knows something. She is avoiding telling me.* His fingers curved over the handle of the cane, bracing himself for the worst.

"Miss Abbott is . . . How are you to work with your injuries?" Lady Cosgrove asked, once again changing the subject swiftly.

"I'll manage," Christopher said, wondering that she would care at all. "Have you any news of Marsali?" He was not going to leave until the woman told him whatever it was she knew. Good news or bad, he needed to hear it.

Lady Cosgrove considered him a moment more, then seemed to stiffen with some sort of resolve. "Miss Abbott would not leave the ship with me. Mr. Luke came to take us to a lifeboat, but she insisted on waiting for you. Later, when I was in the boat, I caught a glimpse of her up on deck, calling your name. The way the ship was rolling in the sea, it is difficult to believe one could stand on the deck at all—without being secured."

No. Christopher refused to believe that Marsali had been swept overboard. Still, he gritted his teeth to keep from crying out his anguish. That Lady Cosgrove would know of Marsali's whereabouts had been his greatest hope.

"I was not aware of other survivors beyond Lydia and I," Lady Cosgrove said quietly.

"Mr. Murphy is alive as well," Christopher said. "It is thanks to him that I am here. And Marsali is alive. I *know* it. If she was on the deck by the boats she must have ended up in one."

"Yes, well . . ." Lady Cosgrove cleared her throat. "Ours nearly capsized several times that awful night. It is entirely possible that others did."

He didn't want to think about that possibility either and refused to consider it yet. "I thank you for your time," Christopher said, wanting only to get far away from Lady Cosgrove and her dire imaginations as quickly as possible. "I wish you and your daughter a happy life together here."

"Thank you." She looked away, as if she felt guilty that they should have such happiness when he did not.

He limped his way to the front door and the waiting butler. It seemed his leg was even less prone to functioning normally now that he had stood still a few moments.

Where are you, Marsali? Where would you go? To Virginia? The possibility that she was even now at Mr. Joshua Thomas's plantation worried him greatly. Yet it was a very real possibility. *If Marsali believed me dead, she would have felt she had no choice but to honor her indenture.*

At the threshold, Christopher turned around once more to find Lady Cosgrove anxiously looking past him.

Discomfited by my injuries, no doubt. His hair had not yet grown enough to cover the scar running down the back of his head.

"If you should chance to learn of my wife's whereabouts

or even see her, I will be found in Virginia, working on or near Mr. Joshua Thomas's plantation."

Mr. Vancer's buggy turned the corner to Fifth Street, bringing into view the towering mansions that made up the neighborhood. To Marsali, every one seemed ostentatious in size. After a few hours away from the city, being surrounded again by grey stone felt depressing. Instead of looking forward to returning to the house, as she had guessed she would, Marsali felt anxious, as if it was a living thing seeking to ensnare her.

They reached the front of the house, and Mr. Vancer alighted from the buggy. Though she was perfectly capable of removing herself, Marsali waited for him to come around to assist her. Two servants emerged from the front doors and started down the steps as if they had been standing there all afternoon, awaiting their return. Marsali wondered if they had and then wondered at the extravagance of it all. Would not such money be better spent on other things—such as helping people like that poorly dressed man down the street?

What is such a person doing here? she wondered, having seen no one who appeared anything other than well-to-do in this part of town. She leaned closer, squinting at him. There was something familiar about him—the broad shoulders, the way he carried himself.

Christopher! Marsali rose up in her seat, leaning over the front of the carriage.

"Miss Abbott, do be careful." Mr. Vancer held his hand out to her, and Marsali accepted it, practically jumping from the carriage. She stepped past him and began walking briskly down the street, about to call out the man when his cane swung into view.

She felt her hope deflate. *It cannot be Christopher. See how he is hobbling. He is probably not even young.*

But he is tall, his shoulders broad.

Many men are tall with broad shoulders, even as they age. She continued arguing with herself.

His hair—that was it. His hair would tell her. If the man was indeed Christopher, his brown hair would brush the back of his collar with a slight curl. He was walking so slowly, and she so quickly, that she was almost close enough to tell.

"What is wrong? Have I done something to offend you?" Mr. Vancer's gentle voice and his hand upon her arm stopped her. Instead of looking at him, she watched as the man with the cane lifted his hat to mop his brow. The skin at the base of his head appeared wrinkled. Her disappointment swelled. *He* is *old.* And his hair in back was cut very short, perhaps the same color as Christopher's, but nowhere near to his collar.

I will simply have to allow my hair to grow . . .

Crushing disappointment swelled in her breast, so much so that she stumbled and might have fallen save for Mr. Vancer's hand at her arm. The man continued his labored walk down the street. Something about his leg was obviously very wrong or possibly even deformed, and Marsali wondered how she ever could have imagined it might be Christopher.

"I thought I saw someone I knew." She looked at the ground as tears stung her eyes.

Mr. Vancer did not say anything but drew her to him, pulling her into his embrace. His strong arms offered comfort, and a tiny sob escaped her throat. "Would that I might take this pain from you, Miss Abbott."

She began to cry in earnest.

He did not chastise her but gently steered her back the way they had come, through the gate and into the relative privacy of the garden. There they sat on a bench, and she wept out her heartache.

"Allow me to help you heal," Mr. Vancer said after some time had passed and at last her tears had dried. "If you will but give me a chance, I promise to make you happy again."

CHAPTER 36

earing a triumphant smile and looking far better than Marsali had seen her thus far, Lady Cosgrove practically floated into the sitting room. "We've made the second page of the *Evening Post*," she exclaimed.

"The newspaper is just now publishing the story of the *Amanda May*?" A month had passed since her wreck—old news for most, though Marsali continued to dwell on it, remembering the horrific events leading to its end with such clarity it was as if they had happened hours ago. "I suppose the papers in America are not as prompt at reporting news as those in England."

"Everything is slower here," Lady Cosgrove agreed, her face resuming its usual, pinched expression. "But this article is not about the misfortune of the ship; it is about *us*."

Why should anyone want to read about us? Marsali set down her embroidery and reached for the paper. "May I?"

Lady Cosgrove handed her the paper and seated herself on the sofa beside Marsali's chair. Marsali had learned to avoid the sofas and love seats when sitting in this room or any other, lest Mr. Vancer join her and assume a place too near her.

"Do read it aloud," Lady Cosgrove said. "I should like to hear it again."

Marsali opened the paper and saw the headline on page two at once. "Fairy Tale to Nightmare—Or Is It?" Her brow wrinkled, and a premonition of unease flared in her stomach.

"Miss Marsali Abbott (19) of Manchester boarded the Amanda May *at Liverpool, England, on 4 September, eager for a new life in America. Miss Abbott, daughter of Charles Abbott, of Manchester, England, came to join her sister, who had made the journey four years earlier. Miss Abbott's parents are both deceased."* Marsali stopped reading and looked up at Lady Cosgrove.

"This is all about me—why should anyone care who I am?"

"Yes, yes." Lady Cosgrove waved her hand dismissively. "That part is rather boring, but keep reading, my dear."

Silently Marsali bristled at the endearment. Never once, throughout the entire four-week voyage, had she heard Lady Cosgrove refer to Lydia as such. Of late Marsali worried that there were times Lady Cosgrove really did believe she was her daughter.

"While aboard the Amanda May *Miss Abbott became enamored of fellow passenger, a Mr. Christopher Thatcher (21), grandson of Eugene Durham, the Seventh Duke of Salisbury."* Marsali glanced down at the ring on her finger, the family heirloom that could no longer be passed down. *At least until I have returned it to Christopher's sisters.* In her letter she had promised to give them the ring as soon as safe passage for it might be arranged.

Safe passage—is there such a thing?

"Grandson of a duke or not, no doubt you would have continued on in a life of poverty being married to Mr. Thatcher. He was a descendaent through his mother, so the title and monies did not go to him."

"He did not need a title or money." Marsali had loved him as he was. *Just* as he was, and she felt certain he would have built a better life for himself here. The one he had dreamed of. She felt suddenly tired and sorrowful. She leaned forward, handing the paper to Lady Cosgrove. "I fear I can read no more."

"Very well." Lady Cosgrove took up the paper, straightened her posture, and began where Marsali had left off.

"It is assumed Mr. Thatcher returned that affection, for Captain Robert Gower (44) of Liverpool, married the two the morning of 25 September, just hours before lightning struck the mast of the Amanda May, *setting the ship afire and sending all of her crew and two of her passengers to watery graves. The only survivors were Miss Abbott and Lady Cornelia Cosgrove—"* Lady Cosgrove cleared her voice suddenly, then mumbled something that began with "fifty."

She skipped reading her age, Marsali surmised. Lydia had informed her—as she'd informed everyone else on the ship—that her mother was fifty-one.

Lady Cosgrove cleared her throat once more. "I seem to have a tickle," she said. "Be a dear and find someone to fetch me a glass of water, will you?"

"Of course." Marsali stood and left the room, trying not to contain her growing resentment of Lady Cosgrove. *She treated Lydia much the same*, Marsali reminded herself— partly a pampered showpiece to put on display, and partly a servant at her beck and call.

But at least I am not in danger here. And I can leave next month.

She found a servant girl to fetch Lady Cosgrove's drinks—water and something a bit stronger, Marsali knew intuitively by now—and returned to the sitting room.

In her absence Lady Cosgrove appeared to have recovered from her tickle and began reading aloud once more before Marsali had even taken her seat.

"Lady Cosgrove's daughter, Lydia, formerly betrothed to

Mr. William Vancer (34) (Vancer Furs, Vancer Shipping) of New York, perished at sea. Upon learning of the disaster, he welcomed both Lady Cosgrove and Miss Abbott into his home indefinitely." Lady Cosgrove paused and removed a handkerchief from her sleeve, then used it to dab at the corners of her eyes.

"Since then Miss Abbott and Mr. Vancer have been seen driving, and the three have hosted a dinner party with a few close friends. At that party, Miss Abbott was seated near the head of the table at Mr. Vancer's right, indicating that the rumors are likely true—that she and Mr. Vancer are helping each other through their grief and may just be able to heal each other's broken hearts. The real fairy tale might just be unfolding."

Marsali brought a hand to her forehead, partly covering one eye and wishing she might disappear altogether. "I did not realize the gossip column merited the second page. It seems this piece is more fictitious than newsworthy."

"Do not be ungrateful, dear," Lady Cosgrove snapped. "Mr. Vancer has rescued you as surely as Mr. Thatcher did—better, in fact. Look what he can give you." Her hand swept the room. Marsali did not need to follow to note the luxurious drapes, furnishings, and artwork. She was well aware of the wealth of her surroundings.

"Note that there was no mention of your poverty or the indenture to Mr. Thomas," Lady Cosgrove said. "Mr. Vancer made sure of that. No one will look down their noses at you here. You will have everything you've ever dreamed of, the life you were born to," she added, causing Marsali a sting of guilt.

The maid appeared in the doorway, waiting there until Lady Cosgrove beckoned her in. When the tray of drinks had been set on the table in front of them and the maid had gone, Marsali was not at all surprised to see Lady Cosgrove pick up the glass that did not hold water.

The older woman scooted forward on the sofa and

reached out, touching Marsali's arm in an almost motherly way. "Dear, you must forget Mr. Thatcher," she advised, her voice softer. "Think of efforts I will have wasted in bringing you here. Mr. Vancer is a fine man, and if you'll only let him, he can give you everything."

"I know," Marsali said, her eyes downcast. *But what if I cannot give him anything—even a piece of my heart—in return?*

"Lady Cosgrove showed me the article in the paper," Marsali said, feeling that to be as good a topic for conversantion as any on her stroll with Mr. Vancer through his gardens.

"Brilliant piece, wasn't it?" he asked, the smugness of his smile suggesting that he'd had much to do with it.

"Did you write it yourself?" Marsali asked.

He chuckled. "No, but I gave them the information needed and showed them its potential."

"What potential?" she tilted her face up at him.

"For the love story of the decade," he said, his lip curving upward as he looked down at her. He patted her hand as it rested lightly on the crook of his arm. "We are the matter of dreams. Women will swoon over such a story, and then they will recall the name Vancer when it comes time to purchase their furs."

Marsali bristled. *Losing one's fiancée and one's husband is what others dream of?* "And if our dream does not go as the paper has so boldly predicted?" She did not see how it possibly could, based as it was on promoting business, as it suddenly seemed to be.

Mr. Vancer ceased walking, turned to Marsali, and took both of her hands in his. "Why should it not?"

She replied with a question of her own. "Why should you wish to marry <u>me</u>? Why, for that matter, did you wish to marry Lydia? No doubt you are one of the most sought-after bachelors in New York, or possibly even the entire States."

"New York, yes. The States . . . perhaps, though there are some well-known Virginians still holding out as well."

She frowned at his arrogance, and he laughed aloud as if he knew her thoughts.

"I am only jesting," he assured her. "The truth is twofold. I have entertained a great many fine ladies with the idea that I might find one I wished to court. But none has ever held my attention for long."

"Perhaps it is your attention that is lacking, rather than the ladies," Marsali suggested, causing him to laugh again.

"That is what I love about you—your candor is refreshing. I shall never be allowed to be vain with you by my side." He released her hands, offered her his arm once more, and they resumed their walk.

Marsali fretted even more. He'd spoken almost as if it was a foregone conclusion that they were a couple, that they *would* be together.

"Why did you suppose that Lydia—Miss Cosgrove," Marsali amended, "would be any different than the other ladies? That she would be able to keep your attention?"

"I did not suppose that at all," Mr. Vancer said, somewhat astonishing Marsali.

"Yet you intended to marry her? And what would happen when you no longer fancied her?" she demanded. "Would you—"

"No." His tone sounded more pained than angry. "When I marry I shall be faithful to my wife. As I would hope she would be faithful to me." He cast a glance at Marsali, causing her further guilt.

I am already unfaithful. I cannot stop thinking of Christopher or comparing the two.

"I agreed to marry Miss Cosgrove for two reasons. First, the Cosgroves are old friends. Our families have a history some generations back. When Lady Cosgrove wrote to me of her predicament, I do not believe she was hoping for an offer of marriage for her daughter."

"Then why—"

"If honesty is your strength, impatience is surely your weakness," Mr. Vancer said.

Marsali sighed, then found herself smiling. "You are right, of course," she admitted. "My apologies."

"Accepted." He gave her hand a gentle squeeze. "Lady Cosgrove's letter arrived at nearly the same time as another letter from England, this bequeathing to me an estate worth a great deal of money. However, to claim the inheritance, I had to be married."

"So your act *was* more than charity," Marsali said, understanding at last what had brought about such an unusual betrothal.

"I admit as much," Mr. Vancer said. "Yet Miss Cosgrove—and her mother—stood to benefit from it as well."

"But you did not know her. What if you did not suit each other?"

He shrugged. "That was always a possibility. I had not seen Miss Cosgrove since she was a girl, and all I remembered of her was that she had a head full of golden curls and chattered incessantly."

Marsali smiled sadly. "She remained very much the same—extraordinarily beautiful and talkative."

"Do *you* think we would have suited well?" Mr. Vancer asked.

Marsali looked up at him once more, as if studying his profile might help her to predict such a thing. "I do not know," she said truthfully. "Miss Cosgrove was quite young and rather prone to emotion."

"Just one year younger than yourself," Mr. Vancer noted.

"Yes, but . . ."

"She had not lived through what you have," he suggested.

"I suppose that might have been our difference," Marsali said. "But she was a sweet girl, ever optimistic and enthusiastic, with a spirit of adventure. I believe you would have liked her quite well."

"Thank you for sharing that with me." They came to a bench in the garden, and he stopped before it, stepping aside and indicating that Marsali should sit. Somewhat reluctantly, she did, and he followed—seating himself too closely to her, as she had feared.

"I have felt somewhat guilty," he explained, "that I am not mourning my intended, as you seem to be mourning your husband of only one day."

"He was my husband for less than one day, but we had four weeks in which to become well acquainted. Had you been given the same, your feelings might be different."

"I thank you for that as well," Mr. Vancer said. "You are generous with your thoughts about others."

Not really, Marsali thought, assuming a great deal of guilt herself.

"But the fact remains that I intended to marry Miss Cosgrove for financial gain. And now that I find myself without a fiancée, time grows very short. If I am not wed by the year's end, I will lose my great uncle's inheritance."

"Do you need it so badly?" Marsali asked. It had not occurred to her that he might live on borrowed wealth or that his business did not do as well as she had supposed.

"Need it? No. Do I want it? Yes, very much so. It will provide the capital to expand my current business, as well as to invest in others I have set my sights upon for some time. It is not about the money so much as the opportunity."

"You are willing to risk a life of unhappiness for this opportunity?"

He did not answer immediately but appeared to be considering her question. "I had not looked at it in quite that light," he said. "After all, I did not intend to marry Miss Cosgrove the very moment she stepped from the ship. Rather, I intended a period of time for us to become acquainted—as you and I are now," he added, giving her a meaningful look. "But, one way or another, I intend to marry by December 31. I must," he insisted. "And if I *must*, I find I should like it to be to you."

His bold declaration left Marsali breathless and set her heart to racing. She had known his intentions from that first day at breakfast, yet to hear him declare them so openly frightened her. Not because he was unkind, for he wasn't, but—*because it is not right. Something about this, about us, is not what it should be.* But to give voice to those words would sound ludicrous, for she could not explain her feeling any better than that.

"I know you do not love me," he continued, causing Marsali to meet his gaze, her own sorrowful.

"No matter," he reassured her. "You are young yet, and time enough has not passed for you to forget your feelings for Mr. Thatcher."

"I am sorry," Marsali said, and in that moment she was, and wished fervently that she might feel differently about him.

"Don't be," he said. "Your depth of emotion gives me hope, actually. That when—*if*—your affection does turn to me—and you must know that I hope it does—you will love me well, with your whole heart."

Marsali swallowed with difficulty, growing more ill at ease by the moment.

"Many marriages begin loveless," Mr. Vancer said. "Many are still arranged, and the couple has little say in the matter. But after they are married, that is when a friendship can be developed and affection formed. My own parents began as such and had a very happy life together." He claimed her hand once more, caressing it lightly with his own, and awakening in her a yearning to be held, to be comforted.

But by him?

CHAPTER 37

M y Dearest Sisters,

I have taken my leave of New Jersey, and some two weeks' travel southwest has found me in a region known as Virginia. The country here is beautiful, and autumn flourishes. Rolling hills, gentle rivers, and dense woods have been my companions during my travels. And amongst all these: farms and a patchwork of well-laid fields. Though I've not yet put my hand to a plough, it seems already that the soil here is rich and a man could support himself well. Indeed, this is much the life I dreamed for myself when in England and should be perfectly content with my lot at this time, were it not for my heartache at the loss of my wife. As the weeks pass, my hope of finding Marsali dwindles . . .

Hat in hand, Christopher left the wide circular drive of the Thomas plantation and climbed the steps to the stately two-story home on the banks of the James River. He knocked briskly, then waited, glancing about as he did. The plantation was bustling with activity on this fall day, the last of October, with men and women scurrying about in an attitude of work. Though he had passed several people, none had made eye contact with him, even when he had offered a friendly smile.

The door opened. It was not a uniformed butler who bade him enter Joshua Thomas's home, but a woman wearing an apron and with a cap on her head.

"Good day to you, ma'am." Christopher gave a slight bow. "I am here to seek an appointment with Mr. Thomas regarding the matter of one of his recently arrived indentured servants."

"If you mean Molly, it were her own fault she fell down that step and broke her own leg. Daydreaming again, I suspect, and now the master getting blamed for it."

Another suspicious injury? "I am not here to place blame on anyone," Christopher assured the woman. "Nor am I acquainted with the misfortunate Molly of whom you speak. I am here to inquire after a woman named Marsali Abbott, who was a passenger on the *Amanda May*, and who was, I believe, indentured to Mr. Thomas."

The woman's narrowed eyes loosened somewhat, though her frown remained. "Come with me," she said at last and led him into a richly appointed sitting room.

Christopher sat in an uncomfortable straight-backed chair near the fire and waited several minutes more, trying to keep both his hope and anxiety to manageable levels. *Marsali could be here.* He imagined glimpsing her out the window, or that she might be the one to return for him. But it was a little boy who next joined him, peeking into the room with a somewhat wary expression.

"Hello there." Christopher leaned forward in his chair to better see the child. The boy was dressed in a fine suit with knee breeches and a matching blue coat. Blond curls roamed this way and that over his head, as if the child's mother had long since given up any attempts to tame them.

"Who are you?" the boy asked, taking another step into the room.

"Christopher Thatcher." He offered his hand as he would have to an adult. "What is your name?"

"Joshua," the boy said. "I mean, Thomas."

"*You* are Mr. Joshua Thomas? How splendid." *If only I was so fortunate.* But Christopher's grin widened. The child appeared well cared for, and if he belonged to Mr. Thomas . . . *Perhaps the man is at least better than my father.*

"What's wrong with your leg?" Joshua asked.

Before Christopher could answer, the same woman who bade him enter the first time reappeared in the doorway, her scowl deepening when she noticed Christopher's companion.

"You are *not* to be down here," she scolded, pulling the child roughly from the room and sending him away with a firm swat on his backside.

"He wasn't bothering me," Christopher said.

She ignored his reference to the boy. "Follow me, Mr. Thatcher."

She led him down a short hall to a study, quite the opposite from his grandfather's in England. Rich furnishings appeared crammed into the space, and dark, heavy draperies covered the window and even much of the walls, bringing an instant sense of gloom as Christopher entered.

"You are here inquiring about Miss Abbott?"

Christopher turned abruptly, unappreciative of being caught off guard, and discovered that an older, slightly stooped, yet strong-featured man had entered just behind him.

"I am," Christopher said. "I sailed on the *Amanda May* with her, and I believe she was to be a servant here."

"And your name?" the man asked.

"Christopher Thatcher, formerly of Yorkshire, England."

"Hmm." The man gave a curt nod and walked around to sit behind the massive desk. He sat carefully, Christopher noted, as if the curvature of his spine pained him. When he was seated, he motioned with his hand for Christopher to take one of the two chairs on the opposite side.

"Now, then, what question do you have regarding Miss Abbott?'

"Is she here?" Christopher asked, trying not to sound overeager. He refrained from leaning forward anxiously, as he felt prone to.

"If you were truly a passenger on the *Amanda May*, then you would know that the ship encountered a storm and was lost just off the coast of New York one month ago."

"One month and four days," Christopher corrected him. *Why does he not answer me directly?*

"If you are here seeking damages, you are wasting your time. Ships are lost frequently; their owners are not liable."

So you are Mr. Thomas. "I am here seeking Miss Abbott, my wife." Christopher met Thomas's gaze. "Is she here?" he asked once more.

"Now I know you are lying," Thomas said, pushing off the desk and standing as if to end their interview. "The Miss Abbott I arranged passage for was not married."

"Captain Gower married us at sea." Christopher rose from his chair as well. "I intended to accompany her and work to shorten her term of indenture. And I intend to stay now, until I have discovered her whereabouts." Something in Thomas's expression made him suspect—the subtle shift of his eyes, his refusal to answer the question Christopher had posed. *He is not telling me something.*

"Miss Abbott is not here," Thomas said at last. "If you have no notion of her whereabouts, it can be presumed she was lost at sea. But even had she come, I would not allow you to stay. Miss Abbott was to be my daughter's lady's maid—a task you seem ill suited for." Thomas's gaze roved over Christopher. "Caring for lady's clothing would hardly seem to be your strength."

"You'd be surprised," Christopher said with little humor. He would *not* be washing dresses here. "As I am surprised that you would refuse the offer of free labor. I am proposing to work for you, in return only for a roof over my head, decent meals, and the possibility of news of my wife."

Thomas appeared to consider him as he came around the other side of the desk. "You haven't the attitude of a servant, and that spells trouble."

"I'm not a servant," Christopher said, wanting that point clarified up front. *I am making the choice to do this. You are not compelling me.* "I am not offering to bring your tea or polish your silver or shoes. But I am a good worker. I love working the land, and I'm not afraid of putting in a full day doing it."

"Papa, Joshua said you had a dashing visitor." A young woman appeared in the doorway and smiled prettily at Christopher. "*Have*," she amended without so much as a blush of embarrassment.

"Susan, this is Mr. Thatcher—*Miss Abbott's* husband." A pointed look was exchanged between father and daughter, arousing further suspicion. "Mr. Thatcher, my daughter Miss Susan Thomas."

Christopher nodded but kept his attention on Thomas instead of bowing over his daughter's hand.

"Mr. Thatcher is of a mind to stay here and work for us, until such a time as news of his wife may be discovered," Mr. Thomas added. "She is one of the passengers whose body was not recovered, so he feels she may yet be living."

Christopher forced back the bile that rose each time he thought of Marsali's body being found washed up on shore— or worse. *She is* not *dead.* Though Mr. Thomas professed that she was not here, Christopher felt more certain than ever that she was alive.

And he knows something.

"Oh, do let him stay," Susan said, sounding far too enthusiastic to Christopher.

Mr. Thomas was silent a long moment, his gaze never leaving Christopher as he considered. Christopher recalled the conversation he'd had with Captain Gower about Thomas and could imagine the man's thought processes as he weighed the benefit of nearly free labor against the cost of a potential troublemaker.

"You're not fit for hard labor with that leg." He glanced at Christopher's cane. "But there are a fair number of lighter tasks needing to be done before winter sets in. We'll give it a trial run." Thomas fixed a look on Christopher that left no question as to who would be the one on trial.

He is more greedy than cautious. Christopher tucked that piece of information away and knew he must learn all he could about Thomas in the coming days. If the man knew anything of Marsali, Christopher would discover it.

"Welcome, Mr. Thatcher. Let me show you around." Miss Thomas linked her arm through his.

I will find Marsali, he silently vowed. And despite her arm through his, he knew he would avoid Miss Thomas in the meantime.

CHAPTER 38

Yorkshire, England, November 1828

"Oh, Helen, you're here at last." Grace rose from her chair to greet her sister as she entered the sitting room at Sutherland Hall.

"I came as soon as I could," Helen exclaimed. Behind her Mr. Kingsley, the butler, hovered, waiting to help with the cloak she hadn't taken the time to remove. "Samuel insisted on driving me over."

"As I would have as well, had Grace been going to visit you to hear news of your brother at last." Nicholas shot a look of approval at his brother-in-law, who had just entered the room behind Helen.

"Thank you, Nicholas," Samuel said. "I am glad we are in agreement on some subjects these days."

"Many of them, likely," Nicholas said, concern creasing his brow as he watched Grace. "I think you should sit down, darling. And perhaps I should read the letters first."

"Carrying a child has not altered my eyesight," Grace said, but she leaned close and rose up on her toes to kiss his cheek, to show that she appreciated his concern. *How I love him.* And how worried she had been for Christopher. Taking up the letters from the side table, she seated herself on the settee and pulled Helen down beside her. "There are three letters here. They all arrived at once—no doubt at least one was sitting at the office awhile—but I propose that we read them in the order they are stamped."

"Yes," Helen agreed. "Just please hurry. I must know that Christopher is well."

"Of course he is well," Nicholas said. "He has written to you, hasn't he?"

"It is only natural that she should feel anxious for news of her brother," Samuel said, a slight reproach in his tone. He crossed the room and seated himself in the chair closest to Helen while Nicholas took one on the other side of Grace.

"Only two of the letters are from Christopher," she explained. "The third came from someone in New York. That is the one with the oldest postmark, so we shall read it first." She picked up the top envelope and broke the seal, then removed the letter. When it was pressed flat she began to read.

"*My Dears Lady Grace Sutherland and Mrs. Helen Preston,*

It is my unhappy fate to tell you that your beloved brother, Christopher, has been missing since the night of 25 September..."

Grace continued reading, her voice rushed and rising in pitch. *Missing, injured, Crayton, married.* It was too much news to take in all at once.

Beside her Helen burst into tears, causing Samuel to jump up and come to stand behind her, his hands on her shoulders for support.

"Will this business with that scoundrel Crayton never end?" he demanded. "We have had word that he is yet well occupied, earning his bread in France, so how is it this Mr. Luke came to follow Christopher?"

"Luke's transaction with Crayton must have occurred before we had put our plan into action," Nicholas said.

"Christopher had booked his passage prior to that time, and if he was being watched . . ."

"Christopher married? I cannot believe it," Grace said, latching onto the least disturbing piece of information. They all knew Christopher had been the most self-proclaimed bachelor.

"He is *missing*," Helen exclaimed. "That is all that matters."

"Not if he has written you a letter, he isn't. Open the next," Nicholas said. Grace hurried to comply, tearing the envelope in her haste.

"It *is* from Christopher." She let out a breath of relief. "I would know his writing anywhere." She read the letter out loud straight through until she came to the line about his missing wife.

"Oh, dear," Helen said, her hands coming to her cheeks. "Each believes the other has perished."

"Read the third letter," Samuel urged. "Perhaps your brother has found his bride."

All four leaned close over the page as Grace unfolded it, her hands slightly trembling. She did not bother reading it aloud, as each was close enough, and four sets of eyes were already scanning the contents.

"He is in Virginia now," Samuel remarked. "That seems a great distance to travel so quickly with the injuries he described."

"I wish you were there to tend him," Helen said, her eyes still searching the paper. "Oh no, he has not found her. He sounds so sad. 'As the weeks pass, my hope of finding Marsali dwindles . . .'" Helen looked up at the others.

"We must write to him at once and tell him that she is well—and in New York." Grace stood and hurried across the room to pull the tassel summoning Kingsley. "Can we have a driver take it to Liverpool today?"

"Of course," Nicholas said. "I will take it myself, if you would like."

"Grace can come and stay with Samuel and me while you are gone," Helen offered.

"If we hurry I may be able to get it on a ship tomorrow evening." Nicholas stood and crossed the room, closer to Grace. "Is that what you would like me to do?"

She nodded and felt her love for him swell. Since learning that she was increasing, Nicholas had hardly let her walk down the stairs on her own. That he would agree to leave her for at least three days to take a letter showed how much he cared for her—and Christopher.

Kingsley appeared in the doorway, his own brow drawn with worry as he considered the four of them fretting.

"I need horses and our fastest coach readied," Nicholas said. "And Harrison is to drive."

Grace placed her hand on Nicholas's arm and smiled her gratitude at his wisdom. Harrison might be their oldest driver, but this errand was of a personal nature to him as well. Undoubtedly he would see Nicholas safely and quickly to the docks at Liverpool.

But from there it could easily take another two months for a letter to reach Christopher. She pushed the disturbing thought to the back of her mind. She would hope and pray for a miracle. And surely they would get one. She and Helen had ended up so very happy, in part at least from Christopher's efforts. He had to have his happy ending as well, even if it was far from home.

It comforted her to think that he had not been alone this whole time and to believe that he would not be for much longer. Perhaps he and Marsali had found each other already.

Samuel helped Helen from her seat, and they came to stand by Nicholas and Grace.

"Would you like me to come with you?" Samuel asked Nicholas.

"No," Nicholas said, not even taking the time to consider. "I would like you here with your wife and mine, lest something happens and one of them requires a physician."

"Very well," Samuel said soberly, and Grace could see the weight he felt. Worrying over Helen's health strained him enough. *That Nicholas should add my care to Samuel's burden . . .*

Is no small miracle itself. Her spirits buoyed, just from thinking how far the two men had come in friendship and trust in the last year. *Surely there must be one more miracle out there for our family.*

For Christopher.

CHAPTER 39

"Ladies, it is time we begin planning our masquerade ball," Mr. Vancer announced as he entered the room, interrupting Marsali in the middle of playing the Irish folk song "Robin Adair." At his announcement, her fingers stilled on the keys of the pianoforte, though the words of the ballad continued to trail through her mind.

What's this dull town to me? Robin's not near.

Where's all the joy and mirth that made this town a heav'n on earth?

Oh, they're all fled with thee . . .

"I have been remiss in not hosting a ball to properly welcome you." Mr. Vancer placed his hand on her shoulder. Instead of comforting, his action felt possessive.

What made my heart so sore?

Oh, it was parting with thee . . .

"Usually the masquerade is held New Year's Eve," he explained. "But the thought came to me today that we must hold it sooner."

"What a splendid idea." Lady Cosgrove clasped her

hands together as a younger girl might, reminding Marsali of Lydia.

Now thou art cold to me.

Yet him I loved so well.

"It will be the perfect opportunity for me to properly introduce Marsali to New York society," Mr. Vancer said.

Marsali wondered *how* he would introduce her. As a misfortunate young lady whom he had befriended, or . . .

"How do you feel about such an idea, Miss Abbott?" He squeezed her shoulder gently, as if soliciting a positive remark.

"There is no need to hold a fancy ball to introduce me to anyone," Marsali said, privately dreading the thought. For all she had wished for her status in life to improve, she did not enjoy the requirements and rigors of society that came with it.

"Who said anything about a need?" Mr. Vancer asked. "This is something I *wish* to do—very much. Please say that you will join me in celebrating with my friends and acquaintances."

"Of course." Marsali gave the only acceptable answer, though her heart had yet to accept that the man she truly wished to be with was dead.

Still in my heart shall dwell

Oh, I can ne'er forget . . .

Christopher paused to wipe his brow before bending over the tub, stirring another batch of the mortar used to chink the barn where they cured tobacco. His arm had been troubling him again until George, one of Thomas's slaves who worked alongside him, had suggested applying the mud to his skin.

The cool mud, when mixed with the crushed leaves of a burdock plant—an annoying little weed in every other respect, so far as Christopher could see—had calmed his wounds as nothing else had. The generously given advice was the start of a fast friendship with and respect for George and many of Thomas's slaves.

"Master's daughter's coming." George inclined his head toward the stables. "She goes riding a lot more these days—since you come."

"Master's daughter is nothing but trouble," Christopher muttered. He finished stirring the mortar and scooped up a generous portion in his trowel.

"For you, especially." George chuckled.

"Oh, Mr. Thatcher," Susan Thomas sang, waving a lacy handkerchief as she walked toward him. *As if I'm blind.* He would have to be to miss her in her burgundy riding habit, her long, golden curls tumbling down her back. She was a striking woman in more ways than one.

"I've news for you, Mr. Thatcher. About your wife."

Christopher nearly dropped the trowel. The mud glopped onto his boot. With a shaking hand, he set the tool aside and looked at Miss Thomas. "Yes?"

"A letter came from Miss Abbott's sister, whom you wrote to. I am sorry to say that she has neither seen nor heard from Miss Abbott."

Christopher lowered his head and let out a defeated sigh. If Marsali was dead, shouldn't he be able to somehow feel it? Instead it seemed the opposite was true. He imagined her very much alive and calling for him to come and find her. Ignoring the tightening in his chest, Christopher wiped his hands on his pants, then held one out. "May I see the letter?"

"I—it is gone," Miss Thomas said. "I did not think you would wish to see it. I supposed that you might not be able to read it, so I took the liberty of reading it for you."

"If I am unable to read, how did you suppose I wrote a letter to my wife's sister in the first place?" Christopher demanded.

"I was only trying to do you a favor." Miss Thomas's lip

jutted out, and she sniffled as if he had hurt her feelings.

Christopher hoped he had. She deserved it if she'd really gotten rid of his letter. "Is it customary in America—in Virginia—to open letters addressed to someone other than yourself?"

"I thought it would be preferable for you to hear such difficult news from me, rather than reading it on your own."

"In the future, please note that I am well able to both read and weather the contents of any correspondence I receive." Christopher resumed his work before he said or did anything more—anything that would have repercussions, like ending his trial run when he still felt that Mr. Thomas was his best hope for finding Marsali. Christopher scooped a generous portion of mud and flung it almost violently at the log wall.

"I shall both note it and report it to my father." Nose in the air, Miss Thomas stomped away in the direction of the house.

"You do that," Christopher muttered. The worst Thomas could do was tell him to leave.

"You're in a mess of trouble now," George said when Miss Thomas was out of sight. His gaze strayed toward the whipping post at the entrance to the barn. "Good thing you a free man."

"I am grateful," Christopher said, thinking not of the consequences but of his continued quest for Marsali. "I'll have to go see Marsali's sister myself, and I haven't any means with which to get there." He would have to walk, as he had walked here; only this time a mountain range stood in his way. For all of Marsali's hope that she and her sister would live close by each other, nearly ninety miles separated the Thomas plantation from the one where Charlotte worked. Traveling there would be akin to going from Yorkshire to Liverpool—only this time he had no coach or horse. He would have to walk—on a leg that still was not strong enough.

CHAPTER 40

My Dearest Marsali,

It was with both joy and a heavy heart that I read your letter. I am so relieved that you have crossed the Atlantic safely, and so relieved you are no longer indebted to Mr. Thomas. But my heart broke at reading the tragic end to your brief marriage. I understand your sorrow more than you know, for Matthew was killed last August in a logging accident at the mill, just a few days after I posted my last letter to you. Since then I have felt devastated in most every way. I wish you could join me here now, but as it is, I am not certain my employer will allow me to continue to stay, as I can no longer contribute any monies for the rent of our cabin . . .

Lady Cosgrove climbed into the carriage behind Marsali. "Just think, dear. One week more, and it will all be official."

"What will?" Marsali asked uneasily, though she was fairly certain to what Lady Cosgrove referred.

The carriage began to roll as she answered. "Your

engagement to Mr. Vancer. He intends to make it official the night of the masquerade ball."

"Without asking me?"

Lady Cosgrove waved her hand dismissively. "What is there to ask? Of course you will marry him."

"I cannot," Marsali insisted. Since the month they had agreed upon had ended and stretched into another, Marsali had been careful not to be alone with Mr. Vancer—lest he decide to propose—a task made easier because November was a busy month in trade for him, keeping him away many hours.

But even had he asked—or even if he did not—she did not feel ready to agree to marriage and would have left his home already had she any idea of where she might go.

Lady Cosgrove leaned forward, placing a hand upon Marsali's and fixing her with a stern look. "You will not throw all of our hard work here away. I have done this for you, and now you shall have everything you've ever wanted."

"Everything *you* wanted," Marsali corrected. "I do not love him," she said, half wishing that she did. Mr. Vancer was kind to her, and she felt no objections with his character. But he did not make her feel as Christopher had. And she could not seem to get past that. Or Christopher.

"Love can come later," Lady Cosgrove said. "You will not get another opportunity like this. If you reject Mr. Vancer's offer, you'll end up a servant somewhere—or worse."

It was not an exaggeration or an idle threat. If Mr. Vancer sent her away, Marsali had no idea where she would go or to whom she would turn. Charlotte had been her last hope, and even she had encouraged Marsali to stay.

"And if love never comes?" Marsali said, as much to herself as to Lady Cosgrove.

"Then you find yourself grateful for what you have—a fine home, beautiful gowns, plenty of food to eat."

All things I have lived without the past years. And all things she could survive without again. *And I can survive without Christopher as well.* But she feared she would never again feel fully alive without him.

Christopher removed his hat and set it aside, then primed the pump in the yard. His leg throbbed but still supported his weight after a day spent on it, working hard. He felt hopeful, both about his ability to walk the hundred miles to see Marsali's sister and even about the possibility that Mr. Thomas would lend him a horse or take him partway.

The Indian summer had allowed Christopher to finish clearing the south field earlier than he'd anticipated. *Surely Thomas will be pleased.* The ground was as near perfect for spring plowing as one might hope, and Christopher wished it was spring already and the winter months did not stretch between. Virginia was a man's dream—at least so far as farming was concerned.

He leaned over, availing himself of the cool water flowing from the pipe, cupping his hands to drink first, then splashing it over his face and arms. Though the nights had grown cool and crisp, by midday the sun still shone brightly. A few of the trees had begun to lose their leaves, but many were still ablaze with color. The garden had been mostly cleared of its pumpkins and squash, but beyond that there was little sign of the coming winter.

He was just replacing his hat when a woman's scream rent the air, raising the hairs on the back of his neck. The crack of a whip sounded, followed by another scream.

The barn. Christopher ran toward it, thinking of the whipping post and the smatters of dried blood on the ground beneath. In the three weeks he had been working here, he had not seen the post used—or noted any other punishments or mistreatment from Thomas. Miss Thomas's behavior had been more troubling, but her implied threats each time they had a disagreement had never amounted to anything.

The screaming had not ceased when Christopher burst through the doors in time to see Mr. Thomas raising his whip once more, aiming at the back of a young slave girl tied to the post. Christopher stepped in front of her, placing himself between her bloodied back and Mr. Thomas.

"Stop," Christopher ordered. "She's but a child. You're beating an innocent child!"

"She's no child—she's near eighteen," Thomas growled. "Not innocent either. She stole from me."

"What? An extra piece of bread because she's starving?" Christopher could see the girl's ribs through the thin fabric of her dress. "You don't want to do this," he said to Thomas.

To his surprise, Mr. Thomas lowered his whip and began coiling it in his hands. "You're right. I don't."

But his tone said otherwise. Christopher's fists clenched at his sides, and he braced himself, expecting Thomas's fury to be redirected at him.

"I'm getting too old for this sort of thing," Thomas said, his voice congenial, as if they were discussing the threshing of wheat instead of the thrashing of another human. "I *shouldn't* be doing it." He finished coiling the whip and looked up at Christopher, their gazes locking. "You should." He held the whip out.

Christopher checked the impulse to voice his refusal and walk away. No doubt that was what Thomas expected, and then he would resume beating the girl.

"My daughter has been after me to make you an overseer," Thomas said. "Let's see if you have it in you to discipline when it's needed."

"Using that whip isn't discipline; it's abuse." Christopher's mind raced, and his gaze never left the whip as he tried to anticipate Thomas's next move.

"Call it what you like, it's got to be done to keep these people in line."

"And who keeps you in line?" Christopher asked.

Thomas's toothy grin appeared. "No one. None around here is up to the task. The same can be said of my daughter. But for some reason she thinks you're the man for the job— and even more, she wouldn't mind being kept in line by you."

This is madness. Christopher had done absolutely nothing to encourage her attention. He took care to avoid her whenever possible. *Even Miss Cosgrove's company was preferable.* She'd been chatty and emotional and somewhat annoying, but Miss Thomas seemed something else altogether. She was a woman with an agenda—one who, he had begun to suspect, would do just about anything to get what she wanted.

Behind him, the slave girl was still tied to the post, her arms suspended above her, her back painfully exposed.

"Are you going to finish, or am I? Or would you like to be through working here?"

I am done. Christopher kept the thought to himself. Feet dragging with obvious reluctance, he walked forward and took the whip from Thomas.

The handle was both warm and worn, and he felt vile just holding it. *How many people has this harmed? How many has it murdered?*

Christopher allowed the coil to loosen, and the whip unfurled, the end snaking through the dirt on the ground. He looked at it a long moment, then turned toward the woman. He raised his hand and drew the whip back, then whirled about toward Thomas as it snapped forward, its stinging tip flashing dangerously close to Thomas's face as the brute hollered and jumped back, losing his balance.

Christopher ran to the girl. Using the knife from his belt, he cut the straps holding her bound. "Go," he said, pushing her toward the doors as he faced Thomas once more.

The man now knelt on the ground, one hand braced on the dirt floor, his head down. Christopher wasn't fooled. Any second now Thomas would jump up in rage, the gun from his belt pointed at Christopher's heart. He couldn't bring himself to care and thought only of the crying girl, of Marsali, and what she might have suffered at Thomas's hand, and of the maid who had died before her.

"It's the weakest of men who hurt a woman, and a true coward who beats a helpless girl." Christopher's voice was filled with hatred. "I'll not have a part of it or anything else to do with the likes of one who does." Turning his back on Thomas, he strode to the doors and hurled the whip outside—over the fence and into the pig's mire for good measure.

Still no shot came. Christopher's heart pounded. *Why is he waiting? What else does he have planned?*

The girl he'd freed stood near the fence. "Look," she said, her hand outstretched as she pointed into the barn. Christopher followed her gaze back and saw that Thomas no longer knelt but lay on his side, unmoving.

"Go," he ordered the girl once more as he strode back toward the barn. "You shouldn't be seen here. If something *has* happened—" For the first time he considered that possibility, and he didn't want the girl to be blamed. "This is my doing, not yours." When she didn't move, he shouted back at her. "Get out of here!" He glanced over his shoulder, relieved to see that she had finally listened and was running off in the direction of the cabins. Christopher reached Thomas's side, then used his foot to push him to his back. He rolled slowly, like deadweight, and his unmoving eyes stared up from an ashen face. His gun was still in its holster on his belt, and his hands were slack at his sides.

"Mr. Thomas?" Christopher dropped to his knees and gave the man a shake. "Wake up." He patted Thomas's cheeks but received no response. Christopher pressed a hand to Thomas's neck and felt a faint pulse. He stood and hefted

Thomas in his arms, then ran toward the house, shouting for help.

Of all the repercussions he had anticipated, this one he was unprepared for.

CHAPTER 41

Following young Joshua Thomas, Christopher climbed the stairs to Mr. Thomas's bedroom. The summons he'd been expecting for days had finally come, and he was not looking forward to the ensuing confrontation. He'd stayed on only because he felt guilt that his actions—however justified they had seemed at the time—had ultimately caused Mr. Thomas to have a heart attack. Christopher had worked doubly hard since then, hoping to somehow make up for that, though he still felt no regrets about aiding the slave girl. And he still did not hold with Thomas's methods.

"In there," the little boy whispered as he stopped before the third door in the second-floor hall.

Christopher knelt before the child. "Thank you, Joshua." He wished he had something to give him—a penny or a stick of candy—though in the month he'd been here, Christopher had discovered that what the child lacked most was attention. Given Mr. Thomas's age, young Joshua had come later in life, and it seemed the man took very little interest in his son.

Christopher had not seen anyone who might have been the boy's mother, neither had there been any mention of Thomas's wife. He guessed she might have died giving birth to the boy—perhaps the reason Joshua's father did not care to spend time with him.

And now I must leave him to his loneliness. It was with some regret that Christopher stood once more and ruffled the boy's hair. "Thank you for being my friend while I was here. But now you must go." He did not want the child to hear him arguing with his father.

Joshua nodded and scampered down the hall, presumably in the direction of the nursery.

When he had disappeared behind another door, Christopher raised his hand to knock upon Mr. Thomas's. His knuckles had nearly brushed the wood when he stilled, listening to a suddenly raised voice coming from the other side.

"And how much longer will you be able to go on like this, Papa?"

Christopher quietly stepped backward. He had expected to have to face Mr. Thomas and felt prepared for that, but he had no desire to have that conversation with Mr. Thomas's daughter in the room.

"I wish to be settled before you pass," Miss Thomas continued. "I do not want to run this plantation alone."

"Won't have to." Her father's voice was feeble. "Harvey will run it for you."

"Harvey will *steal* it from me."

Christopher could imagine the look of petulance upon Miss Thomas's face. On several previous occasions he had witnessed it transform her otherwise pleasant features into something almost gruesome.

"Why won't you ask Mr. Thatcher to be an overseer?" she whined. "You've said yourself that he learns quickly and is capable."

The compliments meant little to Christopher. It would

not matter if Thomas did offer him such a position. He would never work for him—not like that.

"It would be a natural progression to him taking charge," Miss Thomas continued. "And then I could marry him, Papa. He is well bred—the descendant of a duke in England—and he does not know of my indiscretion." She laughed. "He believes Joshua to be your son."

Christopher stifled a gasp. This revelation made little Joshua's circumstance all the more tragic. Instead of retreating down the hall and stairs—as would be proper—Christopher glanced about, searching for any nearby servants, then stepped closer to the door and turned his head to the side to better hear.

"He would find out," Mr. Thomas said.

"It would not matter. By then we would be married, and there would be little he could do." Miss Thomas sighed wistfully. "We would not need to worry about him telling my secret, as some silly maid might. As my husband, it would be in his best interest to keep quiet on the matter. Like the others, he could be made to understand that it was best if everyone believed Joshua came to us through the unfortunate death of a relative."

The circumstances Marsali's sister had described in her initial letter began to fall into place. The need to cover up an illegitimate child could be a powerful motivator. It wasn't mere cruelty leading to the accidental death of more than one lady's maid. *Heavens above . . .* This was murder almost as sure as if he'd witnessed it!

". . . cannot marry him," Mr. Thatcher's voice croaked.

"Yes, I can, Papa. I am only asking your blessing, but if you will not give it, I will convince Mr. Thatcher to marry me anyway, after you are gone. How could any man resist inheriting a plantation?"

Christopher was indignant. He had not wanted his brothers-in-law to hand him property in England, and he did not want it handed to him here. Particularly with Miss

Thomas attached to it. He would have nothing to do with a murderess.

"You will not marry him." Mr. Thomas's voice sounded stronger, and there was a rustling of bedsheets from the other side of the door. "Mr. Thatcher is *already* married."

"No matter," Miss Thomas said dismissively. "He does not know about Miss Abbott, and it isn't as if she is here, so what does it matter?"

Christopher reeled backward as if struck.

"It matters plenty." Mr. Thomas's voice was strained but adamant. "If discovered, Mr. Thatcher would be guilty of bigamy. Wasn't the scandal of your illegitimate child enough of a trial?"

"I dealt with that," Miss Thomas said. "As I have dealt with the problem of Mr. Thatcher's wife. I saw to it that his letter never reached her sister, and I made up a letter from the sister in return. He believes his wife to be dead. It is quite simple, actually."

Christopher turned away from the door, though his inclination was to kick it down and demand justice. But that would only waste more time. And it was entirely possible that he still would not arrive at the truth. Their time for retribution would come.

He hurried down the stairs and out the front door and down the drive. If he had figured the distance correctly and walked without stopping to sleep, he would reach the plantation where Marsali's sister lived by the week's end.

CHAPTER 42

arsali fastened a string of pearls—a gift from Mr. Vancer for the ball tomorrow evening—around her neck and studied her reflection in the dressing table mirror. Four months ago she could never have imagined she would find herself here, in a New York mansion, wearing beautiful gowns and jewelry and with a maid to care for her. It was a lovely change from *being* a maid, yet one she still did not feel entirely comfortable with. She walked over to the window, where she watched the rain as it began to fall from a darkened sky, and she contemplated all that had happened to her in the past two months.

Mr. Vancer had spent a small fortune on her, and with every generosity and gift, she felt he pulled her closer, hooked on a line, much like the unfortunate fish she and her father used to catch. She was nearing the surface now, where escape would be impossible. He would remove her from the hook and place her in his boat, and that would be that.

A soft knock sounded upon her door. "Come in," she called, expecting her maid to appear. Instead it was Mr.

Vancer who peeked his head through the doorway. Marsali turned from the window and met his gaze, feeling a tiny catch in her heart. But it was not love. It was his hook—the weight of guilt eating at her. Mr. Vancer was a good man, but she felt incapable of returning that goodness to him.

"I have a surprise for you." He sounded as eager as a child on Christmas morning.

"You have already given me a gift for tomorrow." She fingered the pearls at her throat.

A grin split his face. "True. But you will like this one better. It has a far greater value than pearls."

Oh my. Oh no. Marsali's gaze dropped to her lap. He was going to ask her to marry him. She had known he wished to present her as his fiancée tomorrow; it was no surprise at all. What was surprising was that in all her weeks here, she had not figured out how to answer him.

He is kind. He will take care of me and provide for me.

I still yearn for Christopher. He made me laugh. We understood one another as Mr. Vancer and I never shall with our backgrounds so different.

"Are you ready?" he asked, pushing the door open a bit farther.

"Yes. Of course," she lied, then put on a brave smile and prayed for the right words, for inspiration and peace in her heart and mind.

He thrust the door open all the way, so that it nearly banged against the wall, then stepped aside, making way for the petite, brown-haired woman behind him.

"Charlotte!" Marsali tripped over her stool in her haste to cross the room and fall into her sister's outstretched arms.

"Oh, Marsali, how I've missed you!" Charlotte hugged her tightly, and Marsali—incapable of stopping a flood of tears, overwhelmed as she was—wept onto her shoulder. A soft click sounded behind them, and she looked up to see that the door had closed and Mr. Vancer had gone.

"I was beginning to fear we should never see each other," Marsali said, still clasping her sister tightly to her.

"As was I." Charlotte lessened her grip and leaned back. "My, but you have grown up, little sister. You look like Mother."

"So do you." Marsali smiled through her tears and then guided Charlotte so that they both stood in front of the mirror. "We look like each other." Both sisters laughed, and then Marsali cried again, relief and the sheer joy of their reunion spilling beyond the borders of her heart.

When at last her emotions had settled, Marsali led Charlotte to sit upon the bed.

"How did you come to be here?" Marsali asked.

"Mr. Vancer arranged it—sent a private carriage all the way to Virginia for me."

"He is a dear man." Marsali felt a swelling of gratitude and was closer to loving him than she ever had been.

"You must be very happy," Charlotte said, brushing a hand over Marsali's escaped curls, as had oft been her habit during their childhood. "How fortunate that he has taken you in—and taken to you." She laughed in that delicate way Marsali remembered from when they were girls.

"I *am* happy," she said, meaning it for the first time since that awful night of the shipwreck. "You're here."

"And I understand that tomorrow there is to be a ball," Charlotte exclaimed. "And *you* are to be the princess of honor." Her gaze grew distant and wistful. "Do you know that I've not been to any gathering resembling a ball since coming to America? We have only country dances in Virginia—sometimes in people's *barns*."

Marsali doubted there could be any dance to top the one she had shared with Christopher on the ship's deck. "Do you wish to go?" Marsali studied her sister curiously. She realized Charlotte was not wearing mourning clothes. Did she not miss Matthew terribly?

"I see what you are thinking," Charlotte said. "You are wondering how I could think of dancing when Matthew is gone."

Marsali did not deny it. "I am not judging you," she hurried to say. "I am only wondering how you have arrived at that point. It feels as if I never shall, and I did not have the years with Christopher that you did with Matthew."

"Neither have you had six months to recover," Charlotte said, causing Marsali to wonder if there was some magic healing that would occur when half a year had passed.

"Of course I miss Matthew." Charlotte sighed sadly. "I always shall. But it is difficult—as it was in England—for a woman to be on her own here and to provide for herself. And I am lonely. And, of course, Alec needs a father."

In her excitement over seeing her sister, Marsali had forgotten about her nephew. "Where is he? I must meet him at last."

"Downstairs," Charlotte said. "One of the maids took him in to feed him some dinner and put him to bed."

"Might I not see him first?" Marsali asked, wondering at Charlotte's seemingly easy adjustment to the household staff in allowing one of them to take over the care of her son—even temporarily.

"Of course you may," Charlotte said. "But first you must tell me all that has happened since you came—and truly how bad it was in Manchester. I could feel the heartache of your letters, though I guessed well enough that you had to be careful with your words."

"I had to take great care," Marsali said. Manchester and her life there seemed a world away. A month across a vast ocean was no small journey. *And one I shall never again make.*

But she did not wish to speak of England and their aunt's house or of Mr. Vancer and his. Marsali wished to recount the details of her voyage on the *Amanda May*. She wanted to tell Charlotte everything about Christopher and to have her understand why Marsali could not forget him. But Charlotte spoke before Marsali could begin.

"Mr. Vancer is dashingly handsome. You are most fortunate."

"Yes." Marsali searched Charlotte's gaze, silently pleading with her to understand. "Lady Cosgrove says that he is going to ask me to marry him."

"That's why he arranged for me to be here," Charlotte exclaimed. "How terribly thoughtful. He is kindness itself."

"He is." Marsali could not disagree.

Charlotte seemed to finally take notice that she seemed less than enthusiastic. "Tell me you are going to say yes," she said. "He must care for you to have gone to all the trouble of bringing me here. I would say it is even probable that he loves you."

"What if I do not love him?" Marsali asked. "Isn't that unfair—to both of us?"

Charlotte turned toward her on the bed and took Marsali's hands in her own. "You have been so fortunate to be sheltered here. Have you considered what might have happened to you had Mr. Vancer not taken you in?"

"I should have had to work for Mr. Thomas," Marsali said.

Charlotte nodded. "And you would have been in grave danger. Something is not right about that household—and you would have been thrust into the thick of it. Even if you had survived your term of indenture, you still would have been obliged to work—hard, as I do. Being a widow in America is not pleasant, secure, or happy. At least if you marry Mr. Vancer, you will have a chance at those. And as for not loving him . . . Love is a *choice*, Marsali. And you must choose to make it now, before it is too late."

"But how? I've tried." Marsali felt more despair than before, if that was possible. If Charlotte did not understand her, no one would.

"You have not tried hard enough," Charlotte said. "You've been holding on to the past instead of embracing the future. It is time you forget Mr. Thatcher and pour all of your efforts into caring for Mr. Vancer. I promise, if you do you shall be very happy."

"I want to be happy," Marsali said, her eyes welling with fresh tears.

"I know." Charlotte scooted closer and hugged her once more. "Trust your older sister and marry Mr. Vancer. I promise you will not regret it."

Marsali accompanied Mr. Vancer into the library as he had requested. Though the door was not completely shut behind them, they were far too alone for her comfort.

"You look beautiful tonight," he said, taking a seat near to her on the sofa. "But, then, I have seen you looking nothing less from the first moment you came."

"Thank you," Marsali said, doubting that she had appeared anything near to beautiful when they had first arrived, tossed about the sea all night as they had been. "I do not begin to know how I shall ever repay you for all of the gowns you have purchased."

"I have a few ideas," he drawled, a twinkle in his eye.

Marsali did not laugh at his joke or the suggestion behind it but forced a polite smile.

"Do not look so alarmed," he said, his teasing voice gone. He leaned forward so she would have to meet his gaze. "I hope you know that I would never force you to anything."

She swallowed, pushing her discomfort down firmly, where it sank inside her like an unwieldy stone. "I do," she said. "You have been nothing but the perfect gentleman to me."

"Perfect may be going a bit far when describing me, but I have come to care a great deal for you." He moved closer yet, so that their knees were practically touching.

"And I you," Marsali said truthfully. *He is a good man. Embrace the future.*

"We have had these three months together, and I feel that we suit each other well. I mean no disrespect to Miss Cosgrove or to your late husband, but I would be less than honest if I did not express the gratitude and pleasure I feel at having you here beside me."

"I am grateful to be here," Marsali said.

"You know what I wish to ask?"

She caught the slightest bit of uncertainty in his words, and it both surprised her and melted the resistance she felt. *I cannot hurt him.*

"I am prepared to answer," she said, mustering courage as she never had before. "Yes, Mr. Vancer, I will marry you."

A corner of his mouth lifted in a slow smile. "That was *much* easier than I expected. I did not even have to ask."

"You didn't—" She brought her hands to her face, mortified. She had been so worried that she would not be able to tell him yes, so focused on what she must say so as not to hurt him, not to disappoint Charlotte or upset Lady Cosgrove, not to ruin her own life, that she had spoken out of turn. Grossly out of turn.

Mr. Vancer pulled Marsali's hands from her face and did not release them. "I am not sorry in the least," he said. "I had worried that you were not ready yet. I am vastly relieved to discover that you are, and that you are as eager as I am for our marriage."

She cringed internally.

"And now I am eager to share our good news with the others. Shall we go in to the ball?" He stood, then held his hand out to her. She took it, and he helped her up. They went out into the hall.

"I will speak to the musicians about halting after this set—so we can share our good news with our guests."

"Go ahead," she urged. "I'll wait here." As soon as he had left her side and began crossing the room to the musicians' dais, Marsali stepped into one of the curtained alcoves adjoining the vast ballroom.

Turning her back to the entrance, she tugged off her glove, then stared down at her hand. Christopher's ring peered up at her, bringing a rush of tears. She looked away, hoping for something in the tiny room to take her mind from the past she so easily slipped into. Through the lone, square window she saw that the drizzle outside continued, as it had for the past several days. She longed to be outside in it, to remember the smell of rain and the feel of the cool drops on her skin as she had stood on deck and spoken her wedding vows with Christopher.

This is hopeless. Marsali squeezed her eyes shut, willing the memory away. How was she supposed to look to the future when everything reminded her of the past and Christopher? She would have to do something to change that.

She opened her eyes and quickly twisted the ring from her finger, then dropped it into the bodice of her dress and replaced the glove.

Christopher is dead. I am no longer his wife. She could not wear his ring if she was to marry another. She must do as Charlotte directed and give Mr. Vancer a proper chance.

Marsali blinked back her tears, straightened her back, and returned to the ballroom, determined, now that she had agreed to marry Mr. Vancer, to make the choice to love him. She would begin tonight. By smiling and laughing with him, staying at his side, and hanging on his every word. She would dance with him and do all in her power to be a delight to him. It was the right thing to do. The only thing to do. And so she would endeavor to do it well. After all . . .

At least one of us should be happy.

CHAPTER 43

urrying through the drizzle, Christopher donned his mask and walked briskly toward the entrance to Mr. Vancer's ballroom. *If my sisters could see me now,* he thought for probably the hundredth time since leaving England. They would not have believed—he hardly could—that he had purposely dressed in costume and was eager to attend a ball.

Upon learning that Charlotte had been picked up by a carriage belonging to one William Vancer of New York City—just hours before Christopher had arrived at her home—he had set off, following her by wagon, foot, borrowed horse, and ferry, believing there was only one place she could be going and one person she could be going to see.

But why did Lady Cosgrove not send me notice? Perhaps she had and Miss Thomas had intercepted that correspondence as well. Regardless, whatever barriers had stood between him and Marsali finding one another, Christopher felt them slipping away. He felt infused with purpose and more alive than he had for many weeks. Very soon—moments now?—he would see Marsali and hold her in his arms once more.

He tugged at the suit his former New Jersey landlady had kindly lent him when he'd stopped at her boarding house for a precious few hours' sleep and a bath. He clutched the muddied card that had fallen from heaven, so to speak, after he had spent an hour posing as a servant hired to help outside for the evening, desperately trying to determine how he might gain entrance to the mansion. Just when he had almost given up and was assisting with the unloading of what he had decided was his last carriage full of guests, he'd found a card and mask that had fallen into the rain-soaked street as the overly excited and flustered occupants of the carriage had disembarked. The ink on the card was now blurred, and Christopher's heart leapt at this fortunate turn of events. The name of the guest it had belonged to was no longer legible, though it was still obvious that the invitation was for tonight's festivities. A masquerade ball . . . honoring Miss Marsali Abbott.

Christopher handed the card to the servant stationed at the ballroom and made his apologies for its condition, citing the rainy weather they had been having. He was given a brief nod in return and moved easily into the ballroom. *No name required.* Perhaps things were done differently here in America. Or perhaps it seemed unlikely that a gentleman would attend a masquerade ball if it was not required that he attend.

Letting out a long breath of relief, Christopher scanned the ballroom for Marsali. He did not see her but on his second pass across the room discovered Lady Cosgrove busily chatting with a group of other women. Even in costume she was impossible to miss, with that ramrod-straight back of hers. With purposeful strides, he started toward her, mask in place.

He waited patiently until a lull in the conversation, then

gently touched her elbow. She turned to him and looked him over, a puzzled expression just visible behind her own mask.

"Good evening, Lady Cosgrove." He inclined his head, allowing his own mask to slip a little so she might see him better.

A hand flew to her chest. "Excuse me, ladies," she said to the other three women congregated with her. "Come with me," she said under her breath and began leading him to a more secluded corner of the ballroom.

"*What* are you doing here?" she demanded when they had reached the relative privacy of an alcove.

"I have come to find my wife—perhaps share a dance or two and then take her home with me." Home was currently a room at a boarding house, but he knew it wouldn't matter to Marsali.

"Shh." Lady Cosgrove pressed a finger to her lips. "Do you wish the entire ballroom to hear our conversation?"

He would shout his request to the entire room if she did not cooperate and tell him where he might find Marsali. "Just show me where Marsali is, and we will leave—together."

"You cannot. She is—no longer your wife," Lady Cosgrove stammered.

"What do you mean?" Panic flared, though reason told him that Marsali was not dead. Masquerade balls were not held in honor of deceased persons.

Lady Cosgrove bit down on her lip and brought a hand to her head as if in a great deal of pain. "She thinks you deceased," she said finally. "And Mr. Vancer is set to publicly announce their betrothal at this moment."

"What of your daughter?" Christopher asked, momentarily brushing aside the crushing pain of Lady Cosgrove's announcement and all its implications, not the least of which felt like betrayal from Marsali. "Is Miss Cosgrove not to marry Mr. Vancer?"

"Lydia is dead," Lady Cosgrove said, a slight catch in her

voice. She removed her mask and looked up at him, a plea in her eyes. "When we landed in New York I told the authorities that Marsali was Lydia, and so we were both brought here. At the time Marsali was not coherent enough to protest, but I did it for her as much as myself. I kept her from Mr. Thomas. As soon as she was well again, she insisted Mr. Vancer know the truth. And these three months we have been here with him, they have fallen in love."

A knife to Christopher's heart could not have hurt any worse. "You never told her that I came?"

"No," Lady Cosgrove admitted with a shake of her head. "At first I was afraid that if Marsali left, I should be asked to leave as well. And then, when I knew that was not a concern, and when you came to find her, I feared for Marsali. I have come to care for her too, you see. Your injuries were so that I did not think you could provide for her. I imagined her toiling long hours each day, the two of you barely getting by with enough to eat, let alone a home to live in or any kind of a decent life. She was meant for better than that. She wasn't born to be a servant. You said so yourself."

"You lied to us both because you thought she would be better off here, living a life of luxury." Christopher grabbed Lady Cosgrove's arm and pulled her toward him. "Did you never once think that ought to be her choice? Do you have any idea what I have been through, not knowing whether Marsali was alive or dead—whether she was alone somewhere and needed me, or—"

"She has not been alone. She has been well cared for." Lady Cosgrove extracted her arm from his grasp. "I am truly sorry. Perhaps I acted in error, but she *is* happy now. Mr. Vancer can provide for her in a way you would never be able to. If you love her, you will leave and let her be."

Outside the alcove the musicians struck the final note of a reel. This was followed almost immediately by a shushing that seemed to flow over the crowd as the ballroom grew silent.

"It is time. Mr. Vancer is about to announce their betrothal. It is for you to decide now whom you will think of—yourself or Marsali and what would be best for her." With that, Lady Cosgrove left him, merging quickly into the guests packed onto the floor, all facing a dais at the head of the hall.

Making certain his mask was still fastened tight, Christopher ducked beneath the sideswept curtain and stepped to the fringes of the crowd. A richly dressed man who could only be Vancer stepped up on the dais.

"Welcome, friends. It has been good to celebrate with you tonight. And now I wish to share with you even more cause for celebration. Many of you are aware of the tragedy that encompassed me a few months ago when my fiancée was killed. The same shipwreck that claimed her life also cost another young woman dearly."

He extended his hand, and a woman took it and stepped up beside him. She turned to face the crowd, a radiant smile upon her face. Christopher wished he could shut his eyes in denial. But they were fixed upon Marsali, standing prettily beside Mr. Vancer in a stunning gown and with wispy curls hanging down on either side of her face.

I have touched those curls. I have kissed that woman. She is my wife. He took a step forward, intending to make his way to the front and put a stop to this farce. She might have forgotten him so easily, but they were still married.

Are we not? Captain Gower had said that common-law marriage was recognized in New York, so for Marsali to marry another should be against the law. Halfway to the dais he paused, uncertain.

With Marsali beside him, Mr. Vancer began speaking once more. "Miss Abbott has been recovering from her own injuries and tragedy these past months."

What injuries? How was she hurt? Christopher hoped she had not been burned. His own pain had been excruciating at times, but it hurt worse to think of her enduring the same.

"It has been a blessing for Miss Abbott and me to turn to one another in our grief." He paused and smiled down at her with a look, which—even from this distance—could not be mistaken as anything other than tender affection.

Along with the knife lodged in his heart, Christopher felt as if someone had punched him and the pain had spread instantly to his limbs and elsewhere.

"Earlier this evening I asked Miss Abbott if she would be my wife, and she has kindly agreed."

Cheers and applause erupted at this news, shaking Christopher from his stupor and prodding him to move once more, quickly now. He had to set this right. Marsali could not really mean to marry another man. *Her affections could not have changed so quickly.*

"I am so very happy for her," a woman beside him said as he passed. Her voice sounded strangely familiar, and from the corner of his eye he noted that her look was too. *Marsali.* His heart lurched. There had been some mistake. That was all. It had not really been Marsali who was to marry Mr. Vancer.

Christopher turned toward the voice and knew immediate disappointment. While the woman had similar features, she definitely was not Marsali.

Charlotte?

"She has had such a difficult life," the woman was saying to another beside her. "I am happy to see that she will be both loved and provided for now. No one could be more deserving of such a happy resolution."

During the time that Christopher had paused, Mr. Vancer had concluded his speech and the applause had died down. Marsali and Mr. Vancer had left the dais, and sets were forming around them. Theirs appeared full already, but that did not mean he could not get closer to her.

"May I have this dance?" Christopher asked the woman who had to be Charlotte.

"You may," she replied with a smile similar to her sister's. She bid her companion farewell and took his hand as they hurried to form the last of a set.

There was no time for introductions, simply a bow and curtsey, and they were off. She was not his partner for long, as he traded with another gentleman as soon as he could, then continually moved into the next closest group, displacing several upset partners along the way as he feigned confusion and murmured false apologies.

At last Christopher had worked his way to the set Marsali was in. When the ladies circled before the gentlemen, he tried to get her attention, but she was not looking his way. The weaving was to come next, and he would have his chance then.

One, two, three of the women passed him. Marsali was next, and he would be able to touch her briefly in passing. He held his arm out, and she touched it lightly. He found her hand and squeezed it, and she looked back as if startled. The next steps came, and Christopher found himself pushed aside from one of the angry men whose partner he had stolen.

Christopher searched for Charlotte but did not see her. No doubt he'd humiliated her in his haste to reach Marsali. He stepped back from the dance, waiting on the edge with those who had not joined in.

Marsali continued dancing with Mr. Vancer as if nothing at all had happened. *How could she not know?* Christopher wondered. *How could she not feel that it was I?* He regretted that he had not thought to take off his mask.

"You see, she is happy." Lady Cosgrove appeared beside him. "I was not lying."

"About that, anyway." There were no words to describe the bitterness and even hatred he felt toward Lady Cosgrove right now. And watching Marsali laugh as she lingered near

Vancer, her hand on his arm, felt as if the imaginary knife was being repeatedly thrust and twisted into his heart.

All these weeks he had been trying to find her. He had walked miles searching for her, had worked for her vile employer—all in the hope that she might be found. And she had been here the entire time, enjoying herself. *Without a thought of me.*

Marsali tipped her head back and smiled up at Mr. Vancer as she had smiled up at Christopher many times before.

He ran his hands through his hair, unable to deny the obvious.

She cares for him. He cares for her. He can provide for her—anything she might want or need. I cannot do the same.

Wordlessly he turned from Lady Cosgrove and made his way out of the ballroom, back out to the street where the rain was turning to sleet.

He had no money to hail a carriage. He had nothing, so he shoved his hands in his pockets and began walking toward the ferry that would not return to convey him until tomorrow morning because he had stayed too long. He had no idea where he would sleep or what he would do next.

Is it better that Marsali is with Mr. Vancer? What kind of life could I have given her?

Rebellion flared for a moment. He had always been able to find work and to protect his sisters. He would have done the same and more for Marsali. He could have given her a good life.

I love her. But none of that mattered now.

His brief marriage was over.

CHAPTER 44

"**A**ndrew Jackson has won the election, and I am not even upset." Mr. Vancer dropped a kiss on the top of Marsali's head before taking his place at the table. "Must be because I am getting married today."

Marsali returned his smile and nibbled at her toast. She dared not eat more; her stomach was in such knots. The last time she had been about to get married, she had felt excited and happy, not as if she wished to cry.

The butler appeared in the breakfast room doorway. "Sir, Mr. Fenington is here to see you about a shipment of furs."

"Right." Still sipping his tea, Mr. Vancer stood. "Forgot I'd told him I could give him fifteen minutes this morning. But that is *all*. Can't be late for my own wedding!" With a fond look at Marsali, he left the room.

She took his absence as an excuse to make her own escape, before Charlotte or Lady Cosgrove arrived at the table. Marsali needed a few minutes alone this morning. Soon enough she would have to dress for the ceremony, but until then she needed a quiet room and a handkerchief and a good cry.

Upstairs in her room, she shut and locked the door behind her, retrieved a handful of prettily embroidered handkerchiefs from her bureau, and went to the window to look out at the city view that would be hers for the rest of her life.

She and Christopher had spoken of a life in the country together. Of their own little farm, of working side by side. The life she was about to pledge herself to could not have been more different.

Marsali sank to the floor, burying her face in her arms upon a seat cushion as the flood began. She cried because months had passed without word, and she could no longer deny that Christopher had died. She cried because she still felt as if she was being unfaithful to him. She cried because Mr. Vancer did not make her heart race and sing as Christopher had. She cried because she knew he did not really love her either—not the way Christopher had. She cried because tonight they would both have to pretend something that did not exist, and then she would have to continue pretending it for the rest of her life.

Her handkerchief was soaked through, and she had started on a second when her door opened. Marsali looked up to see Lady Cosgrove enter, key in hand, with her maid and Charlotte close behind.

"Fetch a cool cloth," Lady Cosgrove instructed the maid upon seeing Marsali seated on the floor and draped over the seat.

"I will be well enough," Marsali said, sniffing loudly and attempting to stop the next wave of tears.

"Your *face* will not be." Lady Cosgrove crossed the room and pulled Marsali to her feet. "Look what you have done to yourself. And with but two hours until we must leave."

"What is it, Marsali? What is wrong?" Charlotte steered Marsali away from Lady Cosgrove and over to the bed, where Marsali collapsed, face down, upon the coverlet and began sobbing anew.

For a few minutes they let her weep while the maid and Lady Cosgrove bustled about the room, readying her wedding outfit, no doubt. Marsali remembered Lydia's silver gown and all the happiness of that other morning, and she cried more.

"You may go now. We will assist her from here," Lady Cosgrove instructed the maid.

Marsali heard the sound of the door shutting once more and guessed that she would now receive a lecture—from both Lady Cosgrove and her sister.

Near the foot of the bed the mattress sank on either side. Reluctantly Marsali rolled over, sat up, and faced both women.

"It will get better," Charlotte promised as she took her hand. "You simply haven't had enough time. I still miss Matthew and love him and think of him every day, but I have learned that I must move on and make a life for myself and Alec. You have been forced to that conclusion early, that is all."

Marsali nodded, though she did not entirely agree.

"It seems ridiculous to think that you loved Mr. Thatcher enough to warrant all this." Lady Cosgrove waved her hand over the pile of soggy handkerchiefs next to Marsali. "You did not talk of love the day Lydia and I helped to get you ready to marry him. Why, you did not even know each other a full month. You have had twice as long to become acquainted with Mr. Vancer."

"But Christopher and I *understood* each other," Marsali tried to explain. "We had each come from difficult circumstances, and those had shaped us into the people that we are, with similar dreams and goals. We did *love* each other."

"Well, you are not going to make a difficult circumstance for Mr. Vancer this morning. He stands to lose a fortune if the two of you do not marry."

"Christopher lost a fortune *by* marrying me," Marsali cried. "He gave me his only thing of value—his grandfather's ring—and he pledged at least two years of his life working to pay off my debt. There was nothing to be gained by his actions."

"Simply because there is something to be gained by Mr. Vancer's does not mean he isn't a good man," Charlotte said. "He is fond of you and will treat you well."

"I know." Marsali fell back onto the pillows, exasperated that she could not make them understand the depth of her feelings. *How wrong what I am about to do feels.*

"If only I could stop thinking of Christopher," she said, tears starting afresh. "But I still dream of him most every night. And when I am awake I imagine sometimes that I see him places—once on the street when Mr. Vancer and I were out driving. I even thought I saw Christopher at the masquerade ball."

"Oh, Marsali." Charlotte's voice was full of empathy, not reprimand.

Lady Cosgrove let out a slow, heavy sigh, as if resigning herself to something. "You did see him at the ball," she admitted quietly.

"What?" Charlotte exclaimed.

Marsali pushed herself up on her elbows and stared at Lady Cosgrove. "What did you say?"

"The truth." Lady Cosgrove's usually straight posture was now hunched, and she looked discomfited. She cleared her throat. "I fear I have done a terrible, terrible thing."

"Only if you are lying now," Marsali said. "Please, tell me."

Lady Cosgrove would not meet her eye but inhaled deeply, as if gathering strength. "Do you remember our conversation one afternoon in my cabin shortly after I had recovered?"

"We had many conversations," Marsali said, clinging to fragile hope. *Just tell me of Christopher.*

"I had said that I admired your willpower and determination. And you told me that I'd more strength than I gave myself credit for." She shook her head sadly. "But you were wrong."

"I wasn't." Marsali sat up and scooted closer on the bed, taking Lady Cosgrove's hand in hers. "I remember now. I told you that when the time was right, you would reach inside yourself and find the courage and strength you needed."

"Yes, well, I have not." Lady Cosgrove sniffled loudly. "When I brought you here at first, I was mostly thinking of myself. I rationalized that I was saving you from Mr. Thomas, but the truth was, I was not at all certain that Mr. Vancer would take me in if I could not supply him with a bride. Lydia—" Her voice caught. "—was gone. But I latched onto the idea that you could take her place."

"But you knew that Mr. Vancer valued your friendship enough to allow you to stay, regardless of my decision or actions. I told you so myself, that first morning after I had spoken with him."

Lady Cosgrove nodded. "Yes, but I knew I should miss your company if you left. A woman my age does not easily make friends in new circles. But with you as his bride, it was possible that I might."

"So you kept Christopher from Marsali because you wished to be her friend?" Charlotte's face screwed up in anger.

"I don't understand," Marsali said. "*Is* Christopher alive? Was he here?"

Lady Cosgrove continued her explanation without answering either of them. "Later, I believed I was doing what was best for you . . . But now I fear I have ruined more than one life with my meddling."

"It may not be too late to mend your mistake." Charlotte's voice softened, and she took Lady Cosgrove's other hand. "*Was* Marsali's husband at the ball?"

Lady Cosgrove sniffed again and gave a slow nod. "Mr. Thatcher was there—and you most probably saw him on the carriage ride as well." She glanced at Marsali, then looked down again, as if she could not bear to see the hurt she had caused. "The first time he came I led him to believe that you had died."

"Oh, Christopher!" Marsali brought her free hand to her heart. She knew what pain she had endured these months, believing him to be dead, and he had been thinking the same of her. "Why? Why would you do such a thing? You knew I was searching the hospitals and the immigrant records daily."

"I was thinking of you," Lady Cosgrove insisted. "Mr. Thatcher had been seriously injured, and it appeared he would be lame for some time—perhaps permanently. I could see only a life of hardship ahead for you, if you remained his wife. I imagined you working to support not only yourself but him as well. But if you stayed with Mr. Vancer, you would never have to work, and you would have everything you ever wanted."

"I wanted Christopher," Marsali cried, anguished to think of Christopher not only believing her dead these many months, but physically hurt as well. "It was not your choice to make."

"That is what he said to me the night of the ball when I confessed what I had done." Lady Cosgrove looked up for the first time since she had started talking. "Seeing you so distraught . . . I realize now that I was wrong."

"Why did Christopher not stay if you told him what you had done?" Charlotte asked the question before Marsali could.

"I convinced him that Marsali was better off with Mr. Vancer and that the two of you cared for one another. Anyone who saw you that night would have believed the same."

Marsali groaned. "I was trying so hard to convince everyone—myself included. I was trying to embrace the future as Charlotte said I must. I was pretending so at least Mr. Vancer might be happy. I have been doing the same in the weeks since, hoping that if I pretended long enough my feelings for him might someday be true." Knowing Christopher had seen her thus left Marsali desperate to find him and explain. To set things right.

"And so Christopher just left—without even talking to me?" Her voice had risen to an angry, frantic pitch.

"He left because he wanted to give you a better life." Lady Cosgrove looked at Marsali imploringly and took her hand. "Mr. Thatcher realized what I already knew—that he cannot provide for you as Mr. Vancer can."

"Where did he go?" Marsali wrenched her hand from Lady Cosgrove's and stood. She looked around the room, trying to decide what she must do next. Wherever Christopher was, she must find him.

"I do not know where he went," Lady Cosgrove said. "When he left that first time, he said he could be found in Virginia on the Thomas plantation. I suppose he went there to search for you."

"I shall start there," Marsali said.

"No, Marsali. You cannot," Charlotte said. "It could be very dangerous for you."

"What will you tell Mr. Vancer?" Lady Cosgrove asked. "He is expecting to marry you today."

"He cannot marry her," Charlotte proclaimed, rising from the bed as well. "She is *already* married. Even you must see that it is impossible for her to marry another."

"A common-law marriage can be annulled easily

enough," Lady Cosgrove said. "And it is not as if the marriage was ever made official—in any way."

"None of that matters. And it will not be annulled." Marsali rushed to the armoire to retrieve her cloak. She threw it over her shoulders as she crossed the room to the dressing table. She opened the top drawer, reaching to the very back to retrieve the tiny, paper-wrapped parcel. When she had taken it from the drawer, she tore it open, then slid Christopher's ring back on her finger. *Where it belongs. Why did I ever doubt that he was alive? I felt it all along. I knew it.*

Charlotte stood before the doorway. "You cannot go to Mr. Thomas's home. It is no safer now than it was before."

"The price for my passage has been paid," Marsali said. "Mr. Vancer showed me the receipt himself, over two months ago. I owe Mr. Thomas nothing."

"And what of Mr. Vancer, who fulfilled the debt?" Lady Cosgrove asked. "You would repay his kindness by abandoning him at this critical time?"

"We never should have *reached* this critical time had you been honest with us both," Marsali said, anger shaking her voice. "I regret that he will be hurt, but I *cannot* marry him now."

"He will lose his fortune *and* suffer public humiliation today," Lady Cosgrove murmured. "Oh! Whatever have I done?"

Marsali stepped around Charlotte and opened the door. "Somehow I think he would choose both over marriage to a woman who already has a living husband."

"Indeed I would." Mr. Vancer stood in the hall just outside her door, his brows pinched and a most stricken expression upon his face. "Forgive me. I did not mean to eavesdrop, but having heard my name mentioned, I paused outside your door and caught the end of your conversation. I gather you are going somewhere—and it is not to our wedding." He touched the edge of Marsali's cloak.

"My husband is alive," she said. "He has even been

here—to your home—twice, without our knowledge. Lady Cosgrove at first told him that I was dead and then later convinced him that I was better off with you."

"But you are not." Mr. Vancer cleared his throat uncomfortably.

"No," Marsali whispered and felt terrible for it. "I love him still. I must find him."

"Of course you must." He spoke with far more understanding than Marsali felt she deserved. Still, she could not force the worry over Christopher from her mind. He was out there somewhere—hurting. Because of her.

"This is quite the turn of events." Mr. Vancer brought a hand to his temples and began rubbing. "In less than two hours we were to be at the church. Explaining to our guests shall be bad enough, but now I am left with only one week before the end of the year in which to find a wife. They are not easy to come by, you know." He gave a harsh laugh.

"I am so very sorry." Marsali touched his hand lightly. "I did not mean for this to happen. I never wanted to hurt you, and I shall find a way to repay every penny you have spent on me."

"You may have to," Mr. Vancer said, clearly jesting but with a trace of bitterness in his voice. "I have already made purchases and invested against the inheritance I was to receive. And now I will be unable to pay my creditors back."

"There is a possible solution," Lady Cosgrove suggested timidly.

"I think I have had enough of your suggestions," Mr. Vancer said. "You accuse Marsali of repaying me poorly when you have betrayed the long-standing friendship of our families in such a manner."

"I did not intend to." Lady Cosgrove rose from her seat at the edge of the bed and crossed the room to the doorway. "When we arrived, I *did* believe Mr. Thatcher to be dead. And when it was discovered that he was not, I did not know how to tell you—I was afraid for you and your predicament and concerned for Marsali and the otherwise harsh future ahead of her." Lady Cosgrove had crumpled a bit but straightened before adding, "And I truly believed that Mr. Thatcher had gone away for good."

"Clearly, he has not," Mr. Vancer said. "Nor would I, were Miss Abbott my wife." He blew out a long breath and leaned his head back, looking up, as if seeking inspiration.

"You can still marry today," Lady Cosgrove said. "Not Marsali, but Charlotte. There is no doubt that her husband is deceased, and she and Marsali are similar in appearance. Why, it is entirely possible that many in the congregation may not notice the difference."

"Aside from her *name*," Mr. Vancer said, clearly exasperated. "And I would rather lose a fortune than force a woman to marriage."

"You would not have to force me," Charlotte said quietly.

"Charlotte?" Marsali turned to her.

"I would not require much," Charlotte continued, looking past Marsali to Mr. Vancer. "A roof over our heads and perhaps an education for Alec—when he is older. That is, of course, if you would not mind adopting a child in the bargain."

"I—would not mind," Mr. Vancer said. He swallowed thickly. "Are you quite certain? We know very little of each other."

"I know that you have treated my sister kindly, and I have hope you would regard Alec and me the same."

"I would," Mr. Vancer said. "I will. I would be in your debt for so great a favor."

It sounded as if they were speaking vows already. Marsali looked from one to the other, astonished at this change in circumstance.

"It is all settled, then," Lady Cosgrove said squaring her shoulders. "Perhaps all will yet be well—for all concerned. Come, Charlotte. You must be readied for your wedding.

And, Mr. Vancer, I believe Miss Abbott is in need of a carriage."

"Yes—please." *I need Christopher.*

"Godspeed, sister." Charlotte embraced Marsali. "If you insist upon going to Mr. Thomas's, make the driver wait. I shall give you the name of my employer, and perhaps you can take my place there. They should be happy to have a woman without a child tagging along as she does her work."

"Thank you," Marsali said. "I shall write to let you know what has become of me."

"You will do more than that," Mr. Vancer said. "You shall have an escort, so your sister and I will not fear for your safety."

"Thank you for your kindness and understanding," Marsali said. "If circumstances had been different . . ."

He smiled sadly. "But they are not, and you must go and find your Mr. Thatcher. I hope that when you do, he realizes how fortunate he is."

CHAPTER 45

January 1829

Christopher rose before dawn, ate a hasty breakfast at the inn, and went out to the stables to saddle his newly purchased horse.

"Good morning, *Amanda May*." He stroked the mare, and she bent her head, nuzzling his hand. "No treats today," Christopher said. "But you help me reach Marsali, and I'll get you a bucket of the finest oats." He'd named the horse after Captain Gower's ship in the hope that she—as the voyage had—would bring him good luck in finding Marsali.

He'd bought the horse just last week, after his sisters' letter had arrived, and with it a bank draft to equal the next five years of the inheritance left them by their grandfather. Neither of his sisters needed the money, and they insisted he was to have it, both to aid in the search for his wife and to start anew in America. In the past he might have argued against such assistance, but the second letter included in the bundle had changed his mind—about everything.

He saddled the mare and climbed up, then left the inn at a brisk speed, eager for the day for the first time in a long time.

He'd lived these past months in a bitter haze, angry at the world and mostly himself for falling prey to the complications of a woman. He hadn't wanted a wife to begin with, but he'd ended up with one anyway. And then he had lost her, and that had hurt worse than his burns or the wound that had nearly split his scalp. The healing took longer too. Well into the new year he still hadn't managed it.

But included in the packet from his family had been Marsali's letter to them—her anguish poured out for him to read personally. What a horrifying experience she'd lived that night of the shipwreck. And she hadn't forgotten him after all. She had searched for weeks. She had shed tears and mourned and hoped and then finally lost that hope. She had believed him alive as long as she could, until the same deception that had tricked him had convinced her that he was dead.

The road forked, and Christopher stayed to the right. From here he had less than twenty miles to travel. And Marsali would be at the end of those.

If only he had not listened to Lady Cosgrove the night of the ball. He and Marsali could have been together these two months. Instead, she had been working at her sister's old post in Virginia. Charlotte had taken Marsali's place at the church and married Mr. Vancer in December.

Christopher had learned all of this from Lady Cosgrove and Charlotte when he had called, one last time, at the Vancer house four days ago. Since then he had traveled over frozen rivers and through bitter cold, eager to get to Marsali as soon as he could.

The miles passed as he lost himself in his thoughts. His gloved hands felt frozen as they gripped the reins, and his new wool cap and coat could not do enough to keep him warm. The winter seemed as fierce as the autumn had been mild. *But spring . . . Spring will be glorious.* A promise of dreams hoped for—and fulfilled.

The distant sun shone directly overhead when

Christopher at last reached the plantation where Marsali worked. He dismounted and tethered his horse to the gate outside, then strode up the walk, his heart pounding.

He knocked at the door and waited, wondering if perhaps Marsali herself would open the door. Instead, an older woman wearing a maid's uniform greeted him.

Christopher doffed his hat. "Good afternoon to you. I am here to see Miss Abbott."

The woman's brows drew together quizzically. "No one here by that name. Are you certain you have the right farm?"

"I am certain." Christopher's heart felt as if it had jumped to his throat. *Marsali has to be here.* "Miss Abbott's sister worked here before her. Her name was Charlotte."

Understanding dawned on the older woman's face. "Are you looking for Marsali—Mrs. Thatcher to those who are not well acquainted with her?"

Relief swept through him. "We are well acquainted." He grinned, while thinking how foolish his mistake and feeling inordinately pleased that Marsali had kept his name. "I am her husband."

"Land's sake!" The woman stepped back as if he had jumped out at her. "Come in." She swept her hand wide, encouraging him to enter. Christopher did, expecting to be shown to a sitting room, as he had when first entering Mr. Thomas's house. Instead, the woman closed the door, then turned and began walking briskly.

"This way," she called over her shoulder. "That poor girl has been pining for you since she came here. She put every penny of her wage into advertisements, asking after you. Every night spent on her knees petitioning the Lord for your return, every morning her pillow wet with tears."

It hurt to imagine Marsali distraught as the woman described; he understood all too well those exact feelings.

The woman led him down a narrow hall and through a kitchen, then out another door. She paused on the step outside, her breath visible in the crisp air. "It's wash day.

Marsali's out in the shed." The woman pointed to a cluster of smaller buildings across the yard. "First one on the left. You'll find her there."

Christopher started down the step when she caught his arm. "Be careful not to startle her too much. She's fragile."

He nodded, then took off across the frozen ground toward the outbuildings. The one used for washing was nearest the pump and also had a large window, presumably to let in enough light for the work to be done properly. He peered through this and felt his heart catch as he caught sight of Marsali bent over a washtub. Her moves were practiced and efficient, her strokes counted, and the garment turned as he had taught her. He felt regret that she had been forced to such a chore, but also a swell of gratitude that she was not above such work and had chosen this life—and searching for him—over a life of luxury with Mr. Vancer. Marsali was fragile but strong as well, as she had proved to him time and again.

He opened the door, pulling it slowly, grateful for the creak of the hinges that would alert her that someone was entering. A fire burned in a stove on the far side of the room, warming both the water boiling on top of it and the small cabin.

Marsali did not turn from her task. "Please tell Mrs. Price that I'll take my luncheon later," she said as she continued scrubbing. "I've just a few more things to wash, and I'll be done."

"Your skills have greatly improved, Mrs. Thatcher."

Her hands ceased moving, and he heard her sharp intake of breath. Slowly, she turned to him, a look of cautious hopefulness in her soulful eyes. "Are you real, Christopher? So many times I have imagined you—have believed that I saw you, only to be fooled."

"I am real." His eyes darted to her dripping hands and the ring he had given her. "You are still wearing my ring and have kept my name."

"I am still your wife." Tears filled her eyes, and he waited no more but swooped forward, pulling her into his embrace. Her hands came around his neck and pulled his face closer, and she kissed him first, as she had done on their wedding night.

"I'm so sorry," she sobbed between their frantic kisses. "I thought you were dead. But I never loved another. I swear it. That night at the ball I was only pretending, as everyone said I must."

"I know." Christopher pressed his lips to her cheeks, her forehead, her hair. He couldn't hold her tightly enough. "I have been a third time to New York, and Charlotte herself told me the whole story." He held Marsali, and she clung to him, as if she might never let go, a rather good idea, considering all they had been through.

"I am here now," he said, reassuring her once more. "I am here, and I will not leave you. We will not be parted again."

Out in the yard behind them a chorus of cheers and applause erupted. Still holding Marsali, Christopher turned them so they could see through the open doorway to the crowd of servants and family members gathered outside. The stout woman who had greeted him seemed to have gathered everyone to witness their happy reunion.

Marsali smiled through her tears. "They have been good to me here," she said.

"I am glad to hear it." Christopher bent low, intending to kiss her again. "But from now on it is I who will be good to you." He wrapped his arms around her waist and pressed his lips to hers in a gentle, slow kiss that elicited more cheering from the group in the yard.

"We will be good to each other," Marsali said when, after several long seconds, they at last parted. She gave him a dazzling smile. "But I fear that if you insist upon kissing me like that, we must make a call upon the preacher today. We are in Virginia after all, and the validity of our marriage may be somewhat in question."

"We will go see the preacher *right now*," Christopher growled. He swept her into his arms and carried her outside. "Never more will there be any questions regarding our status as husband and wife. We are married, and the world had best understand that."

Marsali laughed and wrapped her arms around his neck. "They shall," she promised. "Marrying you was the best decision of my life. It was the *beginning* of my life."

"And mine," Christopher said. And he kissed her once more in front of everyone.

Epilogue

Yorkshire, England, 1842

"Oh, my, but Marsali is beautiful," Grace exclaimed, peering at the long-awaited daguerreotype that had been enclosed with Christopher's last letter. He had been promising to send one for some time, and now that it was here she could not seem to stop staring at it—at them, the happy couple and three darling children.

"And look at Christopher, so handsome and grown up," Helen said as she studied the image of her brother and his family, seated on the front porch of their sprawling home in Virginia.

"I should hope he has grown up at last," Samuel said good-naturedly. "After all, he is thirty-five now. Perhaps the pranks of his youth are at last behind him."

"He never did us any harm." Helen linked her arm through Samuel's. "Have you still not forgiven him for spying on us when we first kissed?"

"Of course I have," Samuel said. "I was never upset to begin with. It was Christopher's brilliant scheming that led me to you."

"A fact you ought never forget!"

All three looked up at the loud voice—one they had not heard for nearly fourteen years.

"Christopher?" Grace reacted first, rushing toward him and flinging herself into his arms with Helen close behind. "I cannot believe you are here," she cried. "That you have surprised us so."

He pulled back from their embrace and flashed his old, lopsided grin. "I told you I was coming. I wrote that you would see me soon."

"I thought you meant in a daguerreotype." Exasperated but terribly pleased, she stuck her lip out in an exaggerated pout. "You haven't changed a bit. Still as mischievous as ever."

"So is your husband," Christopher said. "It was he who suggested I surprise you. He knew of my plan."

As if on cue Nicholas appeared in the doorway behind them. "I'm back." His arms were laden, not with the Christmas parcels he said he had gone to London for, but with luggage belonging to Christopher and his family. Grace could not imagine a finer present.

"Grace and Helen, Nicholas and Samuel, I would like you to meet my wife, Marsali."

Christopher clasped the small woman's hand in his and drew her forward, from the shadow behind him where she and their children had been waiting while he had his fun with the surprise.

"You're even lovelier in person." Grace came forward and hugged Marsali, and Helen followed. "Welcome to Sutherland Hall."

"Thank you," Marsali said as she glanced about the towering room. "It is very—festive."

Grace and Nicholas laughed together.

"It has become somewhat of a tradition," Nicholas explained. "Every Christmas season we try to outdo the previous in lifting the gloom from these old walls. We may have gone a bit overboard in recent years."

Grace followed his gaze to the fresh garland and boughs of holly strung everywhere. "You shall have to take advantage of the kissing balls while you are here," she said, drawing closer to Nicholas. "There is one in every room."

"Even the nursery?" Christopher's oldest son wrinkled his nose as if disgusted, reminding Grace of his father many years ago.

"Even the nursery," Nicholas confirmed. "Don't let your cousins catch you there," he advised.

"Oh let's do call the children in from their play," Helen said. "All but the littlest have gone sledding up the hill."

"Why call them in? We should join them," Christopher said. "Keep your coats on, children."

"You haven't changed," Grace said and felt glad of it.

"That isn't entirely true," Christopher said. He pulled Marsali closer and draped his arm across her shoulders. "When I left here I thought you all were mad, with your tender affections and expressions of love for one another. I couldn't wait to get away from it and be around people who hadn't lost their minds to such."

"And then he met me," Marsali said, a playful smile curving her lips.

They are perfect for each other. Grace had gathered this already from the many letters that had been exchanged over the years, but seeing them together made it all the more obvious.

"And then I met you," Christopher agreed, looking down at Marsali. "And now I know better." He steered her beneath the kissing ball in the room and kissed her right there for all to see.

"He learned from the best," Samuel said, clearing his throat after several seconds had passed and they still had not broken apart.

"True enough," Christopher said, at last releasing a

blushing Marsali. "Everything I know I learned from my wife."

The others laughed. Christopher joined them, but a moment later his look turned serious.

"How blessed to find you all so well. How fortunate we all are."

Grace and Helen nodded their agreement.

"We have found the love our mother never had," Grace said.

"And places to call home," Helen added.

"We have honored Grandfather's legacy well," Christopher said solemnly. "And none of us need fear England anymore."

AUTHOR'S HISTORICAL NOTES

Writing historical fiction is both daunting and fascinating, and as an author I often find myself drawn into the past, researching far more than I need to for the story and having to choose those few events that will most enrich the tale I am attempting to tell.

As *Marrying Christopher* is a work of fiction, there were some liberties taken, regarding the events that took place and particularly the ability to travel by steamship in 1828. Actual facts regarding the ship were accurate, inasmuch as I was able to research them, but Captain Gower's ship was truly ahead of its time—about ten years ahead. Its predecessor, which he references in the story, the American made *SS Savannah*, did sail across the Atlantic in 1819 and was wrecked off Long Island in 1821. Like Captain Gower's ship, the *Savannah* was met with much superstition. In spite of her speed, the public did not embrace steam travel until the late 1830s and early '40s, when the British-made *SS Great Western* began regularly scheduled service across the Atlantic. Like the *Amanda May*, the *Great Western* also had sails and a single smokestack. It's remarkable to think of the progress that was soon to come, with ships like the *Titanic* taking passengers across the Atlantic just seventy years later.

The other vessels referenced in the story, the *Josephine*—the Irish packet ship that rescues Lady Cosgrove and Marsali—and the Black Ball Line "Blood Boats" were both in service in 1828.

The practice of boarding merchant ships and pressing crewmen into service for the Royal Navy was also common during this time period, though far more so in earlier years during the Napoleonic wars and the American Revolution. The opium trade was also a very lucrative—and troubling—reality for the East India Company.

That a young woman like Marsali would find herself on Lime Street in the red-light district of Liverpool was also realistic, with prostitution being a significant problem in Liverpool and other large cities in the 1800s. Disease was rampant, and many young women suffered for having this lifestyle. Some chose it, but often it was seen as the only means for a woman of a lower class to support herself.

America was not without her troubles either, with the issue of slavery heading toward a conflict that would nearly divide the young nation. The sprawling plantations of the south with their tobacco and cotton crops required large numbers of laborers, entrenching the society with a perceived need to continue practicing slavery. Indentured servants were also common, and Marsali's contracted term of four years was indeed generous, with most terms lasting between five and seven years.

Amidst these evils, the world was also entering an age of progress—for better or worse. Joseph Niépce's heliograph was an exciting invention in 1828, and it was not too many years after when daguerreotypes became common enough that Christopher would have been able to send one home to his family.

And though Christopher doubted when Captain Gower suggested that someday men might travel the Atlantic more regularly for business or pleasure, that time was not far distant, allowing us to imagine that families once separated by distances so vast could be reunited again.

Dear Reader,

Thank you for reading *Marrying Christopher*. I hope you enjoyed Christopher's and Marsali's voyage across the Atlantic and their journey to love.

The book you just read is the third in the Hearthfire Historical Romance series. The next novel in this line is set in Scotland during the late 1700s and revolves around the lives of twin brothers who are facing the difficulties of the Highland Clearances following the failed Jacobite uprising of 1745. Watch for previews and teasers on my website in coming months: http://MichelePaigeHolmes.com

Coming this December, also from Mirror Press, is the *Timeless Regency Collection: A Midwinter Ball*. This volume features three novellas by three authors—Annette Lyon, Heidi Ashworth, and myself—all centered around a midwinter ball.

I am equally excited to be one of the twelve authors involved in the Power of the Matchmaker series. Watch for the prequel novella this November and the twelve full-length romance novels to follow, one each month in 2016.

So many wonderful things to look forward to! Thank you for being a part of those. I continue to appreciate those who take the time to read my stories and those who post reviews as well. You make it possible for me to continue doing what I love.

If you would like more information about my other books and future releases, please visit my website at www.michelepaigeholmes.com. You can also follow me on Twitter at @MichelePHolmes.

Happy reading!

Michele

Acknowledgments

I continue to be grateful for the talents of so many who have contributed to this novel. Their dedication and skill make my stories into what I have imagined them to be.

I am especially grateful for fabulous editors Angela Eschler, Michele Preisendorf, Heather B. Moore, and Jennie Stevens. I am also grateful to Heather Justesen for her work formatting the e-book.

Many thanks to Rachael Anderson for designing the perfect cover. I continue to be grateful for her talents and abilities.

Much gratitude goes to my husband and children, for the time they've gone without me. Thank you for your understanding and making it possible for me to pursue my dreams. Bringing to life the words on paper is fun and challenging, but I hope you know I find my true joy in each of you.

ABOUT MICHELE PAIGE HOLMES

Michele Paige Holmes spent her childhood and youth in Arizona and northern California, often curled up with a good book instead of out enjoying the sunshine. She graduated from Brigham Young University with a degree in elementary education and found it an excellent major with which to indulge her love of children's literature.

Her first novel, *Counting Stars*, won the 2007 Whitney Award for Best Romance. Its companion novel, a romantic suspense titled *All the Stars in Heaven*, was a Whitney Award finalist, as was her first historical romance, *Captive Heart. My Lucky Stars* completed the Stars series.

In 2014 Michele launched the Hearthfire Historical Romance line, with the debut title, *Saving Grace. Loving Helen* is the companion novel, with a third, *Marrying Christopher* released in July 2015.

When not reading or writing romance, Michele is busy with her full-time job as a wife and mother. She and her husband live in Utah with their five high-maintenance children, and a Shih Tzu that resembles a teddy bear, in a house with a wonderful view of the mountains.

You can find Michele on the web:

http://MichelePaigeHolmes.com

Facebook: Michele Holmes

Twitter: @MichelePHomes